With his powerful [hands,] blanket off my still [xxxx xx xx xxxx, xxx] long frame beside me. He jerked the ribbons from the ends of my braids, and soon the whole mass of hair lay strewn about on the cot, covering my body almost to my knees.

I lay rigid, torn between terror of what he would do next and an overwhelming attraction for his powerful form. Once more he fell upon me, groaning, swearing under his breath. "It's in the hands of the gods now. Only they can help us, Sieglinde."

The great bearded head lay upon my breast. With his lips, he parted my hair to suck first on one nipple, then the other. My mouth opened and a sound rolled out like that of a creature caught in a forest trap. As the sensuous lips caressed my breasts, I waited, expectant. I wanted this giant to invade my body. My arms lifted to encircle him; my heart beat like a drum.

"*Nein*." He pulled his head away, shoved me brutally back on the cot. "Not yet. I will not take you here." He laughed, a harsh, cruel sound. "That was just a taste. I had to assure myself that you had passion to match your magnificent body."

My whole being, body and soul, had awakened to love. A different kind of love from any I'd ever known. That I was in love with Lothar, I had no doubt at all. The moment he was near me, my blood and heart played tricks on me. It was a thing even God could not control. Whatever, whoever he was, human or divine, the giant, red-bearded, copper-headed Lothar was my destiny.

The Prince of Passion

Rita Balkey

PINNACLE BOOKS   LOS ANGELES

THE PRINCE OF PASSION

Copyright © by Rita Balkey Oleyar

An original Pinnacle Books edition, published for the first time anywhere.

First printing, June 1980

ISBN: 0-523-40662-2

Cover illustration by Gil Cohen

Printed in the United States of America

PINNACLE BOOKS, INC.
2029 Century Park East
Los Angeles, California 90067

The Prince of Passion

PART I

Bavaria

Chapter 1

"Verdammt!"

Those damn thorns again! I pulled my hand out of the mass of roses I was arranging in Lola's favorite Chinese vase. Blood flowed in a crimson stream from a tiny gash in my index finger.

Instinctively, I shoved the finger into my mouth, then just as quickly tore it out again. The brown, wrinkled face of my nurse Ortrud loomed in my memory. "Don't suck on a wound," she always scolded. "It'll bring on the blood poisoning sure as death."

Swallowing hard against a surge of exasperation and anger, I held the bleeding finger over the flowers, and deliberately let the glittering ruby droplets fall on the fragrant petals, like a witch performing some heathenish rite. I imagined my blood to be a fatal concoction, which upon inhaling would bring on a slow, agonizing death. For long, delicious moments I played joyfully, spitefully, with the idea. I envisioned Lola burying her soft face in the blossoms, rubbing her cheeks against the petals, as she did every night when I brought the flowers to her. A short hour later that seductive body would be writhing with the torments of hell, the violent eyes would roll back in their sockets, the pink nipples on that famous breast would turn brown, then black, then . . . I shook my head violently, forcing my mind from its vengeful reverie. God, what had that woman done to me! I cast a baleful glance at the offending roses, a rare variety grown (so the messenger had informed me) in a remote Alpine village. Guaranteed thornless, he'd said. I laughed aloud. What a lie—like everything else in the royal court of Ludwig of Bavaria in the year of our Lord, 1847.

Moving to the ebony cabinet where I kept medicinals, I

3

applied a sliver of elm bark to the bloody threadlike streak. My head ached dully. Tiny pinpricks of pain pushed at my eyelids. Nothing had gone right today.

It was the *föhn,* I muttered, the blistering wind that had been blowing for three whole days and three whole nights, as it did every year. Rising out of the Sahara Desert in far-off Africa, gathering force while crossing the Mediterranean, roaring its vicious way up the Italian peninsula, and over the towering Alps, it descended finally on the hapless people of Bavaria.

The citizens of Munich, the capital, had been especially restless during this year's *föhn.* Last night, sleepless with the heat, I had stood on the bronze balcony outside my chamber. The wind played with me as though it were my lover, caressing my fevered body through the thin muslin night shift. From my vantage point, high above the city, I saw the narrow cobbled streets of the ancient town jammed with people—men, women, children.

Apparently, no one was in bed. The shouts and rumbles rent the soft night air. "Kill the whore!" "Death to the concubine!"

"At *föhn* time, the air is brilliantly clear. A whisper can be heard for blocks. In spite of the heat, I shivered with fear—for myself, for my father the king, for all of Bavaria.

They were shouting for Lola's death. The palace on the Barerstrasse that Ludwig, King of Bavaria, had built for his mistress, the magnificent three-story bronze and marble edifice which had been my home for the past year, was a good kilometer away from the noise and shouting. The night sky was lit up by the host of burning torches. The people of Munich—all rebels now—were clustered thick as flies on the carcass of a horse around the pillar of the Virgin in the Marienplatz, the square in the heart of the city.

Now a mighty shout roared over the ancient rooftops, "Banish your Venus, Ludwig, and give us back our Virgin."

Young mothers would be there, their faces drawn with hatred, sniveling, underfed children clinging to the rough cloth of their full skirts. The men, anger distorting their broad Germanic faces, would be lifting high torches and knives and clubs, pointing menacingly toward the palace of Lola Montez.

But most of them would be the students. They'd be wearing the saucy little cap tipped rakishly over the left

4

eye which was the badge of the Burschen, the vaunted *Studentencorps* that had proclaimed war on decadence. The Burschen hated Lola most of all, for it was she who had persuaded Ludwig to close down their university. It was she, they proclaimed, who had brought their beloved country to the brink of financial and moral ruin.

Now, wrapping a piece of cotton lint around my bleeding finger, I found myself trembling at the memory of last night. In the morning, I'd told Lola about the crowds and the shouting.

"It's getting worse, Lola. We should warn the king. They're bound to storm the palace any night."

"You silly goose. One would hardly think you a king's daughter. You're as fearful as a newborn kitten."

Her tiny pearl teeth had gleamed between her scarlet lips. She stood before the mirror, naked, fresh from her morning bath and rubdown, sipping hot chocolate from a Dresden cup and nibbling a piece of marzipan. I both hated and feared her, this woman who, having been bedded by the famous and notorious of all Europe, was now the plaything of Ludwig I, whom I called father, for I was his bastard. But I had no more rights or privileges than the meanest scullery maid. I was literally Lola's prisoner, slave to her every caprice and whim. Just this morning, she'd ordered Stella, the kitchen maid, to take away my morning chocolate and brioche.

"Fetch some hot water and lemon juice," she barked, ignoring my protests that at fifteen I was still a growing girl.

"Growing girl indeed," she scoffed, arching her finely pencilled brows over violet eyes that could turn soft at the sight of a man, but that now were chunks of ice.

We stood close together as I helped her into her peignoir. "My dear girl, you're getting positively fat. As for still growing—you're a head taller than I, and you're beginning to look like a cow."

Scalding tears of hurt filled my eyes, the warmth of shame suffused my cheeks. I drew back, met her violent eyes with defiance.

"Send out for some bolts of cloth, then. The Sisters taught me how to use a needle. I can run up some new garments."

It was true that the bodice of my frock had popped open

5

halfway down to my waist. My bosom did seem about to burst the seams of the old green muslin.

"I have had no new frocks since coming to Munich last summer." I drew myself up to my full height and assumed what I thought was an imperious look. "After all, if you want me to act like a king's daughter, I must dress like one."

Her beautiful face darkened with rage. "What extravagance! Remember, *liebschen*, it's the king's money you're spending so freely. You may have one of mine for tonight. I wear them but once."

"Really," I replied, my voice heavy with sarcasm. "Which one will it be?" I ran my eyes coolly up and down her figure. "I am certain that any of them will be snug. I refer, of course to the bodice," I added maliciously, and ducked quickly into the giant mahogany armoire to avoid a slap.

Now, hours later, my heart still pounded with anger and frustration. The splashing noise of water running for Lola's bath filled the boudoir. While I waited for the great marble tub to fill up, I fussed around preparing the things for her evening toilette. It took the courtesan two full hours to arrange herself for her nightly rendezvous with the king. And tonight there would be a grand reception in the glittering salon on the ground floor of the palace. The whole court would be there. I should wear this old green muslin just for spite, I thought viciously, and maybe tie the split bodice together with a piece of string.

"Sieglinde!"

Lola's voice from the marble bathroom was sharp, soaring over the roar of the water.

Let her wait. I moved slowly, deliberately, to the dressing table, stopping to position the roses on a rococo table nearby. Because of my height I had to bend over to straighten out the five hair brushes of varying hardness so that Lola need only reach out and pick them up in turn— first the softest and gentlest of them, then working gradually to the stiff-bristled ones. At the edge of the table, I placed the crystal bowl which held the fresh-squeezed lemon juice, milk, and honey mixture which smoothed away the fine wrinkles around her lovely eyes. Pushing thirty, she is, I meditated with glee.

Straightening up, I spread my wide lips in a big smile. The youthful face in the floor-to-ceiling mirror over the

6

dressing table smiled back. I moved a few steps sideways to block out the lifesize canvas of Lola that hung on the opposite wall. Surrounded as I was by the elaborately carved frame of the mirror, I too was a portrait.

"A young goddess, a veritable nymph of the woods!" That was what the old lecher, Baron Von Edel, had called me when I was brought to court last April. "And a genuine, honest-to-god virgin, I presume," he'd added with a wicked gleam in his slanted blue eyes.

A virgin, to be sure. I'd just passed my fourteenth birthday, but already had full, luscious curves at breast and hip, and a proud carriage to go with my exceptional height.

Turning slightly to view my profile, I lifted a hand above my head in imitation of the statue of Venus in the salon. Given the right costume—or none at all—I could pass for a Greek goddess. I lowered my arm to touch the silky skin at the neckline of the green muslin. Even with the brooch with which I had pulled the bodice together the burgeoning fullness spilled over the lacy edge of the dress like bread left to rise too long in the bowl.

"You are like your mother," Ortrud had told me many times. "She was like the Valkyrie of the olden times. They were the handmaidens of the gods, with great deep bosoms a man could lose himself in."

The young King Ludwig had lost himself in the bosom of a golden-haired Valkyrie who'd come with her ailing father from a land in the frozen north. Some said Sweden, others Norway. No one could tell me for sure, because she'd died of the childbed fever hours after my birth at Schachten, the royal hunting lodge. The king, so Ortrud reported, had been desolated at her death. "Kristina was Ludwig's one true love," she assured me.

I spoke to the woman in the mirror. "You are a Valkyrie like your mother. You are a deep-bosomed goddess. One day you will drive men mad. You are not a bastard in the sight of Wotan and Thor."

Child though I still was in many ways, I was keenly and fully aware of my physical assets: a large firm bosom swelling roundly like melons in August, hips curving sweetly to match the bosom, a narrow, well-defined waist, a long, slender neck of a deep ivory hue, a face covered with a faintly golden glow garnered from childhood summers in the clear air of the mountains where I'd grown up. But what really set me apart from the general run of Bavar-

7

ian girls was my hair. I touched it now, the coronet of gleaming braids that sat on my head like a golden serpent coiled in its lair.

"*Gott in Himmel*!" Von Edel had sputtered one evening when he surprised me brushing the waist-long cataract of hair in front of Lola's mirror. "Don't let any other men see you like this, or I wouldn't give your much treasured virginity five minutes."

I pursed my lips against the wave of disgust which rose in my throat at the thought of Ludwig's aging prime minister. He was literally the king's shadow. While Lola and the king tussled in the great silk and velvet canopied bed the thin-faced nobleman insisted on entertaining me. His idea of entertainment was running his dried-up fingers along my bare arms and shoulders, all the while raking my body with hot, lustful eyes.

"Sieglinde, get in here. What on God's green earth are you doing out there?"

"Arranging the flowers for tonight, Lola," I called out sweetly. "There's a regular avalanche of them today. Have you forgotten that tonight's a very special occasion for the king? He's receiving the Benedictine Sisters and giving them the purse for America."

One last curtsy to the girl in the mirror. "You are a Valkyrie," I whispered to her, "a goddess, a handmaiden of Odin. You are beautiful, and one day you will be free."

Then with a swift little dance step, I moved across the lush Persian carpet and down the three marble steps into the sunken bathroom which was the talk of all Europe, and Asia too for all I knew. It certainly had cost a sultan's fortune, Von Edel had remarked.

My foot was on the top step, when a pair of sharp claws dug into my shoulder, right through the worn gauzy material. "Ouch! *Verdammt* again! Am I to bleed to death today?"

Lola's monkey Chou-Chou bent his wizened old-man face to peer wistfully into my eyes from his perch on my right shoulder. Despite the throbbing headache and the pain from his sharp claws, I burst into laughter. In a moment, the warm, wriggling little body was in my arms, snuggled against my bursting dress. Ugly as the creature was, I loved him. With Ortrud dead this year and a half, no sisters or brothers to call my own, I had little else to love.

I dropped Chou-Chou gently to the floor and reached

down to stroke the silky black and white Pomeranian, who jumped from her cushioned basket to nip at my ankles. Miraculously my headache had vanished, the excitement with the animals having brought me out of my depression and irritability. My heart beat with sheer good health and youth. I approached the woman in the tub. She had already turned off the torrent of water from the copper pipe. Helping Lola with her bath was one of the chores I'd been given when Lola had persuaded the king to fetch me from the Schachten hunting lodge. I had been earmarked for the Benedictine convent, and had been trained by the dear Sisters toward that end.

"Nonsense," the king's mistress had declared, "sheer waste. Let the girl see something of life before she buries herself under a black veil." The shrewd violet eyes, which had made Ludwig her love slave, had swept knowingly from my dirty feet in wooden clogs to the pile of gold on my head. "Putting *that* in a convent would be a sin against nature."

Now she rose out of the soapy water like Aphrodite out of the foam, waiting for me to scrub her. The walls of the bath were painted a translucent sea-green and were decorated with richly tinted designs of men and women in various erotic positions. A skylight the length of the room, paned with rose-colored glass, cast an iridescent glow on the entire place, making her white body pink as a newborn babe.

I reached for the rough washing cloth on the little marble table and began to rub in circles, beginning at the shoulders, down the curve of her back, over the rounded thighs. For ten whole minutes, I scrubbed every inch of the seductive form, then drew fresh water from the pipe and rinsed her off. She stepped out of the tub so that I could wipe her dry. Since the tub sunk into the floor she had to lean on me to lift herself out.

At her touch the familiar feeling of being at the bottom of the ocean overwhelmed me. A curious kind of sleepy excitement coursed through my body.

While my mistress chattered unceasingly about the coming evening, I finished drying her, taking extra care with the area under the arms and between the thighs.

"Do the belly once more," she said in her imperious way. "It tends to become fleshy. In the steady, circular motion I taught you."

9

"I am told that men like a soft belly in a woman," I said.

Her sudden laugh filled the little room, echoing harshly.

"And what would *you* know about men, *mein Kind*?"

Lifting my chin with a moist finger, she peered intently into my face. "You're going on sixteen. That bosom of yours would fill any man's arms. Time the king was marrying you off, for your own good."

"Marry—me? Who would marry me?"

Her beautiful eyes gleamed wickedly. "That's no problem. Von Edel, for one. He acts like an old goat at the mere scent of you."

My thoughts tumbled all over each other as I rubbed the alabaster thighs to warm pinkness, swept my hands under and around the full springing breasts. The nipples darkened, became taut, extended. Lola was aroused. Nausea churned in my stomach. Nobody decent wants a bastard, even a royal one. I would never marry. I had no use for men and their evil lusts. I longed for the purity and quiet of the convent where I had known peace and happiness. Being a woman, lying with a man, joining your flesh with his, brought only pain and humiliation.

And yet—as I stroked her flesh I felt her own sensual excitement permeating my own body. Blood every bit as hot as hers was pulsing through my veins. Every night when I rubbed her, the same pulsating, suffocating exhilaration came over me. It was the same sensation I got when Von Edel rubbed his parchment fingers along my bare arm. As hard as I fought the flesh, I could not deny it. Even though I prayed to the Virgin, there was no stopping the torment in my soul. I was a woman, God help me.

After I had tried on and discarded a number of her ball gowns, Lola was forced to admit that they were all too snug in the bosom. So now I stood beside my father the king in a simple flowing gown of stark white chiffon, which fell in soft folds from the shoulder and was caught at the waist with a dark green satin cord. It was a costume Lola had worn at a masked ball last winter. I wore no corset. A thin muslin shift was all that lay between me and the chiffon.

"The Countess of Landsberg," a scarlet and gold clad footman announced from the foot of the stairs.

There had been much discontent throughout the kingdom at Ludwig's elevating a woman who was little more than a slut to nobility. The king's wife, Queen Therese, a royal princess in her own right, refused to compete with the audacious Lola, keeping herself and her brood of four sons and three daughters at·the royal palace at Nymphenburg.

My father's tired old face lit up like a candle as the courtesan came gracefully down the polished glass stairway. She was especially ravishing tonight, the cloth-of-gold dress hugging her curves like a second skin.

"What fools men are, even kings," I thought, irritated at all the fuss. A bare bosom, a peek of nipple, a suggestive glance from heavy-lidded eyes, and the strongest of them turns to jelly.

Ludwig cut a fine figure in his brilliant red and black military uniform, medals strewn across the front. He looked every inch a king. I loved him. He'd always treated me well and had given me a thorough schooling with the Benedictines. I glanced tenderly at his drawn face, remembering the shouting and torches in the Marienplatz last night. This woman made him happy, but the people were in an uproar over his lavish spending and his neglect of duty since she had captured his heart and mind.

"Does she live? Does she breathe? Or is she perhaps a figure of Venus fallen from her marble pedestal?"

A silky cultured voice I knew only too well purred into my ear. Long, tapering, well-manicured fingers pressed on the bulge of muscle just above my elbow. Revulsion rippled through me.

"Venus! But I should be naked for such a pose," I replied, shrugging my shoulder in an effort to rid myself of Von Edel's grip.

The prime minister's hand only tightened on my arm and moved down toward my wrist. Lifting it to his lips, he kissed each finger in turn. "I must beg the king to enact a law against royal virgins looking so seductive."

"The king's guests—the Sisters—I must greet them," I said, sliding my hand out of his grasp.

But the old rake was not easily disposed of. "It will give me great pleasure to assist you in that duty," he smirked, tucking my hand in his with a firm grasp and guiding me toward the four nuns who sat, self-conscious, ridiculously out of place in that resplendent salon, on straight-backed chairs against the wall. All eyes turned to watch our progress. The king's minister, although well past middle age, was

11

handsome, with sharp distinguished features set under a sweep of iron-grey hair.

Naked gods and goddesses balanced on pedestals were set in niches in every wall. There was Venus, stretching her arm langorously, alluringly over her graceful head. A somewhat muscle-bound Apollo fingered a fig leaf that vainly attempted to hide his manhood. Immediately behind the nuns' black veiled heads hung a colorful painting of a Roman orgy, replete with full bosoms and ripe hips, while half-man, half-goat satyrs with grossly distended male organs embraced the women.

No wonder the Sisters sat with downcast eyes, like prim little schoolgirls. I greeted the four warmly, kissing each in turn. I knew and loved them all from the winters I'd spent with them in their convent right outside Munich.

Sister Paulita, the oldest, who had taught me to pray when in despair, to hold my head high, to be unashamed of my illegitimate birth, was to lead the group to America where they would establish a school for the children of German immigrants. "*Liebschen*, you are radiant. Life in a palace must agree with you. I'm afraid you haven't missed us at all." Her dear face glowed with pride and affection.

Tears sprang to my eyes. "Not miss you? Would I miss my right arm? You were all like mothers to me."

We chattered like magpies, the five of us—fat Sister Elfreda, the cook, who had plied me with marzipan and rich dark molasses cookies, Sister Susanna who had taught me to embroider exquisite designs in colored thread on altar cloths, and Sister Emmanuel who had nursed me through childhood sicknesses and who had comforted me most upon Ortrud's death.

Von Edel stood beside me, smiling through his pincenez, charming the nuns. A footman in satin breeches and brocaded jacket offered pastries on a silver tray. Sister Elfreda reached out to help herself to a handful of the goodies. Remembering her sweet tooth, I scooped up another handful and dumped them in her capacious black lap. I hugged her, tears springing to my eyes. "What I wouldn't give to be going with you, Sister. *America*. It sounds wonderful just saying the word!"

"Yes." Sister Paulita spoke up for her companion, whose mouth was full of pastry. "The need is great, especially for strong young people like you. We are old, but we will

12

make a start. Many young Germans are already there in Pennsylvania waiting for us."

Von Edel suddenly leaned forward and clasped the nun's hands in his. "One day, I think, many of us will be in the land of promise. Europe—Bavaria at least—is used up. If I were but a young man—"

A little bell tinkled and the king rose to speak to the glittering assembly. A thousand candles gleamed from three vast gold and crystal chandeliers, as well as from torches set in replicas of Greek and Roman lamps in niches along the walls.

"Used up." Von Edel's apt phrase ran through my mind. Lola Montez, with Ludwig's help, had done her part to use up Bavaria's prosperity. Hatred and resentment swelled within me as I glanced over to the loveseat. She sat, resplendent, surrounded by admirers, her lovely face lifted to the king as Ludwig made a pretty speech and presented a pouch heavy with gold pieces to Sister Paulita. I longed to go with them.

"Waft me to America," I prayed silently, "to the rich virgin land of promise where the air is clean and there are no kings, no courtesans, no puffed-up, overdressed aristocrats draining the lifeblood out of the people."

Von Edel laid a silk-clad arm across my shoulders, dangling his fingers on my bare arm. "Our beloved monarch your father is a genuine Christian, don't you agree, *Fräulein*?"

Resisting the impulse to shake off his touch, I replied, "I know nothing of politics, nor do I care."

"Spoken like a true German woman," he laughed, "but surely your schoolgirl imagination is aroused by the tales of the handsome red-bearded giant who leads the rebel student corps."

"I've heard some wild stories about Frederick Barbarossa emerging from Kyffhauser Mountain where he has supposedly been sleeping since the twelfth century."

As the gay crowd swirled around us, a nameless dread crept over me. The salon reeked of perfume and warm bodies, the air seemed charged with suppressed excitement, as before a thunderstorm in August. But it was only the tenth of June, Corpus Christi Day.

"Death to the Venus," the rabble had shouted last night in the Marienplatz. I glanced down at my breasts and hips swathed in the innocent white chiffon. Von Edel had called

13

me a Venus. What would the student rebels do to me? How could they tell that I was not such a one as Lola?

Like every Bavarian schoolgirl I had grown up with the legend of Frederick Barbarossa, the most flamboyant monarch of medieval Christendom. It was he who had made the Germans the proud rulers of all Europe. He'd been reported drowned while fording an Arabian river during the third Crusade. But superstitious mountain people still nurtured the belief (and had convinced many otherwise sensible people) that he was merely sleeping away the centuries in a forest cave, waiting for the right moment to arise from the dead and become the German Messiah.

Von Edel bent his head close to mine, whispering earnestly, but his words were lost in a tremendous clap of thunder. Or was it thunder? A rumbling as of an earthquake shook the palace. The gloriously shining chandeliers swayed perilously on their chains. The crystal prisms tinkled ominously. The fingers on my arm tightened; the nails bit into my flesh. "The rabble are at our door, it seems," Von Edel whispered, his eyes flying upward to the flickering candles.

The entire room stood as if hypnotized, still as the statues against the walls. Two uniformed guards ran through the room to the loveseat where Ludwig stood conversing with the nuns. They whispered into the king's ear. My father's face whitened. Dismissing the guards, who raced back immediately to the massive bronze gates outside the salon, he rose and spoke to the paralyzed guests.

"The rebels are outside in the Barerstrasse. Remain calm. As your sovereign, I promise you that no harm will come to any of you. At this very moment the royal mounted cuirassiers—"

A deafening shatter of breaking glass interrupted his speech. A stone flashed like a streak of lightning across the room, striking a tall mirror hanging directly over the loveseat. Flying splinters enveloped Ludwig and Lola, falling like a silver shower in a million tiny fragments on the Turkish carpet.

A mighty wailing, like the sound of the damned rising out of hell, rent the air. The richly clad and by now drunken courtiers and their ladies scurried like rats toward the doorways.

I froze, truly becoming the statue Von Edel had called me.

14

"Come, quickly, follow me. If you value your life—and virtue." The old man half-pushed, half-carried me to the end of the salon where the shattered mirror had hung. A second thunderclap resounded.

"They've got cannon, probably mounted on the rooftops across the street," he panted.

"The nuns," I screamed at him. "Sister Paulita and the others."

"They are in no danger. Nuns are hardly what that crowd wants."

We got to the place where the mirror had hung, but Ludwig and Lola had disappeared. Glass crunched underfoot. Von Edel leaned against the wall right beside the loveseat. Magically, the wall swung open to reveal a long, narrow opening behind. Just before the wall closed on us again, Von Edel pulled a bronze Roman lamp from its sconce in the wall beside the loveseat. The king and his mistress were already in the hiding place, clinging to each other like frightened children. Von Edel held the flickering torch to their faces. Stark fear was reflected in their eyes.

"Just making sure it's you, your majesty," he said. "Nobody else knows about this place, but—"

"We are dead. They'll find us!" screamed the scarlet woman who had talked so bravely this afternoon. Short hoarse animal-like sounds came from her painted lips.

"Stop that, you idiot," Von Edel shouted at her. "Someone's bound to hear you through the wall. It is imperative that we all remain absolutely quiet."

Then all at once all the pent-up rage of the past year surged into my veins. "You sorceress! You messenger of hell!" I dug my nails into the soft flesh of Lola's bare shoulder, just as she had done to me that afternoon in the bath.

Words spilled out of me, though I was careful to keep them to a hoarse whisper. "It's you, your extravagance, your insatiable demands, that have impoverished our country. Because of you, you slut, my father may be killed by his own subjects, who once loved him."

I pulled at her golden dress, ripping it half off her body. She cowered, bare-breasted, too shocked to fight back. Ludwig's large grey eyes looked at me wonderingly.

"Please, please, Sieglinde. Control yourself. No time for that now." Von Edel pulled me from the weeping Lola. I collapsed on the floor, great wracking sobs tearing at my chest. We were all lost.

Ludwig removed his military jacket and covered his shivering mistress.

"Here, hold this." Von Edel handed me the torch again. "Don't know how much oil is left in the stem. I've got to work while we have light." Walking swiftly to a wooden chest standing against the far wall, he pulled a little key from his pocket and opened the lock. Turning to bestow a smile of triumph on the king, he said, "I've been expecting an attack."

Then he swiftly pulled out of the trunk armfuls of shabby garments, such as servants or street laborers might wear.

"Here is a change of clothing for all of us. When the rebels do not find us in the palace they will depart. At which time we can make our escape, I'm sure."

The king stood up and began examining the garments in the flickering light. "Very shrewd of you, Von Edel. My compliments."

Despite my revulsion at his lecherous advances, a begrudging admiration for the seasoned old man grew within me. His voice, his whole manner carried an authority completely lacking in Ludwig.

The four of us were quickly attired in the poor rags Von Edel dug out of the trunk. With her black curls covered with a peasant shawl, a long white apron tied over a shapeless gown of black bombazine, Lola looked like any one of a hundred farmers' wives come to the city for market day. "Scrub off that paint," Von Edel ordered, throwing her a piece of cloth to do it with.

The men replaced their tight-fitting white breeches with the loose ankle-length trousers popular among the country folk. I struggled into a white low-necked blouse much too tight for me, and a series of full-skirted petticoats.

As I stood facing Von Edel and the king for inspection, the prime minister shook his head and touched the fullness of breast spilling out of the blouse. "*Nein*. This will never do. You'll be raped before you take two steps outside the building." He handed me a shapeless grey sacklike garment that tied around the middle with a bit of rope.

"Take your hair down," Von Edel barked at me. "Unbraid it."

Quickly I pulled the pins that held the great coiled serpent in place. The two thick white-gold braids lay heavily on my shoulder, falling over my bosom to my waist.

"Here, I'll help you." His hands trembling, Von Edel

loosened my hair from its braided prison, until the great mass of hair lay around me like a golden river. "*Liebe Gott*," he exclaimed under his breath. "How much can a man endure?"

He turned to the trunk once more and fished out a box of black powder with which he dusted my hair so that the gold was dulled to a dirty brown. "Now sit down and braid it again. Even if they catch you, they won't know who you are."

With that, the prime minister snuffed out the torch and slid to the floor beside me. The king's heavy whisper came out of the darkness. "You will be richly rewarded for this night, Baron. Name your price. Even to half of my kingdom."

Von Edel made a dry little sound which I took for a laugh. "Nothing so grand as that, your majesty. Just this little girl of yours will do. With an appropriate dowry, of course, as befits the daughter of a king."

"Take her. She's yours."

Soft whispering and titters were coming from the other side of the room where Lola and the king were sitting. I realized with a shock that with the immediate danger of capture over, the two were actually making love in the dark. I tensed with dread of what Von Edel might try to do. We might be here all night waiting for the rebels to finish ransacking Lola's palace. The sounds of running and shouting still resounded from the salon and the upstairs rooms. Would Von Edel follow the king's example and take me right here on the floor?

But he remained a gentleman, contenting himself with occasionally stroking my thigh under the full skirts. We listened in silence to the obscene grunting, the tiny squeals, the loud sound of kisses, followed by the rhythmic thumping I knew so well from my nights in the boudoir while they wrestled on the great canopied bed. It was true then what people said: the nearness of death intensifies desire.

"Baroness Von Edel," I rehearsed in my mind. I didn't fight the thought. I was a bastard, after all.

At that moment the whole wall burst in on us. Light streamed into our hiding place. Hard-muscled arms swooped me off the floor. My last conscious memory was of my father the king's changing countenance. First shock, then agony, then resignation, as he realized he had been captured by the rebellious Burschen.

Chapter 2

It is the first day of May, *Venustag*, the day of Venus. During the night the god Wotan has wedded the goddess Freya and the earth is fertile once again. The spring *föhn* is blowing, and I am running, my white-gold hair streaming in the persistent wind. I spread out my arms wantonly to greet the new life. The smell of the wild earth penetrates my nostrils.

In Christendom they call it Mary's Day. It is the day to plant seeds. Ortrud had given me a little basket of flower seeds she saved from last year's blooms. I am taking them to the Virgin's grotto to be blessed.

Winter is over. In the night the thunder of the ice cracking in the lake had awakened us in the hunting lodge. I kissed my old nurse on the lips, as was our custom each morning, and set out with my little basket. I would lay the basket at the foot of the blue and white statue. The Virgin would smile upon me.

"Please, Ortrud," I pleaded, "may I dip my feet in the lake? The ice is far out in the middle."

"Go, *liebschen*, go. Greet the new year. The fish will swarm this summer because a virgin has dipped her feet in the water on the first day of May."

My breasts, like little apples, form a curve under my simple frock, which ends at my knees. Next year, when my breasts are fuller, I must cover my legs. Next year when I am fourteen, I will be a woman.

Off with the heavy boots, roll down the prickly wool stockings. "Ahhh!" The water is clear, cold, bracing. I gasp with shivering delight at the touch of it on my warm bare toes. I laugh out loud. I shiver in ecstasy, longing to fling myself into the cold glacial depths, to feel the primal strength of it in my loins.

19

My loins. That part of me which makes me a woman. In this last year the mass of hair has grown full and bushy. The mound of Venus, it is called. The hair there is dark, unlike that on my head, which is almost white and shines in the sun.

But what's that? A monstrous primordial beast has risen from the depths of the icy waters. In an instant it is upon me, its iron claws raking my shoulder, crushing my maiden breasts. Something hard, like a rod of iron, is inside my body, in the mound of Venus.

My womb is split open, my life's blood pouring out onto the damp earth at the lakeside.

"Mother of God, Holy Virgin, save me," I scream, but my prayer is cut off by a cruel paw—no, it is a hand, a large hairy hand which covers my mouth, so that my teeth press into my lips.

I taste blood.

I am being raped.

The beast that is devouring me has a breath that smells of sour beer and vomit. As I struggle upward through layers of pain that sear the insides of my belly I know that the lake at Schachten, Ortrud's kiss, the basket of seeds, are all a dream.

The beast moves in and out of my bleeding loins with savage thrusts. The hairy hand moves away from my mouth, clamps on my breast. "*Gott!* The Venusberg itself! A man could die happy climbing mountains like these."

The voice is young, sounding more like a boy than a man. Moist lips chew at my nipples.

"So this is how I will die," I think, strangely calm. Like a sow in a sty, who has been pushed into the mud by a boar that came wild and choked with lust out of the forest.

O my God I am heartily sorry for all my sins . . . The Act of Contrition learned at Ortrud's knee comes unbidden to my lips.

"The bitch is praying. Do you suppose it's for us?" The words were slurred, as if the speaker were drunk.

"Shut up, you jackass." Another voice. I had regained consciousness by now, but was terrified of opening my eyes and looking at my tormenters. Coarse, ribald laughter followed the last remark. The first voice, the boyish one, protested. "After all, she *was* a virgin. And you said, Kurt, that there couldn't possibly be any virgins in the palace of the concubine."

The man on top of me suddenly spoke, his voice harsh and grating in my ear. "Well, whatever she is, virgin or not, that was the juiciest piece of womanflesh I've ever tasted."

I must play dead, I told myself, clenching my teeth to keep from crying out at the searing pain that flashed from muscle to muscle. Little explosions were going off in my head. They must have struck me with something to knock me out.

The one called Kurt, apparently having enough of me, slid his heavy body off mine. "God, that gave me a mighty thirst. Any of that beer left, Andreas?"

Sound of footsteps, as if they were going into another room. Silence. I waited a few minutes to make sure they were out of sight, then cautiously slitted my eyes open. It was a small dark room of some kind, like a cell. Dull gray light filtered in through a tiny opening high on the stone wall. As my eyes became accustomed to the half-dark, I made out a narrow cot against a wall, and a metal chamber pot that emitted a foul odor. An enormous crucifix with a bleeding Christ on it filled the wall directly opposite where I lay. The floor of the cell was covered with a thin layer of water. I must be in a monastery, or even a convent. But which one? Where? The foothills of the Bavarian Alps were dotted with medieval ruins. I gazed fearfully at the huge rectangular stones that fitted together loosely to make the walls. They were glistening with damp. Probably infested with rats, too.

Suddenly a yellowish glow filled the cell, as one of the men returned. He held a candle in a heavy wooden holder. He stood over me, peering down intently. I kept my eyes in narrow slits, so that he could not tell if I were awake. He was very young, no older than I. His dress was the typical student costume: loose trousers, full white blouse, rakish cap tilted over one eye. "No sound out of her, Kurt," he said, his voice ragged, frightened. "We must have killed her dragging her through the streets that way. Maybe she suffocated under all that hay in the wagon."

Kurt came up alongside. He bent down, touched me on the breast. "Nah. Still pretty warm. Quit worrying. Although if she *is* dead, she's well out of it. From the looks of her, she had nothing ahead of her but a passel of kids and an early death anyway."

"I dunno, Kurt," Andreas replied. "So soft she was, and

smelling so sweet. Somehow—well, kitchen sluts don't smell like that—like perfume. Maybe she was one of those aristocrats in disguise."

Kurt made a noise. "Quit imagining things. So if she's dead, we'll bury her. We can get Brother Matthew to give her a good Christian burial. Fortunes of war, and all that."

"You're right, of course," Andreas agreed. "What's done is done. What we really have to worry about is Lothar. What's he going to say when we have to tell him we didn't get the bitch he wanted?"

"The Valkyrie with the white-gold hair? We did the best we could, you know that. We scoured that palace, all three floors. She must have got away in the first fighting."

"Or more likely someone else took her off."

"Nope." Andreas sounded morose. "Every Bursch knew the orders. *Get the Valkyrie bitch for the Redbeard.*"

Suddenly Andreas leaned his head abainst the stones beside the crucifix and beat his fists several times. His shoulders heaved. He began to cry like a baby, great heartrending, tearing sobs. "I wish to God I was back in Eisenach right now. I'd be helping with the barley sowing. In June the fields are sweet, the sun is warm, the air is fresh—here I am, raping, killing—"

"Christ, stop that sniveling. Fine revolutionary you are—" Kurt's words were cut off by a noise from somewhere above. Then heavy footsteps, like someone marching down a flight of steps.

"Where is she? Where's my woman?"

"Lothar. *Gott bedankt* you're safe." Andreas and Kurt leaped out of the cell to greet the newcomer. They were all hidden from my view since I was not lying directly in front of the narrow doorway.

"Never mind that, where's the girl I told you to get me?"

"We—we couldn't find the one you wanted, Lothar, the concubine's maid with the white-gold hair. She must have got away before we broke in. If she *is* the king's daughter as you said, then—well, maybe she's with him."

"No. I was in the party that grabbed the king and his bitch out of their hiding place behind the wall. And that traitor, Von Edel, too. I thought you two were looking for the little bastard."

"Then it's all over? The king is dead?" Andreas stammered, avoiding Lothar's question about me. "And Lola Montez too?"

22

"No, damn it, we got outside with them, but the royal cuirassiers were all over the place. The Burschen scattered like sheep with a wolf pack after them." Lothar's voice was low, discouraged. "They got away. Now we have to start all over again."

Suddenly a mighty banging resounded through the cellar, as if someone had picked up a piece of furniture and banged it against the ceiling.

Lothar's voice again. "Right now, though, I've got a mighty thirst. From the looks of the place you've been drinking all night."

"Yes, we have at that," Kurt's voice. "It was pretty fierce there for a while. The fighting, I mean."

Lothar gave a little laugh. "You're still standing up. If you ever want to be a good Bursch, you've got to learn to hold your beer."

"Well, maybe it wasn't the beer. But before we marched on the palace last night, we filled up at Hofmann's. And we got ourselves a little bitch last night. A kitchen slut, from the look of her. She was just lying in the street, so we picked her up and brought her here."

"Here?" Lothar exploded. "You fools. This is a monastery, you can't have a woman here. Where is she?"

"In here. That cell over there."

"We're not fighting the poor, you bastards, but the rich. Did you rape her all night? Is that what you're trying to tell me?"

As he spoke, Lothar moved to fill the narrow doorway of the cell. Tall, burly, arms akimbo, he completely blocked out the dim yellow light from the other room. I forgot about playing dead as the giant figure moved into my line of vision. Not only was his beard red and full and long, so long it reached almost to the top of his trousers, but a thatch of coppery red swirled around his head, down over his ears, flowing into the beard. A broad, thick mustache filled the space between his nose and lips. The nose was long, full-fleshed, the lips wide and sensuous. He looked like the pictures of the Vikings of old in the Pinakothek, the magnificent art gallery Ludwig had built in Munich. Or no—something else. A King of the Mountain from one of the fairy tale books Ortrud had read to me. One of those ancient mythical monarchs who were half-man, half-beast. He also reminded me of Frederick Barbarossa. God knows there were plenty of statues and paintings of Germany's first great emperor.

He came swiftly through the doorway, moving like a panther despite his huge bulk. He was so tall his bronze hair brushed the low wooden rafters of the cell. Steel-banded arms encircled my trembling form. I was lifted out of the icy water on the floor of the cell. The giant pressed an ear to my breast. So we stood, locked together, for long minutes, while he listened for my heartbeat. The brilliant coppery mass of hair covered my face, my nose, my mouth, nearly choking me. My breathing stopped. The hands pressing into my back at shoulder and thigh were warm as mother's milk. I had the strange sensation of a sick infant being cradled at her mother's breast.

"Ahhh." A great sigh of relief came from the massive chest. "Faint but steady."

Carrying me into the other room where Andreas and Kurt waited for us, he laid me down gently on a narrow cot, one of many lined up, with some wooden tables on trestles, against the walls. Then, still bent low over me, he pried open both of my eyelids. Stifling a small cry at the pain, I opened both eyes wide, to gaze into a pair of eyes of such an intense green that I imagined myself once again in the glacial waters of Schachten. Even in the wavering lamplight I could see flecks of gold in the sea-green depths.

"Wake up, bitch, whoever you are. You're far from dead. You've got years ahead of you to repent of your sins."

Now the sea-green eyes, after their first soft concern, hardened into granite that has been touched by forest moss. Andreas and Kurt, who had been standing in the center of the room, rushed over to look down at me with relief making their young faces almost comical.

Lothar turned on them, panther-like. "I could kill you, both of you, for this. Now get some blankets, some hot soup and brandy. *Schnell*! Quick! Where's that damn Matthew?" Picking up a long wooden table top, he banged fiercely once more on the ceiling. Footsteps sounded overhead. "She needs some hot soup and brandy."

Words tumbled from my frozen lips. *"Danke. Danke schön,"* I whispered. After the first wave of relief that this monster was not going to rape me, an enormous rush of gratitude overwhelmed me. I wanted to pull down that bearded face, kiss those wide sensuous lips.

24

"Save your breath. You'll need every ounce of strength to pull yourself out of this."

Pulling up one of the wooden benches close to my cot, he straddled it, leaned his head back, surveyed me from head to toe like a butcher purchasing a steer from a farmer. "Hmm. *Gott!* Can't say that I blame those two fools. You are magnificent! Breasts like twin mounts of Venus, thighs a man could prove himself in." He paused, as if reflecting, then in a quieter, sadder tone, "Would to God you were of finer stock."

Neither of us spoke, simply took stock of each other, both wide-eyed. A fourth person had come down the stairs, a monk in a brown robe. A low conversation ensued between him and Andreas.

I stared as if mesmerized, lost in the sea-green depths. My body, which still ached from the night's ordeal, which moments before had been rigid with cold and wet, now burned as with a fever. A frightening, overpowering urge to reach out and unclench those great hairy fists and draw that massive coppery head to my breast took hold of me. I had a mad desire to crush that curving, finely modelled mouth to mine. I who just yesterday had hated all men, had despised the very thought of physical love!

"Here's the soup, Lothar." Andreas held out a wooden trencher with a steaming bowl and a large spoon on it.

"Well, put it down on the bench," Lothar said. "And get a blanket."

Andreas and Kurt wrapped me in a black woolen blanket smelling of mold and damp. I uttered a silent prayer that it was clean and free of vermin. Monasteries were noted for their filth, monks apparently considering godliness above cleanliness.

"Open your mouth."

Lothar held the wooden bowl with one big hand and with the other pressed the spoon against my mouth. I opened obediently and swallowed.

"Good girl."

A flicker of a smile played about his lips and eyes. Just a flicker. Here was a man who would not be easy to tame. He would not be a lapdog, like Ludwig. This was a man used to command.

"Brandy," he shouted at Andreas, who had gone back to sitting despondently at the table, cradling his mug of beer.

Andreas leaped up, but at the same moment Brother

Matthew returned. "Only got two hands, two feet," he muttered, as he handed Lothar the bottle.

"One day you'll die and go to heaven, and then you'll have a pair of wings too," Kurt sniggered from his place at the table.

The thick hot soup, some kind of bean or pea mixture, brought a warm, comforting glow to my insides. The world looked better. But Lothar's face darkened as he continued to feed me. "*Gott verdammt*, Andreas, you did this. You and your damn lust!" He threw the spoon down on the blanket, unwound his giant frame from the bench.

I lifted my head weakly out of the cocoon of blanket. "I'm not sick, I'm perfectly able to feed myself."

The young Andreas, his boyish face white and scared-looking, stood spoon in hand as I struggled up to a sitting position. But suddenly both Andreas and the room and everyone in it began to whirl around. I fell back on the hard cot, nauseated, groaning.

"Woman! You will listen to me." Lothar was back in a great leap from the table where he'd been dipping beer from a large crock. "Do you want to bleed to death? Stay flat on that beautiful back of yours for the next week at least."

Andreas resumed feeding me, his hands trembling, his face white. "You must never disobey Lothar," he whispered, panic in his voice. "When Lothar commands, everybody jumps."

The bowl finally empty, Andreas left me with a chunk of black bread. I chewed slowly, relishing the thick sweetness of it. With each bite my strength grew, and with it my spirits soared. I wasn't afraid of Lothar. Who was he to order me around? I was the daughter of the king of Bavaria.

Once again Lothar towered over me, his eyes cool, appraising. "Well, my Valkyrie—"

"I thought I was Venus," I said, pertly. Two could play at this goddess game.

Shaggy copper eyebrows lifted in surprise. "Spirit, huh? Unusual for a kitchen maid. Just what did you do at the whore's palace?"

"I—I made myself useful." Let him guess.

His big hands dipped down to pick up mine, which lay quietly on top of the blanket. He studied them for a long moment.

"Well, whatever it was, you didn't do it in the kitchen. My guess is that it was done in the bedroom."

I flushed angrily. "I played Venus at the nightly entertainments. I was an actress."

The big hairy head wagged back and forth. "No, not that either. But I'll find out. Meanwhile you are my Valkyrie, a nobler breed by far than the Venuses. The Valkyrie were the handmaids of Wotan."

Suddenly, with the swiftness of a swooping eagle, he bent low and brushed my lips as if to kiss me. The breath from his mouth was warm and smelled of beer. His nearness was making my head spin. I shook it violently several times, trying to regain my sanity. Lothar stood up finally, reached for the brandy on the bench and forced two spoonfuls down my mouth.

Moments later I drifted off in a haze of blessed sleep. The muted voices of the three men drinking beer formed a distant lullaby.

Chapter 3

"Wake up, whore!" The red-bearded face, purple with rage, green eyes hard as glass, pushed into mine.

"Poor little kitchen maid, huh!" he snarled, his beard fairly bristling. He reached down with his powerful hands, pulled the rough blanket off my still naked body with a quick savage movement. "To think that I was ready to kill my own comrades for raping you, thinking you one of the oppressed. You—you who lived in the same rooms with the concubine. You who gave her daily baths. You who touched the rotten flesh of the whore of Babylon!"

Terrified, still half asleep, I stuttered, "I'm—I'm—"

"Never mind. No more lies. I know who you are. I found out soon enough when I rode back to Munich last night. You are Sieglinde, Ludwig's bastard."

He sat down on the edge of the cot, covered his face with his hands. "And to think I wanted you for myself! Now you're spoiled, your maidenhead gone."

But suddenly he stretched out his long frame beside me, pushing me toward the wall. His long thighs against my naked flesh burned like a flaming torch. With shaking hands he jerked the ribbons from the ends of my braids. Soon the whole mass of hair lay strewn about me on the cot, covering my body almost to my knees. I peered down through half-closed eyes at the brownish-gold mess.

"Pretty clever," he barked. "But not clever enough. But I got my prize anyway. The irony of fate, I guess."

Andreas and Kurt stood gaping down at us, wordless, stunned looks on their faces. They reminded me of little children gazing open-mouthed in front of a lighted Christmas tree.

"*Mein Gott*, Ludwig's daughter," muttered Kurt. "Is *she* the one you wanted, Lothar?"

29

"The same, the very same. She's the little bitch all right. Although now that you two have invaded her, I'm not sure I want her."

He turned, white-faced, to the other two, and for the first time I saw the long, thin scar on the left side of his face. It ran from the corner of his lips to the outer edge of his eye. A duelling scar. A badge of honor among German university students. It stood out now like a bloody slash against his pale face.

"Leave me," he ordered the others. Andreas and Kurt turned and dutifully walked up the steps into the monastery. For a long moment Lothar stared down at me. I lay rigid, torn between terror of what he would do to me now, and an overwhelming attraction for that powerful body. He exuded maleness.

Once more he fell upon me, groaning, swearing under his breath. "It's in the hands of the gods now. Only they can help us, Sieglinde."

The great bearded head lay upon my breast. With his lips he parted my hair to suck first on one nipple, then the other. My lips parted and a sound rolled out like that of a creature caught in a forest trap. As the sensuous lips caressed my breasts, my lips and mouth became dry. I flicked out my tongue to moisten them. I waited, expectant. I wanted this giant to invade my body. My arms lifted to encircle him, my heart beat like a drum. I felt that it would leap out of my chest.

"*Nein.*" He pulled his head away from my breast, shoved me back brutally on the cot. "Not yet. I will not take you here." He laughed, a harsh cruel sound. "That was just a taste. I had to assure myself that you had passion to match your magnificent body." He whipped around savagely and with giant strides disappeared into the darkness of the stairway.

I didn't see him for a month. Andreas was left to "take care" of me. Lothar and Kurt went off, he said, to gather the remnants of the *Studentencorps*, the revolutionary army. What had seemed at first a victory, with the capture of the king and Lola, had all turned to ashes.

Eventually, the leaders of the various groups throughout Germany would meet there, in the monastery of St. Emmeran, at Regensburg, to regroup and make plans for a counterattack.

30

"Your father is now in France, in exile. Maximilian, his son, is on the throne," Andreas told me.

So Maximilian was king! To me he was still a little boy, as in the days when he came with his father and mother to Schachten, in the days before Lola Montez had split up the family. I hadn't seen him for ten years at least. It was impossible for me to think of him as king.

As if trying to atone for his sin of raping me, Andreas transformed himself from a drunken boy into a devoted nurse. He ordered Brother Matthew to bring fresh warm water and fragrant pine-smelling soap each morning and evening. While I refreshed myself, cleansing my entire body, he retreated into one of the little cells that lined the walls.

The coarse sacklike garment I was wearing when they carried me off was too full of blood and street filth to put on my clean body. "And I can't very well ask the monks to launder it for you—a woman's garment," Andreas smirked. So I ended up swathed in the heavy brown wool sack that the monks wore, a rope tied around my narrow waist.

Brother Matthew lumbered up and down the steps—like many monks he was very fat—bringing hot food and drink three times daily. There was meat—pork, beef, lamb—and fresh vegetables from the monastery garden—succulent baby carrots, early lettuce, fragrant green onions, and of course the inevitable sauerkraut from the barrels stored in one of the underground cells.

"It's all so delicious," I laughed to Andreas. "Soon I'll be as fat as Brother Matthew."

"Lothar likes his women," he paused, searching for the right word, "solid, well filled out."

Andreas himself never touched me, except the first day after Lothar left, when he helped me wash the dye out of my hair in a deep basin. It took a week of daily washing with strong yellow soap and hot water to restore the gleaming white-gold color. Instead of braiding it up again into the two long coils and piling it on top of my head in the serpentine coil, I let it hang loose and free.

I felt like a child again. This time of waiting, being taken care of by the two men, the boyish Andreas and the fat Brother Matthew, was like a return to the carefree days of my childhood with Ortrud. Inexplicably, I was happy. A curious lightness filled my body.

Day blended into night, the faint light which came from

the tiny slits in the moldy walls making little difference to the darkness in our cellar. Candles burned continuously in the wooden holders on the table. We seemed to be living in a ghostly netherworld of the past.

The rhythmic tolling of church bells marked the passing of the hours. A bell always was ringing somewhere in the city of Regensburg on the Danube. It was a cathedral town, I knew. Once a medieval crossroads, especially important for the salt trade, the town contained many medieval architectural masterpieces—monasteries, convents, and churches. With the centuries, Munich, across the river, had sprung into prominence and had eclipsed Regensburg as a commercial center.

"We are in the City of Bells," Andreas shouted, during a spell of loud booming from the belfry of St. Emmeran's itself. The entire building shook, the ancient stones threatening to spring from their centuries-old positions.

After the first week, Andreas permitted me to get out of bed and stroll around the immense cellar. Andreas and I became friends. We were almost of an age, he being barely eighteeen, I a month shy of sixteen. My heart went out to him and the others who were fighting the courageous but losing battle with the ancient and powerful aristocratic families of Europe.

We had just finished our supper of soup and bread one night, about three weeks after the Corpus Christi Day of my capture. Brother Matthew had lugged a heavy crock of rich, dark lager beer down the steps and plunked it down on the long wooden table. He grinned at us impishly. "Bock beer, the first draw of the season. Drink enough of that, and you'll forget who you are and where you are. You'll become gods."

Two mugs of the heavy aromatic brew simply made me sleepy and full. But Andreas drank freely, his tongue getting looser as the night drew on. He spoke of Lothar and of the *cause*. His thin, pockmarked face brightened, his dark eyes became luminous. "There are those," he said thickly, "who swear that Lothar is Frederick Barbarossa, come roaring out of his mountain cave."

"Well," I replied, "that should be easy enough to disprove. Where did he come from? He must have a mother and father, like everybody else."

He nodded. "Sure, he was just a student, like me and Kurt. Studying medicine at the University at Munich, be-

32

fore the concubine made the king close it down. But still, there was always a mystery about him. He never talked about his family or his home."

"Some people are close-mouthed," I said. "He seems more a man of action than of words."

"Me now, I'd run off home tomorrow quick as sin."

"Where's home?" I asked.

"Eisenach," he replied dreamily. "In Thuringia. My family's been there since the twelfth century. Once we had a house of stone, like this monastery, and many fields. But now we are reduced to a straw-thatched cottage and a few acres of barley."

He reached into the crock, filled up his mug. "It is the birthplace of Johann Sebastian Bach. We are very proud of that."

The pride in his voice as he spoke of home changed him from a snivelling homesick boy into a patriot. Suddenly it seemed that I too felt a great love for my country. The snippy young girl who had said to Von Edel at the soirée, "I take no interest in politics," had vanished. I plied Andreas with questions. "Why is St. Emmeran's the headquarters? A monastery—it seems odd. I thought they were places where people hid from the world."

"Oh no, not in this case. The Church must fight for survival. Like the rest of us." He rose from the wooden bench, cradling the mug of beer in his skinny hands, and walked over to gaze at the crucifix over my head. "It's a holy mission we are embarked upon. Where the Redbeard goes, I follow." His voice was solemn. "There's something almost supernatural about him. Everybody feels it."

Andreas left the crucifix, walked back to the table, leaned his head down so that our eyes met. "Don't you feel it too? Why do you sit here with me, when you could so easily escape? You outweigh me. You're taller than I. In a wrestling match, you'd be the winner." His whole slender body shook like a sapling in a storm.

I remained silent, afraid that anything I said would betray my fascination with the so-called Barbarossa. Suddenly Andreas picked up a zither which he had been plucking on and off for days and began to sing. The songs he sang were old folk tunes, ballads of love and warfare and sorrow, songs about something that had been lost—lost love, lost maidenhood. He sang a song about a maid who roamed the forest like Diana of old, who met a phantom prince and came together with him in love. He left her, never to be seen again, his bright red blood spilled out on the battlefields of a foreign land. The forest girl bore his child in pain and loneliness.

Tears ran down my cheeks. The music, the beer, the shattering events of the past weeks all combined to loosen the pent-up springs of emotion in my soul. "You're quite a troubadour," I smiled, through my tears. I reached out, drew his dark head to my wool-covered breasts, cradled him there like a baby.

Later in the night, Andreas slept in the cot right behind mine, exhausted from talk and beer and singing. I lay wide awake, rearranging my life. A few weeks ago, I had passionately desired to become a nun, to cover my golden crown of hair with the modest black veil like Sister Paulita and the others. But now, my whole being, body and soul, had awakened to love, a different kind of love from any I'd ever known. That I was in love with Lothar, I had no doubt at all. The moment he was near me, my blood and heart played tricks on me. It was a thing even God could not control.

Whatever, whoever he was, human or divine, the giant, red-bearded, copper-headed Lothar was my destiny.

Four weeks to the night of Corpus Christi Day when I was snatched from Lola's salon, Burschen from all over Germany descended upon St. Emmeran's Monastery. I had been asleep for some hours, but it had been a fitful slumber, punctuated by the scrabblings of the rats that infested the ancient walls.

In the darkness, my hands pressed tightly against my breasts, under the rough brown fabric of the monk's robe. Lothar stood by my cot, head bent. Sleepily, unaware that he was not a dream, I took my hands off my breasts, encircled the thick, corded neck and pulled him down on top of me. Tiny, forklike torches appeared in his green eyes. He put the candle down on the floor, lifted me up from the cot, pressed me closely to his chest.

My body arched in response. His lips forced mine apart, his tongue probed my mouth. My arms tightened, my fingers locked together on his neck. My legs parted underneath the blanket.

Then as suddenly as he had picked me up, he thrust me

34

back down. "Not now, my arching Venus. You and I must wait for love."

Wrapping the blanket around me like a sling, he carried me into the cell where I had spent that first fearful night.

"You must be still. Play dead as you did that first night. Burschen from all over Germany will be here at any moment, and you are still the Wittelsbach bastard. If they discover your presence here—well, I can't be responsible. What Kurt and Andreas did to you will be like a warm bath in comparison."

"Yes, Lothar," I whispered. "I have heard of the Burschen and their ways with women. They have been known to kill with lust."

Lothar picked up a tall stone which had been leaning in a corner of the cell, stepped out into the large room, fitted it into place over the doorway. I lay there, isolated, a prisoner. I'd heard grisly stories of dungeons like this, where prisoners were left to rot. But I felt no fear. Lothar's kiss had told me he wanted to keep me very much alive.

Thunderous noises of horses and men's heavy boots soon penetrated the monastery walls.

"Hallo!" *"Wie geht's?"* *"Willkommen,"* all the familiar German greetings passed back and forth outside the walls. But most of all the pious Christian greeting, *"Gelobt sei Jesus Christus!"* Praise be Jesus Christ, spoken by peasants all over Bavaria.

Strange, I thought, that men who could be so Christian could act like savages with a woman. But I had lived long enough at Ludwig's court to realize that the difference between good and bad was often razor-thin.

They came for a long time, clomping down the cellar steps into the *Aula*, the large room with the tables and benches. Soon there was the unmistakable sound of wooden tables being set up, benches being dragged across the floor.

"Beer, beer!" The clop-clop of fat Brother Matthew's clogs sounded on the wooden steps as he supplied the crowd with food and drink. Many of them would have come a great distance, perhaps even from Prussia, to the north. I longed to see them. I missed the excitement of many people around me. At the court there was always a crowd. And merrymaking. Despite Andreas's efforts at entertaining me with stories and songs, the month had been a lonely one.

35

After a while, the noise of greeting and thumping up and down the steps subsided.

"Silence. Still!" Lothar's powerful baritone soared over the ruckus. He made a long speech. Thanks to Andreas's indoctrination, I understood everything he said. He told them that the Wittelsbachs, Ludwig and Maximilian, were as nothing. Not worth fighting. The real villain, the real enemy of the Bavarians and all the German people, was Metternich, the Austrian prime minister.

"The Wittelsbachs have sold us out to the Austrians," Lothar thundered, his voice heavy with anger. "To Metternich, who arranged the infamous marriage of the Austrian Marie Louise with the French tyrant Napoleon."

I was a bastard, a despised person, even if a royal one. But I was beautiful, that much I knew. I had breasts that reminded men of the Venusberg. I had white-gold hair that was thick as August wheat and hung to my knees.

And Lothar desired me.

Now I was part of the people, one of the poor and the oppressed. And I was hungry. I peered up at the slit in the wall. Noises from the river told me it was nearly dawn. Would they never be done with the eternal talking and speechmaking?

"Let us march again," the men were shouting. Mugs banged against the wooden tables. "This time we'll take the palace. Maximilian won't be so lucky!"

And more. "You must be king, Lothar. You are Frederick Barbarossa. The people will love and obey you. You have but to show your face—that beard, the hair."

But Lothar shouted them all down. "No! No. My time has not come. We are like mosquitos jabbing at an elephant. We need more troops. Trained men. We need money for guns, ammunition."

Finally, the meeting began to dissolve. "Go back to your homes, to your studies," Lothar commanded them. "Maximilian has promised to reopen the universities, if we promise to give no more trouble."

"*Auf Widersehen*, Lothar," they said. "We await your word."

Pride welled up within me as I lay there listening. They were true Germans, I thought, obedient to authority, well organized even in defeat. Not like the impulsive French who chopped off heads like carrot tops when they had their revolution fifty years before. And what had it got them? They still had a king. They had simply traded one tyrant for another.

Chapter 4

The midday Angelus boomed solemnly from St. Emmeran's ancient belfry. Lothar grunted as he pushed the massive stone away from the narrow opening to my cell. He strode over to the cot where I lay waiting, spread his long legs wide apart like a colossus, and glowered down at me. "Have you seen any blood in the past four weeks?" he said abruptly. "Since the night Andreas and Kurt," he paused awkwardly, "brought you here."

"Blood," I echoed stupidly. A deep, painful blush started at my toes, worked its way up to my neck and face. Men and women did not speak of such things together.

"Well?" He waited, his face stern, his full lips tightly closed.

"Why no," I stammered, "I am completely healed down there."

The leonine head shook impatiently. "I mean, woman, the monthly blood, the female blood. Not the blood from the rape."

I nodded in a jerky movement, then turned to face the wall. "Yes." I barely whispered the word into the mouldering stones.

"Look at me, woman. We must speak of these things." The narrow cot shook as he lowered his giant frame and reached out a hairy arm to turn me around to face him. But instead of the sea-green gaze I expected, I saw only the coppery bowed head, resting in his cupped hands. He had the attitude of a man in deep prayer.

Suddenly I felt a great pity for this man, who had been pushed into a leadership he obviously did not want or even relish. Something my father the king had once said flashed into my mind, "Uneasy lies the head that wears a crown." This Goliath, this Lothar von Hohenstaufen, had lost a

39

revolution, but they still would make him king. An accident of birth had made him, as it had me, the pawn of destiny.

"I'm hungry," I said, in a desperate attempt to break the tension and to keep my hands from reaching out to console him. Much as I wanted to touch that golden-hued flesh, I knew that a German male would not regard with pleasure any advances from a woman.

"*Gott! Natürlich.*" He jumped up from the cot, leaned over me concerned, the wide mouth parting in a brilliant smile to reveal two rows of gleaming white teeth. A glow of pure happiness suffused the bearded face. "What a fool I am. I was so intent on hiding you from the Burschen that I—well never mind."

He shouted into the *Aula*. "Andreas, some bread and cheese, and be quick about it. And beer. Hurry."

With a swift panther-like movement, he scooped me up in his arms, blanket and all, carried me into the *Aula*, plunked me down on one of the hard benches. He sat himself down across from me, his narrow green eyes dancing with golden flecks. I had the feeling that his soul was surfacing.

"You must eat, my deep-bosomed one. And eat hearty. For I am about to get you with child."

My head jerked up from the trencher Andreas had just put down in front of me. A bit of strong yellow cheese dangled from the corner of my mouth. I swallowed the cheese, managed to stammer, "What—what did you say?" Picking up the heavy stein with both hands I raised it to my lips and took a long gulp of the rich brew. I put it down carefully on the table.

My obvious confusion brought a shout of laughter from Lothar. He hunched his broad shoulders, leaned across the table and brought his bearded, scarred face within inches of mine. The green eyes gazed deeply into mine, as if they would suck the very life force from them. "Oh-ho," he chuckled, "not here, not on this table. Or even on one of those vermin-ridden cots. We will mate like the denizens of the forest, deep in the mountains beyond the Danube. Our child will be like a god, born of purity, of sincere passion, and of heaven."

I remained silent. Surely the man was mad. But I could not deny the raging excitement which swept over me at his words. Every nerve was on fire. The fantasies of the past four weeks, the tormented dreams of his body in mine, were all about to come true.

He went on, apparently not expecting an answer from me. "That's why I asked you about your blood. I had to make sure that my drunken comrades hadn't done the job for me on Corpus Christi night."

We waited for dark to begin our journey. I put my hair into two long braids, twisted them on top of my head into a three-tiered golden serpent. Brother Matthew supplied me with a rough brown woolen cap to cover my head. It was large enough to pull down completely over my ears, hiding every trace of my hair.

Lothar and Andreas prepared some food, muttering in low tones at the far end of the *Aula* about plans and strategems. Lothar talked while Andreas wrote in a little notebook. Charts and maps were spread out all over the long wooden table. St. Emmeran's bell tolled the passing hours. For a long time I watched the two men bent over their work, the dim lamplight casting soft shadows on the dark head of Andreas, catching the gleaming copper of Lothar's cloud of hair. Once or twice he turned around to stare at me, then, wordless, returned to his work.

"*Danke*," I whispered, "thank you, God, for this thing which has happened to me." All the tormenting doubts about my life were forever at rest. How wonderful, how natural. This is what I was born for, to bear this man's child. My body—the bursting breasts, the full curving hips—had been formed not merely for man's pleasure, but to receive a man's seed, to suckle his babe. I would bear Lothar's child, sprung from Lothar's loins. A glorious contentment filled my whole being.

The evening Angelus was still pealing its nightly call to prayer as I followed Lothar silently up the battered stone steps to the monastery proper, through a maze of dark corridors smelling of age and damp. I heard nothing, saw nothing. During my stay in the underground *Aula* I had heard scrabbling footsteps from time to time. But not a monk was in sight. Probably at prayer, I thought.

I looked down at myself. I was a study in drabness. Brother Matthew had given me a brown wool cloak, a rough square with a slit for the head. A piece of rope smelling of oil tied around my waist. My feet were pushed into thick, heavy wooden clogs. I looked more like a sausage than a woman.

Like the wind we rode all night, Lothar in front, I behind him, my arms wrapped around his waist, hands clenched together in front. The horse, a large black stallion, had been waiting for us in the monastery courtyard. By dawn we were in the foothills of the mountains. A freezing rain fell intermittently. We had entered the rocky gorges and steep mist-shrouded peaks of the Black Forest. My cheek pressed against the coarse wool of Lothar's cloak, receiving the strong thrust of his muscles as he guided the stallion skillfully up the steep mountain paths. As we climbed, I caught glimpses of the thatched roofs and long-winged eaves of the peasant huts that dotted the region. Occasionally the dense cover of trees opened up to reveal a broad valley, with a cluster of houses, a white church with a red steeple, a barn with cows grazing nearby. They looked like toys spread out under a Christmas tree.

At length as the sun climbed high in the sky, we left the path and plunged into the dark green tunnel of trees. Maples, oaks, aspens—I recognized the leafy branches from my childhood days at Schachten. Soon we would climb higher into the belt of pines. The high soaring limbs arched over us. We had left the world behind.

The path grew steep and rocky. Soon there was no path at all. The trees were all around us, numberless, the vast shaggy trunks like the pillars of heaven.

"We must walk from here." Lothar leaped down from the stallion, whose sides glistened with sweat and lather, and reached up to pull me down beside him. He looped the reins around a gnarled oak. "Come." He led the way through the forest until we were in a glade of pines. The place was dark and silent as a tomb, with a penetrating fragrance that made me dizzy.

Lothar threw himself on the ground between two giant trees, reached up his long sinewy arms, pulled me downward, lowering me gently so that I lay on top of him. Our lips met. Placing both hands on either side of my face, he kissed me, pressing brutally with closed lips on mine. Then he forced my lips open, reached in with a long tongue, explored the recesses of my mouth. Bone weary as I was from the long ride, my body flamed into response. My tongue darted out into his mouth. His powerful hands on my back, we rocked back and forth with the rhythm of the earth itself.

With a quick movement, he lifted the hem of the monk's

42

garment I wore and rolled me under him. My limbs were bare underneath. I had discarded my bloody undergarments the night of the rape, and had been given no other. He mounted me swiftly, spreading my legs apart cruelly, thrusting deep within me with a power of a thousand stallions. The pain of it seared my loins, darted up into my abdomen. He filled me so completely I felt part of his very flesh. He moved rhythmically in and out of me, his hands spread out on the leafy ground, his massive chest arched. He did not touch my face. A sweet, agonizing sensation coursed through my thighs, concentrated in the space between. Small, clear cries poured out of my open mouth.

Suddenly, without warning, a quaking such as I had never imagined shattered me. I cried out in a combination of fright, surprise, delight. So this was it. Ecstasy. This is what drove men mad, this is what made women cling to men who beat them. This is what made Ludwig of Bavaria the grovelling slave of Lola Montez.

Moments after the shuddering in my loins, Lothar groaned a mighty groan, placed his lips on mine. "Love, love, love, love." That is all he said, murmuring the one word over and over against my open mouth. His long, lithe frame moved in a great continuous pumping motion until at last I felt the jets of his manhood pouring into me.

Passion spent, we lay side by side, Lothar's head on my breast. A soft rain had begun to fall, hardly penetrating the thick covering of branches. I drifted off into a profound sleep, to the music of the rain and Lothar's steady, even breathing.

I woke to the gentle pressure of a hand on my shoulder, Lothar bent over me, tiny crinkles around his sea-green eyes. He was smiling, his lips wide apart, the sliver of scar on his cheek bent in half. "Hungry, love?"

"Famished," I replied, smiling too in response, amazed that I could still speak ordinary words after the shattering interlude of passion.

We ate the hard bread and aromatic sausage from the saddlebag, silently, quickly, gulped hastily from the ale-filled canteen. While I reclined lazily on the bed of pine needles, Lothar watered the horse at a nearby spring.

The sun was high in the heavens as we started out once more on the mountain path, Lothar leading the horse by the halter. There was no way of telling how long we toiled upward. My feet in the wooden clogs felt hot and blistery.

43

Soon thick clouds obscured the tops of the lower mountains. The sun had disappeared completely over the western crags. The thinness of the atmosphere told me we were very high. I longed to stop, to rest a bit, but Lothar's broad a implacable back terrified me, drove the pleading words back into my throat.

Just as darkness descended on the vast reaches of the Black Forest, Lothar veered abruptly and approached a large boulder. Grunting heavily, for he too was slightly out of breath from the climb, he heaved it aside, inch by inch, to reveal the hidden opening of a cave.

The horse tied up again to a tree, I followed him, crawling on hands and knees deep inside the cave. Surprisingly, the earth beneath us was dry, covered completely with a thick layer of pine needles. On and on, deeper and deeper we crept, my hand on his ankle to keep from getting lost in the winding maze. Then he stopped, turned, reached out to me in the thick blackness. "Sieglinde, my love, my beauty, my Venus, my wife. We are home."

All night we lay naked on our piny bed, devouring each other with our hands, our mouths, our bodies. We gamboled like wild forest creatures in the mating season. Lothar's tongue was a thing alive. He explored my mouth, touched my rigid nipples; his huge hands, inexpressibly tender, ran featherlike up and down my trembling thighs, across my abdomen, cupped my rounded buttocks. I was a piece of soft clay in the hands of a master sculptor.

Countless times we soared together to the heights of passion. Time itself had stopped for us. The eternal quiet of the primordial forest, the mysterious brooding dark of the cave shrouded us from the profane world. We slept at last, drained, roped together with our arms and legs like puppies in a litter.

"How could I ever have feared a man's passion?" I whispered to the darkness. Leaning over, I touched Lothar's nipples with my fingertips, reached up to trace the outline of the scar on his cheek. "*Danke*," I uttered the word softly so as not to wake him, "thank you, *liebschen*, for giving me life."

Instantly, his arms tightened about me like bands of iron. "Don't," he cried like a child in sleep, "don't leave me. Ever. You are my very life."

"Lothar?"

"Yes, my Venus?"

"I'm hungry."

He laughed, as I knew he would. But in truth, our night of love had given me a roaring appetite. I joined in the laughter. Our voices echoed hollowly in the recesses of the cave.

Waking fully now, he answered, "Come, let us greet the new day together."

We crawled toward the entrance, my hand on his ankle as before, emerging finally into the soft grey-green coolness of the glade. A chill mist shrouded the mountain top. I shivered in my nakedness. The inside of the cave had been warm, with an even, moderate temperature. Here and there a chink in the arching leafy branches thrust a sliver of light onto the forest floor.

"It's like being in the Marienkirche," I breathed in awe. "A cathedral of trees." I sucked in enormous gulps of the fresh, clear mountain air.

"Yes, wife, it is truly a sacred place. We have made it more so by our love." Lothar walked out a little way, threw out his hands in a wide gesture. "You are standing on Kyffhauser Mountain, the realm of the Hohenstaufens. Our family has dwelt here since the seventh century at least."

"Kyffhauser?" I gasped in astonishment. "Why—why that's the mountain where Frederick Barbarossa is sleeping. Or so the legend has it."

Lothar smiled, drew me close, placed the palm of my hand against the warm flesh of his chest. The muscles were hard and rippled under my palm. He pressed my hand until I felt the pulse underneath strong and steady.

"Yes, so they say," he said, his voice so soft and low I strained to hear the words. "The great emperor sleeps in a secret cave. Let us hope," he bent down to plant a kiss on each of my eyelids, "let us hope that the old Redbeard does not sleep in ours."

A stab of fear, a strange otherworldly kind of fear, pierced my consciousness.

"Some say that Lothar is himself the Barbarossa," Andreas had said at St. Emmeran's. Lothar had known exactly where the cave was. He had crawled expertly through its myriad bends and twists, I following blindly behind him. There had been no hesitation.

Shaking off the superstitious feeling, I tilted back my

head, locked my hands securely around his waist. My words were light, bantering. "The Redbeard would surely be as startled as we, at seeing the two of us. From the pictures of him I've seen, you, Lothar, could be his twin."

The hands at the back of my neck tightened, the sea-green eyes gazed down into mine with a curious mixture of anger and sorrow. As our glances locked for a long moment, I had the distinct sensation that I was drowning, the sensation I always had in Lola's green bathroom with the marble tub and gleaming copper pipes.

"Let us not talk of the dead," he fairly barked out the words. "It's not healthy. Let us rather speak of the living—us and our love. And of those yet to be born."

Church bells sounded faintly from the deep valleys beneath us. His shaggy head jerked up, as if on signal. He lifted his face to the green arch of branches overhead and prayed, his voice loud, clear, authoritative as a priest on a feast day. "Dear God in heaven above, whoever you may be, I ask you to look down upon this union of two of your creatures. Open up the womb of Sieglinde that she may bear the child of our love."

Then, following his command, I repeated after him the sacred vows spoken by men and women when they pledge themselves to each other. "I, Sieglinde, take thee, Lothar, to be my wedded husband, to have and to hold, to love and obey, until death us do part."

My husband kissed me gently on the lips. "There was no priest, Sieglinde, no church, no pope when Adam and Eve became one flesh. You are mine, and I am yours. Nothing on earth or heaven above can change that."

We ate, drank, slept and mated like denizens of the wild. Even in my golden childhood at Schachten, I had never been so much at one with nature.

Each morning Lothar left me for a while, returning with hot food and drink. Although my mind was filled with questions, I said nothing. I imagined myself a fairy princess, held captive in an enchanted castle. The food was simple, but nourishing and well prepared. For breakfast there was hot chocolate and coffee in pitchers fashioned out of some heavy metal, burnished to a dull silver. Sausage, cheeses, sometimes boiled eggs, and always fresh black bread. We did not eat at midday. At supper, when the sun lowered itself on the western peaks, we dined on soup—

46

thick, filling potato or barley or sometimes pea—which he brought in a large iron kettle. We used no bowls, but ate out of the pot with deep wooden ladles for spoons.

"It's ambrosia," I declared, wiping the bottom of the kettle with a chunk of black bread. "Food for the gods. If this keeps up, you'll have me looking like a hippopotamus!"

His ready laugh echoed in the quiet glade. He reached over the top of the kettle and made little circles on my naked belly. "Ummm. No, not a hippo, Sieglinde, but a pagan fertility goddess, with a full, ripe, round belly and thrusting milk-filled breasts."

The weeks passed in this way. I'd lost count of the days, but I figured it was mid-July at least. In the warm afternoons we walked out of the glade, into the trackless forest. Squirrels, chipmunks, weasels, and other small beasts skittered away at our approach, chattering nervously.

"What happened to the stallion who brought us here?" I asked once, hoping for some clue to the source of the food.

"He's been stabled, awaiting our need for him again," he answered quietly. I longed to ask questions about the food, about how long we would live like Adam and Eve, but something in his manner stopped me. Was I afraid of his displeasure? Or was I fearful of breaking the enchanted spell of our forest honeymoon?

We bathed daily in the glacial waters of a mountain spring near the cave, which we had dubbed the Cave of Venus. We walked dripping back to the glade, rubbing each other feverishly, our body heat providing the only drying cloths we needed.

And in the soft twilight, we lay and talked. I told him of my childhood at Schachten, the king's hunting lodge, deep in the Bavarian Alps.

"I was a wild one, even then, given to getting lost in the forest," I said, laughing at the memory. "More than once Ortrud had to call upon the king's foresters to rout me out and drag me home."

I told him also of my girlish desire to become a nun, like my adored Sister Paulita.

"Do you still want to become a nun?" Lothar murmured, burying his face in my hair, wrapping the long wet strands around my thighs like a golden blanket.

For answer I pressed my flesh against his, until I felt his

47

manhood spring to hardness. "I want only your body in mine," I replied fiercely. "Nothing else in life matters. Now or ever."

"Well, what kept you from the convent?" he persisted, drawing away, looking at me quizzically, a glint of sly humor in his eyes.

Anger nearly choked me as I thought back to the hateful days with Lola at the court. "I was fetched to Munich to be Lola Montez's lady-in-waiting. Or rather her little runabout slave. I even had to bathe her. Please—" I buried my head in the hair of his chest. "Please don't make me talk about it. I want to wipe it out of my heart."

Lothar lifted me, carried me back to the clear waters of the spring, splashed me all over with the freezing water. "Let this be a symbol of your cleansing," he said. "From this moment on you will forget all about that whore. Besides—" his mouth tightened, his voice took on a steel edge, "I know all about it. I've had you watched ever since the day you came to the Barerstrasse."

"But how could you? I rarely ventured out of the palace."

"I saw you once, riding in the concubine's carriage. She was playing Lady Bountiful to the poor that day. I made a few inquiries, found out who you were, determined that some day you would belong to me. I knew from that first moment that you, and you alone, would be the mother of my child."

Sudden knowledge flooded me. It all fell into place. "So that's why you ordered Andreas and Kurt to capture me!"

"Yes, you were to be my prize of war."

Hurt, anger, bewilderment, disappointment coursed through me in turn. Anger blazing from my face, I pounded with my fists on his massive chest. "You let them *use* me, take the maidenhead which should have been yours?" Hot tears spilled unbidden out of my eyes and coursed down my cheeks.

His voice was sober but gentle as he replied, "That was too bad, of course. But no harm done in the end. They were looking for a golden-haired Venus. To them you were but a kitchen slut."

"But why didn't you come after me yourself?"

"As leader of the rebels that night, I selfishly reserved for myself the capture of the king and his mistress. But, as you know, I failed even in that."

...tabbing reproach replaced the anger in my heart.
...y I kissed the drawn, scarred face. The ironlike
...htened as if in pain, the long sinewy arms
... me so hard I could not breathe.

...is one assignment that will not fail. Heaven has
...you to be my mate, and to bear my child." His
...ere an oath, growled into the forest.

...we fell together, writhing, twisting on the bare
...watered by the spring, and he took me savagely,
...foreplay. In those times I feared him, for I felt in
...ower beyond that of mere mortality. As his man-
...rst within me once again, I felt that he might in-
...deed be the legendary, the mighty Frederick Barbarossa,
rising from the sleep of centuries to beget a new ruler of
the Germans.

Quick s...
Impulsivel...
muscles tig...
squeezed r...
"Here...

Chapter 5

The moon had run its course twice over and I had not seen my woman's blood. On a furiously wet dawn, early in September, I informed my husband that I was most certainly with child. I glowed with anticipation of his pleasure at the ease with which I had conceived. He seemed not at all surprised, did not even touch me, nor go into raptures of delight.

"Come," he commanded. "It is time." We had just finished our breakfast of chocolate and sausage. Without another word, he beckoned for me to follow him back into the cave, where we put on the rude garments we had worn into the mountains from Regensburg.

"Lothar," I exclaimed, playfully grabbing him round the waist, "aren't you pleased? Many women wait years before their womb becomes fruitful." I don't know what I expected—some sign of joy, a kiss, a hug, anything but this calm take-for-granted acceptance.

The sea-green eyes gave me a cool, measured look. "It has been ordained by powers far beyond our ken. You have nothing to do with it. Now let's hurry and get you up to the Schloss."

Swallowing my disappointment, I followed Lothar out of the glade past the cool mountain spring where we bathed each day. I turned for one last look. Someday I would return with my child and say, "Here is where you were conceived, here among the fragrant trees, in the purity of nature."

We trudged up a narrow stony path, Lothar ahead, I behind, staring at his back. He made no offer to help me. There were few trees here at this height, the pines of our glade being a green spot in the general barrenness. The

51

usual morning mist pervaded, hiding our view of the valleys below.

Suddenly we rounded a sharp bend in the path. An immense pile of blackened stones loomed up out of the mist. Loose rocks and boulders littered the rocky area around the building, which itself seemed to be three or four stories high. It filled with the narrow space at the peak of the mountain.

"Lothar," I gasped, a bit out of breath from the unaccustomed exercise, "can anyone possibly live here? It looks so deserted."

He stopped, turned, clasped me tightly to his breast. I sank gratefully against his comforting warmth. A strange foreboding had seized me upon viewing the Schloss. "Trust me," he said. "Would I endanger the life of my unborn child? You will receive the best of care here."

Once again, I quelled my fears, and followed my husband blindly and obediently into the ruin of Kyffhauser Castle, the baronial residence of the Hohenstaufens. I had promised to love, honor, and obey him, in the sight of God. As I was a willing partner, as I was submissive in his bed, so must I be in all things.

Suddenly, the mountain quiet was shattered by loud, savage barking. Two giant mastiffs appeared from out of the swirling mist, circling us as we walked. They were a wild pair, looking more like wolves than dogs, with massive horsey heads. Teeth bared, they crouched, ready to spring. I screamed, hid my face against Lothar's back.

"Lumpi! Kirnis!" he shouted. "Stop that, you old rascals. This is my wife, Sieglinde."

Then the three of them, Lothar and the dogs, were rolling on the stony ground like a litter of puppies at play. It was hard to tell which was the man and which the dogs. I stood back, trembling. Finally, Lothar untangled himself and ordered the dogs to stay. He came over, took my hand in his, led me to the beasts. "You must make friends with them, Sieglinde, for they will be your guardians in the months to come."

I cringed, rigid with terror. The dogs sat, giant paws fretting the ground, waiting. Their eyes glistened with excitement, their snouts dripped saliva. Shaking uncontrollably like a birch in winter, I knelt on the rocky ground, swallowing hard against a creeping nausea. I threw my arms around the massive neck of first Lumpi, then Kirnis. I

52

couldn't tell them apart. I pressed my lips gingerly to the slimy snouts.

"They're superb watchdogs," Lothar said, roughing up the broad backs of the animals. "Lumpi and Kirnis spring from a line brought over from England over two centuries ago."

Little darts of jealousy entered my heart at the enthusiasm in his voice. He was more excited about seeing the dogs than he had been at the announcement of my pregnancy.

A hard rain began to fall as we moved on toward the Schloss. The mastiffs trotted docilely beside us in the dirt. I reached down and touched the rippling muscles of Lumpi's haunches. At least I thought it was Lumpi.

Lothar smiled approvingly at my effort. "They know you now as one of the household. Just don't try to get in or out of the Schloss without me, or they'll tear you limb from limb."

We came eventually to a narrow wooden bridge that spanned what was once a water-filled moat, but which now held nothing but rocks, dried bones, and bits of household waste. Pointing to the dried-up boat, Lothar said, "That's where Lumpi and Kirnis make their home. The bones are what's left of their meals."

"Or perhaps some unfortunate traveler who thought to seek refuge in the Schloss," I said wryly, with a dry little laugh.

Lothar didn't laugh back, but merely continued silently across the bridge. The moat was intersected by a wide wall of rocks, forming a wall taller even than Lothar, obviously designed to make it even more difficult to storm the castle. On the other side of the wall, which was wide enough to walk on, a second bridge commenced, this one of stone. It was attached to the main building by giant chains, now orange-red with rust.

We walked across the bridge. The dogs, to my enormous relief, leaped down into the moat, running off together over the dried bones. Then we passed under a half-raised wooden grille, crossed with bands of iron, which at one time must have been let up and down to receive or keep out visitors.

"How romantic," I exclaimed, determined not to let Lothar suspect the real panic I was feeling. In truth, I begrudgingly admitted to myself that it had the look of an old fairytale castle such as were found in story books. Thick tangles of wild rose bushes, with a profusion of pink and red blossoms, sprouted through the chinks in the huge unhewn rocks which formed the face of the castle. A cobblestoned passageway led directly into a large squarish courtyard. Practically running now, Lothar approached a massive bronze door and lifted the knocker on which the bearded head of a man was carved.

"Are they expecting us?" I asked, feeling foolish.

"Yes. For some time now. Remember, I've been coming here every day for food. At any rate, the dogs have announced our arrival."

Instantly, the door opened inward to a flood of pale golden light cast by a row of yellow candles set in wooden sconces on both sides of a long, cavernous hallway. Despite the forbidding aspect of the building, the scent of hot wax and cooking cabbage reassured me that I had returned to civilization.

"Karl, may I present Sieglinde, my wife. I have brought her here to you to bear my child."

"*Willkommen, gnädige Frau.* Schloss Kyffhauser welcomes you." The servant bowed deeply, opened wide the bronze door and stood aside to permit us to enter.

I inclined my head to acknowledge the greeting, but could say nothing in response, so struck was I by the overpowering presence of the man. Karl was a colossus, with the head of a bull, a neck like a full-grown tree trunk. I glanced slyly at his forehead to assure myself that no horns sprouted there. Thick black curls covered his scalp.

His attire was just as startling. A dark brown tunic fell to just below thick knees. The fabric seemed to be a heavy satin, the hem richly embroidered in bright reds and yellows. A soft tan leather sleeveless jerkin covered his massive chest. An immense bunch of keys dangled from a rope tied around his waist.

"Karl has been with the Hohenstaufens since before my birth," Lothar said, leading the way down the long corridor. "He will take excellent care of you and the child. If need be, he will lay down his life for you."

A gallery of life-sized statues, armored from head to toe, stood close together against the walls of the corridor. Above them and in the narrow spaces between hung bows, swords, maces, axes, lances, pikes—all of the weapons of the ancient warriors. Everything was covered with a thick layer of dust.

"Here we are," Lothar said suddenly, "this is *Rittersaal*." He parted a thick brown curtain to reveal an opening into a large room. There was no doorway. A vast stone fireplace took up half of one wall. An enormous log fire blazed so fiercely that sparks flew out onto the blackened stones of the hearth.

Lothar led me quickly to the fire. "You'd best take off that wet robe, and warm yourself at the fire. I've got to hunt up the baronin."

The baronin. Who was she, I wondered. I was consumed with curiosity and more than a little anxiety about his family. Would there be a mother? A father? Grandparents? Would I measure up? Would they love me as they did Lothar? All the feelings of inferiority I had experienced as a bastard child once again came to the surface.

"Help Frau Sieglinde with her wet garment," Lothar ordered Karl.

"Your *Grossmama* is most likely in the chapel at her prayers," Karl called out, as Lothar disappeared into the shadows at the far end of the room. The *Rittersaal*, he had called it, the vast meeting room, like the *Aula* in the monastery cellar, filled with tabletops and trestles to put them on. It was the room where visiting knights and their ladies were accommodated, and where knights returning from tournaments and battles bedded down and were fed.

Karl went to a corner of the vast room and returned with a piece of carpet.

"I suggest that Frau Sieglinde disrobe and wrap herself in this bit of wool carpet." He held it up to the fire. For the first time I had a full view of his face. An angry red birthmark, the type commonly called a strawberry mark, covered one whole side of his face. The peasants thought that persons born with such a disfigurement possessed unusual, even demonic powers. Such babies were often done away with at birth. If the servant sensed my shock and repulsion, he gave no sign. His large blue eyes, strangely childlike, were bland and expressionless.

"The baronin will provide you with a more suitable costume when she has completed her worship," Karl said. His voice was gentle, with a suggestion of a caress, much like the voice of a mother to her child. Young boys in church choirs had voices like that—sweet, pure, and lyrical.

Karl discreetly retreated into the shadows in the corner of the *Saal*, as I quickly doffed the wet dirty monk's robe, and wrapped the heavy carpet around my naked body. It smelt pungently of dust and mold, but I was grateful for the warmth. The blistering heat of the crackling fire soon brought on a powerful drowsiness. I sank down into a cushioned armchair, one of many sprinkled around the room.

A number of long wooden tables, set up on trestles, lined two walls. Benches with velvety cushions sat here and there invitingly. An attempt had been made to hide the rough black stones with tapestries, which were so blackened with age and smoke, however, that little of the original color or pattern could be detected.

Gradually, as my eyes became accustomed to the gloom, I made out six narrow windows, actually little more than slits in the stones. Windows in these medieval fortresses were designed not for light but for discouraging the invader. One would have to be an expert archer indeed to shoot an arrow into one of these slits.

A faint noise, like a horse galloping, suddenly sounded from outside the Schloss. My heart lifted. That meant there were some neighbors at least. I wondered dully what had happened to Karl. And Lothar. The smell of the burning pine logs evoked childhood memories of autumn evenings when the smoke rising from the thatched mountain huts below the slopes filled the mountaintop at Schachten with a sweet grey fragrant haze.

Suddenly she was there, looking like an avenging angel, clad in black, her deeply wrinkled face swathed in the white coif of a nun. A broad white wimple spread across her sunken chest. The yellow firelight revealed features so astonishingly like Lothar's that I knew immediately that she could be no other than the *Grossmama*.

"Frau Baronin!" The words excaped me, despite my life-long training that one never speaks first in the presence of the old. And this person was very old indeed—eighty at least, I figured.

The fire cast an orange glow on her green eyes and luxuriant copper brows. Her skin, however, was not leathery like Lothar's, but resembled thin parchment such as documents are written upon. Black-sleeved arms extended to grasp my wrists, pulled me up from the chair, enfolded me, pressed me fiercely to the white breast. The heavy scrap of carpet dropped away, leaving me naked.

"*Meine liebschen*. Finally you are here." The thin old lips continued to murmur endearments into my ear. Soon my cheek was wet with her tears, which ran unchecked into the folds of gauzy white at her neck.

"*Gott bedankt*," I muttered under my breath. My fears dissolved. Whatever else she was, the Frau Baronin von Hohenstaufen was at least affectionate.

At last she released me, stood back, observing my naked figure. "*Gut. Gut*. Lothar did not exaggerate. You have the form of a Valkyrie." The bony fingers stroked my thighs, cupped my breasts, prodded my still firm abdomen. "And those eyes. *Magnificent*. That deep rich brown will mix well with our family green. Yes, my *liebschen*, you will bear the son Germany so desperately needs."

Karl had mysteriously reappeared as we talked. I stooped down to pick up the carpet to cover my nakedness. The old woman struck it from my hand in disgust. "Leave off that filthy thing. And don't worry about Karl seeing your nakedness. He is a eunuch. The sight of a woman's body does nothing to him. He will admire its beauty as he would admire the grace of a bird in flight. Beyond that—nothing. But what a state you are in." She lifted a strand of my hair, brought it up to her delicate nostrils. "You smell of the dirt of the forest, like a wild beast. Come. Follow me." Turning, she headed for the curtained doorway through which Lothar and I had entered.

"Karl," she called out, "throw that filthy robe into the fire. Then bring some hot water upstairs to my chambers. Frau Sieglinde will bathe there in front of my fire."

We walked out of the large Rittersaal into the candlelit corridor. The baronin kept up a barrage of talk, not waiting for me to answer. "Lothar and his whims—sometimes I think it's a streak of madness going back to the Barbarossa strain. The Hohenstaufens are directly descended from Germany's great emperor, you know. Mating in the forest like animals—ugh! However, one does not argue with the head of the family."

So Lothar was the head of the Hohenstaufens. That meant his parents—at least his father—were dead. I resented her speaking of our love that way. But Lothar had called it mating, too. I followed the black form up what was once a grand staircase. The stone treads were worn in the middle, scraps of carpet showing at the corners. It felt strange to be walking around unclothed, but there seemed to be nobody else around. I wondered where the rest of the servants were. A place like this would need quite a few. The room we entered now was a good deal smaller than the Rittersaal. A fire burned here also, the hearth again taking up most of the inside wall.

Karl was there before us, pouring steaming water from a kettle into a round wooden tub set on the hearth stones. The baronin laid a bony hand on my bare shoulder. "I leave you to Karl's practiced ministrations." Then she glided into the shadows at the other end of the room.

Without a word, the burly servant reached out, grabbed me with a firm gentle touch around the waist and lowered me into the tub. As I sank gratefully into the fragrant, soapy water, I wondered what Lothar would think of another man—even if he was castrated—bathing me and fondling my body. As Karl soaped me and rubbed me with a large square of soft linen, I remembered Lola and me together in her luxuriant, pink marble bath. It *was* a good feeling, being bathed by another.

I glanced around the baronin's chamber, to avoid meeting Karl's eyes as well as from sheer curiosity. Richly worked tapestries, like those in the *Rittersaal*, glowed eerily in the half light cast by the fire. Over the hearth, standing out starkly against the grey stones, a bleeding Christ looked down upon us, the long face drawn and suffering. There were no other paintings or ornaments in the room, not even a clock. A Black Forest home without a clock of some kind was indeed a rarity. The clockmakers in these mountain valleys were world-famous for their beautifully fashioned timepieces.

"*Fräulein* is tired," Karl murmured, "but she will soon be clean and new. Like a newborn babe."

"You must call me Frau, Karl," I replied. "I am Herr Lothar's wife. I carry his child."

"Pardon, of course." The high soft voice remained even. "You seem so very young, little more than a child." A friendly grin split the disfigured face and the strawberry mark moved up and down.

"We were married in the sight of God, on Kyffhauser Mountain, the mountain sacred to the Hohenstaufens."

My voice was stern, and I tried to glare at him, but I

58

burst into spontaneous laughter at the completely innocent expression in his blue eyes.

Once he was satisfied that the forest grime and dirt were washed away from every part of my body, Karl helped me out of the tub and rubbed me dry with a soft cloth until I glowed. Picking up a large blanket-like cloth from a nearby bench, he wrapped me securely from shoulders to knees. I felt like a babe in swaddling clothes.

"I go to fetch the baronin," he said. "Please sit here in this deep chair." I sank into it, cuddled in the blankety cloth. It was one of two wide-armed chairs, deeply carved from some richly grained wood, which sat on either side of the fire. Tantalizing smells assailed my nostrils. Definitely cabbage and pork. I had eaten little breakfast, the nausea of pregnancy having been especially severe that morning. I got up from the chair, decided to explore. Beside a narrow curtained-off bed in the corner, a number of heavy wooden chests with broad iron bands across the tops stood against the walls. I could see no windows, not even the slits as in the *Rittersaal*. Heavy, brocaded hangings shrouded every wall. The whole effect was one of antique beauty, a rare quality possessed by houses and people who have been rich and powerful for a long time.

"My son will restore the honor and the glory and the beauty to Kyffhauser Schloss," I said aloud. I returned to my chair to await the baronin's return. I no longer worried about Lothar's continuing absence. He must surely be about family business. We would meet at dinner. We had been together, close as Adam and Eve, for two whole months. It was time we were separated. A man cannot bear the constant presence of a woman, even one he loves very much.

But still, as I sat, cozy and warm by the baronin's blazing fire, I longed for Lothar. I wanted him. Now. Here. The warmth of the bath and the heat of the fire had awakened every nerve in my body. I had a mad desire to stretch out on the ancient stones and receive my lover.

"That hair! Glorious, but we must bind it up. It's not fitting for a married woman, especially one with child, to go about like a forest nymph." The baronin's voice preceded her, so that by the time she stood facing me by the fire, she had grabbed handfuls of my still wet hair that streamed outside the swaddling cloth.

"It is very heavy," I said meekly, almost apologetically.

"When it is thoroughly dry, I will braid it and pile it in a coil on top of my head."

"Yes. Karl can help you. And we'll have a coif for you, like mine. Not a strand must show. It was the custom in the medieval times. The sight of a woman's hair is meant only for her husband."

Meanwhile Karl was pulling the trunks against the wall into the circle of firelight. He took one of the large keys from the metal band at his waist and opened one after the other. Even Lola's expensive wardrobe, the talk of all Europe, paled in comparison. A veritable rainbow of color poured out of the moldy old trunks. Reds, blues, yellows, greens, purples—all rich, radiant hues. The fabrics were just as varied: deep velvets, gleaming dully in the firelight, rustling silks, smooth satins, coarse textured homespuns, fine linens. And extraordinary lengths of the same white gauzy stuff that was wrapped around the slender patrician head of the baronin.

First, Karl spread lengths of unbleached linen on the carpet; then, as his mistress handed him the garments, he spread them out, one by one, for our inspection. There were bodices, skirts, cloaks, charming frocks with long sleeves and heavily embroidered hems. The baronin said nothing, merely shook her head in approval or disapproval as each piece was spread out.

"Ah-hah! Here it is." She handed Karl a pretty frock gaily patterned with little purple flowers resembling violets. "Hold it up against Frau Sieglinde."

The old woman's face lit up like a girl's; a faint rosy blush suffused her yellow cheeks. I longed to reach out and clasp Lothar's *Grossmama* in my strong young arms. She could be the mother I had lost at birth. But the years of training held me back. One simply did not take liberties. The Frau Baronin was beautiful, even in old age, a sleek, handsome animal, like her grandson Lothar. Her glowing skin reminded me of the glow from Lola's alabaster lamps. Surely the hair underneath the imprisoning white coif was a coppery red, like the brows.

Dutifully I rose, divested myself of the white swaddling cloth, allowed Karl to hold the dress against my naked form. The old woman frowned, pursed her thin, narrow lips, shook her head. "No. No. That won't do. That frock is for a maid. Too virginal."

Then suddenly she found what she was looking for. "Ah,

at last, the bridal gown!" She held up a frock of deep, rich forest green, worked with tiny flowers of an even darker green. The fabric appeared to be a fine, lustrous silk.

"The verdant color is symbolic of fertility, something which you have already proven," she smiled, patting my abdomen affectionately. Karl slipped a thin linen shift over my head, then the bridal gown. As it slipped over my shoulders, he reached in with gentle hands and pulled out my still damp hair.

There were white ribbons down the front of the bodice opening, which Karl proceeded to lace. I gasped in pain as he pulled the ribbons tight. My full breasts spilled up over the edge of the low neckline.

"Wait, Karl, you're tying the ribbons too closely together," I gasped. "I can hardly breathe."

The servant's own breath seemed to be labored, as he worked directly in front of my face. A curious excitement emanated from the gigantic body. His calloused fingers trembled as they brushed against the warm softness of my flesh. A momentary repulsion seized me at his touch. He was a eunuch, a freak. But immediately I softened and pushed the unkind thought to the back of my mind. Full of compassion, I lifted my arms and rested my hands lightly on his broad shoulders. He flushed and smiled.

"There, Frau Sieglinde," he said. "I've loosened the ribbons. You should be more comfortable now. Although—" he drew back, surveyed me from head to foot—"it *is* like a second skin."

"No matter." This from the baronin, who continued to busy herself among the garments pulled out of the trunks. "She'll be wearing it just for today. Here are some slippers to match." My feet slipped easily into the dainty slippers. They too were fashioned of green flowered silk.

"Is there a mirror? I'd like to see myself," I said, whirling around so that the full green skirt billowed out gracefully. If Von Edel could see me now, I thought gleefully, he would no longer think me a Venus. I was a genuine medieval lady of the manor.

"Schloss Kyffhauser has no mirrors," the baronin replied. "Looking glasses only encourage vanity and licentiousness. There is not even glass in the windows to see your reflection in. When the weather turns cold, we simply board them up."

The absence of mirrors did not shock me. Many deeply

61

religious Bavarian homes considered looking glasses insti-
gators of sin. I already knew the baronin to be a pious
woman. Lothar had gone to fetch her from the chapel
when we arrived. And she was wearing the religious garb
of a nun. Many German women put on the medieval black
and white of the religious life and wore it to the grave.

Karl moved over to where the baronin was still handling
the garments from the trunks. I sat down in the armchair,
which was upholstered in red velvet, and started to
straighten out my hair for braiding. It was going to be difficult without a mirror. But years of practice should be of
some help.

"Here, let me help you with that." The baronin snatched
the long strands of golden hair from my fingers. "The rate
you're going we'll be here the rest of the afternoon."

I gladly relinquished the job to the old woman, grateful
that she hadn't asked Karl to perform this task too. He
might be castrated, but his masculine presence disturbed
me. First she split the thick mass into two large sections,
using a large comb she pulled out of a deep pocket in her
black skirt. "Hold this side," she commanded, handing me
the hair. I smiled. Ortrud used to sound like that. Then,
quickly splitting the other half into three even strands, her
surprisingly nimble fingers formed a long, heavy braid. Finally, the serpentine white-gold coil reposed once more on
my head.

"Feels heavy," I remarked. "I've been spoiled by our two
months in the forest. How many are in the household," I
asked, as she sank down in the armchair opposite mine,
fatigued by the exertions of getting me dressed and
groomed. "I mean, beside you, me, Karl, and Lothar. Are
there any women servants?"

The thin lips pursed. "Karl is the only servant I need. He
does any cleaning necessary. And all the cooking. Oh, of
course there's Klaus, who sleeps in the byre with the cow
and the horse. He grows many of our vegetables, and jour-
neys to the village monthly for supplies."

Panic welled up once more within me. *No women, besides the old Grossmama!* "Then Klaus may be sent for the
doctor or the midwife when my times comes."

A deep frown creased the parchment brow; the coppery
brows drew together to form a straight line. "There will be
no need for such outsiders. Karl and I will take excellent
care of you and the child."

"But—" I opened my mouth to protest, bewildered at the thought of having a confinement so far from civilization. What if something should go wrong? What if the babe should lie awkwardly in the womb? Women were known to die, along with their infants, at such a time.

Rising from her chair, she cut off further conversation. "Let's not discuss such matters now. Plenty of time for that. You must banish all fears from your mind. It is not healthy to be anxious."

Picking up a roll of the gauzy white cloth from the floor, she wound it round and round my head and neck so that nothing was visible but a slim triangle of flesh—forehead, eyes, nose, mouth, chin. She stood back and surveyed her handiwork. "You could be she," she breathed. "It's uncanny."

"Who?"

"Adela. The first wife of Frederick Barbarossa."

Then her skinny fingers were in mine, and she was pulling me out of the chair, across the dusty carpet, past the array of medieval costumes toward the stairway. "Come. Karl will have dinner laid for us in the *Rittersaal*."

My heart leaped. Lothar would be there waiting for us. Would he too be attired in the medieval manner? A quick picture flashed across my mind, formed of all the paintings I had seen of medieval knights.

Chapter 6

Dinner was laid on a low wooden table pulled onto the black stones of the hearth. With a pang of disappointment I noticed only two place settings. "Will Lothar not be joining us?" I asked, trying to keep my voice even and casual. I must not let this woman think me an immature child, subject to sudden moods.

"Lothar?" The baronin pulled a great carved chair, richly upholstered in burgundy velvet, close to the little table, sat down, settled luxuriantly back on the cushions. "*Nein, liebling*, your husband will not be joining us. Not today, or for a long time to come."

"But—but why not?" I almost shrieked at her. Waves of shock and fear rippled through me. I clutched the wooden back of my chair so hard the carved edges dug into the soft palms of my hands.

A secretive, almost evil look crept into her eyes. Her lips curved in a humorless smile. "Lothar is gone."

"Gone?" I echoed stupidly. "Gone where? And why?"

"As they say in the Bible, he must be about his father's business. You will not see him here in Kyffhauser Castle until after the child is born. Now please be seated, so that we may get on with our dinner. The food will be getting cold."

I pulled out the chair, sat down mechanically, adjusting the green folds of the bridal dress around me. My mind jumped from thought to thought, trying to take in the stupendous news. It was some mistake—a horrible joke! "But that is impossible," I cried, "he could not leave without at least bidding me goodbye."

The black-veiled head bowed low, the bony hands folded piously in an attitude of prayer. Quelling the angry words on my tongue, I followed her example and mumbled with her the traditional words of thanks for the food.

"Hand me your plate, please," she ordered. I did so. She piled it high with meat and vegetables. "Your duty now is to eat, rest, pray, and dedicate yourself to useful, pleasant occupations."

The face which met my anguished gaze across the low table was no longer the kind and loving one that had dressed me and braided my hair. The parchment skin had smoothed into a mask. The eyes were cool, even heartless.

So that was the galloping noise I had heard upstairs. Lothar had saddled the horse and departed. Like a thief in the night. Despite my resolve, the hot tears welled up from the depths of my soul. I spit out the food I had been attempting to chew, bowed my white coifed head in my hands. Deep, wrenching sobs shook me from head to foot. I pushed the chair back, started to rise.

Instantly the old woman was beside me, strong hands restraining me. She pushed me back into the chair with a surprising strength. "Sit down," she muttered between clenched teeth. "You will learn to control yourself, to behave like the lady of the manor. Why do you think I went to the trouble of dressing you like that?"

I sank back down in the chair, still sobbing. The baronin returned to her side of the table and resumed her eating. After a while, my sobs dwindled. She was right, of course. No amount of weeping would bring Lothar back.

"We are not properly married," I said after a while, picking up the goblet of red wine. "The child will not be recognized—he will be a bastard. Like his mother," I added bitterly.

She cupped her rosy goblet in her hands, and walked away from the table into a far corner of the *Rittersaal*. "Come here, child." I rose to follow her.

We stood in front of a faded tapestry that covered a good third of one wall. I could barely make out the figures, but one of them seemed to be a king with a jeweled crown. His robes were ornate, resembling those of a priest dressed for Mass. A golden globe, like a sun, rose over his head. Undulating rays emanated down on the figure. I strained forward in order to see the face of the king. The hair under the crown was a fiery red, and reached past the shoulders. A long beard, full and bushy, extended to the waist.

"That is Frederick Barbarossa, the progenitor of the

Hohenstaufens. The duchy of Swabia, where Kyffhauser Mountain stands, belongs to us, along with all the land along the Danube. The usurpers—the Wittelsbachs and the Hohenzollerns—have stolen it from us."

She led me back to the table. "Every male of the family is dedicated at birth to the restoration of our lands. Once that is done, the throne of Germany will be ours. That is what Lothar must do with his life. What you must do is bear the son. The next sun-king."

The old eyes glittered in anticipation. "You were selected for your ample proportions. As well as your gentle breeding, of course."

I could bear it no longer, this callous way of discussing the love that I shared with Lothar. "No. No. It's not true, what you say. Lothar loves me, as truly as any man ever loved a woman."

She lifted a black arm into the air. "Be still, you fool! You were bred, as a mare to a stallion." The cultivated voice became shrill. "Love! Schoolgirl drivel! Where is he now, your lover? He lay with you only long enough to fill your womb."

Her green eyes glowing, she fairly leaped from her chair. "Imagine, a baby in Schloss Kyffhauser. I must go to the chapel and pray for your safe delivery." Off she went, black skirt flying, fingering a black-beaded rosary she'd pulled out of a deep pocket, leaving me with my wine and my thoughts.

A sudden chill shook my body. I turned toward the fire, leaning my head against the burgundy cushion, unutterably weary. Her spiteful words lay like drops of acid in my whirling brain. As I gazed somberly into the fire, waves of loneliness and self-pity overwhelmed me. But gradually a fierce rage took its place. Lothar *had* run off like a stallion, once his work was done. Not that it seemed like work at the time. He had certainly enjoyed our lovemaking as much as I.

The hot, scalding tears flooded my cheeks. But they were angry tears this time. I pushed the chair back and stumbled to the center of the *Rittersaal*. The faded sun-king tapestry wavered in front of me. I hurled myself blindly on the carpeted floor, beat my clenched fists against the dust of centuries. My slipper-clad feet thumped up and down helplessly. Faster and faster, harder and harder I pounded, as if I would sink through the very floor into oblivion.

Gradually I became aware that great gentle hands were lifting me up from the floor. A mat of black curls touched my bare breast. Pale blue eyes stared fixedly at my bosom. They were the eyes of a man who has crossed a vast desert and has suddenly stumbled upon an oasis.

"You will injure yourself—and the child." His eyes lifted from my bosom, met mine. His gaze was steady and comforting. Of course he knew of Lothar's secret departure. He had very likely provided him with food for the journey down the mountain.

"Now you must retire to your sleeping chamber for an afternoon's nap," Karl insisted. "The baronin's orders. She would be very displeased if she finds you still here when she returns from her prayers."

At the head of the stairs, Karl led me past the curtained doorway to the baronin's chamber where I had bathed and dressed, then stopped at a heavy wooden door at the far end of the corridor. "This is a tower room," he said. "The view is magnificent." Taking a key from a large bunch that hung at his waist, he inserted it into the lock right below a huge brass door pull. When it refused to open, he drew back and gave a mighty kick with his booted foot. The old door flew open with a rasp of old hinges.

"Oh!" I gasped with pleasure. I had expected still another dark, dismal chamber but this one literally glowed with light shed from a heavy silver candelabra set on a medieval chest much like the ones from which the baronin had pulled all the clothing.

A brightly canopied bed took up one entire wall. The curtains were of a damask-like fabric heavily embroidered with a pretty woodland scene. A long cushioned bench sat against the other wall. On the chest beside the candelabra lay a number of exquisite toilet articles—brush, comb, a hand mirror, all intricately worked with gold leaf on a moss-green background. The coverlet of the bed was of silk. The entire room smelled of spring.

"What is that wonderful fragrance?" I asked, sniffing the air.

"A special blend of pine needles and herbs," the servant replied, obviously pleased at my reactions. His gaze, as he stood by the bed, rested on my bosom. "The quilt is of down. I made it myself when I heard of your coming. I'd been saving the goose feathers for years for Lothar's bride."

Unconsciously I held up my arms, extending them in a

swift luxurious movement over my head, in the Venus-like pose I had assumed that Corpus Christi Day when I admired myself in the mirror. With the movement, my breasts, heavier and fuller than usual because of my pregnancy, finally escaped the bondage of the tight bodice. My nipples, rigid now with the chill of the room, thrust themselves into the air.

Startled, I gazed at them like one transfixed, uncertain what to do. Instantly the big bull of a man was upon me. He buried his crisp dark head in my neck, clamped his mouth on my right nipple. He sucked, like a starving infant. Automatically my arms descended to rest on his shoulders.

A fierce hot desire flamed up in my loins. Lothar had loved to suck on my breasts. Karl's giant hands pressed deeply into my soft shoulders. I moaned, arched my body toward his. Then suddenly I remembered what the baronin had said. *A castrate.* Would such a man act like this? I could not afford to find out. Although I carried Lothar's child, he might rape me right here. I struggled in his iron grip. But my writhings only maddened him, so that he clasped me even tighter to his strong frame.

"Be calm," I told myself. "Remember the child in your womb." I pressed against his thighs, searching for the familiar hardness of manhood as I had done with Lothar. Nothing. Nothing but a softness.

Then as quickly as he had assaulted me, Karl tore himself away and threw himself on the floor. He hugged my knees with his giant hands. "Forgive, forgive, *liebe* Frau Sieglinde," he sobbed. His sweet high voice was raw with agony. "I would sooner die than harm you or your unborn babe."

The tear-streaked face looked up at me. The birthmark stood out red and angry. "Although I can never love a woman in the way of other men, I still feel a desire, a strange kind of passion. Your breast—I have never seen a lovelier sight—your skin so soft—your eyes so deep, soft and brown—please forgive me."

Before I could utter a word to console him, Karl stood up and stormed out the door. I heard the sound of the key turning in the lock. I moved over to the window in a trance, leaned out the narrow opening to take several gulps of clean fresh air. My heart was going like a triphammer.

I stood for a long time at the opening, breathing slowly,

steadily. The view, indeed, was magnificent. After the band of barren rock and sand, a wall of green arose to meet my eyes. A faint haze and the delicious aroma of wood smoke declared the presence of huts on the slopes and in the valleys below. The storm that had soaked Lothar and me in the morning had dissipated. The declining sun cast a bluish glow on jagged snowcapped peaks to the west.

A low growling rose from below. I bent down and watched as the dogs rounded the corner of the Schloss, scavenging in the dry moat. "They'll rip you limb from limb," Lothar had warned.

There was no hope of escape from this place, no way I could get down the mountain to the village. I was condemned to remain here for the seven remaining months of my pregnancy. Weary suddenly, I turned to the bed. I released the rest of my body from the medieval dress and fell full-length on the silk coverlet that Karl had made for me.

In moments I was fast in a dreamless sleep.

A shaft of brilliant sunshine streamed across the bed. I woke up with a start. The heavy silken quilt now covered me. I lay naked between the sheets. A fresh gown, green like the one I'd worn yesterday, was tossed on the little wooden bench. Also a new length of white cloth for my coif.

Karl! Of course. He had the key to my room. He had slipped in and covered me with the quilt.

Unlike the too-tight bridal dress, this frock was cut more simply, falling in soft folds from tiny gathers just under the bust. But like the other, the neckline was cut low in a sweeping, graceful curve. Those medieval women must have frozen in the winter, I thought crossly.

Reaching for the soft linen, I twirled it round my still braided hair like a scarf, then brought it down to my neck. There was plenty of it to stuff into the opening of the dress so that not a trace of skin showed of neck or bosom. I picked up the gold and moss-green hand mirror and gazed at myself approvingly. The baronin had lied. She had said that there were no mirrors in the Schloss. Obviously she didn't know about this one.

When Karl kicked open the door with my breakfast, I reached for a brioche even before he could set the tray down on the chest.

"Taste the coffee, Frau Sieglinde," he beamed. "It is a secret blend of my own."

"Delicious." I drank two cups as he watched me, anxiously awaiting my verdict. "You are a genius with food, Karl. I failed to compliment you on the superb dinner of yesterday."

I reached for the second brioche. "I'm grateful that the baronin's medieval living style does not extend to food. I don't imagine there was coffee in the twelfth century."

"No," he replied, smiling, "the baronin may dress as in the past but she eats in the present. She will be delighted at seeing you so attractively gowned and coifed this morning."

The burly servant seemed exuberant and much relieved that I chose not to speak of his passionate embrace of yesterday. He strode to the window as I ate, peered out. "A fine day. The sky is clear and blue. It will be perfect for our walk," he declared.

"A walk—sounds wonderful. I relish the outdoors. You know that the Baron von Hohenstaufen and I lived for two whole months in the forest. Just like Adam and Eve."

He dashed out into the corridor, returned shortly with the pair of wooden clogs that Brother Matthew had given me. "You'd better slip these on," he said. "We've had a very rainy summer, and the grounds are mired in places."

In minutes, we had left the gloom of the Schloss for the bright morning sun of the courtyard. Yesterday when I had approached the Schloss with Lothar, the driving rain had obscured my vision. But now as we walked slowly on the moss-covered stones of the barbican, the dark outlines of the building rose up more clearly. Many of the stones had fallen out of place and lay scattered on the ground. The slit-like openings which served as windows were staggered in an uneven pattern so that it was hard to tell just how many levels the dwelling contained.

"What happened to it?" I asked Karl, as I picked my way among the broken stones.

"Many wars," he answered. "And of course the ravages of time. The Hohenstaufens have many enemies."

"How long has the baronin made this her residence? Curious, that she should live so far from civilization."

"The baronin has lived here since her husband and son—Lothar's father—were executed in the revolt of 1830. That rebellion also came to nothing. Her home in Regensburg was confiscated and all the family treasures stolen by the government."

"How sad! And Lothar? Did he grow up here with her?"

"No." Karl stopped, wrinkled his face in a puzzled frown. "One day, about five years ago, he simply appeared. He just knocked on the door."

We had rounded the far corner of the ruin and were back in the courtyard area. Here too most of the buildings were a pile of stones.

"And you, Karl? How long have you lived here on Kyffhauser Mountain?"

"I was brought here as a child of ten from the State Orphan Asylum in Regensburg. The baronin has been very good to me. I owe her my life."

It was on the tip of my tongue to ask about his castration, but I could not bring myself to utter the dreaded word. Instead, I prodded him further about Lothar and the revolution.

"After the Thirty Years' War which ended in 1648," he told me, "the family was driven from the throne."

We moved now toward the outbuildings behind the Schloss proper. "Are Lothar and his *Grossmama* very close?" I inquired.

"Oh, yes. They talk a great deal together. About politics and—" Karl stopped in front of a decrepit-looking stone building. "Here is the byre where Klaus sleeps. He never comes into the Schloss."

"The byre can wait." I pulled on Karl's leather sleeve. "Tell me what else Lothar and the baronin discuss when they are together."

"Well, for the past few years, she has been persuading him to find a strong girl of good family and father a son."

Again I felt the dart of fear that I had been used. Lothar would never come back to me. He had his son. For me he cared nothing. A deep sense of hurt coursed through me once more, as it had when he'd left so secretly yesterday. He had not lingered in the forest glade a moment longer than necessary. I hated him, I told myself, as I followed Karl into the byre where Klaus lived with the milch cow and the horse.

"Klaus. Are you there?" We were in the dark manure-smelling little building.

"*Ja.*" A strong old-man voice came from inside. Klaus appeared and gazed at me silently.

"So this is the bitch," he said briefly, then returned to squeezing a round of cheese between two boards.

I flushed but said nothing. I could not afford any enemies in this isolated place.

Outside again, Karl led me to a great pile of rubble. "This is the family burial ground." He crossed himself in reverence. "When the Schloss was intact, it was the site of the chapel. It was the custom in those days to inter the bodies of the family beneath the paving stones of the chapel."

A sudder of premonition ran through me. "Dear God," I prayed silently, "spare me and my babe from this forsaken place."

My tour of the Schloss ended in Karl's kitchen, a dark cavernous room with a multitude of drying herbs hanging from the rafters. There was a fireplace here, too, big enough to roast an ox.

"This is my wife, my darling," he said, moving to place a loving hand on the corner of a huge iron cookstove. He pointed to the herbs. "There is all that is needed for sickness of any kind."

Seeing them there eased my fears of the coming birth. Ortrud also had been skilled with herbs, and never had believed in doctors. We finished the morning's excursion seated across from each other at the wooden table, sipping from a flagon of mellow wine. I had removed the confining coif in the heat of our walk. Karl's gaze continued to fix itself on my bosom. It no longer bothered me, however. I felt I could handle him.

On the eve of All Souls' Day, November second, the child leaped in my womb for the first time. I rejoiced in the tiny pain. The baronin had told me that movement generally appeared in the fourth month. That meant I had conceived in early August. The baby would be born toward the end of March. Five months to wait before Lothar would come and carry me away from this prison.

When I announced to the baronin that I felt life, her old face lit up like a candle. "*Gott bedankt*. March, then, or early April."

"Could I not go into the village with Klaus," I pleaded, "where there are other women? And a midwife?"

The parchment face darkened with displeasure. "I have spoken to no one in the village for twenty years. Besides it is most important that the child be born in the Schloss.

Karl and I will serve as midwives when your time comes."

As hard as I tried to be cheerful, my loneliness and despair were deepening. I missed the busy, frantic life of the court, where we had parties every night, where there was always someone to gossip with. Each day followed another with unbending monotony. After breakfasting in my room, I took my walk with Karl. Then back into the *Rittersaal* for dinner, and an afternoon of sewing on endless baby garments. And endless listening to the baronin drone on about old Hohenstaufen glories.

Late afternoons I dozed, usually in my chamber, but as the winter came on, Karl spread a quilt on a wide bench in the kitchen where the crackling wood fire warmed me as he prepared our supper. Sometimes I told him about Lola and the king, my father. The pale blue eyes darkened with anger, the strawberry birthmark took on a purplish hue.

"Has he a wife, this king?"

"Of course," I replied, "a good and faithful one, and seven healthy children."

"Then it is a grievous sin that he has played the wanton with a harlot. It is a good thing that Lothar and his friends drove him into France." His burly hands lifted the lid of the cookstove and jabbed viciously at the blazing fire within. "It is a grievous sin," he repeated, "when men allow their passions to destroy their proper loyalties."

The great black head shone in the light of the fire, the blue eyes glittered with tiny fires. "Nothing is greater than honor. That is the highest duty."

Seeing his anger, and remembering his great remorse after his own fit of passion on my breast, I gave up any idea I had of seducing him into helping me escape. He would never betray the baronin, to whom he owed his very life.

Chapter 7

As my figure thickened and became cumbersome, my sleep became more fitful. I tossed feverishly in the high corner bed. I felt suffocated under the enclosing curtains. Even though my chamber was unheated, I threw off the linen to sleep with my bare ugly body uncovered, exposed to the chill night air.

Concerned about the dark shadows which appeared under my eyes, Karl mixed a light herbal concoction into my bedtime chocolate. "This will banish the bad dreams," he promised. "It is tincture of wolfsbane, just a tiny amount."

Wolfsbane! I knew it well. A deadly poison, if taken in enough quantity, it was extracted from the pretty bluish flowers that grew along mountain streams. Finally a delicious drowsiness overtook my tense muscles, and I fell into sleep.

Dreams chased me through the night. I dreamed of Lothar and the Cave of Venus. His lips were on mine, his tongue a tiny darting snake devouring my mouth. His muscular flesh pressed fully on mine as we lay together breast to breast, thigh to thigh, knee to knee. I arched up, straining toward the delicious consummation, madly waiting for the hard feel of his thrusting manhood in my moist, anxious flesh. But it never came. I woke with a cry of agony and frustration. Sweat poured from every pore of my tortured, clumsy, lust-filled body.

"Lothar!" I cried out, sitting bolt upright in bed. There was someone in the room. "Lothar? Is that you?"

Then, as my eyes slowly cleared from the effects of the drug, I saw the figure standing at the side of the bed, gazing down at me, regarding me with eyes so filled with love and pity and tenderness that I instinctively held out my arms.

It was Karl. He was naked. His right hand held a taper. For a moment he stood still, frozen, like one of Lola's Greek statues. As our eyes probed each other's naked, suffering souls, he turned slightly, put the taper to the single candle in the silver candelabra on the chest.

I stared dumbly at his mutilated manhood. My hands trembled. I had an uncontrollable impulse to reach out and touch it, caress it, murmur endearments as to a hurt child. Instead, I forced my eyes upward to his chest which was a forest of thick, black curls. My head spun, I buried my face in his firm knotted abdomen. The hot blood drummed in my throat, warning me that this man could not give me what I longed for.

Finally he spoke, his sweet high voice barely audible.

"Here I am," he said, "such as I am. I am yours. Do with me what you will."

Karl plunged both rough calloused hands into my tousled hair which hung thickly on his naked body, the tendrils reaching down past his thighs. He pulled with both hands, but ever so gently, so that the lower half of his body from his waist to his knees was completely shrouded with my hair.

Then, pushing me down on to the bed, he slid me over against the wall, so that his giant frame could stretch out beside me. Slowly, almost out of my mind with want and longing, I drew my burning face out of the thick hair, away from his warm body, leaned my head back to rest on the feathery pillows.

"Woman, woman, thou art life itself," he murmured, as his big hands roamed all over my body, exploring every curve, under the arms, the moist places under the heavy breasts, the armpits. Then he began to rub in little circles, starting with my breast, moving over my distended abdomen, down the length of hip and thigh, until he reached the dark, warm moistness between my thighs.

Suddenly, quick as a viper's tongue, he thrust his long forefinger into the quivering opening. I cried out at his touch.

"Lie back, Frau Sieglinde," he urged. "Just lie back and let me play with you. Give yourself up totally to sensation."

With a long, drawn-out groan, he flung himself on my breasts, sucking greedily at the dark brown, rigid nipples. Every nerve in my body burst into flame. I could not be still, as he commanded. I flailed about, twisting my yearning body under his touch. I stroked his damp hair, kissed the strawberry birthmark hungrily, desperately, tenderly. I sucked greedily at his thick sensuous lips, tearing them away from my breasts. All the while he played with me, as a master musician strokes his instrument. Stroking, stroking.

Suddenly, like the sun and the moon exploding together, all my senses burst asunder. All the long, bleak months of denial were released in the animal cry of triumph which burst from my fevered lips. But even my ecstasy was tinged with fear. "The baronin," I whispered hoarsely. "She will hear us."

Karl's muttered reply brought a smile to my lips, the first in many days. "You, Frau Sieglinde, are not the only one to drink the wolfsbane tonight."

And with that the big lovable man fell fast asleep, the ugly red cheek warm and comforting on my breast. For the first time since Lothar left me my fear was gone. I felt calm, at peace with myself and the world.

"We will leave this place," I whispered fiercely into the crisp dark curls. "You and me. Wherever I go, whatever I do, you will be with me. Always, Karl."

That nightmare night was the turning point in my life at Schloss Hohenstaufen, for that night Karl and I reversed our roles. He became the child, I the mother he had never known. The child in me died forever, and I was born again—a woman. A woman who was keenly aware of her power to sway men through their passions.

Together, Karl and I would flee this prison. We'd leave it to the haughty baronin and her memories and her ambitions. Let her get herself another vessel, another womb to bear the savior of the Hohenstaufen glory.

"I am Sieglinde," I whispered into the night, as I had whispered into Lola's mirror on Corpus Christi Day six months ago. "Daughter of Ludwig von Wittelsbach, king of Bavaria. Sister of Maximilian, his successor. I will not become a pawn of destiny. I am a woman. I will be loved. I will be happy."

The single candle burned low, sputtered out as dawn crept over the Kyffhauser Mountain. I slept at last, to be awakened by the slow, careful movements of Karl slipping out of my bed.

"It is dawn, Frau Sieglinde," he said. "I must go before

77

the baronin awakens." He smiled groggily, smelling of sleep.

I reached to grasp both his warm hands in mine. "Karl," I urged, "let's leave the Schloss. Today. Tonight at the latest. You can drug some meat and throw it to the dogs."

I leaned toward him, arching my back so that my swollen breasts brushed against his nakedness.

"No, no, it cannot be." He moved swiftly toward the door. "Where would we go? How would we live?" Fear haunted his childlike blue eyes.

"Oh, anywhere," I said impatiently. "What does it matter? Into the village, or back to Regensburg, or even all the way back to Munich. It's only a few days' hard riding."

He glanced uneasily at my protruding belly. "Even a half-day's riding might bring on your labor prematurely. The child would be injured, or even die. Besides—" He ran to the window, pried off the rough pine board. "Look!"

I rose up in the bed and looked out the window at a world that was completely, totally, blindingly white.

"We'd have to take Klaus's horse," he said. "Riding as you and Lothar did in the summer is one thing—but now the wind would cut you to the bone before we had gone ten kilometers."

I sank back dejectedly, disappointment plain on my face, my eyes cloudy with unshed tears. "When?" I asked. "When, Karl?"

"When you are delivered safely and the babe is well. Spring. April at the earliest."

At my silence he continued, rubbing my hands between his to warm them. "Just three months, four at most. In the meantime, I will come to your bed every night." He paused, then went on awkwardly, "To bring you comfort."

He left me then to start the day's chores. I sank back on the pillow, secure in the knowledge that I had a friend, a protector, a confidant, and yes—even a lover.

As with Christmas, the New Year came and went without notice. To the Baronin von Hohenstaufen, one day was like another. She ignored all holidays. The present had no meaning for her. She lived in the past and, awaiting the birth of the child in my womb, in the future.

Every morning, as we faced each other over the low table on the hearth in the *Rittersaal*, she ticked off the days remaining until my confinement, like a bell tolling in a steeple.

One raw February morning, she said, "Just a month to go, if what you tell me about your time with Lothar is true. Stand up, girl," she commanded.

I lumbered to my feet, extricating myself with much effort from the deep cushioned armchair.

"Hmm." She pursed her thin lips, made sucking noises. "Turn around." The coppery brown knitted in a straight line over the green eyes.

"You look ready to deliver," the old woman said. "How can I be sure the child is really Lothar's?"

"Why don't you send for him," I retorted, stung as always at her suspicions. "He will tell you of the night he broke my maidenhead."

Her white-coifed head reared back. "No need to be vulgar. Birthing is woman's work. Lothar will not be needed until the time for the christening at least."

After she'd left, Karl came into the *Rittersaal* with a fresh trout he had fished out of the icy lake, and fried it in sweet butter in an iron skillet right over the coals in the great fireplace. My appetite had been poor the last few days, and he knew my fondness for the mountain trout. I reclined uneasily on the long wooden bench where I rested every afternoon for a few hours. Karl had spread a thick warm wolfskin over the hard surface.

After I'd finished the trout, and some apple cake fixed with raisins and rum that I loved, I dozed to the sounds of the big servant clearing away the cooking things. Suddenly, a sharp swordlike pain shot through my loins. I sat up, with a little cry. All the blood drained from my face into the lower part of my body. A strange excitement coursed through my brain.

It had come. I would give birth today. I waited. Karl had gone into the kitchen. Another sharp pain, much sharper than the first. I screamed as still a third tore through my loins as if it would cut me in half. Labor wasn't supposed to happen this fast. Something was wrong.

"Karl, Karl!" I fell back on the furry wolfskin, breathless.

I must have fainted, for the first thing I saw as I struggled up through layers of unconsciousness was Karl's angry birthmark.

"Go away," I screamed at him hysterically. "You'll mark the child."

He grabbed my fists, drew me to his chest. "Still, still,

liebschen, still, still." Crooning softly, he rocked me back and forth.

Then the baronin was there, her stern old face aglow with anticipation, her sea-green eyes aglitter, shooting sparks of gold.

"I knew it," she said. "I had a premonition. Brew some tea with a drop or two of wolfsbane, Karl. Just enough so that she can sleep between the contractions."

"I want to go to my bed," I moaned, thinking longingly of the feathery quilt. "I want Lothar. Send for Lothar. He should be here at my side."

"Be still, save your strength," she snapped. "You'll need every shred. I couldn't fetch Lothar even if I wanted to. He's in the north of Germany right now. It would take at least a week for the message to reach him, another week for him to get here."

Karl fetched the tea and held it to my lips. The scalding liquid set my insides on fire. Then as the old woman barked out orders, he set up a long wide board on two wooden trestles to form a waist-high table. He spread a number of clean linen cloths on it.

"We can watch your progress much better at this height," the baronin said, as the servant lifted me tenderly and placed me on the table.

"Don't go away, Karl." I pulled at his hand. "Don't leave me."

The big lips parted in a smile. "Always, Frau Sieglinde, always I am here."

The pain consumed me, blotting out all sense. Karl's rough hand pushed the wet hair from my streaming forehead, and wiped my face with a cloth soaked in cool water and vinegar.

"Up with you." Incredibly the baronin and Karl were forcing me to walk, holding me up between them. Round and round the *Rittersaal* we went. Her aristocratic voice was biting. "Stay on your feet as long as you can. The child will come more quickly."

I licked the salt from my sweat-drenched lips. I heard the animal sound of my own hoarse, labored breathing. A giant hand with talons of iron clutched my lower back. I dropped to my knees, my two tormentors dropping right alongside me. I heard as if at a great distance a cry like that of an animal being torn alive.

"Push, you slut, push." A harsh voice grated in my ear. "Stop your caterwauling and push."

I clenched my teeth, dug my nails into the hands that held me, bore down with all my might.

"It is time," the baronin shouted.

Karl moved behind me, clasped me firmly round the waist with his grip of iron, held me up while the old woman spread my knees apart.

"Here it comes." Her voice pierced the thunder in my head. "The head is emerging."

"Push, you slut, bear down." She shouted in my face, covering me with her spittle.

"I am dying, I am dying," I groaned through crusted lips. "Lothar, Lothar, my husband, my love, we had such a little time, such a little time."

Then a cup of scalding tea was being held to my lips. I gulped down the bitter wolfsbane tea.

"That'll keep her quiet for a while. Her job is over."

And Karl's softer voice, "And a good job of it too. A splendid babe."

Dimly I felt a sinuous, twisting sensation between my thighs as the old woman pulled the baby from my bleeding womb. I wanted to speak, to bend my head and gaze upon the form of my newborn child, but my muscles had turned to water. The wolfsbane had taken hold.

The voices again: "There's another. Quick, the scissors. Who would have thought!"

"Get them near the fire." That was the baronin. "Wrap them up tightly in the cloths."

Then a deep merciful blackness descended upon me.

I never saw my little son. Karl had buried him, wrapped only in the linen cloth, under the pile of rocks where the ancient Hohenstaufens slumbered through the centuries. I grieved but did not pray. Surely no prayers were required for that innocent soul which was now among the angels in Heaven.

My daughter, being a full month premature, demanded my unflagging attention, and took almost constant feeding. At first the tiny rosebud mouth could suck on the nipple only a few seconds at a time. But I persisted, thrusting the engorged breast between the sweet lips every half-hour at least until at last she drew the milk hungrily from me.

Her head was covered with an unmistakable red fuzz. I called her Kristina, for my Norwegian mother. At the end of the second month she had filled out nicely, the wrinkles in her flesh rounding out to mounds of fat.

"For this you were born," Karl beamed, approvingly. He would sit for hours, gazing at the two of us, the child at my breast, jumping up to change her cloth, or fetch some little thing I needed. His happiness in my daughter was boundless. His big face glowed as if a thousand candles had been lit inside his head.

I had not seen the baronin since the night of the birth of the twins. "Is she ill?" I asked Karl, truly anxious for the old woman. She had delivered me safely, despite all my fears, and for that I was grateful.

He shook his head. "The baronin is simply weary from the ordeal and the excitement. And of course"—a shadow crossed his face—"she has gone into deep mourning for her lost grandson. She spends most of the day and half the night in the chapel, on her knees."

Just as he spoke, however, she was there, in the arched doorway, holding the thick curtains apart with her long slender hands, the rich black velvet of her winter robe gleaming dully in the firelight. She stood there a moment— only a moment—but long enough for me to feel the hatred palpable and alive, streaming from the coifed figure, quenching the warm room with the chill of death.

"How is my grandchild?" she asked in a sweet voice, completely unnatural to her.

"She is well," I replied with a laugh, trying to keep my voice normal, to mask my uneasiness. "Very well indeed. She seems to have her father's constitution."

"Here, let me have her." Her long black-clad arms reached out and lifted the baby from my breast. "In truth, she is a handsome child, the picture of health. But alas, I have known many such to fail suddenly. Blooming one day, gone the next. We must be vigilant, guard her at all times from drafts and unexpected noises—"

Her pessimistic chatter was depressing me so I interrupted. "Has the Frau Baronin been ill? I have missed you the week since the birth of the child."

She did not answer my question but instead continued to gaze at the child in her arms. "I have been remiss, but now I intend to exercise my rights as a doting grandmother. I will care for the child at all times, except when she is at the breast."

The old woman turned and began to walk swiftly toward the curtained doorway.

I sat up paralyzed with fear. "Where are you taking her? The Schloss is too cold except for this room. She cannot bear the cold as yet."

"Calm your fears," she called back from the doorway. "She is very strong. She is a Hohenstaufen. She is so strong in fact that she killed her brother." Her voice was muffled now, but distinct as she entered the chilly corridor with my child. "The sister has killed the brother."

Like a madwoman, I leaped from the bench, calling out, "My baby, my baby, please, please—" I ran across the *Rittersaal*, clutched frantically at her robe, fear like an icy hand squeezing at my heart.

"Karl," the baronin shouted, "come and see to Sieglinde. She is not herself."

Then Karl's big arms were around me, pulling me away from the baronin. "Come, come back to the fire," he coaxed. "The baronin would not harm her very flesh and blood."

He laid me down on the bench and covered me lightly with a blanket. "Don't take on so, she only means to be of help. There is a fire in her chamber, just as warm as this one. The child will come to no harm."

But I knew better. I clung to him, despairing. All I could hear were those dreadful words, *The sister has killed the brother*. I knew with a mother's instinctive knowledge that the old woman meant to take revenge on my Kristina for living, while the tiny Frederick had died.

Restless, I busied myself with my toilette, neglected because of the constant nursing of the child. Karl fetched a bowl of warm water and some herb-scented soap. I drew the shirt from my rounded shoulder and bursting breast, rubbed the soapy cloth thoroughly all over my naked body.

"Let me help, it will go faster." Karl sprang to my aid, rinsed off the soap with clear fresh water, rubbed me dry with soft linen cloths. I leaned back against the cushions and let the gentle giant arrange my hair. The two thick braids done at last, there was no sound in the room but the crackling of the logs on the fire.

After what seemed an eternity, the baronin was back

with the child. I reached out greedily, clasped the swaddled bundle tightly to my bosom, bent over the little face. I kissed the tiny cheek. Cold as ice. As I loosened the swaddling blanket, I felt the cloth around her little bottom. Wet, cold and clammy. I wanted to lash out, to rake my nails down the length of that smiling parchment face, to gouge out the Lothar-like eyes. But I clenched my teeth and held my tongue. She must not even suspect that I would take the child and leave. But leave I must, tonight, Karl and I and the baby. I was certain now that the baronin would kill my daughter.

It was all so easy, I could hardly keep from laughing out loud. The baronin joined me for an early supper and soon after Karl had served the mugs of steaming chocolate, the old coifed head was nodding on her wimple. The wolfsbane had done its work once more.

When we were certain she was asleep for the night, I dressed quickly in a heavy woolen garment such as the Black Forest peasants wore. A length of rough brown wool covered my coiled hair completely, extending down around my neck, falling down the front of my dress.

"We must look like a poor mountain family travelling to Mannheim in search of work," Karl said.

Karl would carry the baby on his back like a bundle of wood, with a board strapped to her extending over her head and a wool cloth pulled over it to form a kind of roof as protection from the snow and wind.

The dogs he had taken care of earlier, with the wolfsbane and a juicy chunk of fresh meat. "Those hounds won't be barking much for days," he promised, grinning widely.

I ran to him impulsively, hugged him fiercely. I had been so wrong about him. His loyalty for his mistress was as nothing compared to his love and devotion to me and Kristina. "You are a real man," I whispered into his broad chest. As we stepped out into the courtyard, Karl pointed to the heavens. "Smells like rain. Good. That means our footprints will be gone by morning."

I followed Karl past byre and garden, past the slumbering Klaus, who had also drunk the drugged chocolate that night, and into the scrub pines. The path wasn't nearly as steep as I had feared, but leveled off soon into a kind of plateau.

Just as we passed the rocky graveyard, I stopped and

uttered a quick prayer for my lost son. Karl didn't appear to notice, but, stooping, picked up a stout branch and thrust it into my hands. "You'll need a walking stick," he said briefly. But I felt his sorrow, too.

The moon was high but soon a few clouds flitted across the heavens, and just as Karl had predicted, a light spring rain began to fall. Faster and faster we trudged. I lost all track of time, the only thought in my mind to put distance between me and the madwoman in the Schloss.

Bells resounded faintly from the village halfway down the mountain. I counted ten resonant strokes. As if on cue, a fretful whimper came from the wooly bundle on Karl's back. The pressure in my bosom also told me that we must stop.

"Karl," I said, my breath whistling painfully in my lungs, "the baby must be fed. And I must be relieved."

"*Ja, ja,* we stop soon. There is a place I remember well from my childhood. It is a good dry place where we can sleep out the night."

Shortly we came to a low stone wall, like so many in this part of Germany, the remnants of a line of fortifications built by the Roman legions. Karl stopped, and with his stick scraped away the thin covering of snow.

"Aha, *Gott bedankt!*" he cried at last. "This is the place, just as I remembered." He stooped low over the wall, and lifted up a number of large stones to reveal a hole in the ground.

"Come," he commanded in his new authoritative voice. Obediently, I took his extended hand, and stooped with him to peer into the hole.

I gasped in amazement and delight. "Wh-what is it, Karl?"

"Part of the Limes. You have surely heard about the Limes."

"Of course. Every German schoolchild knows about the famous line of fortifications left by the Roman legions. You mean that it is actually—" I stopped, breathless with wonder.

"The same. It is just one of many I uncovered on this mountain, which no one else has ever seen. As a boy, when I had been beaten by the baronin and wanted a place to lick my wounds, I came here."

Karl as a boy. Somehow I had never thought of him as

anything but this kind, gentle giant of a man. "Karl, what was it like, growing up in that place, with that gloomy, praying old woman?"

"Not now," he said briefly. "Right now we must settle for the night." He led me deeper into the cavelike space, then motioned me to lie on the ground. It was soft and comfortable from a thick layers of pine needles that had been brought in. My heart pounded in remembrance of the Cave of Venus.

"You are sure, Karl, that no one knows about this place?"

I sank down gratefully on the soft piny bed and uncovered my breast. Karl unstrapped Kristina and laid her on my breast. The sound of her eager sucking filled the little room.

I shivered with relief and delight. "Ahhh. That feels good," I whispered.

His hearty laugh filled the cavelike space. "No need to whisper. Nobody here but ghosts of Roman legions."

He stretched his great frame alongside mine, shoulder to shoulder, thigh to thigh. The rhythmical pull of the tiny mouth on my nipple set up a stirring response in my loins, a familiar primitive urge. Gradually the sucking noises tapered off, finally stopped, and the infant once more fell asleep. Pulling the nipple from her mouth, I moved to cover my breast. But Karl reached over with his hand and pulled the woolly cloth away from the other breast as well. For the first time since before the birth, he kissed and licked my soft warm flesh. Despite my efforts at control, I found my legs parting, my hands reaching out to clasp him more firmly to me.

He stopped to lift the baby, laid her on the ground on the other side of me. An overwhelming compassion swept through me. I must know his story. When finally we lay peacefully in each other's arms, surrounded by the silence of the centuries, I asked, "Karl, I must know, how did it happen? Why were you castrated?"

"When I was a boy of twelve, a slut of a servant girl lusted after me. She would come to my bed at night to torment me. I was a full-grown man by that time. But I knew it was a wickedness for a man and woman to bed together without the blessing of marriage. "I threw her out of my chamber. Many times. Finally, enraged, she accused me falsely to the baronin. It took three men to hold me for the necessary operation. The baronin said that it was for my own good and the welfare of my immortal soul."

"How wicked," I cried. "But you are not a slave, this is the nineteenth century, not the twelfth when such things were permitted."

"You forget," he said bitterly, "that the baronin lives in the twelfth century. And I was a waif, abandoned by my parents, cruelly marked at birth. Where could I go? To whom could I turn? I too was grateful to have food in my belly and a roof over my head."

We slept till dawn, his head on my breast, his tears running into the little hollow beneath, where they dried from the heat of my body.

Chapter 8

We headed for Mannheim, about 150 kilometers to the north. Karl said it was the nearest city, a crowded place where a man and his wife and child could easily lose themselves. What was more important, it was a place where Karl could find work on the docks. Mannheim was the largest port on the Rhine and hundreds of ships of all descriptions, both passenger and cargo, sailed in and out of there each week.

As though a kindly Providence were watching over us, the weather turned warm after our night in the Limes cave. The air was clear and crisp, much like the föhn weather in the south, but without the persistent nagging wind.

Stopping only to suckle Kristina, and partake frugally of the bread and sausage Karl had stashed into a leather bag, we walked through half-frozen fields which in the summer would be sown with maize and tobacco.

The second night Karl found another ruin for us to settle into, this one a dilapidated outbuilding which once had been part of a farm. The place smelled of mice and damp, but it was dry and warm. And there was a well nearby that yielded fresh, clear water.

The third day, even my mountain-trained legs accustomed to long treks in the hills around Schachten, began to weaken. So it was with great relief that I saw the line of poplars which Karl had said stretched along the Rhine for ten miles immediately outside of Mannheim.

I stood beside him on a softly rising hillock, for the terrain was nearly level now, and gazed at the thrilling panorama below. I caught my breath at the sight of the river. It was my first view of the famous Rhine of story and legend.

"Oh, Karl," I breathed in a hushed voice, "it is more beautiful by far than all the stories could tell." A warm

April breeze had sprung up. The sun shone brightly in the noonday sky. The blue-brown river stretched like a broad silken ribbon, flecked with little whitecaps where the wind ruffled the waters.

From what I could see of the city itself it was a smaller version of Munich, with the same narrow streets lined with tall houses. Wooden piers and wharves lined the riverbanks, which seemed to be jammed with people. Craft of all kinds choked the river, especially around the wharves. There were chubby freighters which had panted their way from the south loaded with coal from the Ruhr, some with lumber from the Black Forest. Each little boat pulled at least three or four barges. Among the tugs and barges, slim graceful packets rocked at anchor, sails furled, gaily colored flags snapping smartly in the April breeze. Squat steamers, identified by the half-circle of paddle wheel in the center, belched thick black smoke into the clear noontime air.

My heart lifted. I felt as if I could soar right into the air and land on one of those steamboats to sail into some exotic foreign land. "Oh, Karl, let's hurry." I tugged at his sleeve. "I can hardly wait. Let's go straight to the docks."

He looked soberly into my glowing face. "Are you not weary? We should find a lodging of some kind first, with a real bed and milk and beer for you."

"Nonsense. I'm not tired anymore. Please." Breaking away from him, I started down the hill toward the town, running like a child just let out of school.

His hearty masculine laugh followed me. We reached the line of poplars and followed them directly into the town. "I keep forgetting," he chuckled, "how much of a child you still are."

The sun was so warm, I took off the wool cloak and tore the scarf from my hair which, loosening from its pins, fell down around my body in golden tangles. I made no attempt to bind it up again. Somehow the wind-tossed tendrils represented my new-found freedom.

Every foot of the mile-long wooden landing place was covered with teeming humanity. Judging from the great variety of costumes, all of Germany seemed to be represented. I recognized some of them easily—the leather knee breeches, white shirts and richly embroidered suspenders of the Bavarian, the tall, elaborate coiffeur and swirling white skirt of the Frisian. Large, burly sailors with woolen caps pulled down over their ears and wearing thick blue jackets moved in and out of the crowd. Little clumps of people surrounded them, mothers, fathers, sweethearts with their arms entwined about them, saying their farewells. I thought of Lothar. Tears misted my eyes and a fierce chilling loneliness held me like a vise in its grip. But I banished it, lifting my head to the skies. I was a Wittelsbach. The proud blood of kings and queens flowed in my veins. Besides, I had Karl.

Looking over the heads of the throng, I caught sight of him. He was talking earnestly with a group of workers loading hay from farm wagons onto a barge moored at the river's edge. "Don't move," he'd cautioned me, before wandering off to seek some workers to talk to. "Or I won't be able to find you in this crowd, big as you are."

His dear face had been wrinkled with concern for me. "Karl," I promised, "I am a woman now. What could happen to me? But I promise not to move."

Reassured, he'd gone off, Kristina still strapped firmly to his broad back. Caught up in the excitement of the place, I wandered off, like a child on Christmas morning, weaving in and out of the chattering people, dodging farm wagons and drays loaded with baggage for the steamers. Suddenly a hand clamped down hard on my shoulder and spun me completely around. A pair of the blackest, wickedest eyes I'd ever seen flashed down at me. "*Lieber Gott,* what have we here? A sun goddess come down from Mt. Olympus to shed her beams on our poor benighted Mannheim, I swear."

The man was young, undeniably handsome in a dark, aristocratic fashion. Thin, exquisitely outlined lips curved in a smile. A tiny white cap no larger than a saucer reposed at a rakish angle over his left eye, held in place by a ribbon under the finely modeled chin. The thin face was crisscrossed with knife-like scars, some healed so as to be almost invisible, others still maintaining a reddish-purple hue.

"Burschen!" The vaunted, much feared student corps, noted for duelling and womanizing. Three others, dressed exactly like him, quickly formed a little circle around me. All wore white gloves, tall boots, white breeches, close-fitting jackets ornamented with bright royal blue braid at neck and sleeve edge. Silk ribbons of the same blue color stretched diagonally across their breasts.

91

"Sir, you presume," I said icily, struggling to free my shoulder from the grip of the gloved hand. "Please release me, or I shall be forced to call the Polizei."

Shouts of derisive laughter greeted my remark. A gloved hand found a place on my other shoulder and the thin laughing face moved closer to mine. "What do you say, comrades, is she a goddess or isn't she? Surely no human maid was ever blessed with such a fountain of gold." He removed a hand from one shoulder, yanked fiercely at a strand of my hair. I squealed with the pain.

"Come, comrades. Feel." The four of them crowded round me, their scarred faces bent low over my breast, which swelled out of the poor tight frock. Eight hands stroked my hair, my neck, the top of my breast. They murmured glowing phrases.

"Why, Sebastian, the sun itself is captured here. A shame to waste it on the clods of Mannheim. In Heidelberg you will be truly appreciated. We will put that treasure to good use."

As they talked, they pushed me slowly, inexorably out of the crowd toward the edge of the wooden wharf. My screams were lost in the general uproar of the waterfront. I knew with sinking certainty that no policeman would risk his life by interfering with the Burschen. The clubs of duelling students were known the length and breadth of Germany for their skill with the sword.

My screams and struggles brought only amused looks from the people on the wharf. "Burschen having fun with a girl," they were thinking, "nothing a peaceful law-abiding citizen would want to interfere with."

I remembered a poor girl in Munich, daughter of a cobbler, who had been taken right out of her father's shop, ravaged, kept for weeks in the Burschen headquarters. She'd come out of the experience with a bastard child, and no hope for a decent husband. In my plain, drab frock, with my dirty, unkempt hair flying about, I looked for all the world like a poor idiot farm girl in town for the day with her father.

"Ho there, you!" The four Burschen hailed a farmer who was just leaving the wharf with his empty wagon. When he pretended not to hear their call, one of them ran in front of the horses, waved a gold piece in the air. "A double florin, just for yourself. Take us to Heidelberg. My poor sister"— he pointed toward me—"is subject to fits and must be taken home immediately. In the name of mercy, help us."

The sight of the two-florin piece glistening in the sun dispelled any doubts the farmer might have had. Fits were common enough, God knows, and I certainly could be anyone's sister. He reined in his team with a shout.

Two of the Burschen jumped into the wagon, leaping like gazelles over the low sideboards. The other two, who had been holding onto me firmly, hoisted me up, the two in the wagon leaning down to grab my feet. The wagon started up with a jolt and we all ended up on the hard wooden planking in a heap.

"Holy Mother of God," I shrieked, struggling to my feet. "My baby, my baby. She'll die without my milk." Out of my mind with fear and rage, I ripped desperately at the woolen dress, split it open to expose my breasts. I lifted them, one in each hand, cupping them so that the hard nipples extended. "See, see, you fools. The milk. I am a nursing mother. Take me back to the wharf at once."

Whoops of joy greeted my plea. "Not only is she a goddess," the one called Sebastian exclaimed, "but she gives the food of life." They reached out to touch my full, tender breasts with gloved hands. "Don't worry, your brat can do without you for a few hours."

They leaned back on the sides of the wagon, long white-clad legs extended, arms folded arrogantly on the beribboned chests. I sat down in the center of the wagon, pulled the dress feebly back together in a vain effort to cover my nakedness. I had to escape, but knew it would mean death under the hooves of passing horses to jump out of the wagon. As we jolted through the narrow cobbled streets, men and women gaped at us and shook their heads. I knew better than to stand up in the wagon and shout at them. Now that I was half naked, I really did look like an idiot girl.

Nearing the edge of town, the driver pulled up in front of a church where a wedding was in progress. A band was playing right in the middle of the intersection of two streets. Every inch of space was clogged with people in Sunday finery. The bride and groom were just emerging from the church. She was attired in the traditional black and white of the region, with blue and red streamers flowing from her elaborate headdress. Three or four young girls, obviously bridesmaids, stood proudly by.

The Burschen turned from watching me to gaze, intrigued, at the wedding party. I rose in the wagon, pulled the torn bits of garment away from my breasts, and shouted as loud as I could at the mob in the street. "Help me, please help. I am being stolen. My child will die without me."

The little band stopped playing, the bridal couple turned, astonished at the sight of a woman standing half-naked, hair streaming in the wind, in the bed of a farm wagon.

I shouted into the sudden silence. "I am the daughter of Ludwig, king of Bavaria. If you will help me, you will be richly rewarded."

Sebastian arose, clasped me round the shoulders, pulled my garment up to cover my breasts. "She is mad," he spoke to the people in the street, who stood open-mouthed. "Yesterday she was the Virgin Mary. Today a royal princess. Tomorrow, who knows?"

Screams of laughter erupted from the crowd. "Ludwig's daughter, eh? Well, king no more is he. He's gone now, *Gott bedankt*, and his whore with him."

The townspeople drew aside to let the wagon pass. Sebastian pushed me down brutally into the splintery wood of the wagon bed. Lightning streaks of pain shot through my head and neck. The hoots and derisive shouts of the people followed us. "The Burschen and their loose women. They should be banned from the streets. Go back to Heidelberg and stay there."

Thinking me unconscious, the Burschen made no further efforts to hold me, but sat lolling against the sides of the wagon, their long white-breeched legs stretched to the middle of the wooden floor. Sebastian's gleaming leather boots rested on my belly.

"What shall we name her? Freya, Venus, Aphrodite?" asked one.

"Venus! What this country needs is a good dose of paganism," Sebastian offered.

One of them kicked me in the thigh, then reached over to pinch my breast through the wool of my dress. I flinched, but didn't open my eyes past the slit through which I was watching them. Let them talk, I thought. I'd listen, keep my eyes and ears wide open and figure out some way to escape.

"From the way she fought, I'd vote for Brünnhilde, the

94

war goddess of the old Teutons, or Gellona, the Roman warrior goddess."

"Look at those breasts, those hips, that hair. She's built like a Valkyrie."

After interminable twistings and turnings, the wagon started a steep ascent. I slid into the rear end and groaned loudly as a searing pain shot through my head.

"*Mein Gott*, have we killed her?" The one called Luther bent his head to my breast, pressed a heavy thumb into my throat. I felt my pulse beating wildly against his thumb. I shut my eyes completely.

"No, just unconscious. Probably hit her head too hard on the floor when we pushed her down. She's all right. You can't kill this kind."

"Let the *Mensch* alone." *Mensch* was the street word for prostitute.

"*Mensch?* Don't look like a *Mensch* to me. Just some idiot girl loose from her keepers. We'll have our fun with her and dump her back on the wharf tomorrow."

"Maybe even a couple of florins for her trouble, to ease the pain."

"Hey, do you suppose she really has a baby?"

"No, stupid. Nursing mothers don't wander around the docks with their hair streaming down to their waists. They all have some story. Being a nursing mother is one of the favorites."

The absence of street noises, and the appearance of dense wooded regions at the roadsides told me we were entering the mountains. As we neared our destination, the talk switched to politics.

"Y'know, if ol' Redbeard himself, the Barbarossa, knew there was a woman like this around, maybe he'd come out of his cave in Kyffhauser Mountain."

"I heard he'd been seen, or at least some Goliath of a man with a beard almost to his waist, red as the inside of hell."

"Bah. Foolish old woman's talk. It's just Lothar von Hohenstaufen who almost got Ludwig and his whore Lola Montez. He's got red hair, and a lot of people think he's Barbarossa resurrected."

As they talked, my brain worked feverishly. The derisive laughter of the wedding party had given me an idea for escape. I would pretend madness. "*Mutter Gottes*," I groaned, as a signal to them that I was waking up.

"Forsooth, the nymph awakens."

"No nymph this, but a full-blown fertility goddess. Astarte herself never had such nipples."

"Yea, verily, our cup overfloweth."

I groaned again, louder and longer, turned over and flailed about with my arms, all the while moving my hips in a seductive motion.

"Comrades," Sebastian shouted in glee, "I think we will feed among the lilies tonight."

I sat up, looked around wildly. "Release me," I demanded. "My father the King of Bavaria will have your heads for this."

Sebastian arose, faced me. "For one night in your arms, O Venus, I would happily sacrifice my life." He swept low in a gallant bow.

"There is a curse on me," I replied gravely. "Given at my birth. He who takes my maidenhead will burn in hellfire forever."

There was a moment of stunned silence. Then the wagon, having reached the top of a steep mountain road, started abruptly down the other side, throwing Sebastian headlong into my lap. He lay there, helpless with laughter. I joined in the general merriment, throwing my head back, stretching out my arms above my head, twirling my hips from side to side in a frenzied manner, like a priestess dancing before a pagan idol.

Maddened by the movement of my flesh beneath his head, Sebastian buried his scarred face between my breasts, moaned several times and then proceeded to make little snuffling noises like a wild boar rooting in the forest. The others had fallen silent, eyes wide, mouths open, saliva drooling from open mouths. I shook my head so that my white gold hair fell down in front of my face, covering Sebastian completely.

In a few minutes we were in the ancient walled town of Heidelberg, which lay at the foot of a narrow gorge. The wagon labored up a rutted road to a crumbling ruin perched on a precipice overlooking the swift-flowing Neckar River. The Burschenhaus was a handsome circular building set back from the road and half hidden by clumps of shrubbery and trees, bare now of their rich summer foliage.

I was lifted out of the wagon, the driver paid off, and the

wagon rumbled back toward Mannheim. Continuing my masquerade, I whirled round and round the driveway, throwing my hair about like a Spanish dancer. The Burschen skipped in and out of the trees, chasing me and shouting for all the world like children on a holiday.

Finally, breathless and glowing, I allowed myself to be led into the building. We walked into a large meeting room, much like the one at St. Emmeran's. About fifty students were seated at the long wooden tables. Some sipped wine, but most drank beer from large, elaborately carved steins. All were smoking little cigars. The place reeked of beer and smoke.

Sebastian lifted me up and ran with me to one of the tables. Sweeping steins, bread, and cheese to the floor, he stood me on top of the cleared space. "Holla, *Kameraden!* Harken! The White Caps now have a mascot. The Reds have their dancing bear, the Blues their clown, but we—" He twirled me around. "We have a love goddess."

The entire room became still. All eyes fixed on me. My eyes blazed. I threw back my shoulders, so that my breasts protruded. I swivelled my hips.

Suddenly the room exploded in laughter and catcalls. "Looks more like the village idiot to me," called one.

"Disbelievers, eh?" Sebastian, enraged, walked to the wall where a number of duelling swords were hung, drew one off the hook and returned to the table. In a lightning stroke, he deftly cut the miserable peasant garment from first one shoulder then the other. In a moment, the drab brown wool lay in a heap at my feet. Then, working the point of the blade expertly between my shoulder and the strap of the cotton shift, he snipped that too. I stood motionless, too stunned to speak, my naked body revealed to the gaping students.

After a breathless hush a din arose like all the demons in hell, and they were dancing around me, chanting in Latin. Some grabbed the torches from the sconces on the walls and brandished them wildly about their heads. A burning torch was thrust into my hand. I held it out, shouting now along with them at the top of my lungs.

"Hail Freya! Hail Venus! Hail Astarte!" They called out the litany of the fertility-love goddesses of all antiquity.

Sebastian, who had remained on the table with me, suddenly tore the torch from my grasp and hurled me to the

97

rough wooden table top. One hand under my waist, he drew me to him, bent his head to my breast. His feverish lips clamped on my nipple.

With a whoop, another student was at the other breast. Shivers of repulsion shook my body. I writhed desperately in a futile effort to free myself. But my movements only served to goad the two men. Having drunk his fill, Sebastian chased the other student away and threw the whole length of his body on mine. Forcing my thighs apart with his powerful hands, he quickly thrust himself into my body and satisfied his lust. He was obviously the leader of this drunken mob, and as such was privileged to be the first to invade the goddess.

When he'd finished, he stood up and called out triumphantly. "She is fine. Deep, warm, satisfying. Tonight we will install her officially."

I lay rigid, semiconscious, too stunned to continue my pretense at madness. Tonight, I was sure, would mean my death. It was not uncommon for young women to be raped to death by the Burschen.

A thin grey light outlined the squares of the tall leaded window. I lay on the floor in a tiny room, about the size of my sleeping chamber at Schloss Kyffhauser. A pile of dusty tapestries had been thrown on the floor in a crude attempt to make a bed. There was no other furniture in the room. I looked around hoping to find a chamber pot at least. Nothing. The chill of centuries penetrated my naked body.

I stretched, and cried out with the pain in my lower extremities. The events of the previous day came back to me in a rush of remembrance. Had I been raped once, twice, many times? After Sebastian had thrown me on the table top and fallen upon me, the rest of the night was lost in a merciful haze.

Shivering with the cold I rose and moved to the window to look out at the prospect before me. Heidelberg itself was lost in the morning mist, but I could make out a number of houses clinging to the side of the mountain immediately below. Thin wisps of smoke from breakfast fires curled heavenward from chimneys sticking out of brown rooftops. A church bell chimed in the distance, calling the faithful to early Mass.

My darlings, Kristina and Karl, were out there somewhere. I bent my head to rest it in my cupped hands, prayed desperately, "Kristina my darling, don't die. Please, Holy Mother of God, for the sake of your Beloved Son, keep her alive."

I ran my hands all round the edge of the casement, looking for a latch. But the window was firmly plastered in the wall. Making fists of my hands, I drew back and punched with all my strength through one of the little panes, then another, until the sound of splintering glass shattered the stillness of the morning. But the strips of lead remained firm and fixed.

Maybe I could find a hammer, a tool, a knife. Desperately I rummaged through the pile of cloaks, rugs, and wall hangings on the floor. Nothing. Finally I sat down, impotent with rage and frustration, and bawled like a baby. I picked up one of the tapestries, wrapped it around me, then threw it off again. The stiff gold emobroidery touched my engorged nipples, causing unbearable pain.

Suddenly the door opened behind me and a hand was laid on my shoulder. Hair flying, I whipped around to face a pale young Bursch. "Don't touch me, you swine. The agonies of hell upon you and your children and your children's children!" With both fists I pounded his face and neck.

He knelt beside me, put both hands on my bare shoulders and shook me violently. "Stop it, Sieglinde, stop it. Don't you know me?" His narrow pockmarked face was inches from mine.

"Andreas?"

"The same." A broad smile split his narrow face, and the sweet gentle caring look I remembered so well from the month in St. Emmeran's returned to his luminous eyes.

"What—how?" I asked, bewildered at seeing him here. "What are you doing here?" Then, before he could answer, realization flooded me.

"You're part of them, aren't you—those animals masquerading as men." I pulled on the white jacket, yanked off the saucy white cap. "You stood by and let them degrade me. Me—Lothar's wife!"

A nervous fear crossed his face. He loosened his hold on me, walked to the broken window. "Yes, I saw them bringing you in. I—I watched as Sebastian raped you in the sight of the entire Corps. I even picked up a torch and danced around our "goddess" with the rest of them."

99

"Why?" I cried out bitterly. "Why, Andreas? How can you call yourself a man?"

He turned to face me and the torture on the young face moved me to pity, as it had done that first time after he and Kurt had nearly raped me to death. "You must understand. I was drunk. As usual. We are always drunk. It helps us forget that we have failed in our revolution. Oh, Sieglinde—" He fell on the floor beside me, grasped both my hands in his, pleading for mercy. "Sieglinde, I am a coward."

I clutched at him frantically. "Please get me out of here. My child will die without my milk." A sudden hope struck me. "Get Lothar. Where is Lothar? He'll kill them all when he knows where I am and what they have done to me."

Great round tears rolled down his scarred countenance. "I do not know where Lothar is. No one knows. He could be dead. I wish to God I could get him for you, Sieglinde. If he were here, in charge as he should be, this thing would not have happened to you."

His voice lifted. "I will get you out of here. But not now. The time isn't right. Already they are in the great hall preparing for the duelling this morning. Later, afterwards, when they are celebrating, I have a plan."

"Later, when? How long do you think a nursing mother can wait?"

He glanced fearfully at my swollen breast. "Can't you take some of it out? I remember my mother—"

"Yes, yes, of course," I said impatiently.

"But you must promise me one thing."

"Anything, Andreas, anything."

The tenderness in the dark eyes gave way to lust, he glanced at my naked thighs, touched with trembling hand the dark triangle. "Since that night Kurt and I ravaged you, after abducting you from Lola's palace, I have thought of no other woman. I know you are Lothar's, and that I can never hope that you could feel any desire for me, but—"

I shrank back. Even Andreas, the kind, the sweet, the gentle. I was nearly choking with disgust.

"Just one night," he pleaded, "one night to lose myself in your arms—one night all to myself."

The throbbing pain in my breasts decided for me. What was one night in the arms of a coward to my daughter's life? "Yes, Andreas, anything. Even two nights."

He rose from the floor, avoiding my glance. "I must go

now to help prepare for the duelling." He opened the door to find Sebastian with hand upraised ready to turn the handle.

"Well, so here you are, Andreas. They're looking for you." The thin curved eyebrows raised cynically. "Surely you have not—" A sardonic smile crossed the scarred face. "Well—all for one and one for all, I suppose."

The sound of Andreas's boots was still echoing in the corridor when Sebastian hurled himself on the floor beside me, drew me to him, rolled over on top of me. I dug into his neck with my nails, but he merely laughed and thrust himself into me as he had the night before in the great hall When he had done, he rolled over, adjusted his clothing, breathed a sigh of satisfaction. "That was very good, my dear, very good indeed. No better way to start the day."

Chapter 9

Sebastian carried me into the large meeting room once again and installed me in a huge heavily cushioned chair. The vast fireplace was empty. I shivered in my nakedness.

One of the students brought me some steaming coffee, hot sausages, and a small loaf of hard black bread. He seemed very young, like Andreas, and I thought I detected a look of pity in his eyes. One of his ears had been cut off, probably in a duel.

Thinking him a friend, I leaned down and whispered, "May I have something to cover me, a cloak or a blanket?"

His eyes lit up with compassion and he dashed out of the room to return moments later with a richly embroidered cloak. I huddled under it. No one appeared to be paying attention to me. Then I settled back to watch the preparations for the duelling, confident in Andreas's promise to free me. It was my only hope.

If it were not for my degradation as "goddess" and the uncertainty about the welfare of Karl and Kristina, I might have actually enjoyed the spectacle about to unfold before me. Rivalry between the many duelling societies throughout Germany was fierce and of long standing. Although killing was not the object, many young men died when a razor-sharp sword found a vital spot. Most of the young men I'd known in Munich proudly wore the scars of duelling contests on their faces. I knew it was serious business with the Burschen. As was the prize—me. I would be handed from one to another, being the property of the winner for the day, or until the next contest.

Everyone was getting ready for the morning's contest. A dummy with a mask and an iron arm with a sword in its hand stood in a corner. Several students slashed away at it, practicing their thrusts. The chief object in the fencing was to cut the face of the opponent. Left untended, these cuts became vivid scars of the type that crisscrossed Sebastian's face. The eyes were protected by heavy lead goggles, the neck by tightly wound bandages. The rest of the body, including the legs and thighs, were bound with heavy cloth or leather. Some of the students were busily wrapping the men who would be duelling that day, while others sharpened sword blades on a large grindstone turning on a wheel.

Soon, with the hot breakfast inside me, I relaxed and settled back to enjoy the spectacle. A contagious excitement filled the vast room. Duelling had been outlawed, of course, for many years, but the police closed their eyes to the whole business.

Finally, at a signal from Sebastian, everyone took his assigned place. The first two contestants stood in the center of a large cleared space, eyeing each other in the outlandish goggles, waiting for the signal to start. Two students, also heavily padded, stood behind them as "seconds." Andreas stood with pad and watch in hand to keep the time. I stared directly at him, willing him to look back, but he returned my gaze with no sign of recognition. His face was wooden.

"Go!" shouted Sebastian. The two combatants began to thrust at each other with such lightning rapidity that my eyes could not follow them. They danced lightly and gracefully at each other, darting about like youngsters in a deadly game.

"Halt!" The seconds leaped forward and laid their swords over those of the two duellists. A thin stream of blood streamed brightly from a cut in the head of one of the young men. I gazed, fascinated, as it wound its way down over his padded body to the floor.

"Surely he will die," I thought. I rose instinctively to go to him, but in a split second, a large man came running out with a pan of water and some lengths of white cloth. The wounded combatant retired to a corner where the surgeon washed off the wound and bound it up.

The duels went on all morning, the blows coming and going like flashes of light. I sat on my throne, waiting. Who would be the winner? As each bout ended, the victor was permitted to rest for two bouts, then he must challenge again. Most of the bouts lasted but a few minutes.

Finally, the bells from the churches in Heidelberg told me it was noon. Sebastian led a stocky young Bursch with coal-black hair to my throne. The winner. He looked like a bear, with heavy black brows jutting out over eyes like coals.

"Hail, Holy Astarte, O beauteous Venus with the golden breasts which pour forth milk like honey to our famished lips!" Sebastian bowed low, brandished a torch.

He held up the still padded arm of the winner. "Heinrich of Eisenach will be your consort for a day and a night." The Bursch glared at me, his eyes flaming with lust, his breath coming and going in irregular gasps.

I looked around desperately for Andreas. The Burschen were divesting themselves of their padding and goggles and were busily setting up the long wooden tables and benches. Great platters of food and large crocks of foaming beer were being carried into the room.

The human bear moved closer, pushed aside the heavy cloak, lay a heavy hand on my knee. He licked his lips in anticipation. "Off with the cloak," he whispered. "I must view my prize."

Suddenly Andreas was there beside him, gently lifting the hand from my knee. "King Heinrich, you must eat first, refresh yourself. Our goddess is a demanding lover. What will she think if you do not measure up?"

Miraculously, Heinrich followed Andreas to a nearby table. "*Ja, ja,* I must eat. She will wait." He sat down, drew a roast chicken toward him and began to chew noisily. Meanwhile Andreas hoisted himself on a high stool, and began to strum a zither and sing in a soft melodious voice. Another student took his place beside him, and blew on a thin pipe that produced a flute-like sound. The music had little melody, but the throbbing, insistent beat soon worked a change in the students. Many, having finished their meal, came forward, as they had last night, and began their devilish dance in front of me. Someone had brought in a copper brazier filled with burning coals and placed it on the floor at my feet. An icicle of fear stabbed at my heart. What was it for? Were they going to brand me? Was I to be subjected to some fiendish fire torture?

I glanced pleadingly at Andreas who sat on the stool, strumming and singing as if he were alone in the room. The men who were dancing began to sweat, and to chant in

Latin and German: "Astarte, Venus, Freya, Brünnhilde, goddess of life and love! Fill us with your body, bestow on us your radiant flesh."

I never took my eyes off Andreas, waiting for his move. Had he forgotten his promise? Then, as I watched, he quickly reached under his jacket and pulled out an object that looked like a small ball of fur. "A sacrifice," he shouted, leaping down from the stool and throwing the zither against the wall so that it shattered to pieces. "We must have a burning sacrifice in honor of our goddess."

The dancers, startled at the abrupt cessation of the music and the noise of the zither splintering, never noticed that Andreas had thrown the little ball of fur on the red-hot coals.

Almost immediately a smoke arose from the brazier, so dense I could see nothing. In moments a cloud of it surrounded my throne, choking me and causing great tears to roll from my eyes. It soon became suffocating.

Shouts filled the room as the acrid smoke penetrated every corner. I felt myself being lifted out of the chair and carried through the choking, sputtering, cursing students.

"Keep your eyes closed," Andreas hissed into my ear.

In moments we had left the suffocating hall. I let out a long breath, sucked in the clear fresh air greedily, opened my eyes. Tears still coursed down my cheeks. A closed carriage waited just outside in the driveway. Andreas slid me out of his arms onto the soft leather seat beside him. "Here." He handed me a wet cloth smelling of vinegar. "Blink your eyes a number of times to encourage the tears. You'll soon be cleansed of the poison."

As I dabbed at my smarting eyes, conscious that the carriage was moving swiftly down the mountain, he said apologetically, "Sorry I had to do that, but it was the only thing I could think of."

"What was that horrible stuff you threw on the fire?" I gasped, more in admiration now than fright.

"A powder, made from a bitter herb well known to any magician or sorcerer. That furry object I threw on the fire was a dead rat that I soaked in the poisonous brine all night. It'll burn for quite a while. They won't miss you for at least ten minutes."

By the time we reached the cobbled streets of Mannheim a light snow was falling. I turned swiftly to Andreas, who sat quietly beside me, wiping his own eyes. I pulled the brocaded cloak tightly around me. "We must go immediately to the wharf to find Karl and Kristina."

"No." The face that turned to me was hard and impassive. "First you must pay your debt to me. By this time your big servant, if he is as shrewd as you say, will have found a suitable wet nurse. The city is teeming with them. Every day babies are born who die, and mothers are left with bursting breasts."

I opened my mouth to argue, but just at that moment the carriage came to a halt in front of a large, square dwelling with a single tower in the Italian style. "We are here," Andreas said. "Come, hop down, there is no time to waste. Already Sebastian may be after us."

Since I was without shoes, and the snow was falling heavily now, the driver hopped down from his high seat, tied the reins to a hitching post at the end of the narrow drive, and carried me up to the front portico.

"Put her down," Andreas ordered, then reached into his jacket pocket, handed him a two-florin piece with one hand, and pounded on the door with the other. A small, modest sign to the side of the door read MADCHEN AKADEMIE. FRAU ANNA BECKER.

A girls' school! A wave of blessed relief swept through me. It would be a haven, after all I'd been through. I had visions of neat white beds in clean, well-scrubbed rooms. There would be sweet-faced if stern teachers. I imagined my shivering body slipping between snow-white sheets smelling of the sun. There would be hot chcolate in the morning and at bedtime.

The door was opened by a little man so hunchbacked he was almost doubled over. We entered. He closed the door behind us. Nobody spoke. Andreas and I followed him down a long corridor into a small parlor filled to overflowing with bric-a-brac and overstuffed furniture. A small fire struggled feebly in a fireplace of red and purple streaked marble. Andreas plunked himself down on a long low davenport. I sank down gratefully beside him, still clutching the cloak around me.

"Don't open your mouth," he muttered. "Let me do the talking."

I glanced round at the paintings, which covered practically every inch of the dark flowered wallpaper. Every one of them, without exception, was of nude men and women in various erotic poses.

So that was it! No wonder Andreas thought nothing of bringing me here like this. Frau Becker's *Akademie* was no girls' school. It was a brothel. Well, at least I was out of Heidelberg and that hellish monastery. I would leave as soon as I got some clothing.

But despite my raised hopes, terrible scenes flitted through my mind of Kristina slowly languishing away for lack of milk. The fat little cheeks would become thinner and thinner, the sparkling eyes, so like Lothar's, would become lustreless. The tiny plump fingers would turn into matchsticks.

Suddenly, unable to keep quiet any longer, I turned on Andreas and touched his cheeks with both my hands. "Andreas, I know what this is. Please, let me go to find Kristina and Karl. I promise to come back here as soon as I find them."

He laughed wickedly. "Not a chance." Then—"Hush, here they come."

"Andreas, what have you brought me now?" A tall stately woman stood before me, glistening black hair pulled smoothly back from a pale aristocratic face. Finely modeled brows arched over the sharp nose and cheeks in a manner that reminded me of the Baronin von Hohenstaufen. She was dressed simply and severely in a black skirt and white blouse with tiny ruffles at wrist and high neck.

A slender hand extended to push the rough cloak away from me. She took my forearm firmly, pulled me to my feet. "Jesus Maria," the woman exploded. "You've really done it this time, Andreas. You've struck pure gold!"

She smiled at me in explanation. "Andreas is always bringing me the girls when the Burschen are finished with them. There is nowhere else for them to go."

Then she proceeded to examine me, pinching me here and there like a basket of peaches at the market, exclaiming all the while. "Is it real? That skin! Like silk! Nicely curved thighs, not too fleshy, just right, the kind men want but can never find. But, *mein Gott*, that hair!"

I stood silent, waiting for her to notice my breasts. Finally, she touched them, caressed the curve of each, touched the nipples, and as I had expected, exploded again. "*Mein Gott*. Milk! Have you a child?"

I opened my mouth to speak, but Andreas interrupted. "Her baby disappeared when the Burschen took her. I—I

108

promised we would search for the child—and her husband."

The woman, whom I presumed by now to be Frau Anna, looked at Andreas in consternation. "Well, go and do so. I am never so desperate for girls that I have to rob infants of their very life. Find the child and bring it here. And the husband too. I'll care for the girl until you return."

Andreas did not move. "I have something coming to me in payment for her escape." He cleared his throat nervously. "One night alone with her."

What happened next would have been comical if the circumstances had not been so tragic. Frau Anna leaped upon the poor young student with fangs literally bared, like a cat protecting her newborn kittens against the family dog. Even Lola in her most devastating tantrums had never looked so magnificent.

"You swine! Get out of here and do as I say. You'll get what is coming to you all right. But not tonight."

White-faced, Andreas ran out of the little parlor and was well into the corridor when Frau Anna leaned out of the portiered doorway and shouted, "Or I'll sic the whole Polizei of Mannheim and Heidelberg after you and your precious Burschen."

She returned and put a protecting arm around my shoulders, with the other ringing a little bell standing on a marble table. The look from her sapphire eyes was so affectionate, so motherly, so wonderfully kind that I gave in to my pent-up emotions at last and collapsed, senseless, on the flowered carpet.

She was the first thing I saw when I woke to bright sun streaming from the tall uncurtained casement window. Perched on the edge of the bed, she gazed down at me with lovely hazel eyes. A halo of fuzzy red hair, just like Kristina's covered her round little head. Pert brown freckles marched up and down her nose and across the softly curved cheeks. She literally sparkled with youth and life. Even the drab grey smock she wore couldn't disguise her curvacious figure.

"Good morning, Sieglinde. My name is Bettina."

I sat bolt upright, confused, trying to remember where I was.

Her laugh was a delicious sound, like a mountain stream running over stones down a hillside. "If you could only see the expression on your face," she said. "Wait." Rising from the bed, she went to a little dressing table near the window, returned with a gold-handed looking glass, held it in front of me. The face that gazed back at me was wan and dirty.

"Take it away," I groaned, pushing at her hand. I sank back on the bed, tears of sorrow and despair coursing down my cheeks. Another night had passed without Kristina.

Instantly her arms were around me. "Sieglinde, don't take on so. Frau Anna has every policeman in Mannheim looking for your baby and your precious Karl. She'll find them—if they are to be found."

"If?" I screamed at her. "I left them only yesterday—no, it's been two days already. They *must* be found."

Bettina went to the door and called out "Heinz," then came back to enfold my hand in hers. "What you need is something hot in your stomach. Things always seem better when your belly's full."

She was right, of course. I simply had to remain calm. I gazed at her, amazed at her loveliness. If she lived in this house, she must be a prostitute. But she was not the faded, coarse-looking kind of person I always imagined those women to be. And the room—it was not dingy and dirty as rooms were supposed to be in brothels. The place was as beautiful as Bettina. Bright wallpaper with an edelweiss pattern covered every surface, including the ceiling. The white spikey flowers with their light green leaves marched straight across the door, so that you couldn't tell unless you looked hard where the door knob was.

The door knob itself was of clear, sparkling crystal. A marble-topped beside stand, a large mirror over the dressing table, and a chaise lounge covered with bright fabric completed the furnishings. I felt as though I were in a mountain meadow in the springtime.

"Is this a—brothel?" I asked, hesitating at the word. "And you are a—" I couldn't finish the question for embarrassment. She looked like Sister Paulita might have looked when she was young. Her eyes were clear, fresh, innocent.

In moments the food was there, brought by the hunchback who had answered the door. The tray groaned under a heavy burden of hot fried bratwurst, crackly potatoes, fresh green beans prepared in the kind of sweet-sour sauce

Ortrud used to make. I picked up the mug of steaming chocolate, drained it in one gulp.

"Bettina," I said, "could you lend me a dress and cloak? I'd like to go into town immediately and search myself for Karl and Kristina."

She avoided my eyes. "Frau Anna has charge of all the clothing. You'll have to ask her yourself."

"You mean," I sputtered, amazed, my mouth full of food. "You have no clothes of your own? What do you do when you want to visit friends?"

"I have no friends," she said abruptly, "at least not in the vicinity."

"But," I persisted, "what about your parents, your family? Do you never go out at all? Surely that drab thing you're wearing is not your only garment."

"My, you are a question box. Better finish your dinner so Heinz can take it back to the kitchen. The kitchen girls don't like stragglers."

As I ate, my eyes swept the room again. No chiffonier, no armoire, no chest of drawers of any kind which might hold clothing. Surely they had seductive garments in which they entertained their customers. I cleaned up my plate, in a hurry to be rid of the servant and to ply Bettina with questions.

"There, now, that's a good girl, you've eaten it all," she exclaimed when I had finished. Heinz picked up the tray and went out the flowered door. But instead of remaining with me, Bettina left with him. She turned the key in the lock as she left. "I'll come back in a few minutes, as soon as I get Frau Anna's orders about you."

Wrapping the blanket around me, I got up and walked over to the long window. The view was breathtaking. The house was even higher than the ruin where the Burschens held their duelling and commanded an impressive sweep of the town, the river, and distant snow-capped mountains. Steep-roofed gabled houses nestled against each other, spilling down the mountainside like dominoes. Smoke curled up from hundreds of chimneys. I saw the barges, moving slowly up and down the Rhine, which glittered like the gold of the Nibelungen in the clear April sunshine.

I resisted the impulse to jump out the window, which was wide open. How far would I get with nothing but a blanket around me? The Polizei would pick me up immediately for a madwoman or an idiot.

111

Girlish laughter and muted talk drifted through the closed door. There was a lot of running up and down the stairs. For all the world like the Benedictine convent, I thought wryly.

True to her promise, Bettina returned. We sat close together on the chaise lounge. "Frau Anna says I'm to sit with you until she comes up to see you."

We talked like two schoolgirls after "lights out." She too had been raised by the nuns, in a little convent outside Berlin. "Very strict they were too," she said ruefully.

"Bettina," I burst out, "Why? Why do you do it? Sell yourself, I mean?"

She burst into a hearty laugh, threw back the coppery head. "For money, you goose. What else?" Then her freckled face darkened, the sweet mouth became pensive. "My mother died from bearing ten children, one each year. She washed other people's dirty linen to keep the food in our mouths."

"Your father? What about him?"

"He was a brickmaker, made good money when he worked, but he spent most of it in the beer halls." She shook her head defiantly. "My body is mine, to do with what I want. Some people use their brain, some their bodies. Men like my body. I make them feel like men. That's my talent, I figure, and I'll make no apologies to anyone."

"Bettina," I cried, "I didn't mean—" I stopped, confused. I sorely needed friends. My heart yearned for them.

"Now," she said, patting my hand affectionately. "It's your turn. Tell me about yourself."

My mind worked quickly. I longed to throw myself in Bettina's arms and spill it all out: my abduction from Munich, my rape, my forest marriage to Lothar, Lothar's desertion; but something warned me to hold back. In this year of revolution all over Europe, you couldn't be sure of anybody's politics, even a prostitutes's.

The lies came easily to my lips. "There's nothing much to say. I grew up with the Sisters, then my mother died when I was fourteen. I married Karl at sixteen and had Kristina just two months ago. There are a lot of men in Karl's family, more than the family farm can support, so he thought we should come to Mannheim to find work for him."

The hazel eyes peered at me inquisitively. "Hmm. Then you've never really had to work for a living."

"No, except for work around the house, of course."

She picked up my hands which were lying on top of the blanket. "These don't look like they've been in soap and water much."

I pulled them away, conscious suddenly of their soft whiteness. "Well, Karl has been doing everything since Kristina came. And we've been traveling for weeks, you know."

The speculative look again. Then, after a pause, "You know, you could make yourself a small fortune, in just a few years at the *Akademie*. With that statuesque form, those mountainous breasts, that incredible hair—"

My face went white. I sat up and pulled the blanket around my nakedness. "Me? Sell my body? Why, it's a sin against God and the Church." Even as the words passed my lips, I felt the lie deep in my soul. I had lain with Lothar, and let him take my body, without the church's blessing. But somehow, this was different.

Bettina went on talking. "Everybody sells something. A wife sells her body to her husband, not only in bed at night, but from dawn till dusk, in the kitchen, the laundry, the garden. She wastes her youth, her beauty, and for what?"

"But that's different." I protested. "They surrender to each other in love."

"Love? Ha! You *are* a child, aren't you? Men are interested only in possessing your body. As far as a man is concerned, you are not a person, but a delightful plaything—a toy."

"But that's not true. There is such a thing as real love, real respect between men and women."

She threw me a shrewd look. "Karl, your husband. Does he respect your opinions? Does he ask your advice about anything at all?"

I was silent. The lies had to end. I fell back on the bed. "I don't feel like arguing about it, Bettina. Right now all I want to do is find Kristina and Karl."

She was instantly contrite, kissed me on the cheek. "What a complete fool I am. Please forgive me, let's be friends."

"Of course, Bettina." I murmured, returning her embrace, grateful for the warmth of her firm body against mine. Who was I to condemn anybody?

At that moment the flowered door opened to reveal Frau Anna's statuesque figure. Her costume, I was to learn, was

113

always the same. Stiffly starched blouse, pleated, or some-times with tiny ruffles running down the front, tucked into a skirt of some heavy cloth. She smelled of starch and soap.

I sat up, asking eagerly, "Is there any news? Have you found them?"

She didn't answer, merely came to the bed, sat down, wrapped me in her starched arms. Her cheek against mine was wet with tears. Then she drew back, thrust a cup of something hot under my nose. "Here, drink this."

I recoiled. "No, I have just had two cups of chocolate. I'm not thirsty."

Her face was white and cold. "You forget, my child, that I have the power to turn you back to the Burschen. Would you like that?"

Bewildered, I gazed into her eyes. Where had the kind-ness gone and the compassion I had seen last night?

"What is the liquid?" I asked, weakly.

"A herbal infusion to dry up your milk. You'll be in for real trouble if something isn't done immediately about your condition."

With her free hand she kneaded my right breast. "They're already starting to cake."

I winced with the pain, but managed to say, "Why must I dry up?" But even before the words were out, I knew that my baby was dead.

She put the cup on the little marble table. "You must be brave, *mein Kind*, braver than you have ever been in your whole life." Turning, she motioned to Bettina. "Leave us, please."

When Bettina had gone, she turned back to me, took my face in both her hands. "Now is the time, Sieglinde von Wittelsbach, to prove your royal blood. You must act like a daughter of a king now. Your child is dead. Your *husband* too."

For one frozen moment my heart stopped beating. The blood drained from my body. A scream began somewhere deep down inside my heart. Then as the reality struck my consciousness, I pulled away from the soft hands, opened my mouth, let out the scream.

"No, no, it can't be. You're all lying. It's a plot to keep me here, to make me a prostitute. You won't let Bettina go into town, you won't give them any clothes, you're making it all up—"

A whirl of long tapered fingers crossed my vision, as

Frau Anna slapped me several times right across the face. The screaming stopped, I fell down, head spinning, on the pillow. Meekly then I drank the soothing liquid in the cup.

She went on talking, as I lay dazed, my whole being a cauldron of seething emotions. "I am not lying, you little goose. Why would I resort to such methods to keep you here as one of my girls, when I can have any girl in Germany for the prices we command in this establishment?"

The drug she'd given me was very powerful. I tried to answer that I would be no prostitute under any circumstances, but my tongue slithered around in my mouth, and I couldn't shape the words.

The story was brief. There'd been a fight on the docks. Karl had accused some Burschen with red caps of knowing something about my disappearance. The Polizei had been called and he'd ended up in the town jail from which he'd attempted to escape during the night. He was slain by the police bayonets.

"The baby—Kristina?"

"She died with Karl. It seems that he had sneaked into the women's section where the baby had been taken for the night, and during the struggle with the Polizei she was crushed to death. She was still strapped to Karl's back."

"How—how can you be sure it was Karl?" I stammered.

Frau Anna smiled. "I don't imagine there are *two* men in Mannheim, of the size and shape you describe, with strawberry marks on their cheeks and babies strapped to their backs."

Heinz came limping back into the room with a package in his withered hands. "I thought you'd want some proof," Frau Anna said, "so I sent someone to the Polizei for something you'd recognize."

She tore the paper off the parcel, laid it on the bed. It was Karl's jerkin. I picked up the soft, leathery stuff; the dear, familiar odor of beer and smoke rushed up my nostrils.

Choked with grief too unbearable for words or thought, I sank into blessed unconsciousness.

Chapter 10

The days came and went, morning, night, another morning, another night. I was conscious of dim voices talking. Someone was binding my breasts, lifting me off the bed, cruelly pulling a cloth round and round my body, tighter, tighter. I moaned with the pain.

"It's got to be tight to do any good at all." That was Frau Anna's crisp voice.

Then Bettina's, lower, softer, "But it's cutting into the flesh."

Frau Anna again. "Remember, nothing to drink at all. Remember, Bettina, and you too, Heinz, no matter how much she moans and begs for water."

Then came a morning when I woke to see the white spikes of the edelweiss clearly outlined. I counted. Five petals to a flower. My belly hurt. I had a tremendous thirst. Snatches of conversation came from the corridor. I tried to call out, but my throat was so dry I choked on the words. With a supreme effort I rose in the bed, tugged at the suffocating bindings. I couldn't even get the tip of my little finger between the cloth and my skin.

"Here now, what do you think you're doing?" Frau Anna had come into the room.

For one wild hopeful moment, I pretended that she really *was* a headmistress, a gentlewoman whose fortune had been squandered by a drunken father, and this place actually *was* a high class school for girls, and I had just been through a near-mortal illness.

But Frau Anna's first words dispelled even the tiniest hope.

"Let's have a look at those breasts, my girl. Time you got to work."

"Work? Surely you don't expect me—"

She cut me off, ignoring my protests. "Hmm. The cloth is bone dry. Off with it, then."

Hoisting me up in the bed with surprising strength, she began to peel off the cloth. My imprisoned breasts sprung free. Tears sprang to my eyes from the blessed relief.

"Ahh." I murmured. "That feels good."

Frau Anna smiled broadly. "*Mein Gott*, but they are magnificent. Providence has smiled on you, Sieglinde, king's daughter or not. It's rare that one sees breasts so full and yet so firm."

The strong yet soft hand caressed the curve of my breasts, going slowly from one to the other. The dark eyes gleamed with strange delight. A tiny smile played about the thin lips. "*Ja, wunderbar!* I have many customers who will pay double, even triple for something like this. You will become rich, *liebling*, in just a few years at my *Akademie*."

A nagging rebellious thought tugged at me, and I burst out, "But Frau Anna, I'm not sure I *want* to be a prostitute."

"My dear girl, you have no choice. What else could you do? Go into domestic service?" Flinging the down comforter to the floor, she raked my body with her cool, appraising eyes. "With that body, you wouldn't last a day. No *hausfrau* who wants to keep her husband in her own bed would hire you. Besides, you owe me for a week's keep here."

I was silent, fighting back the hot tears and the feeling of helplessness which swept over me in hot waves.

"Where else would you get such a life as this? Every need taken care of, pampered, warm, well-fed, lots of companionship, interesting men, a different companion every night."

"But I couldn't just give in. To do something I'd been raised to think of as sin—I have relatives, my husband has relatives." I said.

She sighed, sat down on the chaise lounge, the black skirt billowing gracefully about her. Her voice took on the hardness which alternated with softness in her character. "You spoke, in fact you rambled, during these last days when you were semiconscious from the drug we had given you to dry up your milk and help you recover from the shock of your experiences with the *Burschen*."

"Talked?" I echoed the word, my thoughts dry, prickles of fear tugging at my throat. "Talked about what?"

"Oh, Andreas filled me in on what you didn't tell me. Something about Ludwig, and Lola, and Ortrud, and Schachten. Oh yes," she beamed, at the look of terror on my face. "I know all about you. And your so-called *husband*."

"That's blackmail," I whispered. "You would keep me prisoner here?"

The dark smooth head bobbed slowly up and down. "Yes. You'll thank me for it some day." She walked quickly to the flowered door, called into the corridor for Heinz. "I would strongly advise against flight to Mannheim, Sieglinde. The white slavers would have you before the day was out. Lucky the Burschen got you that first day or you'd be all the way to England by now. Maybe on a boat to South America. You'd be enslaved as completely as if you were a Negro from darkest Africa."

Heinz stood in the open doorway, awaiting instruction.

"I think, Heinz," said Frau Anna, "that Sieglinde is in great need of a bath."

I walked naked behind the hunchback down the carpeted stairs, to the foyer where I had first entered, then through a large kitchen, down another pair of steps. The house was quiet as a tomb.

"The girls are not yet up," Heinz spoke without turning around. "Usual rising time is two o'clock. Then the bathtub will be busy. We have plenty of time to give you a good scrub."

The cellar was above ground level, since the *Akademie* was on a slight hillock, and was well lit by a series of little windows set into the stones. Through the windows I could see evidence of a large garden with dense shrubbery. No worries about privacy, anyway. In one corner, right next to a large white porcelain stove, like so many in Bavaria, was a tub, fashioned of marble streaked with grey and pink. It was filled to the brim with warm, scented water. I eased into it, anxious to cleanse my body of the many days' sweat.

Memories of Lola flooded back as the little man rubbed me vigorously with the flannel cloths that hung on a rack by the stove. Did the touch of my flesh excite him as Lola's had excited me? I wondered, as his strong fingers dug into my soft flesh, paying special attention to my inner thighs, under my arms, my breasts.

At his command, I slid down into the water, so that my

hair could soak, lifting my feet to the far edge of the tub which, although long, couldn't hold my length. "Looks like seaweed," came a laugh from behind me as Heinz massaged my scalp till it tingled. My hair lay in great wet swatches around me, white with suds.

I picked up a hand mirror I'd noticed on a chest within arm's reach of the tub. "I look just like the statue of the Lorelei at that bend in the Rhine—you know the famous nymph who sits on a great rock at a treacherous bend in the river—"

"And lures hapless seamen to their death as they crash their boats against the rock," the little man finished for me. Then he scuttled to a large sawed-off barrel nearby, dipped his bucket into it, returned with rain water to rinse my hair.

"Do you bathe all the girls?" I asked, to break the awkward silence.

"I should say not," he responded. "Just the bad cases, like yourself. Frau Anna was afraid you'd be too weak from your ordeal to scrub yourself adequately. Besides the sweat from your three days in bed, and your breasts, there was a lot of real honest-to-God dirt. Where have you been? In the woods?"

"Yes. My husband Karl and I walked all the way from the Black Forest to Mannheim. We had no chance to bathe."

I shook my head to banish the depression that sprung up immediately at the thought of Karl and Kristina, and with Heinz's help crawled out of the tub. He spent a long time rubbing my whole body until it glowed pink. He led me to a cot near the tub.

"Lie down," he ordered. The mattress was hard. There was no pillow. "Now comes the best part, better even than the water and soap."

The gnarled hands began to pummel me with a ferocity of a drummer in a band, beating, beating, on the tightly stretched skin. I lay with my head turned sideways and caught quick glimpses of the shrivelled arms, with thick corded tendons at the wrist. He worked methodically, from shoulders down past the rib cage, onto the rounded thighs, working especially hard on the buttocks and inner thighs.

"The soft parts of a woman's body go first," he said, panting from the exertion. "I do this once a month to every one of our girls. They are known all over Europe for their soft yet resilient flesh."

I lay prone and silent, giving myself up completely to his ministrations, feeling the life slowly ebbing back into my abused, exhausted limbs and muscles.

Back up in my edelweiss room, I stood at the tall window, wrapped in a warm flannel shift. It was just like the one Bettina had worn that first day. The town lay quiet, wet and sodden under a soft steady rain. April. In a month I would be seventeen.

Well, I was back where I had started. Nobody. A bastard child soon learns that she owns nothing, that anybody owns her who can take possession. Lothar would never find me now. Once in a place like this, a girl is lost forever. Even if he did, he would not have me, after other men had tasted my flesh.

"Frau Anna says you are to come down to dinner." I turned to see Bettina, her red curls and sunny freckles lighting up the doorway. She wore a simple flannel robe just like mine. The hazel eyes widened. "You look marvelous," she said. "Quite a change from when I last saw you."

At the genuine look of friendship and warmth in her face, I rushed to her, threw my arms around her sweet little form. "Oh Bettina, it's good just to be alive."

The dining room was brilliantly lit by a multitude of candles set in sconces along the walls. Over the table, in the center of the ceiling, hung a large crystal chandelier, every little taper burning. The effect was dazzling. Colorful paintings in elaborately carved gilded frames lined the spaces between the many windows. I had no time to examine these art works in detail, for Bettina motioned me to a chair beside her own along one side of a long table.

The girls walked in silently, one by one, each in the identical gray flannel robe, and stood behind her chair, hands behind her back, exactly as we had been taught to do at Sister Paulita's.

Although I was eaten up with curiosity to see what the others looked like, I refrained from staring and concentrated instead on a huge mural painted on the wall behind the head of the table. It was a typical Bacchanalian erotic scene like the ones on the walls of Lola's palace on the Barerstrasse, with nymphs and satyrs, half-man, half-goat creatures noted in mythology for their lecherousness. Great bunches of flowers and grapes were distributed among the prancing forms.

"Keep your eyes down," hissed Bettina, who'd noticed me staring at the mural. "Here comes the chief."

At that moment Frau Anna swept into the room, dressed as always in the impeccable white and black, hair gleaming like wet ebony in the candle light. Then, sitting straight-faced directly under the pagan mural, she ladled out the soup from a blue and white Dresden china tureen, with all the sober style and dignity of a headmistress. The soup was followed by fish with a magnificently delicately flavored sauce, tiny pearl onions floating in it, and finally a great mixture of vegetables in a brown roux.

Despite my good intentions, I had finished before the others, and sneaked a glance up and down the table at the girls. All striking, in different ways. A stable of real thoroughbreds, I thought to myself, not without a little pride that I had been asked to join them.

My eyes came to rest on the person directly across from me. Head bent, she was intent on putting a fork to the last of the vegetables. As if conscious of my gaze, she looked up, straight at me, and I gasped in astonishment. She was either a man or the most masculine-looking girl I had ever seen. Strong nose, with a slight curve in it, deep, penetrating grey eyes, set deep in a finely boned face, high, broad, sweeping forehead, lips firm and pink, with a decided indentation in the upper lip. And that hair! A rich, rich black, blacker than Karl's, or Frau Anna's, so black it seemed to emit glints of blue, as a lump of coal. The brows went straight across, thick, hairy, untrimmed, meeting over the bridge of the nose.

"She looks like a god." A nagging thought—could this be one of those women who favor other women? I had heard of such things, and that certain houses kept such people to please female clients. I was helpless to tear my eyes away from that piercing gaze. But soon the sharp commanding voice of Frau Anna shattered my hypnotic gaze.

"Sieglinde, please rise so that we can get a good look at you." I stood up, looked down at my plate, embarrassed.

"Girls—and Ymir—allow me to introduce Sieglinde, who has come to live with us." Slowly, she went round the table, introducing each girl in turn by name, Ilse, Hilde,

122

Annelies, Berta, Adelheide, all good Germanic names, and all good Germanic faces of exceptional beauty.

I noticed that she had skipped over the mannish-looking one directly across from me, whose grey eyes had never left off gazing at me. "I have saved the best for last," Frau Anna concluded. "This, Sieglinde, is Ymir, who as I'm sure you've noticed by now, is not a female, but a male. And a very attractive one, at that."

A man! In the same drab grey shift worn by all the girls. But of course! I experienced an indescribable feeling of relief. So he wasn't a pervert, as I had imagined.

"Delighted," Ymir smiled a dazzling heart-catching smile. His teeth gleamed in the brown face.

Frau Anna spoke again. "I am handing you over to Ymir for indoctrination. He performs this very valuable service for us in addition to servicing the occasional female client who knocks on our door."

Frau Anna rose, folded her napkin primly, slipped it into the ring. "You are dismissed," she told the table. "In case anyone has forgotten," Frau Anna continued, "today is our monthly costume review. I expect you all, fully dressed, to report to the salon at five."

Ymir's hand in mine as we mounted the carpeted stairs together was firm, warm, and strong, bringing back heart-breaking thoughts of Lothar. But no two people could be more different, I thought, sneaking sidelong glances at his handsome darkness.

"Ymir," I said, trying desperately not to think of the forthcoming indoctrination, "what kind of name is that? Surely it isn't German. Sounds a bit Russian."

He laughed, a pleasant deep throaty sound, stood aside to allow me to enter the edelweiss room before him. Then he carefully closed and locked the door with a key before answering my question. "No. It is Scandinavian. It is the name of a giant. According to Northern mythology he was the first living being. He was nourished by the cow Aud-mulla."

I was delighted. "Why, I too am Scandinavian. My mother was Norweg—"

I never finished the sentence. For without a sign of his intention, he swept he into his arms, pressed his full sensual lips firmly on mine, forcing my lips apart, searching my mouth with his tongue. His arms tightened. I was too surprised to resist, but found that I did not want to. I flamed into response, pressing back against his lithe body with all my strength.

We staggered toward the bed, still clasped tightly together, moving as one. He pushed me down violently, tore off his shift, revealing his stunning nakedness. His body was perfect, like the Greek statues in Lola's palace. His manhood was hard, outthrust toward me.

"Take it off," he commanded. "That hideous thing. And be quick about it. " Trembling, I did as he bade, lay there waiting, my eyes dilated, my legs falling helplessly apart on the soft blanket.

For an endless moment, he towered over me, gazing down at me with grey eyes that widened in disbelief. Tiny forked flames danced in the narrow grey eyes. *"Lieber Gott!* A feast for the gods!"

Then he was on me, all over me, his manhood pressing first into the space between my breasts, creeping on my soft belly, pressing, pressing, downward until finally plunging into the place that waited, moist and anguished, for invasion. I dug my hands into the tight black curls as I had done to Karl, but this time there was pure sensation of a splendor such as I had never imagined.

I was a woman now, having borne a child, having known pain, passion, want. I was all female, straining with backflung head and arched back toward this man with a strange Scandinavian name.

"Please, please," I moaned, "hurry, hurry."

His reply was brief and violent. "No, damn you, you wait until I'm ready. I am no boy tossing in the hay with you."

Three, four times he brought me with practiced movements to the very peak of ecstasy, only to hold back. I thought I would go mad. When I could bear it no longer, when I was moaning hoarsely, incoherently into the pillow, he began to move in and out with slow, steady, firm thrusts, playing me like a master violinist.

We reached ecstasy together. Shudders of pure pleasure tore through my every muscle. We were truly one body.

Afterward, we lay side by side, not speaking for a long time, savoring the feeling of well-being and the satisfaction of having found a perfect partner. But I was troubled. I had responded like a moth to the flame. Passion had consumed me utterly. And my child was dead less than a week. I had sworn true love to Lothar in the forest.

"I am a wanton," I said. "Minutes after seeing you for the first time, I melted in your arms."

He lifted his head and peered down at me, his sweetly curved lips brushed mine. "Wanton? Perhaps. I would say rather total female." Cool grey eyes gazed deeply into mine. Such eyes the Vikings must have had, I thought. Glorious eyes. Demanding. Domineering.

Then his seriousness passed, and a warm smile lit up the high-boned face. "Well you passed the first test with flying colors." He laughed a long, hearty laugh, nuzzled his nose and mouth into my neck. I shivered with delight.

"Test?" I asked, puzzled.

"Yes, the caveman-approach test. I rushed at you that way to see how you would respond instinctively. But—" his face serious again—"it was not all in the line of duty. I wanted you the very moment you walked into the room with Bettina. I knew I would take you the moment we got upstairs."

"You've made a fool of me," I protested, tears and anger fighting against each other in my voice.

"The first thing you must learn, Sieglinde, if you are to be a success in this business, is that lovemaking is never foolish. Violent, clumsy, mechanical, even vicious—but never foolish."

I could not deny the glow that still remained from his practiced lovemaking. "Do you fall for all the girls immediately?"

"Of course not, you goose. With some of them, Gertrud for instance, I have to grit my teeth and work myself up to even becoming aroused."

"But they're all so beautiful, even Gertrud. She is like a queen of the night."

He sighed, a tired weary sound. "In my profession, beautiful women soon become ordinary. It's the price I pay, I suppose. I become jaded. But you, Sieglinde, you truly stirred my senses as they had not been stirred for a long time. You are a masterpiece."

Now I was laughing too and rolled over on top of him. "Maybe it's the Scandinavian in both of us."

We were friends. Now I had two of them, Bettina and Ymir. I decided to find out more about this *Akademie*.

"What about our garments, Ymir? When do I receive

some more attractive things to wear?" I pointed with disgust to the heap of grey cloth on the floor.

He pushed me off, then rose, went to the window, stood gazing out. Even his back was perfect. Smooth tight buttocks, wide shoulders, narrow waist. His tall, muscular form was outlined in the afternoon light.

"We at the *Akademie* are not like other houses of this nature, which cater merely to the pleasure seekers. Frau Anna feels we are professionals at our calling, every bit as respectable as doctor, lawyer, or even a professor at a university. We exist for the patron who wants something unusual, more stimulating than the ordinary *Gasthaus* along the waterfront can offer."

"What do you mean, unusual?" A fear pricked my heart. Visions of bestiality and whippings rose before me.

"Each girl is an actress, trained in a variety of roles. Bettina's repertory, for instance, includes Rhine nymph, Egyptian goddess, schoolgirl, and scullery maid—whatever a customer has a hankering for. Even a nun."

"Nun?" The word shot out of me like a bullet. "Nun?" I repeated, more softly, still not quite believing what I had heard.

"Yes, many of our clients have nursed a secret desire to possess a nun, a desire that commenced in boyhood. You can understand, I'm sure, the craving for purity, sweetness, the unattainable."

"But how can a prostitute who has known many men pretend to purity and sainthood?"

"Easy enough, with a few lessons and some practice. And of course, the appropriate costume. A man sees what he wants to see in a woman."

I sat on the bed, cross-legged like a child, mulling over the startling things Ymir was telling me. "Then—you're never just yourself? Always something else? Like an actress?"

"Precisely." Ymir had the air of a teacher lecturing a rather stupid pupil. "Men want something exotic, completely different from their wives or other women they know. Frau Anna's *Akademie* is a fantasyland. When a customer enters these halls he leaves the outer world behind."

"And you," I couldn't help asking the long-thighed man standing in front of me. "What roles do you assume?" I smiled. "Besides, of course, that of trainer of apprentices."

126

He looked startled, a shadow crossed his eyes, then he reverted immediately to his calm demeanor, and the mask came back. "Usually our female clients want me in my natural naked state."

"An Adam to their Eve?" I said banteringly.

"Sometimes," he said, leaping from the window, hugging me fiercely, growling into my neck, baring his teeth and taking little bites on my bare shoulder. "Sometimes I tie a loincloth around my hips and become a savage from darkest Africa. The women eat it up."

"I'll bet." I laughed despite myself. "What's your favorite?"

He released me, stood up again, looked thoughtful. The dark brows lifted, the smooth olive forehead wrinkled. "That's hard. I'd have to say, I think, Frederick Barbarossa. It seems my favorite client, a sea captain's widow, has become obsessed with the legendary Hohenstaufen monarch. Or at least his statue that stands in her town square."

He doubled over with laughter. "So I put on this long shaggy red beard down to here," he pointed to his waist, "a fancy medieval outfit, and presto—she is in ecstasy for a week."

My heart lurched into my throat. I stuffed my fist into my mouth to keep from crying out. Then I said, calmly, "Oh no, that you could never be. You—you don't have the coloring, or the size, or—"

He cut me off, not noticing my agitation. "Enough of me and my roles. You are the one who has to dress up tonight for the first time. I must school you in the proper gestures, the words, the walk."

He strode to the doorway, called out for Heinz, who appeared, as always, immediately. The hunchback was carrying a great box which almost hid him from sight.

"Put it on the floor, Heinz, and then you may go."

The little man did so, then backed away and remained standing in the doorway as if reluctant to leave, his eyes resting on me. I was still naked.

Ymir lifted his head from the box. "Heinz, please leave at once." His voice was cruel. The little man scuttled off fearfully.

As I watched Ymir drawing colorful fabric from the box—sheer chiffons of pale hues, some flesh colored, others sea green or palest blue, brocades and velvets richly dyed

127

and heavily embroidered—my mind slid back to the baronin and her moldy chests. Once again I felt like a doll, who was being treated like a piece of antique statuary.

Ymir flung piece after piece of fabric around my body, pulling tightly here, loosening there, tying it with a bit of gold braid at the waist, or between and under the breasts. A length of palest sea green chiffon worked here and there with sparkling green stones made me into a mermaid.

"Perfect Lorelei," he exclaimed. "All you need is a golden comb or a harp. We have many calls for Lorelei, but none of the girls has enough hair to make the illusion a good one."

We settled finally on a Daphne costume for the afternoon's review in the salon. A piece of rich forest green velvet fell just to my knees, caught at the waist with a band of artificial leaves, glossy green, interspersed with bright red berries. A crown of laurel leaves sat on top of my hair, which flowed loosely to my waist.

"You remember Daphne," Ymir instructed, "the maiden who was daughter of the river god and was pursued by the Greek god Apollo. To preserve her virginity, the king of gods, Jove, transformed her into a laurel tree."

"Yes," I said, "It has always been one of my favorite tales. I shall love being Daphne."

The grey eyes looked at me quizzically, brows lifted. "For the wife of a peasant, you are well educated. Methinks you are not exactly what you seem."

The blood rushed to my face, but I said as calmly as I could, "I had a little schooling. All Black Forest children know the ancient tales of both the Germans and the Romans."

My apparition in the mirror brought a gasp of delight. Innocence, freshness, fertility, with a hint at virginity, were all there. I looked as if I had just stepped out of the primeval forest—a maiden untouched, unseen by man before this moment.

Ymir was ecstatic. "That's it. That's the look." He seemed to be breathing heavily. A look of wanting had come into his eyes, as before when we had first come upstairs.

"Wait here. I will go and costume myself."

I was still preening in the mirror and rehearsing the look of fertile virginity when Ymir returned wearing a laurel crown just like mine and a rich green bunch of leaves over his genitals. Beyond that he was completely naked.

"Behold," he turned round and round like a model on a stage. "Apollo."

My heart raced, my eyes glittered. How wonderful to make life a game, to forget the cruel realities of death and desertion. I could leave Sieglinde behind, I could (at least for a few hours) become Daphne, a maiden who had never loved and lost, who had never had her own baby torn from her arms.

The salon or drawing room of the *Akademie* was at the rear of the great house. A wall of tall windows overlooked a deep garden that stretched up the hillside. Now, in April, the bare-limbed trees showed bumps where buds swelled, ready to burst at the merest hint of hot sun. Numerous flower beds were now brown moist earth. A neatly trimmed high hedge completely surrounded the space. The hedge appeared to be at least eight feet high.

Ymir led me away from the window to a straight-backed chair, in a long row of them. "Sit here, don't talk to anyone. You'll destroy your Daphne mood."

I sat down obediently, head down, eyes closed. One, two, three, four, five—I counted the chimes that rang ponderously from the great clock in the corridor. Then Frau Anna's voice broke in. "Good. I compliment you all for being so punctual."

"Open your eyes," hissed Ymir into my ear. I did so, and saw the other girls, eleven of them, sitting in identical chairs, all with sober faces, all dressed differently. A tense excitement permeated the room, as before an opening night at the theater.

"Gertrud." At the sound of her name, the tall dark beauty from the Black Forest rose, walked slowly toward the chair where Frau Anna sat, turned round, then moved up close so that Frau Anna could examine her costume in detail. She was stunning dressed as a gypsy. I had seen plenty of them in my childhood at Schachten. A snug-fitting red satin bodice was slit all the way to the waist, barely covering her full breasts. A skirt of brilliant reds, greens, blues, in dazzling patterns, swirled from her narrow waist. Both arms were covered with bracelets halfway to the elbow. Even her ankles tinkled seductively with gold and silver circlets.

The girl named Ottilie walked in tiny steps, swathed to the knees in a tight silver cloth mermaid outfit. Jeweled combs highlighted her honey blonde hair which hung wetly down her back. Her nipples, also wet, poked through holes in the silver cloth.

Each girl, in turn, rose as Frau Anna called out her name, performed and got approval. The older woman kept up a running commentary, so that everyone benefited from any criticism. A skirt was unsuitable, a bodice too tight, a costume too crudely sexual.

Adelheide was a stunning Egyptian goddess, her smooth black hair pulled back tightly from her high cheekbones. Long, red, curving nails, body swathed in gold cloth, eyes heavily outlined in black, she could have stepped out of a museum. Bettina was transformed into a bewitching peasant girl, with snow white blouse, dipped low in front and full swirling skirt. Shock waves ran up and down my spine when Berta presented herself as a schoolgirl, complete with white blouse, blue jumper, ribbons in her hair. She even carried a satchel full of books! I was enthralled.

"Sieglinde, I've saved you for last, because you and Ymir are to perform."

I am a virgin, I am a virgin. I am running from my ravisher. I repeated the words to myself as I walked, shaking with fright, in front of the watching eyes.

Ymir rose, came swiftly toward me, fierce determination and lust written all over his handsome face. He reached long, strong arms toward me. I ran the length of the spacious salon, darting in and out of the furniture, hiding momentarily behind the window draperies, like a child playing hide and seek. Ymir pursued. My blood raced with the excitement of the game.

After five minutes of running about, Frau Anna shouted, "Let him catch you. Our customers are not athletes."

I slowed down at the end of a velvet couch. Ymir caught hold of me roughly by the shoulders, pressed me fiercely against his long body. The hardness of his manhood pressed against my thighs.

"Fight, fight," Frau Anna shouted again. "Fight for your virtue."

I struggled free, for I was almost as strong as he, then started once more around the room, Ymir in hot pursuit. The girls were laughing, enjoying the game themselves.

After three rounds of hide and seek, I flattened myself against a wall, exhausted, and let him take me.

We sank, bound together, to the couch, lay there kissing passionately. Ymir wriggled his long body until he lay directly on top of me. The throb of blood in my veins made me oblivious to everything. I forgot about Frau Anna and the other girls.

"Bravo, bravo!" The sound of shouting and hand clapping, foot stamping as the Germans like to do, gradually sunk into my consciousness.

Frau Anna's voice cut through the turmoil in my brain. "You may stop pretending now, Sieglinde."

Pretending! But I had not been pretending. I wanted Ymir. The spirit of the mock chase had inflamed my senses. Reluctantly, it seemed, Ymir released me. We sat up slowly on the soft cushions of the couch.

Frau Anna was smiling, her thin lips spread wide. I had not thought she could look so happy. "You'll do just fine, Sieglinde. That was excellent. I should think that with some practice, you will be able to assume a great many roles. Except"—with a glance at my breasts—"a boy, of course."

Chapter 11

For two whole delirious weeks, Ymir and I made love continuously in the lovely edelweiss room with the view of brown-roofed Mannheim. At various times I was a gypsy, a mermaid, a peasant girl, a queen of England, a queen of Russia—but most of the time, a goddess. I was Brünnhilde, Freya, Ishtar, Aphrodite, Venus, Isis, and (Ymir's favorite of all) Ceres, the mother goddess of the whole universe. For that role I dressed in wheat-colored velvet or chiffon and carried a sheaf of wheat.

We ate with the others at the regular hours, then retired again to my room for more "lessons." Twice each day we took the air in the garden, which was moving into early summer. The tulips were a riot of color and the hard bulges on the once bare limbs had burst into tender green leaves.

The garden, Ymir told me, was a very important part of the "program" at the *Akademie*. Little man made streams meandered through the grass and flower beds. A water wheel at one end produced a miniature water fall. Rocks, hedges, even an old stone wall added to the romantic atmosphere.

I fairly glowed with health and well being. Once more I was loved, cherished, desired. I pushed to the back of my mind the fact that he was a stud, a man who was schooling me in the acts of love. Despite the fact that he was simply preparing my body for others to enjoy, I convinced myself that Ymir loved me, Sieglinde. Lothar had ceased to exist. He had never been real, I told myself. He had faded into the past, like everything and everyone I had ever known. There had always been something supernatural about him. Maybe he really was the Barbarossa reincarnated. After impregnating me, he had returned to his mountain cave to

133

sleep another five centuries, I told myself. As for Karl and Kristina, they had been real enough. But it hurt too much to think about them. So I didn't.

Ymir taught me how to act coy, to appear to withdraw, to drive a man frantic with want and longing. "But don't overdo it," he cautioned. "Many of our clients are elderly. Their powers are diminished. You must know when to stop teasing and submit. If you can bring pleasure to these men, you will soon be a wealthy woman. In fact, Frau Anna has considerable trouble keeping girls because they are quickly carried off by titled or wealthy merchants and established in a mountain or seaside villa as a cherished mistress." He gave me a sidelong glance. "Would you like that, Sieglinde?"

"Mistress." I repeated the word thoughtfully. I thought of Lola, who had been a pampered, spoiled darling, then of my bliss as Lothar's wife. Now I was a plaything for jaded men. "No." I said firmly. "I want to be Number One. I want to be a man's wife, legally, in every way."

His smile was sardonic. "You may never have that choice. Few men will marry an ex-prostitute, a woman whom many, many men have known."

Then I asked the question that had been nagging me ever since I had first met Ymir. "Why do you stay here Ymir, doing this kind of work? Surely you could have any woman you wanted, rich, famous, even titled."

A troubled shadow crossed the handsome features; the eyes that turned to me seemed filled with unshed tears. "Someday, Sieglinde dearest, I will tell you my story. Now is not the time—nor the place."

At last the day came when Ymir announced that I was ready. "Your training is complete. I will so inform Frau Anna."

Our last night together fell by coincidence on the eve of my seventeenth birthday, May 1, 1849. The cool grey morning lit up the panes of the window as we reached ecstasy together for the third time that night.

"Ymir, my darling, my own," I whispered passionately, overcome with emotion and the sheer animal joy of our lovemaking. "I love you with all my heart and soul and body."

The long lithe body stiffened, then leaped out of the bed, as if a hot brand had touched him. "Don't say that," he shouted at me, "don't ever say a thing like that." His voice was hard. The eyes which a moment ago had been clouded with passion now shot out little rays of hatred. "No one loves Ymir and Ymir loves no one."

Putting on his grey shift, he made for the door. "Training's over," he said, his hand on the knob, without turning to look at me.

After he left, I lay in bed for a long time. "Happy birthday," I told myself. "You are seventeen, you have a profession. The oldest in the world. Soon, in a year or two, you will be rich, you will leave this place, and this Germany which has brought so much heartbreak to you. You will hold your head high. You will be your own woman at last."

It was a good feeling.

"He is very lonely," Frau Anna said, "and very rich. But impotent—so far, none of my girls has been able to help him."

His name was Ernst Grauberg and he would be my first client. "You will need to call upon all the training Ymir gave you, and more, to give him pleasure."

There was more. The man was sixty-six, from Hamelin, and owned three steamships which belched their way up and down the Rhine pulling barges filled with coal.

I was excited and more than a little tense. The fee would be split three ways, she said, "one-third for me, one-third for the house, and one-third for you."

As she had said, Herr Grauberg was no stallion. Short, tubby, white hair but plenty of it, small beard. He looked like Saint Nikolaus who came with his bag of goodies on the sixth of December. But the kindly old "saint" was burning with lust. He had ordered a Lorelei so I greeted him resplendent in diaphonous chiffon. My long white-gold hair streamed loosely about me. Heinz had provided me with a golden comb studded with glittering stones.

The May night was fair, although the smell of a morning downpour still pervaded the garden. The little man sat on an iron bench watching as I went through the gyrations of the water nymph role.

I sang, *Ich weiss nich was soll es bedeuten, dass Ich so traurig bin* . . . the well-known song of Schubert's that tells the legend of the siren of the rocks. *"I don't know why I am so sad . . ."*

Nothing happened. He continued to sit there, motionless,

with a hungry, yearning look in his little blue eyes. Desperate, I climbed down from the rock, moved swiftly to the bench, took his pudgy hand and led him to the wooden water wheel that turned ponderously in the corner of the garden. "Make it run," I urged. "You are Neptune, god of all the oceans. You make the storms that wreck the ships of Ulysses."

Dutifully, he turned, first slowly. mechanically, never taking his eyes off me, then speeded up, faster, faster, until he was fairly panting, the wheel turning, the water splashing, spraying wetly on both of us. His red face glistened with sweat and water. My costume clung wetly to my body, outlining every curve.

Suddenly he moaned, clutched me to him with his fat arms. We both fell on the soft wet ground still damp from the morning rain, and he took me like a savage, spreading my legs hurtfully, plunging into me with swift, trembling movements. Herr Grauberg was no longer impotent.

Next day at dinner, Ymir winked at me across the table, mouthed the words, "You passed with flying colors." I smiled back, although my heart still ached for the sure, masculine feel of his arms.

Herr Grauberg had engaged me for a whole week. On Saturday, as we all lined up for the weekly inspection, Frau Anna told me that I had earned two florins.

"Only two?" I gasped in disbelief. A scullery maid earned as much.

Her thin aristocratic face was impassive. "Of course I had to deduct certain sums for your keep, the initial trouble we had with you, the drugs for drying up your milk—and after all, Sieglinde, you are still on probation, you know. One battle does not make the war."

That afternoon, during recreation time, Bettina dropped into my room to talk. I had asked her at dinner to help me with my mermaid act. Herr Grauberg had become aroused when I became wet, so I figured that I could become a success not only at the Lorelei, but at anything connected with the water.

"You've got to make swimming motions," she said. "Just wriggle like a fish on a hook." She moved across the room, threw herself on the floor, moving her petite form sinuously. We both ended up laughing helplessly.

Oh Bettina," I said, my chest fairly hurting, tears of joy

running down my cheeks. "You are the dearest thing to me, just like the sister I never had."

The hazel eyes veiled with pity. She sat down on the bed beside me. She buried her bronze curls in my arms. It felt so good to hug another human being for the pure joy of it, without the specter of lust connected with it—just pure, simple, deeply felt love. Like the love I'd felt for Karl.

"How sad," she said in her sweet Berliner accent, "to be an only child. Are your parents still alive?"

Once again I hesitated. I longed to confide in this girl, but could I trust anyone with the true facts of my parentage? Frau Anna said she knew all about me, but was she really telling the truth? Or did she say that to frighten me, to keep me from running away? Bettina looked innocent enough, but suppose she told someone else, a client perhaps, in an unguarded moment?

She wriggled out of my arms, looked intently into my face. "What is it, Sieglinde? Is there some deep dark secret about you? You say you come from the Black Forest, a peasant family, yet your speech, your hands, somehow don't fit."

"Yes, Bettina," I admitted, "I haven't told you the whole truth. My mother died shortly after my birth, she was from the north, from Norway. My father was of the nobility—one of those countless little dukedoms in the south. You know, there's a Schloss on every mountain peak."

It was near enough to the truth to salve my uneasiness.

"Oh. That accounts for your magnificent stature, your incredible hair."

Then she told me her story. Abandoned as an infant on the doorstep of a church, she'd grown up in an orphan asylum, and at twelve was farmed out to work as a servant. One day, while running an errand in the village for her mistress, she'd been abducted and cruelly raped. Afterward they shipped her to England for prostitution. "Liverpool," she uttered the word with loathing. "The cesspool of the world.

"Eventually," she went on, "I was shipped to Argentina, but the ship floundered in a storm. After drifting in a lifeboat for a week, we were picked up by a British ship and brought back to England."

As she reached this point in her story, she stopped, unable to go on. I began to weep, knowing what she was about to tell me. Disease. The most dreaded word in the world of

137

the prostitute. The disease which makes it impossible to bear children, which closed off a woman's womb forever.

"The British authorities deported me back to Germany. I ended up here in the *Akademie*, picked up by one of Frau Anna's Polizei. Heinz cured my sores in a month with his herbs, but—" now the tears spilled heedlessly down the freckled cheeks—"once you have that disease, it never really goes away. It festers inside you, waiting to attack the infant in the womb."

I knew what she was talking about. I'd seen them, the pitifully deformed, with no legs, no arms, horribly disfigured, sometimes raving idiots. They begged on street-corners, or were shut up in foul institutions for an entire lifetime.

"Oh, Sieglinde," she clutched my hand so hard it hurt, "please don't stay here. Get away as soon as you can. Just as soon as you get enough money for passage to America."

America! The land of promise. The El Dorado of the poor, the oppressed of Europe. Why not the Land of Redemption for reformed prostitutes? America—the land where you could be illegitimate, and nobody held it against you.

My eyes glowed. "Nothing would make me happier."

Bettina pulled a square of linen from the pocket of her shift, blew her snub nose long and loud. The sweet face that moments ago had been tear-streaked, now glowed with excitement. "I'll be twenty-one next month. In three years of working for Frau Anna I've saved 150 florins, enough for a second-class ticket to America. I could have gone last year, if I'd been willing to go steerage, but from what I've heard about that—"

"Yes," I agreed, "half the steerage passengers perish from starvation or disease."

Three years, I thought. I'll be twenty-one by that time; the same age as Bettina now. Would I too be diseased, like her? I was reassured by the thought that Frau Anna's girls were examined each month by Herr Doktor Glanzend from Mannheim.

After she left, I sat on the bed and dreamed about going to America. But at two florins a week it would take years. And I'd forgotten about the three-year contract—an apprenticeship she called it—I had signed in Frau Anna's office.

* * *

Life at the *Akademie* settled quickly enough into a routine. By the end of May I was working every night. Frau Anna was pleased. "I'm booking you weeks in advance," she told me at our Saturday review in the salon. Later, in her little office, a tiny room off the kitchen, she showed me my "credits" on the financial statement for the house.

"Ten florins!" I exclaimed in dismay.

"After all," she bustled, "you are still a neophyte."

I swallowed, screwed up my courage. "May I have it, please?"

The sapphire eyes narrowed, became glacial. "You are well aware that such a thing is impossible. No money will be issued you until the end of your apprenticeship."

"I must have it," I insisted. "I want to bury my child and my husband decently. I want to erect a gravestone. Just a simple marker."

"They will rest well enough where they are for the present," she said coldly. "When you have served out your apprenticeship you will have enough money to erect a mausoleum if you so desire. Or—" she cocked a cynical eyebrow—"even transport them back to the Black Forest. Isn't that where you came from?"

"It isn't fair—or even Christian," I said angrily. "It's like slavery."

She leaned back in her chair, gave me a malicious glance. "What if certain people in power were told who you really are? The Wittelsbachs of Bavaria have many enemies in this area. The Burschen of Heidelberg would be most interested, I'm sure."

Although my heart was beating furiously with frustrated rage, I said nothing more. I was literally enslaved for three years. There was nowhere to turn. The Polizei? She had them in the palm of her hand. A good many of them were steady patrons of the *Akademie*.

Much of what I had to do for and with my clients was repulsive to me, but sometimes I'd be lucky and draw a handsome steamboat captain or a wealthy landowner tired of his mistress. I was young and strong, the blood was hot in my veins, and more often than not I found myself entering into the physical act of love with an abandon which brought release to my tormented soul.

And Frau Anna was right of course about Karl and Kristina. Their bodies might be in Potter's Field with murderers, beggars, the rejected of the land, but their souls were in heaven.

One beautiful rose-filled day in June, Bettina celebrated her twenty-first birthday, and just as she had told me, she announced to Frau Anna and the whole *Akademie* that she was off to America. She'd booked second-class passage on the steamer *Thomas Jefferson* sailing out of Bremerhaven the very next day. She came to my room to say goodbye, radiant in a walking dress of apple green cashmere, the skirt trimmed smartly with rows of black velvet ribbon. A bonnet of darker green velvet with layers of white lace under the brim sat primly on the red curls.

I smiled through my heartache at losing my best friend. "Oh, Bettina, you look so proper—and innocent!"

We both laughed. "At least I don't look like a street-walker. I'm listed on the passenger list as a widowed schoolteacher from Freudenthal. In fact, I'm sharing my cabin with a very elderly woman who is traveling to join her son in America." She clasped me in her arms, hugged me hard. Then she was gone, promising to write from America. We would be together again, she said. She would become rich and send for me. I believed her. I *had* to believe her.

That evening being a Saturday, Ymir and I were scheduled to do a performance for the weekly costume review. We were to play Mars and Venus whose love affair had convulsed the gods on Mt. Olympus with ribald laughter. But Ymir's version of Mars was no bumbling lover, as in the myth. Dressed splendidly in bright red tights that outlined every muscle of his supple brown body, he could set anyone's pulse racing, even a jaded Venus.

I wore a very brief pale yellow costume of sheer chiffon with figures of planets and stars pasted in strategic places. A glittering crown rested on my golden tresses.

Mars cavorted around me invitingly, reaching out frantically while I ran and skipped about, eluding him. Ymir's hands touched my breast, grabbed me for a few moments, pressed me down almost to the floor. His breath came heavily, his eyes glittered with fierce desire. I marveled at his acting ability. When we'd finished, there was spontaneous applause. We were to put on the skit for a group of patrons at a party in the grand salon the following evening.

140

"You should go on the stage, Ymir," I murmured against his lips.

His eyes burned into mine. "I'm not acting," he growled.

We took our bows. Sudden joyous knowledge flooded through me. Ymir truly loved me and wanted me, as much as I desired him. We would escape together, he and I, and flee to America, the land of the free. There we could go on the stage and make our fortunes.

My mind was filled with fantasies about escaping Frau Anna and her *Akademie*. There was nothing now in Germany to hold me. My child was dead, my family in disgrace, and my husband, my beloved Lothar, had disappeared, perhaps forever.

But one evening, the past rose to confront me.

Chapter 12

My patron for the evening was Andreas, who had returned at last for his "payment" which he'd demanded for rescuing me from the Burschen. My heart warmed at the sight of him in the salon. He had proved a true friend in the past. Perhaps he could help me now.

He asked me to go into the garden with him and do my Lorelei performance. "Your fame has travelled up and down the Rhine," he said. "So I decided it was for me." Like my first patron, the little man from Hamelin, Andreas was not as virile as he would like to be.

Although my heart was not in my acting—my arms ached for Ymir—I must have done a good job. My instinct for perfection overcame whatever inner turmoil I was feeling.

"You have made a man of me," Andreas exulted later, as he dressed in the pre-dawn dark in my room. Because mention of Lothar would have marred both my performance and his, I had refrained from asking about him before this moment. But now the words spilled out.

"Andreas, where is Lothar? Have you heard from him? Is he still alive?" The pockmarked young face darkened. "Nobody knows, Sieglinde. I wish to God I did. The last I heard he was on his way to America to raise money. All I can tell you is that the revolution in Germany is dead."

He pulled the window open, violently. "Come here Sieglinde, stand by me."

I did as he asked, wrapping the light blanket around my nakedness against the chill coming in from the open window. "Feel it?" he urged. "Do you feel Lothar?"

I gazed out the window into the murky dawn. The smell of wood smoke from breakfast fires assailed my nostrils. A tremendous *Heimweh*, a homesickness, overwhelmed me. My head dropped into my hands and I sobbed openly.

143

Instantly Andreas enfolded me in his arms, rocked me back and forth like a child. "Sieglinde, darling—do not weep for Lothar. If he could, he would be at your side. You are part of him, and he of you."

"It isn't just Lothar, and his long absence," I sobbed against his white Burschen jacket. "Oh, Andreas, my life is ruined, I am a slave to Frau Anna, and I seem to have banished Lothar from my heart."

I told him about Ymir, and about my passion for him, and my dreams—fantasies really—about escaping with him to America. "Help me, Andreas, help me. For love of Lothar, if for no other reason." When I had finished, his pockmarked face was white.

"You must leave this place without delay. There must be a way."

Now it was his turn to hold his head in his hands. After a long moment, he looked up. "This Ymir, where can I see him—talk to him? Perhaps we can work out something together."

I smiled ruefully. "You mean, another smoke-out?"

"No," he nodded gravely, "not this time. More subtle techniques must be employed. Frau Anna is too clever for such crude tactics. But trust me," he promised, with a last kiss.

A week later, tormented with impatience about Andreas's promise to help me escape from the *Akademie*, I decided to work through Heinz. I could trust him, I knew.

The kitchen was hot, the day being sultry. Yarmila the cook was in her usual place at the table, sewing on a large piece of blue cloth. The wizened creature looked up, a startled look crossing her face. "Why aren't you dressed? Aren't you entertaining a patron tonight?"

"But I *am* dressed, Yarmila. The patron requested that I wear a bag of a gown, with a rope around the middle. I guess he wants a lady monk."

She shook her head. "Queer things, these rich men. Oh—to answer your question, Heinz isn't here. He went into Mannheim to the bank with Frau Anna. They'll be gone until after supper."

It was with a heavy heart that I opened the door to my patron for the evening, wondering what sort of perverted person had ordered a girl dressed like a scullery maid.

"You!" The word exploded from my lips. "What are you

144

doing here?" The figure stood in the dimly lit corridor like a ghost out of the past.

"More to the point, my dear Sieglinde, what are *you* doing here?"

Same oily smile, same sophisticated mocking tone to the voice. The hair seemed greyer, the face a bit thinner. One thing remained the same: the smoldering lust in the glittering steel-blue eyes. Franz Von Edel took off a high silk hat, bowed graciously in his courtly way. "I must admit to some surprise at seeing Ludwig's daughter in a brothel. A high-class establishment, to be sure, but a brothel nonetheless."

"Come in." I took his hand, and pulled him into the room. It was a treat just to look at him. He was dressed like a fashion plate, in a pearl-colored summer cloak edged in ermine over a ruffled shirt. A gold-handled cane rested elegantly over his left wrist.

He never took his eyes off me. I smiled, remembering with a rush of gratitude how he had rescued me and my father the king from the student rebels. It wasn't his fault if the scheme had backfired, in my case at least.

"Now I can truly thank you, Von Edel, for what you did—or tried to do for me."

A shadow crossed the handsome features. "Yes, I heard that you were captured after all. Was it very bad?" He stood the cane in a corner, slipped off his white gloves carefully, slowly, finger by finger. The hands were just as I remembered—long and hard-knuckled with smoothly filed nails. He put the gloves on the nightstand beside the single candle and moved his delicate fingers to my face.

"You are older, my Venus. By more than just the year or so that has passed. The girl I knew in Lola's palace is now a woman."

The old man leaned forward, touched my lips lightly with his, still cupping my cheeks in his hands. My lips trembled under his, then impulsively, with a violent movement, I pressed my body to his. A woman, was I? Well, he didn't know the half of it.

I deliberately maneuvered the lower half of my body so that my thighs pressed insistently against his. I would seduce him. Von Edel would take me out of here. I would make him so mad with desire that he would carry me off before morning. His manhood leaped in response, becoming hard in moments.

"Whoa there, not so fast, young woman." Von Edel

pulled my hands from around his neck. "Give an old man a chance to warm up," he laughed.

But I could tell he was pleased. His eyes sparkled in the old way. I moved to the nightstand and lifted the stopper from the crystal decanter of brandy, poured a little in each of two wide brandy glasses.

"Will this help?" I asked archly.

Smiling broadly now, he took the glass, his aristocratic face pink with pleasure. I moved to the chaise longue, beckoned to him to sit beside me. Once I had thought him repulsive, but now he seemed like any other man, ready to leap at a woman and take her like a stallion. At least he was clean, which was more than could be said about some.

"Take off that damn rag," he said draining his glass. "And pour me some more brandy. This time don't be so stingy with it."

Our glances remained locked, as I stood up, untied the rope, and slipped the shapeless rag down around my feet. I stood naked, my breasts outthrust, the nipples taut, expectant. I arched my back slightly as Ymir had instructed me, to bring my entire body into full view. Especially the dark traingle of the mound of Venus.

"Yes," he said thickly. "You have changed. Now you really are a Valkyrie, a woman fit to service the very gods themselves."

I fell to my knees, moved slowly forward, lay my head in his lap, let him play with my breasts. Then ever so slowly, as he drained the decanter of brandy, I undressed the old man, from the soft wool cloak to the shining calfskin shoes.

Finally I spoke, as we fell together onto the floor. "Why did you want me dressed like this?"

"Don't you remember? This was how I saw you last. I wanted it to seem that we were back in that little room in the concubine's palace. It was my way of erasing the whole year."

I hurled myself away from him. "Then you knew all the time I was here?"

He leaped off the floor, picked me up like a doll and threw me on the bed. "Of course, you ninny. I knew all the time where you were and what was happening to you. I know all about your little idyll in the cave with the Redbeard. I know about the birth of your twins, about the Burschen, and what they did to you—"

Enraged now, I beat my fists against his chest, which

146

was matted thickly—unexpectedly—with dark curls. With lionlike strength, he pinned my hands to the pillow, moved smoothly on top of me, drove into me with the force of a lightning bolt. I wriggled beneath him, trying to throw him off. But my movements maddened him all the more. In moments he had reached fulfillment, and I lay under him, helpless, feeling the shock waves of his ecstasy rolling over me. We lay like that, locked together, our sweat mingling in the hot August night.

"I'm sorry, forgive me please," he muttered into my tangled hair. "I have waited so long and my desire was so great—"

"It doesn't matter. We have all night," I replied softly, my anger gone. If he were to help me at all, I must please him, no matter what he demanded. All night he demanded, sometimes like a mad dog, biting my breasts, my thighs, my neck with sharp little bites so that I cried out with the pain. Sometimes he was a starving man, fairly eating me up like a succulent dish of sweetmeats. I surrendered myself utterly to him, this friend of my father's, but to my own amazement, despite calculated planning going on in my mind, I found myself moaning in ecstasy.

At last we both lay, spent, in the predawn darkness. "Dreams do come true, my forest nymph turned Valkyrie," he murmured, crooning into my ear, his gentle fingers caressing my nipples.

"Von Edel," I said abruptly, "once you asked King Ludwig for my hand in marriage. Do you still want me for your wife?"

"Wife!" He laughed, cynically. "That is out of the question now, Sieglinde. You are secondhand goods. God only knows how many men have filled you with their seed. But mistress—well, if you can guarantee a performance every night like the one you've given me tonight, yes."

He rolled over directly on top of me. We rocked back and forth on the bed. "Yes, yes, a thousand times yes. I will set you up as no woman has ever been set up. Lola Montez would turn green with envy."

"Then you are still wealthy, in spite of being in exile?"

He nodded. "The new government simply tied up all the money in the banks. They knew nothing of the family jewels and other treasures hidden in the mountains. My family has an old Schloss there—a ruin **actua**lly."

"Do you know the baronin?" I cried, with a stab of fear.

"Of course. Everyone does. Nutty as a fruitcake. The old woman has some wild dream about that redbearded grandson of hers taking over Germany." He rolled off me again, sat up, chin in hands.

"The Prussians are taking over Germany. All the little dukes and barons in their charming little Schlosses on top of the mountains in the south will soon be begging in the streets." He lay his hand on my belly, rubbed thoughtfully in little circles.

"There's one provision, Sieglinde, if you want to tie up with me. We must live in America. Would you mind that very much, leaving your homeland?"

"Mind? Mind?" Overjoyed, I threw my arms around him, pressed the hard old body to mine, unable to speak for the joy in my heart.

"I've thought of nothing else for months. Oh, yes, yes, yes."

PART II

The Voyage

Chapter 13

By noon of that same day, the Baron Von Edel and I were on board the Rhine steamer the *Rising Star*, bound for the new port of Bremerhaven on the North Sea. There we would embark for America on the next available ocean steamship.

He had left my bed at dawn and returned three hours later with a bagful of gold coins. Frau Anna had started to make a fuss about my leaving so suddenly, but the mound of gold coins on the desk in her little office quickly silenced her objections. Von Edel suggested that I remain in the kitchen with Heinz and Yarmila while he arranged my "release" with the woman.

"You'd only get in the way," he said. "I'll handle this. You must remember—I am the diplomat."

Their voices soon became loud and angry, however, and carried clearly through the closed door.

"She's too good a property to let go just like that," Frau Anna's normally well-modulated voice approached a shriek.

Then Von Edel's heated response: "Six hundred florins is twice the value of your so-called apprenticeship. I consider my offer more than generous."

So after kissing Heinz and Yarmila goodbye and promising to write I was off with my new lover to America. In the carriage, I could hardly sit still for sheer excitement. Like a child, I peered out the little square of window at the busy rush of noontime traffic in Mannheim, remembering the last time I'd traversed these narrow twisting streets, in the back of a hay wagon with the mad Burschen. I thought I would die that April day. But ironically it was Karl and Kristina who lay in unmarked graves somewhere out there at the river's edge.

"Goodbye," I whispered to my dear ones. "*Auf Wiedersehen*—for now." Once again my heart made a solemn resolve. "Some day I'll return and take you home with me—wherever I am—and you will rest in consecrated ground."

Overcome with emotion, I turned swiftly and kissed the Baron on the lips as he sat writing on a little pad. He looked pleased, but pushed me back on my side of the seat. "No time for that now, Schatzie," he chuckled. "But here—take out your high spirits on this."

He pulled out from an inner jacket pocket a piece of paper, which I recognized as the apprenticeship contract I'd signed with Frau Anna. "Tear it up," he ordered, "and throw the pieces out the window." The wind picked up the tiny pieces and blew them about like snowflakes in the dark narrow street. I laughed. Snow in August. So there it goes, I thought, one life ends, and another begins.

"Welcome to the *Rising Star*, Baronin. I am Captain Schneider."

I turned from gazing at the wide river to greet a tanned Viking in a smart blue and gold uniform. Von Edel had gone below with the steward to check out our accommodations, leaving me standing at the rail, gazing out at the Rhine, glimmering blue-grey in the noonday sun.

Sometime during the busy morning, Heinz had run into Mannheim and fetched me a fashionable costume to wear on the boat. The silk dress was a deep, deep blue, the full skirt trimmed lavishly with row upon row of narrow black velvet ribbon. Wrist-length sleeves ended in a cascade of fine champagne-colored Brussels lace, which spilled out gracefully over my hands. A bonnet of lustrous brown silk, thickly lined with more lace, covered my coiled braids. I had coaxed a few wayward strands out of the coronet to blow attractively in the wind.

The bodice, not being fitted to my figure, was of course a snug fit, and my bosom bulged invitingly above the low neckline, which was edged with tiny brown velvet rosettes. A brown velvet cape tied loosely at the neck and reached to my waist.

I opened my eyes wide to stare questioningly at the captain, knowing full well the effect of the brown accents on my eyes. The gentleman glowed approvingly. The sailors glanced furtively at me as they passed back and forth. I was a sensation, and I knew it.

"We are privileged to have such distinguished passengers

152

aboard," said the captain, bowing deeply from the waist. "As you know, we are a cargo vessel, but at the baron's insistence, I have given up my cabin for your journey."

I nodded, extended my lacy hand, but said nothing. If this masquerade were to be successful, I must begin to act like a lady of quality.

Von Edel, strangely enough, gave up his constant adoring attentions and left me alone most of the time. I saw him only at meals, he being preoccupied with two other men to whom he did not introduce me. From their dialect, I knew them to be Prussians. So the willing Captain Schneider became my guide for the journey down the Rhine from Mannheim, informing me proudly, in detail, of the amount of goods transported up and down the historic river by the day, by the month, by the year. As we glided past the lush vineyards which cover the hillside banks, he lent me his glass, so that I could see more easily the heavy grapes ripening in the sun.

I resisted the impulse to wave and call out greetings to the passengers who lined the rails on the steamers plying their way upstream. I gazed with appropriate wonder at the many mysterious gloomy castles which perched formidably atop steep crags overlooking sharp bends in the river.

"Those were the abodes of the predatory river pirates," the captain said. "Thank God they are no more. Many a ship disappeared without a trace. Now it is perfectly safe to run the river."

"What about the fabled Lorelei?" I inquired lightly. "Isn't the famous siren still a threat to hapless seamen?"

He laughed, throwing back his handsome head. "This evening you will see for yourself. We will be passing Bingen, where the famous rock is located." When the massive salt formation hove into view it was shaped exactly like the prow of a giant ship. The sun hovered over the river like a glowing disc, making molten gold out of the sparkling river.

Sensing an unusual interest on my part in the Lorelei rock, the captain assembled the crew just as we passed the bend in the river, and commanded them to sing the melodic song by Franz Schubert which celebrates the story. "The beautiful maid sits gleaming on the rock and combs her golden hair . . ." they sang out lustily. I lifted my head to the heavens and gazed defiantly at the rock. At that moment I decided to *become* Lorelei, the siren who

153

breaks all men's hearts. Men would love me, but I would not love them. Love was for the young, the foolish, the unschooled.

"Magnificent!" I gave the captain a brilliant smile. "Truly magnificent," I murmured as the song of the seamen swirled around me.

The following day we left the broad river for the canal which connects it to the Weser, and thence through the flatlands of northern Germany to Bremen. The port itself, Bremerhaven, had been constructed just ten years before to divert much of the immigrant traffic from the overcrowded French port of Le Havre.

The two mysterious Prussians who had been conferring with Von Edel left us here. A makeshift city had sprung up around the new port, an untidy assemblage of wooden barracks-like buildings, windowless sheds, even tents, to house the thousands of emigrants who poured into the port from all over Germany and northern France. Many of them—whole families—had no shelter at all, but slept and ate on the rough wooden planks of the wharf until they could get berths on an America-bound ship.

"So many of them," I exclaimed from the window of our room in one of the older, more expensive hostels. "Germany is being emptied like a keg of beer. Why are they all trying to emigrate?" I looked down in pity at the crowd. Some sat tiredly on their sea chests, others stretched out on shabby cloaks, actually sleeping amid the din of loaded drays moving in and out, loading and unloading. Seamen milled about waiting for the tugs to take them to their vessels.

"Politics," Von Edel said briefly, "and hunger. Some, like us, have fallen out of favor with the government—you yourself are in great danger, Sieglinde, from the student rebels. I must caution you—"

"Yes, yes," I cut him off, not wanting another lecture on not disclosing my true identity as Ludwig's daughter. "But these people don't look politically dangerous to me."

"The potato rot has devastated vast areas of our country. The farmers are starving. Many have had their lands taken away by the banks—land which was in the family for centuries."

We lingered a week in Bremerhaven waiting for our ship. Von Edel forbade me to leave the hotel, but sent out for a seamstress. She and her assistant, a snip of a girl, man-

154

aged to run up an adequate wardrobe for me. "Hardly the wardrobe of a baronin," he remarked, "but it will do until we reach America. The fashions may be different over there. We don't want you looking like a greenhorn."

I was immensely pleased with the four frocks: two cotton morning dresses, one silk afternoon gown, and one rather showy black velvet.

"We may be asked to sit at the captain's table," he said. "And you will have also for dress occasions the blue and brown Heinz purchased in Mannheim." Another bonnet, an ankle-length wool cloak, an assortment of fine India muslin chemisettes completed my seagoing outfit. For shoes I still had to be satisfied with slippers, since a cobbler needed more than a week to make a sturdy pair of shoes.

The baron of course was already equipped with an extensive wardrobe consisting of fine linen shirts, heavy silk cravats, snug fitting white breeches which tucked into the tops of shiny leather boots. We made a distinguished-looking couple as we left the hotel early in the morning for the little river steamer that would take us and our luggage to the *Ocean Monarch*. She was by far the largest and most impressive of the various sailing steam craft which crowded the harbor.

"Two hundred thirty feet long, thirty-nine feet wide, thirty-one feet deep," crowed Von Edel. "And plenty of headroom in the cabins." You'd think he'd built the ship himself board by board. But I had to admit that with the huge paddle wheel amidships, and the snubnosed ends, so different from the slim graceful sailing packets, and the black smoke belching thickly from two big smokestacks, that she looked just like a fat comforting German hausfrau among a group of slender schoolgirls.

Von Edel rattled on praising the ship as we chugged across the inlet. "She's got sails of course, just in case the engines fail, but they won't. Finest in the Northern Star fleet."

I looked into the spray from the choppy water. "She's beautiful." I breathed to quiet him. "She's freedom," I said to myself.

We stood on the deck, awaiting a steward to direct us to our cabin, our two small seachests beside us. Suddenly Von Edel exploded. "*Verdammt!* What rotten luck. Look what's coming aboard."

A group of about twenty men were clambering up the

rope ladder from the tug that had followed ours. Young and agile, they fairly leaped over the rail in their eagerness to get aboard.

"Burschen," I exclaimed. But no—these were not quite like the students who had made me their "goddess" at Heidelberg. There were no saucy cocked hats, no beribboned chests. Instead the prevailing costume was large wide-brimmed hats and white shirts of a soft flowing fabric. Instead of the tight breeches and hobnail boots, they wore long trousers flaring at the ankle. Their shirts were open at the neck. Some had bright colored scarves tied loosely around their neck.

Von Edel leaned over the rail and spat into the ocean. "Forty-eighters! Intellectual swine. Rabble-rousers, malcontents. They've been leaving the country like rats scuttling from a sinking ship. Well, we'll just have to avoid them somehow. Just hope they'll all be put in steerage."

"Forty-eighters?" I turned to face him, puzzled.

Sliding his hand under my elbow, he guided me forcibly away from the rail toward the center of the ship. "Let's get to our cabin. They're bad news for us." Then, at my look of puzzlement, he explained. "The student revolutionaries who stormed Lola Montez's palace on the Barerstrasse and nearly disposed of you for good are called Forty-eighters, because of the year of the great rebellion. Now that their cause is lost for good, they're all shipping out for America."

"But," I protested, pulling against his arm, "shouldn't we greet them as comrades? Aren't we, like them, refugees seeking haven in America?"

The baron's handsome face darkened with rage. He didn't like me to argue with him. "No," he snapped. "Let's get out of their sight. I'll explain in our cabin."

The steward's man had caught up with us by that time, and engaged in low conversation with Von Edel. I took the opportunity to sneak furtive glances at the Forty-eighters as they streamed past us. None had much luggage. Some carried flimsy boxes, some musical instruments in cases. One rather small, chubby individual staggered under a large pile of books in a net bag. They stared openly at me. I wore the silk afternoon dress, my cloak flying open. I found myself smiling back.

Having settled our affairs with the steward, Von Edel dragged me into the companionway leading to the second-class section and we lost sight of them. But in moments the strains of a familiar song drifted over the noise of the ship. *Nun ade du mein lieb' Heimatland—Now goodbye my beloved homeland.* I longed to be out there with them singing the bittersweet melody of farewell. Despite my happiness at going to America, tears streamed down my face. I reached blindly into my reticule for a handkerchief and blew my nose vigorously.

Our cabin was little more than a closet. There was no porthole, merely a few slits at the top of the wall for air. A brocade bell pull hung by the door. Dark shining wood panelled the interior, giving off a rich but gloomy effect. One oil lamp was nailed to the wall, the other nailed to the small bedside table. Two bunk beds, one on top of the other, took up half the space, a commode and our trunks the remainder.

There was scarcely room for two people to move around. Von Edel slammed the door shut behind us, shoved me down on the lower bunk. His hand flew out to slap me across the face, first one side then the other. Then encircling my neck in a vise-like grip, he bent over me, his eyes glittering with fear and jealousy.

My heart was hammering so hard it thundered in my ears. This was a strange, new, savage Von Edel. "That's just a sample," he ground out between clenched teeth, "of what you'll get if I catch you even looking at one of those Forty-eighters. You're mine. I bought you. I own you body and soul."

I lay on the bed, stunned, too frightened to move. He drew off his pearl colored pants, folded them neatly, lay them carefully across the trunks against the wall. Without a word, he lifted my skirt to cover my face and took me like an animal, grunting throughout. I decided not to struggle. I did not want to die before reaching America. The moment the boat docked and we were on dry land again, I would disappear on the dock. It would be easy to do. Landing places were always scenes of mass confusion.

I sat up in bed and watched silently as he stood up and adjusted his clothing. "He is simply your ticket to America. Hold your temper," I told myself.

"Get up, make yourself presentable," he barked at me. Seeing that his temper had cooled, I ventured the question, "Why must we fear the Forty-eighters? This is an American ship, is it not? We will be under the protection of the American captain."

He reached into an inner waistcoat pocket, pulled out an official-looking document. "I am in the employ of Frederick Wilhelm, the King of Prussia. Bavaria is lost. Maximilian is no Ludwig. Germany must unite. The only monarch worthy of the name is the Prussian Kaiser."

Genuinely puzzled, I asked, "Then why are you going to America? Shouldn't you remain in Germany?"

He opened the cabin door, motioned for me to precede him into the passageway. "To raise money, you ninny, and to stop your precious Redbeard. He's in America right now keeping the revolution alive among the emigrés." His eyes glinted greedily. "Lothar von Hohenstaufen's death is worth a lot of money to the Kaiser."

We walked rapidly down the second-class companionway, past rows of closed cabin doors. Von Edel talked softly, rapidly. "I'm hungry. All this running has made me ravenous. I'm not in the habit of discussing politics with my women. You have but one job, my Valkyrie—to keep your body ready for me at all times."

The noise of singing and merriment reached us before we got to the door of the salon. German music, German talk. My heart quickened. I could bear anything Von Edel did to me for a few weeks. America was worth it.

The scene in the salon, which was midships behind the paddle wheels, was lively. Singing lustily, mouths wide open, beer steins in hand, a group of Forty-eighters was gathered around a small band. I grinned. We could have been in a Munich Ratskellar. The dining area was also inviting. I moved automatically toward a long table laden with an assortment of meats and vegetables and desserts. Beer and wine, even fresh milk, stood about in pitchers. I remembered seeing several cows being hoisted up into the vessel by rope.

A steward approached us, smiling. "If the baron and baroness will kindly make their choices, we will serve you at a convenient table."

Von Edel frowned, grabbed my elbow again. "Must they drive us out of the salon?" he muttered. Then to the steward, "The baronin and I will take our meals in our cabin. I will return to place our order—but my wife has developed a sudden indisposition. You understand."

We ate in the stuffy little cabin, my appetite ruined by

my keen disappointment at not being in a hospitable salon. "You are not to leave this cabin without me," Von Edel ordered. "With those Forty-eighters all about, and your natural whorish disposition—"

"Not even to use the privy?" I inquired archly, pointing to the commode that slid under the bunks. "Must I squat like an animal in front of you?"

He flushed. "I will escort you to the privy and wait outside in the companionway for you."

As it turned out, I didn't have to worry about the Baron accompanying me to the privy. Or to the salon. Or anywhere else on the *Ocean Monarch*.

By midnight, the movement of the ship as it got underway with the tide, combined with a freshening of the wind, had a disastrous effect on the old aristocrat. By dawn, my lover lay helpless on the lower bunk. He had vomited frequently and copiously during the night. His face was ashen. He could scarcely talk.

Trying hard to suppress my glee at such an unexpected turn of events, I said sympathetically, "What you need is some strong tea, laced with a soothing herb. I have something in my reticule." Before sailing, Bettina had warned me (she had read all the immigrant pamphlets) to carry some seasickness remedies. I had asked the seamstress in Bremerhaven to fetch something for me.

A pull on the bell cord summoned a fresh-faced young seamen. In my halting English I ordered some breakfast for myself and some hot tea for the baron. When it arrived, I engaged him in conversation, heedless of the baron's threatening glances. "You must pardon my English," I said. "But I have not practiced very much."

He laughed. "Your English is excellent—but you should come into the salon, madam, and talk to the other passengers. Most of our passengers are German emigrants, but we have a number of Americans also returning to their homeland."

A feeble protest came from the bed. "The baroness will not eat in common with the other pass—" but poor Von Edel never finished the sentence. He hung over the edge of the bed, sunk again in nausea.

"Pardon, Sir, but the aroma of your wife's meal is causing you further distress. It is wiser that she not eat in the cabin."

So it was settled. Jealous as he was, Von Edel could not deny me food. I spooned the tea into his mouth, as he lay exhausted on the pillow, and gradually his paroxysms subsided, and he fell asleep.

With a light heart, I donned one of my pretty morning frocks, a flowered cotton, decided against a bonnet—after all it was still August, and hot. I brushed my hair vigorously till it shone and was free of tangles, then piled it up loosely in coils, jabbing a few jeweled hairpins here and there to hold it in place. Finally, I laced a long violet ribbon in and out of the coils. I also decided against a cloak. Walking around a ship was hardly like walking down a street in Munich or Bremerhaven.

Once in the narrow passage, however, I couldn't resist turning the opposite direction from the salon to go back up on deck. I had to reassure myself that I was really out on the vast Atlantic Ocean. To my surprise, the wind was strong and a driving rain was blowing all over the promenade. There was no one at the rail. Bucking the spray I leaned over the rail, laughed uproariously into the wind, heedless of the salt spray drenching my fine new frock. It was cotton. It would dry quickly.

"*Bitte.* Pardon me." A voice from behind caused me to whirl around. A large red face loomed out of the wet. A burly sailor, very tall, dressed in the usual dark blue peacoat, a duffel bag slung over one shoulder, rushed past, bumping me slightly in his haste.

My heart jolted. That voice, the soft, Bavarian accent, was oddly familiar. I gazed at his retreating back a long time, until he disappeared in the mist. Forget it, I told myself, the ship is packed with Bavarians. They're all going to sound like Lothar.

The raw sea air had cleared my lungs of the foul smell of the cabin. I dove back through the hatch, headed for the salon. My dress was thoroughly wet by this time and clung like a second skin, outlining sharply every curve of bosom and hip. The strong wind had loosened a good bit of my hair from the coils so that it blew about my face like a cloud. I had a passing thought that I should repair to the cabin and make myself presentable, but somehow I felt more like a schoolgirl on holiday than a baronin of Bavaria.

"*Bitte, gnadige Frau, wollen Sie Bier?*" No sooner had I entered the salon than five of the Forty-eighters surrounded

160

me, all talking at once. Their eyes were filled with a genuine warmth and friendliness. Many had left sweethearts, even wives, behind. A quick glance around the salon told me I was the only woman present.

"Speak English to me, please," I urged. They buzzed around me, hurriedly introducing themselves as we moved toward a wide circular table next to a stove in which a roaring coal fire crackled merrily. All the furniture in the room was nailed firmly to the floor against the wild pitching of the ship.

I caught some of the names—Theodor Prange, Emil Poesche, Ignaz Fremden, Leopold Siegel. All bowed gracefully from the waist, sweeping their broad-brimmed hats across their knees to the floor. Leopold, a tall charmer with a rich cluster of blond curls and merry blue eyes, who appeared to be the leader of the little group, called for brandy. We arranged ourselves at the table, lifted our glasses.

"To America," sang out Leopold.

"To America," we chorused.

The heat of the stove, along with the general merriment and the sense of exhilaration from being free of Von Edel for a while, brought a warm glow to my entire body. I began to perspire. Leopold and the others told stories of their student escapades. I laughed so hard my hair fell down completely, untidily, about my shoulders. Tiny wet curls clustered on my forehead and cheeks. I pulled out the long violet ribbon, shook the coils loose. My hair lay in golden folds almost to the floor.

"That hair—I've seen it before," called out a little man with thick eyeglasses who had been quietly reading a book as we drank and laughed.

"Oh, Emil," Leopold responded. "Germany's full of girls with long golden hair."

"But not in Bavaria!" retorted Emil, reaching out a hand to pick up a long strand. He put it to his nose, sniffed. "From her accent, the baronin betrayes herself as a native Bavarian."

A silence descended on the group around the table, which soon extended to the entire salon. All eyes were upon us. Emil's voice rose to a shout. "You're one of them. You were with the whore the night we stormed the Barerstrasse palace. And I saw you with the Montez one day in the street. You were in a carriage with her—"

The little man rose, hurled his glass to the floor, smashing it into bits on the flowered carpet. "I do not drink with traitors—or whores!"

He stormed out of the salon. After a moment of stunned silence, Leopold said shakily, "It's nonsense of course, Frau Baronin. Please—you must understand, and forgive. Emil's fiancée was killed in the street fighting in Munich."

But the furtive shifting look of Leopold's eye told me that he, too, recognized me as Ludwig's bastard daughter. The brandy had loosened my tongue and I said boldly, "It's true what he said. I did live in the palace of Lola Montez. But I was not like her—I had no choice, Ludwig ordered me to——"

Leopold reached for my hands which were clenched tightly in my lap. "Forget it, it's all in the past, we're on our way to America where there are no kings, no concubines."

A large, corpulent, red-faced American had joined us in the commotion. He had apparently been drinking steadily all morning, for his voice was thick and slurred as he said, "Tha's right—stop talking politics. Boring subject anyway. In America, it's money that talks. Nothin' else." He waved a pudgy hand at the waiter. "Another round of brandy for my friends!"

The pudgy hand took mine away from Leopold. "Name's McGreevey, ma'am, Nathaniel McGreevey." He took the seat Emil had vacated. "Scotch-Irish, three generations in America." He leered at my bosom openly, but I could not be offended, he was so full of good spirits. I was grateful to him for relieving the tension. I let him squeeze my hand. I liked the warm, fleshy, sweaty feeling.

All of the Forty-eighters, except Leopold, moved away from the table, back to the little band. The music started up again, and the singing. After a third round of drinks, we were laughing helplessly at McGreevey's quaint, ribald descriptions of life in America.

"Ho, what's that now?" McGreevey looked toward the door, where a woman, dressed completely in black from head to toe, stood uncertainly.

Upon seeing me, her face lit up, and she ran to our table.

"Oh, thank God," she exploded, "a woman. Do you speak English?"

"A little," I smiled. Her delicate face was thin, drawn. I took her hand.

"Someone, please—I need help! I can't get anyone to answer the bell. I've called and called and finally I had to leave her—"

"Who? What is it?" She was trembling. "Are you ill?" I asked, concerned.

"No, not me," she replied, "my little girl, my Rosie." Tears streamed down her cheeks. She reached out to place a beseeching hand on my arm. "I don't know what to do"

I leaped up from the table, drew my hair back hastily, tied it in place with the violet ribbon. "I will come," I said calmly. "I know something of medicine."

As we raced out of the salon, I turned and shouted at McGreevey. "Get the ship's doctor, hurry," then followed the woman to her cabin. As we walked, she explained that she was a widow, her name was Lauretta Chambers, and she was returning to America, her home, after a stay of some years in Europe. "My husband was a diplomat," she said. "He died suddenly this summer in the terrible cholera in Paris."

She had undertaken, with her little daughter, the long overland journey from Paris to Bremerhaven because she'd been told that the German ships were freer from disease than the French.

"But now, in spite of all my precautions, I fear my child is deathly ill. I fear the cholera, which took my husband in just two days."

We were inside the cabin by now. The child was indeed a pitiful sight, the little face was white as the pillow on which it lay, the tiny eyes half open, glazed. Soft brown hair clung wetly to the sallow cheeks. I fought back quick tears, seeing my dead Kristina in her place.

I laid a hand on the child's forehead. "No fever, Mrs. Chambers. It is only the seasickness. My husband, the Baron Von Edel, is also suffering from it. I understand half the ship is down with it. That is why you could not get a steward. They are all busy tending the sick."

A ghost of a smile flitted across her pale face. "You're sure?"

"Reasonably sure—of course I am no physician. But I'm sure when he sees the child, the ship's doctor will concur with my diagnosis. In the meantime, I have an herb which has helped the Baron to fall into a peaceful sleep."

"You are a baroness? A real baroness?" Mrs. Chambers exclaimed, wonder in her voice.

I nodded, kissed the woman quickly, impulsively, on the cheek. I wanted to be friends. "Please—now that I will soon be an American like you, please call me Sieglinde."

"What a lovely name. I am Lauretta."

In moments I was back with the hot tea from the salon, and sprinkled in it a few grains of the herb from my reticule. Together we spooned some of the hot liquid into the limp little mouth. A loud knock on the door proved to be the steward with another man who carried a small drawstring bag.

"This is Dr. Gerhard," the seaman announced. "He will examine the child."

The doctor brushed past the seamen, entered the room head bent without acknowledging the introduction. He didn't look much like physicians I'd seen—no frock coat, silk hat, gloves—but simply wore the peacoat and black wool cap of the ordinary seaman.

"The poor wretches in the steerage have been keeping me occupied," he mumbled, moving immediately to the bed.

It was the same soft Bavarian accent I'd heard that morning on deck. The seaman who had bumped into me was the ship's doctor. Now he turned to look me full in the face as I stood behind him. "What have you given her?"

Amazed recognition flared between us. We both uttered a single word. "You!" in an indrawn whisper.

It was Lothar! The beard was gone, the shaggy brows had been dyed a dark brown, but there was no disguising the green eyes flecked with gold, the thin scar from mouth to eye.

But immediately the haunting, smoldering light in the green eyes changed to a cool impassive stare. The shaggy brows drew together in a straight line, as they always did when he was being stern and thoughtful. "I repeat madam, I must know what the child has taken internally."

My heart was knocking against my ribs. I was finding it hard to breathe. Mrs. Chambers waited for me to answer the question. Miraculously my voice sounded almost normal as I forced myself to speak. "Ah—it's merely an herb against the seasickness, to calm the stomach. My husband, the baron—"

The black wool head jerked up sharply, he rose from the

bed. "Your husband? Is he also ill? Why have you not called me?" The voice was angry, sharp.

I drew myself up to my full height, faced him squarely. He would not intimidate me any longer, I thought. "Yes. I am the Baronin Von Edel. We occupy Cabin 6, just a few steps down the companionway."

He turned abruptly, devoted himself to examining the child and spoke no further to me. I opened the cabin door, ran blindly down the passage to the door which led to the deck. On deck, the wind was still blowing, but the rain had stopped. I walked rapidly back and forth, the length of the ship, heedless of the curious glances of other passengers and the seamen passing by. My hair had loosed itself from the violet ribbon and blew around me like a cloud. I tried to sort out my emotions. After the first shock it seemed perfectly natural that he should be here, on this ship. He too was fleeing to America from his political enemies. He was a hunted man. Von Edel himself was hunting him down for the Prussian Kaiser. The disguise was natural, too. He had been a medical student at Munich.

I was filled with a towering rage—not against Lothar, but against myself. My blood was pumping furiously through my veins. My pulses raced. My mouth was dry. I still loved him. He could still make a simpering idiot out of me. With one glance of his sea-green eyes!

Suddenly I found myself in front of the hatchway opening which led to the steerage section. As Von Edel and I had waited on deck yesterday, I had seen the shabby poor—men, women, children, old, young, middle-aged— pouring into the black hole like so many cattle. My heart had constricted with pity at the time, and gratitude that I was not among them.

Now a heart-wrenching din, a mixture of weeping, wailing, moaning, and even raucous laughter, rose to greet me. I stood for a moment, uncertain, then plunged down the steep narrow steps. Something was leading me, something beyond mere earthly power. My muscles seemed to be acting on their own accord.

"Dr. Gerhard" had said he was occupied with the people down there. He would undoubtedly have to return below decks when he had finished treating Rosie Chambers. Halfway to the bottom the choking stench of packed humanity took my breath away. It was the smell of a thousand privies. It was like a dream of hell. The people were animals packed in a cage, with no sight of God's heaven but what they could snatch through a dirty smeared porthole.

A narrow aisle divided two rows of bunks which were stacked three deep, the space between so narrow a child would have trouble sitting up. Sleeping bodies lay everywhere so that I had to pick my way carefully to avoid stepping on outflung hands and feet. Old women with colorful peasant scarves marking their humble origins sat on boxes, staring meekly, dejectedly, at nothing, or making a feeble attempt to control the children who ran about wildly. A group of black-clad nuns sat on their luggage, reciting the rosary in a soft monotone. Several passengers crowded about them.

An old man walked about, sprinkling vinegar from a bucket onto the sawdust-covered floor. A baby snuffled at its mother's breast. A young couple, fully clothed, moved in the act of love, grunting and murmuring unashamedly in sight of all. Several older men looked on, their rheumy eyes glittering in the dim yellow light of the lamps swaying from the low ceiling. A bony hand reached out to grab my ankle as I passed. I stood, waiting, until the old peasant, grinning toothlessly, relaxed his grip.

At the far end of the ship, I spied a stack of boxes, trunks, bags—luggage and cargo, I presumed. I sat down, ignoring the stares of the curious. With my hair all about me, windblown, untidy, in the simple cotton frock I wore, I could easily pass for a young farm girl. I leaned back against rough wood and closed my eyes. Three glasses of brandy, the excitement of meeting a lover I had sworn to forget, the faint smell of tar and salt, worked their will on my body. I slept.

Chapter 14

A hand of steel clamped on my shoulder and sharp nails dug through the thin stuff of the dress. My eyes flew open to meet Lothar's deep, penetrating gaze. This time, he let the naked, haunted look blaze unashamedly. His other hand clamped on my other shoulder, I reached out instinctively to put my hands on the rough, weathered face. My finger traced the thin outline of scar.

For a long moment we stood thus, commanding time and space to roll back. We were alone once again on Kyffhauser Mountain. The whining horde of steerage passengers simply melted away.

"If ever you loved me," he said finally, speaking through lips which remained motionless, "you will protect my disguise."

If ever I loved him! Just the nearness of him set my senses reeling. All the cruel, biting words I had so carefully rehearsed through the long months of loneliness and despair were forgotten now, lost in the thunder of my bursting heart. I swayed toward him, waiting for his kiss.

The black head bent, the shaggy brows touched my forehead. Then, abruptly, he threw himself away from me. "Not here," he growled. "It is not safe, or seemly. I—I must see to the sick. You must return to your cabin."

"Lothar—Lothar—I must see you alone, I must talk to you, explain—" My voice rose hysterically. The old men who had been watching the lovers now turned their full attention to us.

Lothar pushed me roughly down from the box, started walking me through the narrow aisle. "Keep your voice down, act natural," he hissed. "It is too dangerous to talk here."

"Where then?"

He seemed confused. The hands on my shoulders tightened. My heart soared. He still loved me, or I wouldn't be having this effect on him. "In the surgery, behind the engines. Tonight. No—we must not be seen together. On deck is the safest place. Midnight, by the stack of lifeboats right next to the paddle wheel."

The rest of the day passed in a daze of dreams and plans. I could not eat, couldn't bear the thought of joining the fat American and the Forty-eighters in the salon. After tending to the still nauseated Von Edel, I climbed wearily into the upper bunk, tried to rest, but every nerve, every fibre in my body was singing: *Lothar, Lothar, Lothar.* I would see him tonight, alone. In the dark. At midnight.

I waited until she ship's bell struck eight times to announce midnight. The ship was quiet; even the noise from the salon finally stilled. A pale half-moon flitted in and out of a cloudy sky. There was the delicious smell of rain in the air. I worked my way stealthily to a crevice between the end of the stacked lifeboats and the framework of the giant paddle wheel.

My feet were bare, the dress was the same flowered cotton I had worn all day. I had made a pretense at piling my hair on top of my head. As I crouched against the wood of the ship, the strong, acrid smell of tar filled my nostrils. It was a good smell, cleansing and pure, after the foul, stuffy cabin and the steerage this morning. A sailor on watch walked past quietly but did not glance my way. The dull throbbing chug-chug of the engines drowned out even the splash of the sea against the ship.

"Sieglinde." A mere whisper out of the dark. His lips touched the tender lobe of my ear as he whispered my name.

"Lo—"

His hand, warm, moist, covered my mouth. "I warned you. I am Doctor Gerhard." He looked cautiously up and down the deck, slipped into the little space beside me. We touched, face to face, shoulders, thighs, knees.

"I want you," I whispered. "My woman's body wants you. There will be no talk." I pushed my breasts against him, slipped off the shoulders of the flimsy frock and leaned back. He could not deny me. I would not let him.

His lips brushed my nipples, hot, searching, then sucked greedily for a long time. Then he pulled back. "Wait."

Panther-like he bent down to the lowest lifeboat, slipped

off the canvas covering, lifted a number of long fragrant pine boards out of it. Carefully, without a sound, he slipped some of the boards into the top boat, some in the middle boat. "Damn fools," he muttered, "loading cargo into the lifeboats. If we should need them in a hurry, God help us."

At last, he extended his hand toward me, pulled me into the bottom lifeboat. It was actually below the level of the promenade deck. He had left some of the boards in the boat to make a kind of bed. As he slipped in beside me, he pulled the canvas top over us to hide us completely from prying eyes.

The pine smell was strong under the cover. We were back in the Cave of Venus on Kyffhauser Mountain. Roughly, he pulled down the rest of my bodice to my waist, then pushed up the skirt of my frock to meet it. His powerful hands were pulling my thighs apart, and the fine cambric undergarments I'd chosen with such care in Bremerhaven were being ripped ruthlessly open. In moments his manhood was inside me—a hard, silken sheath. In and out, in and out, harsh, demanding, ravenous. The thunderous chugging throb of the engines at our backs matched the stormy rhythm of our lovemaking.

Lothar's breath whistled into my ear as he reached for his fulfillment. I soared to meet it. His shout of triumph mingled with the noise of the engines. I moaned, twisted under him, tormented with the ecstasy that still eluded me. Desire still burned hot within me.

He rolled his heavy body off me, murmured panting, "You must forgive my hasty lovemaking, Baronin, but your nearness overwhelmed me. No doubt you are accustomed to a more gracious kind of coupling. I understand Frau Anna's girls make a distinct art of the whole business." His voice was like steel, a stranger's voice.

"Then—you know?" The warm tingle of desire in my blood slowly turned to ice.

The massive head turned. He pulled off the black cap. The shorn copper locks shone dimly in the faint moonlight. "Who doesn't? All of Europe knows about you and your "career." You weren't satisfied to be the mother of my child, the Hohenstaufen heir—you had to sneak off like a cat in heat, with a tomcat of a servant."

"No," I shrieked.

He clapped a hand over my mouth. "Be still, woman."

"No," I whispered hoarsely. "I loved your child as my

own body. The baronin—your beloved *Grossmama*—hated the baby. Lothar, you must listen—you must know the truth."

Again, the hand slapped across my mouth, this time knocking my head back against the hard boards. "Truth," he snarled. "In your mouth the word is a mockery. You've become the whore of the most infamous traitor of all—the notorious Baron Von Edel. The Prussian Kaiser has paid him to hunt me down and kill me."

"Dearest, I didn't know—he doesn't even know you are aboard."

"See that it remains that way. Or I would not hesitate to kill you both as you lie wallowing in your lust."

The hate in his voice told me it was useless to argue with him. This was neither the time nor the place. My beloved's soul was infested with the pestilence of hatred and distrust. Words at this time would be more than useless.

"Beloved."

"What is it now?" He knelt in the boat, adjusting his breeches, preparing to leave. He had finished with me. But I had not finished with him.

"I love you. I want you. Whatever I am, or become— that will never change."

I turned on him, pushing him down beside me with a violent thrust. "You will not leave me like this, unsatisfied. I demand that you love me again, and again, and again—"

Then I was all over him, hauling myself on top of his body. Our noses, lips, breasts crushed together. I slipped searching hands under the heavy peacoat, tossed it aside. My heavy breasts hung invitingly in his face. He took the bait. All the night long, as the ship's bells marked the hours, the engines throbbed beside us and the moon shifted uneasily in and out of the cloudy heavens, I lay with my lover. Demanding. Taking. We spoke little, only the murmurs, endearments, the shouts, the agonized groans of ecstasy.

That night I was transformed. In my night with Karl I had become a mother. Now I became a Valkyrie, demanding love from my god-lover.

170

Chapter 15

A stormy dawn streaked the North Atlantic sky as I crept back to my cabin, after extracting a promise from Lothar to meet me the following night in the lifeboat. I felt drained but exultant.

When I reached the woman's privy in the second class section, I met Lauretta Chambers, who was just leaving. "You're up early," she remarked.

"It is the baron," I replied, sighing heavily. "Even with the sedative herb, he is restless. I am up during the night with him. How is Rosie?"

"She is well, all thanks to you." She put a hand on my arm, smiled broadly. "I can't tell you how much you comforted me—but wait, perhaps I can." She reached into the black reticule hanging from her arm. "Here." She handed me a small white card. I peered down at it in the pale light of the lamp.

Leland Chambers. 18 Gramercy Park South, New York City.

"Leland Chambers is my father-in-law, Rosie's grandfather. We will reside with him. Being a diplomat, my husband never was able to establish a permanent home in America."

"Gramercy Park South," I repeated. "No. 18. A lovely name for a street. The baron and I will plan on calling on you when we are in New York."

"More than that," Lauretta said urgently. "If you need any help of any kind, or advice—" she hesitated, then plunged ahead—"forgive me, my dear—even money— please call upon us."

Then she was gone, too embarrassed to continue the conversation. How kind, I thought. Americans must be

171

lovely people. McGreevey had been kind, too. So affable and easy going.

Inside the cabin, I felt Von Edel's face. It was brittle and dry, and cold as death. For a moment, a wild hope surged within me—maybe he would die before we even reached America. No one would be surprised. The mortality rate on these Atlantic crossings was often fifty percent. At my touch, the lacklustre eyes flew open, lighted up momentarily with the old sardonic flash. "Always the whore," he whispered, then closed his eyes once more, dismissing me.

I slept the rest of the morning and through the afternoon, went to the salon at dusk for supper. Leopold Siegel approached me. "Good evening, Frau Baronin," he bowed gallantly. "We have missed you. Have you too caught the seasickness?"

"No," I responded, laughing, seating myself beside him on a low couch. "But the baron is very demanding, just like a child."

I had changed the rumpled cotton for one of the afternoon frocks, an elegant blue silk, with tiny rows of lace at neckline and wrists. My breast swelled whitely over the low decolletage. I leaned back on the couch, allowed Leopold to feast his eyes.

He leaned close, said in a soft whisper, "A perfect wife— and so beautiful too. It isn't fair."

Except for the two of us, the room was empty. Even the redfaced McGreevey was absent. "I'm afraid," explained Leopold, "that the malaise of the sea has thinned our ranks. The voyage threatens to become tedious."

A sudden bucking of the ship hurled us against each other. I straightened up and Leopold said, flustered, "A storm is brewing. Don't like the look of the sky. The whole ship's crew has been running frantically around fastening everything down."

Instead of being frightened, however, I became exhilarated. Leopold managed to catch a steward to order some brandy for us. We sat, as the darkness descended, sipping glass after glass of the rich, cloying drink. Leopold never took his eyes off me. A sense of my power swept through me. I could have him, I thought. I could have any man I want. But in my deepest heart I knew there was only one man who could satisfy my hunger. And *he* would be waiting for me at midnight in the lifeboat.

As the time approached, I looked anxiously at my companion. "Perhaps I should see to the baron. He may need something." Bidding Leopold a fond goodbye, I walked unsteadily down the narrow passage to the cabin. Gradually I became aware that my feet were getting wet through my slippers. A layer of water was sloshing about in the corridor, seeping under the cabin doors.

Thoroughly frightened out of my brandy-induced high spirits, I rushed into the cabin, shook Von Edel awake. He sat up, his grey head rumpled and struggled bravely to open his drugged eyes. "Look," I commanded, "sea water. The ship is sinking."

Groggily, he leaned over the bed, peered at the floor. Just then one of the trunks slid across the room, jammed up against the bunk, pinning his arm. "*Gott in Himmel*, a real gale," he shouted. "But I've been in worse than this on the North Sea. All ships roll about like this in a storm." He fell back on the pillow.

Disgusted with his lack of concern, and thinking now more of Lothar than of Von Edel, I threw on a warm cloak and ran out onto the deck again. Sheets of water were sweeping in great arcs over the rail and splashing against the bulwark and the lifeboat where Lothar and I had lain last night. I fell to my knees and inched my way along the ship, staying close against the bulwark until I reached my crevice of last night.

Then, suddenly, with a nerve-shattering sound, the steerage passengers tumbled, screaming, from the black hole of the hatch. "Holy Mother of God, save us—ten feet of water down there—we'll all drown like rats—would to God I'd stayed in Bavaria—better to starve than be eaten by sharks—"

Several burly seamen were attempting to push the crowd back down the hatch. But a lad of ten or so escaped them and ran out on the slippery deck. At that moment a giant wave crashed over the ship and we all watched horrified as the boy was swept out to sea.

"There, now, you see," the sailors shouted to the stricken crowd. "You're safer below. There is no danger of the ship's foundering."

The fearful mob crept quietly back down the dark stairway to await what fate held for them there. I crouched against the ship in my crevice. If an inch of water had seeped into our second level cabin, how deep must it be below decks? Lothar was down there somewhere, in the midst of that kicking, screaming mob!

Panic rose in my throat. I ran to the hatchway, pounded like a madwoman at the closed door. A giant hammer of a wave rose high over my head, smashing me to the deck. I sprawled, clinging desperately to the smooth wooden planks to keep from being washed overboard into the sea.

Slowly, agonizingly, I inched my way toward the lifeboats. A searing pain ripped through my shoulder and arm, as wave after wave crashed about me. The whole world had turned into one vast, cruel whirlpool of freezing water. After an eternity, I reached the bottom lifeboat. hauled myself painfully into it, lay there, my breath whistling in my throat. At least I'd be first in the lifeboat. I was safe. But Lothar—where was he?

Then gradually the roar of the crashing waves stopped, as if the gods had said "Enough." The violent lurching of the ship stopped. I peered out of my hiding place to see the moon shining brightly in the heavens. We would not sink, after all. Von Edel was right. One need only remain calm and trust to the mighty engines and the sleek lines of the ship to withstand the most violent storm.

The ship's bell tolled eight times. Lothar was there, suddenly, lying beside me. I clung to him like a dying person, spoke to him through chattering lips. "Lothar—must you spend so much time in the steerage? I feared for your safety during the storm."

His arms tightened around me. "It was pretty bad down there for a while. We had to extinguish all the lamps and the cooking fires. Just hope no one starts a fire, or lights a lamp when I'm not down there to watch them."

Next morning, I came out on deck to meet a brilliant September day, still, windless, but cold. Black smoke from the fat smokestacks drifted down over the deck, covering everything in sight with soot and cinders. Von Edel had taken a little gruel at dawn and was in better spirits.

Ten days—two weeks at most, the steward said, we would be in New York. I stood at the rail, my mind working feverishly. True to my promise, I had not spoken to Lothar of our situation, of my alliance with Von Edel or of what we would do when we all got to America. But that Lothar and I would be together, I did not question. I'd

174

work it out somehow. I laughed aloud at a school of fish darting in and out of the foamy water.

Lost in thought as I was, I sensed, before I actually heard, the excitement in the direction of the hatch to the steerage, a kind of buzzing as of bees in a pear orchard in August. The buzzing became a wailing—a bone-chilling, drawn-out keening. I turned to see once again the black mass of humanity thundering out of the black hole. Dear God, was there no end to their misery? At the same moment I heard the first terrible cry.

Fire! Once the dread word had pierced the sunny morning, I knew I'd been smelling it for some moments, but took it for the smoke from the ship's engines.

They tumbled all about me, pushing me to the rail, shrieking for the lifeboats. Black smoke poured out of the hole, along with the bodies, followed the next instant by the orange tongues of flame. Men were tugging at the lifeboats, cursing at the ropes that lashed them to the deck and the bulwarks.

Then the blue-coated seamen were there, moving among the people. "Keep calm, everyone—there's room in the lifeboats for all. Everyone will be saved," they chanted.

Precious minutes were lost in pulling the piled-up lumber out of the boats. My eyes smarted now from the heavy acrid smoke. Tears streamed down my face. Lothar! I must find him. If he perished in the fire—maybe, dear God, he was still down there! Life without Lothar was no life at all.

I worked my way through the screaming crowd, toward the hatch. I stopped a seaman running past. "The doctor!" I screamed, "Have you seen the doctor?"

He stared at me, wild-eyed. "Are you mad, woman? Get in the boat. It's every man for himself now."

"Women and children—women and children in the boats." A man stripped himself of all his clothes and jumped over the rail into the water. I watched him swim with a strong sure stroke toward a lowered boat.

"Every man for himself," the sailor said. My mind leaped. Von Edel! I must get to him. I had drugged him into sleep. The smoke would get to him before the noise. If the baron perished, I would be guilty of murder, as surely as if I'd poisoned him.

The narrow second-class companionway was choked with smoke. Somehow I held my breath long enough to

175

push into the cabin. The bunk was empty. Back out on deck, hot licking flames ran like darting swords from one end of the ship to the other. A piece of rigging fell burning at my feet.

"Please—help me, I must find my husband. I clutched frantically at a seaman who was guiding some children toward the rail and the waiting lifeboats.

Suddenly a voice boomed in my ear.

"Sieglinde! *Gott bedankt*, here you are!"

It was Lothar, the black cap gone from his copper hair, the stubble of beard clearly visible now in the glare of the flames.

He grabbed me, held me close a long moment. "Lothar," I sobbed hysterically, "I must find Von Edel. Please help me find him. I must save him."

He drew back as if I'd struck him. "So it's the old lecher whom you love after all." The green eyes widened with hurt and amazement. "After the last two nights you still ask for *him*."

"Come on," he said savagely, "I'll find your lover for you. If it's the last act of my life."

Flames licking at us, we stumbled through the hysterical mass of passengers. Some had climbed the rigging to escape the flames, only to be hurled back to the deck as the furled sails caught fire. It seemed impossible to distinguish one person from another.

But suddenly, miraculously, I caught sight of a familiar maroon silk robe. He was screaming, "I'm blind, I'm blind. Lead me to a lifeboat, someone." The Baron fell into my arms. I lowered him to the deck and cradled him against my bosom. His face was puffed up, with tiny blisters forming all over the aristocratic features.

"Don't die, Von Edel, don't die. You'll send me to hell if you do." I sobbed.

A wall of orange approached us, swept over us. Bits of wood flew through the air. One hit my shoulder, but I brushed it off, only dimly sensing the pain of the fire.

"Drop him. He's dead. Save yourself." Lothar pulled me away from the burning body of the baron. Then he was carrying me, lifting me over the railing. "Jump. You're a strong swimmer. Make for one of the lifeboats. Some of them are only half-full."

In moments I was sailing through the air. "No—no," I screamed, "not without *you*."

But with a mighty heave he threw me into the ocean. The water was icy, but I surfaced, the strong practiced muscles of my youth reacting instinctively. I turned to look back at the ship, searching desperately for the tall black figure with the copper head. Had he jumped too?

The sea was a mass of charred wood and bodies, some swimming, some floating face up. A faint pitiful cry sounded nearby. "Mama, mama." A little girl was clinging to her mother's body. I swam toward her, but she sank beneath the waves before I reached her.

The sun had risen high in the heavens, as the morning reached toward noon. I swam steadily away from the burning ship, toward a lifeboat that seemed to be almost empty. The men at the oars stroked rapidly away from the *Ocean Monarch*, fearful of an explosion from the engines. I could see swimmers trying desperately to reach the lifeboat, but the men ignored their piteous cries.

A noise like a million thunderclaps rent the air. A thousand fireworks shot up into the bright blue shy. Hypnotized, I gazed at the burning hulk, watched horrified as it plunged within seconds into the deep. A churning whirlpool formed around it, sucking the last of the passengers on board into the depths of the ocean.

"Goodbye, Baron Franz Von Edel," I chattered through frozen lips. "Thank you for wanting me—thanks for bringing me this far."

It was all bad dreams rolled into one. Treading water, I loosened the slippers from my feet, slipped off my dress. There. I could swim twice as fast in my chemisette. Resolutely turning, concentrating only on saving myself, I swam surely, vigorously toward the lifeboat I had seen earlier. Then my way was blocked by a nun, still in her habit, holding a small child aloft. "Please," she shouted over the waves, "save this child. You are a stronger swimmer than I."

She hurled the child at me even before I got to her. It was a light burden, but slowed me down. My breath rasped in and out of my tortured lungs. Now and then, through blurred eyes, I glanced at the child's face to make sure it was above water. The men at the oars continued to row swiftly away from me.

Resting for a moment, I laid my cheek against the child's. Thank God, she still breathed. Brown circles of freckles stood out on the pale cheeks, dark wet hair clung to the small head. I started in sudden recognition. It was Rosie, Lauretta Chambers's daughter. The poor young mother must have perished.

I prayed swiftly. "Kristina, Kristina, my own dear dead one. For you I will save this child." With a last desperate lunge, I covered the distance between us and the lifeboat. Rands reached out to haul us to safety: I fell into blackness.

When I opened my eyes, I saw nothing but a pair of hobnailed boots. I was on my stomach, my face turned to the side. My head was splitting open. I groaned.

"She's coming round. It's all right, then. Such a strong young woman. So brave, to save the child that way—but then that's a mother's love for you."

Another voice, vaguely familiar, gruff, replied, "The child is not hers. I met her on the boat."

The child. I must see Rosie. I pulled myself up, choked, spluttered, then fell back down again.

"Atta girl. Get it all out." Strong fists pounded into my back, then began a vigorous massaging movement. "Get it all out," the familiar voice continued. "You must have swallowed a bucket of sea water."

Then the hands were turning me around, face up. The red, fleshy face of Nathaniel McGreevey hovered over me.

"The child—Rosie—is she—"

"She's all right," he replied heartily. "Don't you worry about a thing."

I sank back on the floor of the boat, trying not to think of another lifeboat, with a layer of fragrant pine boards—

"Here now, don't pass out again." Something burned down my throat. "I guess we can spare a spoonful of this brandy for the little lady."

McGreevey's eyes were bloodshot, glistening. He lifted me up, carried me to one of the wooden seats, sat down beside me. As full consciousness dawned on me, I realized that I was almost naked. The thin cotton of my chemisette had ripped in several places. My nipples poked pinkly through the lace. Instinctively I folded my arms across my bosom.

"Here, slip this on, my dear." There was a tearing sound. The nun who had begged me to save Rosie pulled off her underskirt, held it out to me. Her veil was gone, but the white muslin undercap remained, preserving her modesty.

I slipped the heavy homespun garment over my head,

tied the drawstring over my breast. It felt warm and comforting. At least it was dry.

"Rosie, where is she?" I whipped around to look the length of the boat. An elderly man, wearing nothing but a frock coat over his nakedness, was holding the child in his lap. McGreevey reached back and put Rosie in my lap. She was awake, but the brown eyes held a look of wonder and shock. "Schatzie, schatzie," I crooned. "Sweetheart, you are alive. Your mama will be found. We have but to pray for it."

But she spoke not a word, simply clung to me. I enfolded her with the voluminous folds of the nun's skirt, glancing furtively round the boat. Twenty people, most of them men, about half of what it would hold. I sat leaning wearily against McGreevey, while Rosie slept.

The nun, whose name was Sister Prudentia, proved her name by producing a rather substantial hunk of cheese, which she doled out in little bits to each of the survivors. There was no water. The canteens which were fastened to the sides of the lifeboat were empty.

"Is that a shark?" McGreevey touched my arm excitedly. "See that hump over there?"

"Be still, you fool," a thick German voice yelled from the rear of the boat. "It's a dead body. Stop frightening the women."

Immediately Sister Prudentia picked up the crucifix that dangled at the end of the black rosary around her waist. She kissed it, and began to chant, softly, "Glory be to the Father, to the Son, and to the Holy Ghost."

In minutes, we all picked up the refrain. My lips moved in the timeless prayers I had not said since leaving the convent of the Benedictines. All afternoon we prayed, as we drifted slowly away from the other lifeboats. One decade finished, Sister Pruentia started another. The sun dipped over the watery horizon.

"Rosie, Rosie," I whispered into the soft hair, which had dried and lay in sort ringlets about the little face. She whimpered, made childish sucking noises in her sleep. I judged her to be four or five years old.

As night darkened the North Atlantic sky, I lay on Nathaniel McGreevey's broad shoulder, Rosie in my arms, thinking, reconstructing my life. I would become a nun. I would find Sister Paulita, in that place called Pennsylvania.

I would devote my life to serving the poor and the orphaned, such as this little lost one in my arms.

Our constant prayers must have pierced the wall of heaven, for at dawn we were sighted and picked up by the sailing packet *Maris Stella*. Just four days out of Liverpool, her white sails billowed gracefully in a brisk ocean breeze. She was the most beautiful thing I'd ever seen.

Since the packet was jammed with emigrants from famine-ridden Ireland, and the pestilence raged below decks, the twenty survivors of the *Ocean Monarch* were forced to bed down on deck. The concerned seamen supplied us with warm clothing and blankets.

"Plenty more where those came from," remarked one sardonically. "The dead don't need no blankets."

"But they are filled with the pestilence," I protested to McGreevey, "and maybe vermin too."

"Better than freezing to death," he answered, tucking me and Rosie securely into a wind-sheltered corner. "You'll know what I mean when night falls. We're headed for Canada; the ship's taking a far more northern route than the *Ocean Monarch*.

There was no extra food, but the ingenious McGreevey found us some ale and a loaf of hard bread just mouldy on the edges."Hardly a feast," he grinned, "but it'll sustain life."

The big man settled himself down beside us for the night. "Yup," he said smugly, "as I said, money can buy anything." He reached into his waistcoat, pulled out a handful of gleaming coins wrapped securely in a leather bag. "Your husband, the baron, perhaps he too will be picked up."

"I saw him die," I replied simply. "He is at the bottom of the Atlantic Ocean."

The pudgy fingers worked their way into mine. "Oh— sorry. But you have people, relations, in America?"

"No one, but there is a nun I knew."

"They will send you back, if there is no one to vouch for you."

I took the bait. "Mr. McGreevey, will you be my sponsor? And the child's?" I asked.

In the darkness, I felt his hands loosening the drawstring of Sister Prudentia's underskirt. Then his hot hands were on my bare breasts, caressing, reaching down to the waist. The big head bent down, the lips, moist, seeking, began sucking the nipples. "I will be your protector," he whispered hoarsely. "Or else you will be snatched right off the docks into white slavery, the child sent to an almshouse."

Rebellion rose swiftly within me, but died immediately. He was right. A protector should have payment. I could lose him in New York just as I had planned to lose Von Edel.

Next day, McGreevey managed to find a red velvet dress with a long train, which fitted me. A lace bertha covered the shoulders. "It's a bit fancy for the occasion," I laughed. "But I can't go ashore in a nun's underskirt. Where is the owner?" I asked fearfully.

"Very much alive," he smiled broadly. "She was easily persuaded to sell it. Said she could get three more in New York for the price I paid." Using the same techniques, he obtained warm cloaks for both me and Rosie.

"You look like a decorated Christmas tree," he said, after I had donned the frock. "At least it's warm," I said, grateful to the big man.

After a week more at sea, the exciting cry of "Land, land" ran through the *Maris Stella* like wildfire. Some fell upon their knees and thanked God for His mercy. Others capered about, shouting and singing. The steerage passengers emerged at last, yellow-faced and emaciated. They stared around them vacantly.

My first view of America, the Promised Land, was not to be New York, but the St. Lawrence River, hundreds of miles to the north in Canada. Because of the pestilence on board, every passenger had to be inspected by the health officer before being permitted to leave the boat. If sickness were found, a long stay in the Quarantine Hospital was guaranteed.

A half-hour later McGreevey, Rosie and I we were on the island, standing on the dock, waiting to board one of the numerous river steamers waiting at the wharf to carry emigrants south to the United States. After stopping at Quebec, we would sail through Lake Ontario, then to Albany by way of the Erie Canal. Finally the Hudson River steamer would take us to New York.

The *Naomi* was the largest of the steamships moored in the St. Lawrence, with two decks, and a magnificent salon twice the size of the one on the *Ocean Monarch*. A rich green and gold carpet stretched from end to end. Vast armchairs, sofas, and little tables were arranged invitingly for the comfort of the passengers. Crystal chandeliers blazed light even in the middle of the day. To my amazement enormous vases of fresh flowers stood about.

Walking to our cabin we passed a number of lifeboats lashed to the deck. Waves of unbearable remembrance washed over me. Lothar is alive, I told myself. I must not give him up yet.

The handle to our cabin door was gilt, the interior larger than the one Von Edel and I had shared on the *Ocean Monarch*, richly furnished in glossy wood. A handsomely bound Bible sat on the bedside table. Stubby candles burned cheerily in crystal holders with clear glass chimneys. There was even a small iron charcoal-burning stove.

"It's enchanting," I exclaimed. "Do all Americans travel in such grand style?"

"Those with money do," answered my companion. After a hasty wash-up at the lavatory in the corridor, the three of us, looking like a slightly overdressed, prosperous American family, proceeded to the salon for our noonday meal.

Once again I was overwhelmed at the profusion of food and drink spread out on the snowy white cloth. "So much," I murmured, "and so many new and different delicacies. How will I know what to choose?"

Rosie between us, we traversed the length of the buffet. Fresh fruit, looking as though it had just been plucked off the tree, every conceivable variety of meat—whole legs of lamb, fresh roast pork, ham, bacon, sausages and great slabs of beef which McGreevey called "steak."

He reached for a plate from a stack of them, placed a steak on it, with some potatoes and green vegetables. "There's a start," he said, beaming. I peered down at the meat, dubiously. "It's not cooked," I exclaimed. "The blood still flows from it."

Again the big man let out a whoop. "Try it. We call it "rare."

You're gonna love it, you'll come back for more."

With the help of a steward, we finished making our selections of food, and found a table with a view of the river. The salon was crowded, but there was no music or conversation among the passengers as on the *Ocean Monarch*. Everyone piled his plate high with food, sat down and proceeded to eat quietly, silently. McGreevey had finished a plateful and gone back for a second helping in the time I fed Rosie some custardy rice pudding. After a few bites, the weary child fell sound asleep against my bosom. I ate spar-

182

ingly of the rich, heavy beef and rather enjoyed finishing my meal with some cheese and apple. The air in the salon was thick with cigar smoke. All of the men were drinking heavily. McGreevey downed three or four large tankards of rich dark ale. I sipped some light wine.

It was three o'clock before we retired to the cabin. Rosie curled up in a pile in the upper bunk. I covered her tenderly with the wool blanket.

Our accomodations on the *Maris Stella* had not been conducive to sleep. I looked forward eagerly to crawling into the lower bunk. Without a word, we both undressed, silently, quickly. McGreevey smelled of beer, steak, cigars, and sweat. He stood aside, motioned for me to crawl into the bunk before him, against the wall. "Wouldn't want you to roll out during the night," he whooped. Then he pinched me heartily on each buttock.

"Ouch!" I turned, prepared to be angry, but instead found myself giggling. I bit him lightly on the neck. He bit back, first on my neck, then on each breast. We wrestled playfully, then becoming impatient, he mounted me. My loins flamed in response. It seemed the most natural thing in the world to be here with this man, moving, sweating, in the timeless act of love. What else does one do after eating a hearty meal, after being rescued from a fire at sea? One affirms life. I let myself be sucked into his vibrant masculinity. Tomorrow I would think of Lothar and love. Tonight I belonged to this rich, strong, virile American.

Half expecting him to be a crude lover, I was pleasantly surprised. He moved in and out of me expertly, lifting his heavy body easily, with the sure instincts of a fine animal. Shouts of pleasure came from us as we reached simultaneously for a shattering fulfillment.

Afterwards we slept, back to back, buttocks pressed together, the rest of the afternoon, through the long night, waking with the sun the next morning.

At Montreal our steamer docked for five hours to unload and pick up passengers before moving into the waters of Lake Ontario. Nat left the boat to go into the town and returned carrying two large leather portmanteaus of clothing for his little "family."

"Pretty provincial stuff," he apologized as he spread out the things in the cabin for my approval. "But once we're in New York, I'll buy you a roomful of Paris gowns."

PART III

New York

Chapter 16

Finally, on a raw October morning, when the mist hung thick over the Hudson, we steamed into New York. The *Naomi*'s whistle echoed hoarsely as we blasted our way through the forest of ships' tall masts and smokestacks to moor at the river's edge, along with hundreds of vessels of every kind.

Hurriedly dressing Rosie and flinging on my heavy cloak, I ran with her on deck, leaned on the rail and raked the busy scene with hungry eyes. By the time the ship settled in its berth and the gangplank was lowered, the sun was up. My first impression of the fabled city was one of brilliant sun shining on roofs and church steeples. At least, I reassured myself, New Yorkers are God-fearing people.

McGreevey's gold greased our way through the immigration procedures. I had no passport, nor did Rosie. No one in the city knew me. There was only my word that I was a decent, self-supporting, law-abiding emigrant. I feasted my eyes on the wharfside tumult. There were the usual drab dockside buildings—shipping offices, cargo buildings, saloons, seedy hostels. Carts, wagons, and shabby hacks jostled for space on the wooden wharf with fine lacquered private carriages.

A small boy, with a face black as coal, sidled up to us. "Fetch a hackney, Mister?" He looked up at McGreevey, grinning amiably.

"Sure." McGreevey threw him a small coin, which the lad bit before stuffing it into his ragged pocket. I stared at him unashamedly. He was the first Negro I had ever seen.

Immediately, an open carriage pulled up in front of us, the driver restraining with difficulty a pair of matched bays. "You'll have to do for yourself," he shouted down from his perch. "Can't let go these animals in all this hullabaloo." McGreevey picked up the portmanteaus, threw them on the luggage rack. "Come on," he shouted irritably, "let's get out of this mess."

Swooping Rosie up from the wharf, he plunked her down hard on the high leather seat. She looked frightened, her brown eyes soft with unshed tears. I lifted my foot to step, then turned, hesitating. A stream of people were going in and out of the door of a long unpainted wooden building over which swung a large lettered sign that read GREAT WESTERN SHIPPING OFFICE.

McGreevey's hands were boosting me up. "Should we not inquire about the survivors of the *Ocean Monarch*?" I inquired. "Before we leave the docks, that is. Perhaps Mrs. Chambers, Rosie's mother, has been picked up."

And Lothar, too, I said to myself. Lothar may be out there somewhere in the dockside mob, looking for me. But the big American shook his head, sat down beside me, leaned over to speak to the driver. "The Astor House, and make it snappy." Then to me, "Our misbegotten vessel was owned by the Northern Star Lines, and sailed from the East River, the other side of the city. They'll have the list of survivors over there."

"When can we—" I started to ask, but my question was lost in the shouts of the driver and the shrill clatter of the carriage wheels as we careened bumpily onto a narrow cobblestoned street. I stared about me, open-mouthed, clutching Rosie desperately with both arms to keep her from falling out. The city was like a thousand Munichs on Corpus Christi Day. Not only was the narrow street choked with vehicles of all kinds, from closed carriages to open wagons loaded with ice and hay and boxes tied precariously together with baling ropes, but pedestrians darted in and out of the traffic like scurrying rats, seemingly unconcerned about life and limb.

"Look out," I screamed as we nearly collided at a busy intersection with a long horse-drawn carriage.

"An omnibus," McGreevey said proudly. "It can handle forty people at a time."

"Looks more like sixty packed in there," I remarked, looking back in wonder. Had we survived fire, shipwreck, the vast Atlantic Ocean itself, only to be slaughtered like sheep in the New York streets?

Eventually we left the congested riverfront district and entered a street which appeared to be considerably wider but was no less crowded. Tall buildings, some five and six stories high, towered on either side. "Welcome to Broadway, the greatest little street in the world," shouted my companion. The Astor House was a tall marble structure, which stretched almost an entire block along Broadway. A liveried footman stepped up smartly as our carriage halted in front of the broad marquee, and extended a black-gloved hand to help me alight. I looked down with distaste at the filth in the gutter. Inside the hotel, however, a different world emerged. A large brilliantly lit foyer swarmed with smartly dressed men and women. A number of the women appeared to be alone.

Following my glance, McGreevey remarked, "A man need never be lonely in New York." He paused, looked at me significantly. "Entertaining the male sex is just about the best way for a woman to earn her keep in New York."

We were given a large room facing Broadway.

"Looking out at the passing parade will keep you occupied—and out of mischief—when I can't be with you," he grinned as I sank down gratefully on a luxurious velvet couch and rested my feet (after slipping off my dirt-encrusted shoes) on a hassock with a richly embroidered cover. My eyes swept the room, feasting on loveliness: delicately shaded wallpaper, accented by fine wood panelling on doors and windows, an ebony table with mother of pearl inlay, sofas and chairs upholstered richly in crimson and gold.

"That mirror's nine feet high." McGreevey stood in front of it, preening, smoothing back his iron-grey hair with a practiced hand, before replacing the high silk topper.

"It's finer than anything I've ever seen in the king's palace," I gasped in admiration.

He shot me a quizzical look. "And what would you know about the king's palace?"

"Well—" I stammered, then quickly recovered. I'd almost revealed my true identity. "You forget, sir, that I was the wife of a baron of the kingdom of Bavaria. I grew up in the court."

His laugh came quick and boisterous from the marble-topped commode where he was splashing water on his face. In a few quick strides, he was beside me, pushing his wet face into mine. "All right, sweetheart, you can stop the game now. You're no more a baroness than I am king of New York. You are a whore. Pure and simple. Well—

trained, I will admit, but still, for all that a whore, every bit as much as those gals strolling around in the lobby downstairs."

Rubbing his big face dry with the towel, he threw it on the floor. "But I'm not complaining. You just go on doing what you've been doing in bed, and I promise you a full belly and a queen's wardrobe."

A little tug on my skirt reminded me that Rosie was listening to all this. "The child," I whispered, panic in my voice. "Please be careful."

"Damn the child." The face that had shown such kindness on the *Maris Stella* and the river steamer now became ruthless and cruel. "Get rid of the brat. Today. Take her to Gramercy Park. I've got to run off now—business to attend to. When I come back tonight, that kid better be with her relations."

Then he was gone, after promising to order a carriage for us downstairs at the desk.

He was right, of course. We had done what we could for Rosie, all that anyone could expect in the name of Christian charity. Now it was up to her family to care for her and search for her missing mother. Rosie had run to the window, stood looking out at the Broadway traffic below, her brown eyes wide open, her face alight. In her excitement, she leaned out so that her little feet lifted off the floor. I ran to close the window.

"Don't ever lean out like that, darling," I said, pulling her inside. "You'll fall out—and it's six stories to the sidewalk."

" 'Linde, 'Linde," she said. My heartstrings caught. It was the first words she'd spoken since I'd picked her out of the water. She was repeating my name. Seeing my wide grin, she repeated, " 'Linde."

"Tante Linde," I prompted. I knelt down, clutched her to my breast. Tiny arms encircled my neck.

"Tante Linde," she whispered in my ear, then broke into childish laughter. Overcome with emotion and relief that she had finally come out of the stonelike silence, I wept for the first time since the day Von Edel had taken me from Frau Anna's.

I rang for fresh water, washed the grime off Rosie's face and hands, and dressed her in the pink frock and fur cape McGreevey had bought in Montreal. I still wore one of the muslins, although I knew it to be extremely out of fashion, judging from what I'd seen in the Astor lobby downstairs. The bright flowered print, very full skirt, heavily embroidered flounces, made me look like a peasant dressed up for a feast day. By now it was noon, and the sun had vanquished the earlier threat of rain. I donned the heavy cloak, which hid most of the dress and fitted on one of the simple bonnets.

We would pass, I decided, as we stood in front of the tall mirror. Then we walked down five flights of carpeted stairs to the lobby to await our carriage. As we walked, I talked to the child to make sure she didn't lapse back into her long silence.

"You're going to live with your grandfather. Won't that be nice? They live in a lovely house in Gramercy Park."

She looked up at me, a wondering look in her childish eyes. "Mama, Mama?" Her voice was faint, as if she were uncertain.

"Her too," I said with a forced gaiety, "and grandfather."

"Mercy Park," she chanted, mimicking me, "Mercy Park."

"No. 18, Gramercy Park," I instructed the driver, then settled back on the leather seat, busy with my own thoughts. She is not yours, I told myself. You knew you would have to give her up. You can have children of your own. Someday. Someday. But when? I had borne two, lost two. My own true love, the only man whose children I would ever want, the only man who had truly captured my soul, lay in the chill waters of the Atlantic Ocean. Or did he?

I glanced out the little window on my side of the carriage. The line-up of cabs, wagons, gigs, omnibuses was if anything thicker than it had been on the waterfront. Lothar could be out there, somewhere, anywhere. We could pass each other in the street and never know it. Once I delivered Rosie to her grandfather, I would simply order the driver to take me to the East River. If there was any news of Lothar, I need never see McGreevey again.

A shriek of delight from Rosie brought me out of my reverie. Our carriage had stopped, completely hemmed in by the crush of afternoon traffic. The rider swore softly, continuously. A fat black-eyed man stood right next to our carriage, squeezing an accordion. A spry brown monkey hopped from one of the man's shoulders to the other, doffing his little green cap in response to Rosie's laughter. Excited squeaking sounds emerged from the animal's mouth. Soon my laughter joined hers. My spirits lifted. Live for today. Lothar was alive. I would find him. A church, a magnificent Gothic structure much like the Marienkirche in Munich, caught my eye. Of course! There was Sister Paulita. I would find *her*, ask *her* for shelter until I could find some useful employment. The pastor would know of her, surely. Comforted now that I had a plan, I relaxed and enjoyed with Rosie the remainder of the long journey up Broadway.

Eighteen Gramercy Park South was a neat brick residence exactly like the others which surrounded a small green grassy park bounded by a spiked iron fence. Wide white marble steps, immaculately clean and glittering in the afternoon sun, led up to a curved portal, faced with marble.

"Impressive," I murmured. "Rosie may be an orphan, but at least she'll not be in want."

A maid in a neatly pressed uniform, white lace cap on her dark curls, answered my knock.

"Please inform Mr. Chambers that I wish to speak with him."

"Who?"

"Mr. Leland Chambers. I believe this is his residence."

She looked me up and down, then said, "You a Dutchie? You looking for work?"

"Am I a what?" I responded.

By this time another maid had joined her. They stood in the doorway, regarding me and Rosie. They giggled. "You sure talk funny."

"I have just emigrated from Germany," I said stiffly, offended at their rudeness. "You talk funny too. Where did *you* come from?"

"Ireland." Then, making to close the door, she said, "Nobody here named Chambers. You got the wrong house."

"Is this No. 18 Gramercy Park South?"

"Yes, but—" She reopened the door, looked at us thoughtfully. "That name Chambers rings a bell. Wait, I'll go ask the mistress."

A tousled imp of a little girl peered out at us through the lace curtained window. Rosie stared at the girl, who promptly stuck out her tongue, pressing it flat against the glass.

In moments, a dark-haired young woman appeared. "I

am afraid you have come a year too late," she said softly. "May I be of assistance?"

"Do you know where I can find Mr. Chambers? It is most urgent that I locate him." I pointed to Rosie who stood quietly at my side. "This is his grandchild, Rose, whose father is dead in France, and whose mother was lost at sea."

The woman clapped a soft white hand to her mouth. A diamond ring on the fourth finger sparkled richly. "Oh, merciful heavens. How tragic. How very tragic. They died, the old man and all the servants, in the great cholera last summer. We moved into the house right after Christmas, months later. And I—I'm afraid there are no relatives, except a son who was in the diplomatic service—but, of course, that would be the child's father."

"Who is dead," I repeated flatly.

The street lights glowed in a murky twilight as Rosie and I left 18 Gramercy Park South. Mrs. de Hoeck had promised to send word to the Astor House if Lauretta Chambers showed up. The driver of our carriage sat on his high seat, asleep, his head deep on his chest. I shouted up at him.

"Please take us to the East River docks, please. To the Northern Star Shipping Company," I commanded, hoisting myself and Rosie up the high step.

He shook his head groggily. "Nope. The gentleman said only to take you here. Nowheres else."

He flicked the reins and we started the long, slow trek back down Broadway to the Astor House. My mind was troubled, but I was not really worried about McGreevey's reaction when I returned with Rosie still with me. He surely would understand that I simply could not dump the child in the streets. If he caused any trouble, I told myself, I would simply pack up and leave him. I didn't need him. There were three maids in Mrs. de Hoeck's house. I could find employment quick enough while I waited for some news of Lauretta Chambers. I was a mere seventeen, and strong.

The sweet haunting sounds of church bells filled the air. Must be six o'clock. We were approaching the intersection where Rosie had laughed at the monkey and where I had seen the beautiful church. "Stop the carriage, please," I pounded on the wooden driver's seat. "We will get off here and walk the rest of the way."

A sweet-faced young Irish girl ushered Rosie and me

into one of the many receiving parlors in the rectory of the great church. A young priest, also Irish, judging from his rich brogue, appeared shortly.

"Yes? You asked to see the pastor. I am one of the curates. May I help you?"

His face was kind, his eyes tender and compassionate. I found myself pouring out the whole story of the fire, of our rescue at sea, and of searching for Mr. Chambers, only to be told of his death.

"So you see, Father," I finished. "The child and I are quite alone in America. Except for a nun—Sister Paulita of the Benedictines from Bavaria. She emigrated to a place called Pennsylvania. I—I thought perhaps you would know of her address—" I stopped, feeling suddenly foolish.

He lifted handsome black brows. "Pennsylvania? That's a long trip by stagecoach from New York. Do you have any money?"

"No. Nothing. These clothes came from the kindhearted charity of another survivor."

He reached into a drawer of a small desk, pulled out a piece of paper, wrote something on it. "Here is the address of a shelter for destitute females and orphans. They will take care of you until you can find employment. As for your Sister Paulita, I'm afraid I have no knowledge of her. America is a vaster place than you can ever imagine."

Out on the street again, I looked at the address. Someplace in the Bowery, I read. There was no money in my reticule. My stomach told me it was suppertime. Darkness had descended completely now. There was no help for it then. We would have to return to the Astor House and face Nathaniel McGreevey.

Nathaniel McGreevy was livid. "What in the—" He whipped around angrily, turned his contorted face toward the child. "That brat still with you?" Sweeping up a half-empty bottle of whiskey from the little table, he lifted it to his mouth, drank long and deeply.

Then he stretched his great bulky body out on the couch, started unbuttoning his trousers. "C'mere, girl. Been waitin' long enough as it is." His voice was thick and slurred. I tried to elude him, but his hands grabbed hold of my skirt, pulled me down on top of him.

"The child," I whispered hoarsely. "Let me go."

He ignored my pleas, started rooting with his mouth under my neckline. "To hell with the child." He gave me a shove. I fell on the floor. "We'll just take care of the brat first—then to the business of the evening."

The drunken man lurched menacingly toward Rosie who, seeing his face, started to scream. Before I could get to my feet, McGreevey grabbed her, forced the little mouth open, poured down a quantity of the raw whiskey. She gagged and choked, the tears streamed down her frightened face. Rosie fell to the carpet. I picked her up, cradled her against my body, her face hidden from the drunken McGreevy. I edged toward the door.

Sensing my intention, he put down the bottle, moved toward us. "Oh no, you don't, my little whore. You still owe me—" A loud cracking sound filled my brain. McGreevy smashed a hammy fist right into my cheek. The room spun around. A thousand firecrackers went off in my head. Fiercely, instinctively, I bent my head to shield the child.

He pinned us against the door, arms spread on either side of the wall, his face close, menacing. Rosie whimpered against my cloak. I thought fast. If I persisted in trying to escape, he might do actual physical harm to the child. I moved to the chair, sat down quietly, rocking her back and forth in my arms. Eventually Rosie fell asleep, enough of the whiskey having gone down her throat to bring on a blessed unconsciousness. I laid her gently down on the couch and covered her with a blanket from the bed.

Then I turned back to the drunken McGreevy and started taking off my garments. In an instant he was upon me. The fluffy peasant-like cotton dress was torn to shreds as he drove himself into me again and again. He sodomized me. He chewed the moist parts of my body—my mouth, the deep place between the thighs. I endured it all, throughout the long night, hoping only that Rosie would not awake and witness my degradation. I had always been told that a man sodden with liquor became impotent, but this man put the lie to that.

I woke to a pounding on the door and to Rosie's muffled weeping. McGreevey was gone. Wrapping a blanket around my nakedness I opened the door to a uniformed hotel maid.

"Have orders, ma'am, that you are to vacate the room by seven. Being that it's nigh six, thought I'd best check on things—" She gasped, her blue Irish eyes wide with shock. "Merciful Mother of God, what happened to you?"

"What do you mean?" Gradually I became aware of a dull throbbing pain on the side of my head. I stepped over to the nine-foot mirror. The left side of my face was horribly swollen. A deep purple bruise stretched from forehead to chin. "I—I had an accident walking back to the hotel last night—" I said weakly, but I never finished my excuse.

The maid's eyes became dark with compassion. "You poor thing," she murmured, "he must have had the drink in him for sure. I'll fetch you some ice for that—though it's probably too late now to do any good."

"No—don't go, please. Don't leave me." I reached out to the woman, like a drowning man to a raft. "The child and I are quite alone. I—I don't know what to do. We were shipwrecked and have nothing—I know no one in America except the man who—"

Strong arms took hold of mine, drew me softly to the ample white bosom. "There, there now, don't take on so. Bad enough for the kid to be cryin' without you startin' the waterworks too. I see the likes o' you every day at the Astor House."

Her voice had that soft lilt to it that I had noticed in all the Irish I'd met—the maids at Gramercy Park, the young priest. We sat down on the bed. Her strong fingers began kneading the muscles in my arms, working their way down my shoulders and back. "Hmm. Nothing wrong with you. Good body. If you don't mind a bit of scrubbin' and emptyin' slopjars and such, I can get you on here at the hotel. We got a reg'lar army of chambies workin' here."

"Oh, anything, anything," I smiled through my tears. "All I need is enough money to get to Pennsylvania and take care of Rosie."

She nodded, her dark curls slipping out of the white muslin cap. She reached out a work-reddened hand to tuck in the wayward strands. "One thing at a time. First, you two will have to get out of this room." Her eyes clouded over again with sympathy. "Happens all the time. Men have their fun, go off leavin' the poor girl with a kid."

"Oh, it's not like that. I—I lost my husband at sea. It was a fire—"

"Just as you say, love. You don't have to tell me a thing." She made for the door. "My name's Annabel O'Toole. Get something on and come down to the kitchen. Ask for me."

After she'd gone, I threw on the other cotton frock from

Montreal, dressed Rosie quickly in her rose outfit, stuffed the torn dress and our cloaks into the portmanteau which McGreevey had left us. Then, following Annabel's orders, we walked down six flights of stairs to the underground kitchen. We entered a steaming wonderland of good food smells, and bustling cooks tending great vats and skillets on a gigantic black cookstove which stretched the entire length of one wall. Enough cutlery and pots to fill ten tinkers' shops hung from the wooden rafters overhead. A whole army of white-clad men and women sat at long tables eating breakfast.

Annabel rushed up to us as we stood uncertainly in the doorway. "Come on. Breakfast gong'll sound in half an hour, and we'll have to start makin' up the rooms while the guests are eatin'. The boss says any friend o' mine is more than welcome. But you got to work hard."

Her arm swept toward the stove, as she pushed Rosie and me down on a long bench. "Gas," she said proudly, "everythin' in the hotel is gas, 'ceptin' some of the rooms still has candles. Some folks don't like the smell o' gas."

Rosie and I helped ourselves to generous helpings of steaming oatmeal, fried eggs, crispy bacon. There was even a tall glass of cold milk for the child.

"My, your little girl sure has a good appetite. She'll get rid of that puny look in no time." Annabel hovered over us, beaming.

Our meal done, we followed Annabel into a filthy alley directly behind the hotel. Like all gutters in the streets of New York, this one was running with refuse, both human and animal. A row of ramshackle unpainted wooden buildings flanked the other side of the alley, which bore the unlikely name of "Prosperity."

The O'Toole family home consisted of two very small airless rooms in the rear of one of these buildings. Annabel led me through a narrow, pitch black hallway to a room with one tiny window facing a sunless courtyard. I glanced out furtively. Some ragged children played on a heap of rubbish. The door of a rickety wooden structure swung on one hinge to reveal a common outhouse.

"We work and eat in this one," Annabel was saying, "and sleep in the other." The wood floor of the other room was covered completely with filthy mattresses. Several greyish blankets and a few lumpy pillows were spread about. The place had a rank close smell of unwashed flesh.

We returned to the kitchen. A swarm of chattering, dark-haired, blue-eyed children, ranging in age from infancy to about ten, stood around a large wooden table, shucking oysters. Besides the table and an old wood cookstove, there was no other furniture in the room.

" 'Taint much," Annabel said, a wry smile on her pleasant features. "But at least it's dry. Don't do no cookin' since Tom, my husband, brings all our food from the hotel. Oh, here he is now."

A burly Irishman stooped as he pushed inside the narrow doorway. Each hand carried a large bucket of oysters. Annabel put an affectionate arm about his big shoulder. "He keeps an eye on the kids for me," she explained. "His job is to keep all the houses around here supplied with oyster work."

Tom smiled at me, revealing two rows of gleaming white teeth. He reeked of masculinity and good health. Even the children's dirty faces were pink and glowing.

Although my nostrils rebelled at the fish odor of the oysters combined with the sharp odor of human flesh and urine, and excrement from the privy in the courtyard, I smiled at Annabel in gratitude. Anything was better than a public almshouse, or the shelter recommended by the young priest. At least both Rose and I would be earning our keep. It was agreed that she and I would share a mattress for one dollar a week. My wage as a chambermaid was to be three dollars a week and all the food the both of us could eat.

The children shrieked when they saw Rosie's beautiful pink dress, gathering round her and chattering like children anywhere. But immediately Tom ordered them back to work. Rosie took off her cloak and fell in with the crowd, an apt pupil.

"They ain't all my kids," Annabel explained as we made our way across the alley to the hotel. "Just five of 'em. Some of the kids in the neighborhood work in our kitchen." I learned also that the patrons of the big hotel consumed "millions" of oysters each day. "Some like 'em fried, others slip 'em down raw," she said. "But mostly it's stew oysters that's needed. As fast as the kids can shuck 'em."

I spent the next two hours filling large soup bowls with the famous milky oyster stew. Each bowl cost fifteen cents and contained at least twenty small oysters and a pat of butter. Bread, butter, relish, and salad made up the rest of the meal. Like all of the big hotels in New York, the Astor House featured a free lunch. For the price of a drink or two, a patron could have all the food he wanted between the hours of twelve and two.

Annabel outfitted me in a voluminous white muslin uniform which wrapped around the waist and tied in the back. A matching ruffled cap covered my hair. She stood back to survey me. "By God, Sieglinde, even in this tent you look luscious. You'll have to step lively, I'm thinkin', just keepin' ahead of the pinchers."

"Pinchers?"

She answered my question by reaching out with her hand and giving me a hearty pinch on the buttocks.

"Oh—that!" I laughed shakily, remembering McGreevey's habit. "Don't worry, I can handle anything. I'm as big as most men. And stronger."

By nine o'clock that night, I wasn't so sure. Most of my day had been spent dodging wandering hands, answering a firm "no" to offers of bed and board for "favors" rendered, and in one instance, actually running out of the room and down two flights of stairs, with a drunken patron in hot pursuit. Apparently being a "chambie" at the Astor House was a hazardous occupation, involving a lot more than emptying slopjars and making up beds. By the time I got back across the alley, to the O'Tooles' two rooms, the moon was up, and I was bone-weary. My stomach churned from the tension and excitement of the unaccustomed activity.

Rosie was fast asleep, still in the pink frock, her soft brown hair spread spiderlike on the filthy mattress. After covering her with her fur-lined cloak, I flopped down beside her and threw a protecting arm across her tiny body. She smelled to high heaven of oysters. In moments, still wrapped in the white muslin chambie uniform, I too had dropped off into a deep, dreamless sleep.

Chapter 17

A week passed, one day following another in the same pattern. I never saw Rosie awake. She was asleep when I left at dawn to report for breakfast to the hotel kitchen and asleep when I returned after dark. Tom O'Toole reported that she was doing fine. "A real little worker," he said. "Puts out her share."

Her "share" came to fifty cents a week, for working most of the day over an oyster bucket. I had two dollars for the week's work. At this rate, I figured, it would be spring before I could get enough money together to pay coach fare for both of us to travel to Pittsburgh to look for Sister Paulita.

When I mourned that fact to Annabel, she said cheerfully, "What's the hurry, dear? Winter's comin' on anyways, and with the snow in the mountains down there, you'll have to take a train—and that you could never afford."

She looked at me curiously. "Besides, I thought you said the kid wasn't even yours, that her mother might show up on a survivor list. 'Course, if you really want to make a lot of money, you could work nights, a different kind of work. Then you could see more of the kid during the day."

"What do you mean," I asked. "What can I do at night?"

"You can be a saloon girl," she replied. "With your figure, and that gorgeous hair—they'd take you on in a minute. You ain't been in New York long enough to get that pale, washed-out look. If not here at the hotel, then for sure at one of the places up and down Broadway."

The saloon was the large room behind the heavy curtains at the far end of the main dining room. During the daytime the curtains were pulled shut, and the place was quiet. But at night, after the dinner hour, I noticed patrons—all male—drifting from their tables toward the curtains and disappearing on the other side.

I got my chance to see the mysterious place the very next day, when I was assigned, along with Annabel and a whole squad of other chambies, to scrub the vast plush carpet in the saloon. Because of the American male's addiction to tobacco chewing, the richly figured plush carpet was heavily encrusted with dried brown spittle. Gleaming brass spittoons stood everywhere, but most of the time the chewers missed, or didn't even bother to aim. Stomach churning, I set to work on my hands and knees, wielding a stiff brush and lots of strong yellow soap. All of the chairs and other furniture had been moved out, and large fires started in the porcelain coal stoves to dry out the carpet before that night's performance.

The room was ornate. A heavily carved wood bar filled one whole side of the enormous wall, a brass-plated foot rest running its entire length. All four walls and the ceiling were splashed with larger than lifesize colorful paintings of nude men and women in various romantic poses. Dazzling crystal and gold chandeliers cast a brilliant glow over all. To my amazement, bronze figurines of Greek gods and goddesses stood about on pedestals against the walls. The saloon of the Astor House was, I concluded, a combination of Lola's salon and Frau Anna's elegant parlor where Ymir and I had played our seductive games.

Now I understood what Annabel meant. I knew perfectly well what kind of place this was, and what went on each night. As we scrubbed throughout the morning, Annabel, kneeling beside me, offered more information about being a "saloon girl."

"Pay's good," she panted, as she dug her brush into the rug, "wouldn't mind doin' it myself. Tom and I could get ourselves a little place of our own uptown—wouldn't have to live in no pig alley. But—" she grimaced—"he won't hear o' me displayin' my body that way."

"I have no Tom," I said. "Nobody to object. And Rosie need never know about it. All I need is a few weeks' work and we can both go to Pittsburgh."

"Wait 'till you see what they do before you make up your mind." Annabel showed me where I could stand that night to get a good look at the "goings-on" in the saloon. "You don't want to let yourself be seen in there," she advised. "Someone might get the wrong idea about you."

202

My peephole was in the corridor which led to an outside door through which porters carried the cases of liquor and beer to stock the bar. I walked casually up and down the dark narrow place, pretending to be cleaning, and when the porters had finished their work, I moved up to the doorway and opened it a crack.

The place was packed with men of all ages, sitting on chairs or standing shoulder to shoulder against the lurid walls. Cigar smoke made fragrant clouds in the air. The chairs were arranged in rows so that a broad aisle was formed through the center. Probably the stage, I thought. Waiter girls moved about serving drinks to those who did not want to stand at the bar. Their short skirts barely cleared their buttocks. Shiny red boots reached to the knees. Snug bodices boosted white breasts to thrust invitingly upward.

At ten promptly a small orchestra struck up a lively tune and a handsome middle-aged man dressed in a flowing blue and red cape sprinkled with glittering stars stepped right on top of the bar. An expectant hush fell over the crowd. "Gentlemen," he called out. "Besides our usual attractions, tonight the Astor House Saloon is proud to present an entirely new production of Lady Godiva of Coventry. Our performer is a lovely young virgin from Germany, who speaks no English, and has known no man."

The rousing music slowed down to a sultry, erotic beat. The drums beat insistently. I heard the whinny of the horse before I saw it. A magnificent white stallion was being led into the saloon by two young boys, about twelve or so, dressed in nothing but slim black loincloths. The white figure of a woman was strapped to the horse's bare back with pieces of rough rope. Her head was down, a curtain of coppery hair mingling with the horse's mane to sweep the carpet. The horse stepped daintily, head high, unmoved by the crowd, to the end of the runway then turned around to return.

As the group approached the center of the runway the second time, one of the boys dropped his end of the reins, and loosened the coils of rope. The woman sat up, swaying seductively as if awaking from a deep sleep, stretched white slender arms over her head. When she had reached a full sitting position, she parted her hair with her fingers, flung it back, gazed fearlessly out at the crowd of men.

She was completely naked, her supple breasts firm, upstanding. The nipples appeared to be colored with rouge to make them stand out starkly against the creamy flesh. Suddenly, a roar arose from the throng of men. Shouts, catcalls, whistles, filled the saloon as the boys led the horse slowly from one end of the aisle to the other. I stared, utterly fascinated, as she approached the doorway where I was hiding. I looked her full in the face.

Bettina! There was no mistaking that creamy complexion, snub nose, sprinkle of saucy freckles. Her sparkling green eyes were clearly visible in the glaring light of the chandelier. Bettina! My dear friend who was coming to America to marry a rich American, to become respectable. The sweet face that stared straight at my doorway was waxen and impassive. She might have been carved of marble.

Unable to bear the sight any longer, I turned and ran into the filthy alley, blinded by the hot scalding tears which sprang to my eyes. So that's what Annabel meant by being a "saloon girl."

That night I lay awake for hours on the lumpy mattress, cuddling Rosie against my heaving bosom. Much as I longed to go to her, I could not reveal myself to Bettina. She must not know that I was aware of her degradation. Furthermore, I could never become a "saloon girl," not for all the money in the world. My body had been abused and used by men since that Corpus Christi night at the Barerstrasse palace of Lola Montez. Now it belonged to me. I would give to no man ever again—except in love.

Christmas Eve, late in the afternoon, I dressed Rosie in the pink frock and furlined cape McGreevey had bought her, and set out for our weekly walk down Broadway to the East River docks. I donned the rich crimson velvet with the lace bertha from the *Maris Stella*. In our matching bonnets, we looked quite festive.

"We won't have to take a back seat to anyone in the Broadway parade," I exclaimed, kissing Rosie. The child had blossomed since that black morning in October. The little cheeks had filled out, the arms and legs that had been like matchsticks were sweetly rounded out. She never spoke of the fire, or the lifeboat. Or of McGreevey.

Annabel looked a bit troubled as we talked in her kitchen. "The steward won't like it, your takin' a half day off on a big holiday like Christmas," she said.

"Please cover for me. I'll give you my wages for the whole day. I guess I'm superstitious but it seems that if I skip a week going to the dock, well—that would be the week Lauretta Chambers turns up alive."

"Yeah, people have a way of doin' just that. Just yesterday a sailor who'd been given up for dead suddenly turned up. Seems his shipmates swore they'd seen him washed overboard. Found his wife livin' with another man. A real mess."

With an effort I wiped all emotion from my face. "My husband died in my arms. But I did not see Mrs. Chambers die. There's always the hope—"

The Irish eyes softened. She put an arm about my waist. "Our prayers—mine and Tom's and the kids too—go with you, Sieglinde, although it'll be hard on you givin' up the kid after all this time."

Now as I gazed at Rosie hungrily, wishing she were truly my own, the deep soft brown eyes, so much like mine, sparkled up at me. In her arms she cuddled a rag doll I'd whipped up out of the bright flowered cotton McGreevey had torn from my body that first night in New York. I'd forced myself to stay awake every night an extra hour or so for a week before Christmas embroidering black eyes, a wide upturned crimson mouth. I'd even made little brown freckles to march across the nose and cheeks.

Annabel kissed us both and the children waved a cheery goodbye before returning to their oyster buckets. "I have this feelin'," she said, "in my heart—" she clapped a work-roughened hand dramatically to her bosom—"call it Irish intuition, that today's your lucky day."

My own heart was far from optimistic, however, as Rosie and I stepped through the double glass front doors of the Astor House. Two and a half months of devouring the survivor lists in the newspapers had yielded no results. Even an advertisement I could ill afford in the *Post*, the most widely read newspaper in New York, had been fruitless. So each week, on my half day off, Rosie and I took the long walk to the Northern Star shipping office to make sure there was no word.

The clerk there had become our friend and had promised to send word if there was any news at all of Mrs. Chambers—or of Dr. Gerhard. He had been curious about my intense interest in the whereabouts of the ship's doctor.

"He saved Rosie's life. He was very kind," I said simply in answer to his questions.

A leaden sky had been promising snow all day. Now as we joined the throngs on Broadway, the temperature was close to freezing and I pulled my cloak close against the biting wind. Richly attired men and women crushed shoulder to shoulder on the sidewalk in front of the hotel. There was to be a gala polka and champagne party tonight in the main dining room. The saloon, too, would have a new production billed as "Mrs. Claus and her North Pole Maidens."

Since the night I had seen Bettina naked on the horse as Lady Godiva, I had not set foot in the ornate showroom. I longed to go to her, to talk to her—but dared not. Secretly I suppose I was afraid she might talk me into becoming part of the repertoire. I wasn't sure I could resist the temptation to become once more what I had been at Frau Anna's *Akademie.*

Finally we crossed Water Street, then Front Street, then on to South Street, the busy cobblestoned thoroughfare which ran along the length of the East River. I always hurried through this last part of our walk, for we had to traverse the rough Bowery section where both the houses and the people bore dirty, bloated faces. A regular rabbit warren, it made our Prosperity Alley look like a royal palace.

At the corner of Maiden Lane and South Street, we had to wait a long time before the street was clear enough to cross to the wharf. The lamplighter, just climbing down his ladder after lighting the gas arc at the corner, nodded to us pleasantly. "*Guten Abend,*" he said, his German still thick and rich, "*Freuliche Weihnachten.*"

"Happy Christmas to you," I replied, glancing nervously at the tavern on the corner. Loud singing and raucous drunken laughter poured forth from the row of saloons on that side of the street. A group of men lounging at the corner leered at us openly, but made no move. Every week they saw me come here to this corner with Rosie. Every week they leered.

The office of the Northern Star Lines was the last in a row of square clapboard structures, once painted but now weathered to a deep grey by the wind and spray. Rosie ran to open the splintery door. The knob was molded in the shape of a man's head and she delighted in turning it. The

206

rusty hinges groaned noisily. Inside, the usual smell of dampness, tar, unwashed bodies, and whale oil filled the bleak little room.

The old man behind the long wooden table looked up and pushed back his visored cap to grin at us. "Didn't expect to see you two on Christmas Eve," he said, "but you sure look pretty, both of you."

He rose, shuffled out from behind the table to put a friendly hand on my shoulder, leaned down to peck Rosie on the cheek. He smelled of pipe tobacco and whiskey. "Lucky you caught me. About ready to close up and go home. Boardin' house is havin' a big party tonight." The rheumy old eyes glittered in anticipation. "How about comin' along? Be such a crowd there no one will notice one or two extra."

"No, thank you, Mr. Stone. I appreciate your invitation," I replied kindly.

While I walked around the room reading the latest lists of survivors of shipwrecks and sinkings, he carried on a sprightly conversation with the child. I heard the sound of the drawer pulling out. "How about a sweet tonight for the little lady?"

Three or four times the door squealed as customers walked in and out to make brief inquiries. The lists were old ones. After the onset of winter, the crossings diminished, and consequently the number of disasters. Nothing new. I should have known, but something impelled me to come down here each week and read every name on the lists. There was always the wild hope that by sheer accident, by merely being at the waterfront, I would catch sight of a tall figure with a coppery head. Just being at the waterfront brought me somehow nearer to Lothar.

"Come, Rosie," I said finally, pulling the child away from the old man. "It is dark outside, we must be getting home. It will take us a long time to walk back."

"Mama!" Her shriek coincided with the raspy sound of the opening door.

"Rosie! My darling child, can it be you? Oh my dear God!"

Lauretta Chambers stood in the half-open doorway, her thin arms outstretched to clasp the screaming child to her breast. All in black, she was thinner, almost gaunt.

For a few moments there was no sound in the bleak little

shipping office. Mr. Stone stood behind his table, tears streaming unashamedly down his old brown cheeks. He drew a large dirty handkerchief from his pocket and blew his nose with a loud blast.

I stood speechless, watching the reunion, happiness and sorrow mixing themselves together in my heart. We talked incoherently at first. This was her first trip to the dock to inquire after her child, Lauretta explained. She had been ill for months since the fire.

"I was out of my mind," she told us, "I didn't know who I was. When the *Ocean Monarch* sank, something—a bit of wreckage perhaps—hit me on the head. I was pulled into a lifeboat, senseless. That is all I remember until yesterday morning, when my memory suddenly returned. After hunting up my family, I came directly here to make inquiries about Rose."

She turned to a young man who stood quietly behind her, observing the tableau. "My brother, John Ryan. Rose and I will be staying with him and his family in their home overlooking the Hudson."

In answer to her inquiries, I told her nothing of McGreevey or my work at the Astor House or of the hovel in which we lived. My story of the rescue of Rosie and myself was briefly told. Tears of gratitude filled the mother's eyes. She fell upon me, kissing my cheeks, my mouth. "We are forever in your debt, my dear Sieglinde." Her eyes clouded. "Another, more selfish person, would have simply put the child in an almshouse and gone her own way."

"No, I could never do that," I said quietly. "No one could who has ever been a mother herself."

Her eyes flicked over my crimson velvet. "You look well. The baron—you're sure he perished?"

"Yes, he died in my arms."

"How are you living? With whom? Have you friends? You're welcome to come home with me. John's home is very large."

"The city is filled with German émigrés. We—help each other. Eventually I will receive the monies from the baron's estate." My voice was gay and filled with confidence. From the corner of my eye, I saw Mr. Stone open his mouth to speak, to tell her of my lies, but I glared him into silence.

Rosie rested in her mother's arms, her brown curls falling over the black cloak, the doll in the flowered dress squeezed tightly between mother and child. Lauretta

208

looked troubled, but said merely, "Please, you must come to visit. A short steamboat ride will get you there." She scribbled an address. "You—" she paused significantly, "and your—friends." The guarded look in her eyes told me she didn't quite believe my story of prosperity.

"Of course I will—in the spring," I replied. "Rosie and I have become attached to each other. I think it best that she now becomes reacquainted with her mother."

The compassion in her eyes was too much for me finally and I ran sobbing out of the door. I waited in the shadows behind the building until their carriage rounded the corner of Maiden Lane.

The crowd on the wharf had thinned out. I walked freely along the sturdy wooden guard rail, raking the forest of masts and smokestacks with hungry eyes. Lothar could be out there on one of those dark ships. He too, like Lauretta, could have lost his memory. He could have been pressed into service as a common seaman—it happened all the time.

I stopped underneath the flickering light of a gas street lantern, squeezed my body between the iron post and the guard rail. The flickering light cast ghostly shadows on the moored ships. Longing washed over me in sickening heart-wrenching waves. I bent my head to gaze into the murky waters and let the tears flow unchecked. Now I was truly alone, with not even the comfort of Rosie's soft arms around my neck each night. The cold river water slapped against the pilings, the moored boats creaked mournfully in the wind. A light snow had begun to fall. I shivered, from the cold and from my own despair.

It would be so easy to lean over, just a little more, to loosen my hold on the splintery rail, and simply fall in. No—that was no good. I was too good a swimmer. Some other way. I could go back to the hotel, lock myself in one of the rooms, turn on the gas. Every week, it seemed, some unfortunate soul died under the gas at the Astor House. Simply turn on the gas, without applying a match, and lie down. Like falling asleep, they said. I banished the thought as soon as it formed in my brain. It was one thing to consign myself to hell by destroying my body—but there was another now. There was a new life in my womb, conceived in August under the North Atlantic sky.

Suddenly I was wrenched out of my morbid reverie. Strong cruel fingers grabbed hold of my shoulders and spun me around to face three drunken men, all wearing the woolen cap and blue peacoat of the sailor.

"G'wan. I saw her first. She's all mine." The sailor whose face bent down to peer into mine gestured widely with his one hand, while holding tightly to my shoulder with the other.

The others did not move. "Looks like a Dutchie to me," said one. "Tha's the way I like 'em. *Big*." He gestured obscenely in the air, describing two large curves.

"You new? Ain't seen you down here before. Where's your room, Dutchie?" The third one reached out to sweep off my bonnet. "Gawd, lookit all that hair."

After the first few startled moments, I remained calm, deciding that the best strategy was not to struggle. They had obviously mistaken me for a streetwalker. "You presume, sirs," I addressed them in my haughtiest tones. "I have just seen a friend off on the steamship over there, and I am awaiting my carriage."

The three of them doubled up in laughter. "*You presume, sir*," they mocked. "Hear that accent. Could cut it with a knife."

I started to walk away, but in an instant they were upon me, pinning me to the guardrail. Once again the first man shouted at his friends. "She's mine. I saw her first." He grabbed hold of my arm. With iron fingers he started pulling me away. Immediately my other arm was pulled in the opposite direction. A searing pain shot through my shoulder blades as the men tugged at me viciously. They were all around me, blocking my vision. It was Mannheim again, but instead of scarves and little white hats, my attackers wore woolen caps and peacoats. But it wasn't Mannaheim, I told myself, suppressing panic. This was America.

I opened my mouth and let out a bloodcurdling screech. There were always some blue-uniformed policemen patrolling the sidewalks across the street in front of the row of saloons. "Help, police, help me." I screamed, but a coarse hand immediately covered my mouth. I sunk my teeth into the soft flesh.

"Listen to that!" they whooped, "a whore calling for a policeman."

Desperately I started swearing at them in German, using all the curse words I'd ever heard. I kicked out with my feet, first at one, then the other. By this time a crowd had gathered and stood around watching the fun. One thought ran through my mind: I would not be raped again. I would sooner die. And Lothar's new baby with me. "No, never," I shouted desperately.

Like a wild man, the sailor nearest me caught me round the waist and bent me over backwards. At the same time a second kicked me behind the knees so that they buckled. I fell sprawling on the wharf, my head striking one of the wooden posts of the guard rail.

"Unhand that woman, or I'll blast you all to kingdom come." The voice was like thunder over Kyffhauser Mountain, heavy with German gutterals, and came from a tiny thickset man with wide sandy brows shading small eyes which even in the darkness gleamed piercingly. A sandy beard, neatly trimmed, nestled in the ruffle of his shirt front. Bits of sandy hair struggled from underneath a giant silk topper. A nose broad of base and too long for the face made him look like one of the Christmas elves in the store window.

In his pudgy hand, he brandished a shiny black pistol which he slowly turned, back and forth, pointing now at one tormentor, then another. I lay quite still, with bated breath, waiting for the sailors' reaction to the newcomer.

The men backed away, edging into the crowd of onlookers. "Don' mean no harm. Jus' havin' a little fun with the lady."

"Pick her up, Max, and be gentle about it."

A giant of a man who'd been standing behind the little German bent over me swiftly, helped me to my feet. As he did so, I noticed he also had a gun strapped to his vest.

Finally a policeman elbowed through the crowd. "What's the trouble, Mr. Stammler?" The German replaced the pistol in a holster under his frock coat. "No trouble, officer, just some sailors too long at sea."

The policeman looked dubious, raked me from head to foot with a searching eye. "She a friend of yours, this lady?"

"Yes, officer, I know the woman." Stammler never took his eyes off me.

"Well, all right then." The officer started moving away. "Just thought maybe she was a streetwalker. Can't keep 'em off the wharf."

Still watching me steadily, Stammler replied, "She's no

211

whore, officer, be assured of that. We had made an appointment to meet here tonight."

As the crowd dispersed, disappointed at the outcome, I looked with grateful eyes at the little German and his big friend Max. "*Danke, danke sehr!*" I exclaimed. "Now if you can help me find my bonnet," I continued in English, "I'll be getting home."

"There it is," Max yelled, pointing to a round object floating between two vessels. "I'm afraid my chivalry doesn't extend to jumping into icy waters to rescue a lady's bonnet."

"It's not worth much, anyway," I laughed ruefully.

"Shut up," Stammler rapped out abruptly. "And turn around."

Bewildered, I stopped talking, turned around several times while he examined me, his tongue making little clucking sounds. Finally he reached out a gloved hand and touched my hair with a kind of reverence. "How long is that, when you let it down?" he asked, his voice thick and husky.

"Past my hips," I replied mechanically.

He turned to Max. "Well, what do you think, Max, will she do?"

Max grinned from ear to ear. He was a bear of a man, reminding me strongly of Karl. Black curly hair, blunt features, the blue-blue eyes of the Black Forest peasant.

The little man grasped my right hand in his, pumped it up and down vigorously. "Allow me to introduce myself. My name is Rudi Stammler. I run a café on Broadway. If you want work, come with me. With your looks and that superb figure, you don't need to walk the wharfs."

"What—what could I do?" I asked, suddenly fearful. It was all so fast. I must think before I got myself in another mess.

He started walking away. For a moment, I stood under the lamp, the snow falling around me, then ran after the two men. Stammler turned around so fast we bumped into each other. Suddenly his arms were about me, to keep me from falling down again. "If ever I saw a girl who needed a man around—" His voice rose irritably. "Do you want a job or don't you? Rudi Stammler doesn't have to ask twice."

"Why yes of course I want a job—"

"Well, *schnell* then, shake a leg."

Within minutes I was inside a carriage of the expensive closed landau type, being carried back uptown. Max and Stammler ignored me, after seating me between them, talking across me about business matters. I found myself listening with total absorption as they discussed how much beer and ale and hams and pork haunches and barrels of sauerkraut and pickles would be needed until spring. It seemed that they had been at the wharf negotiating purchase and delivery of food for the restaurant.

The flaps of the little windows were down, so I could not occupy myself by looking out at the crowded street scene. I settled back to admire the truly magnificent costumes of the two men. Both were rather flashily dressed in comparison to the ordinary Astor House patron. Max sported a double breasted waistcoat of light colored satin, the broad lapels of which were turned back to reveal a rich brown fur lining. Ruffles of a fine linen shirt spilled out under a brightly patterned silk cravat. A heavy gold brooch shone dimly from the center of the silk. Rudi, on the other hand, resembled more a bird of paradise, with an elaborately embroidered vest under a cloak lined with a startling tartan plaid. His short fingers were heavy with rings. But somehow, even with the finery, they didn't look like pimps. Max was big and comforting, but about Rudi there was a strange compelling quality, a warmth and kindness that I sensed immediately.

I relaxed, settled down for the long slow trip up Broadway. Bleecker Street, he had said. Way past the Astor House it was. It would take at least an hour, with the Christmas Eve traffic.

Chapter 18

Rudi's café was in the heart of the theatre district, at the corner of Bleecker and Broadway. The landau was forced to stop in the middle of the street because the crush of vehicles prevented our approaching the sidewalk. People milled about, thick as the snowflakes which now fell heavily from the sky, clothing everything with a magic mantle of white.

Men and women, wrapped snugly in glossy furs, were pouring into a garishly lighted theatre. A large placard on the side of the building featured the picture of a naked man tied to a horse. *Mazeppa* was printed in large block letters on the marquee. We made our way precariously to the sidewalk, Max blazing a trail for Rudi and me with his broad shoulders.

"The first real snowfall of the winter," Rudi sang out joyfully. His pixie face split into a grin from ear to ear, as if he personally were responsible for the weather.

"At least it covers the dirt in the streets," remarked Max. "Even the pigs go home when it snows."

We stopped in front of a drab brick building which appeared at first to be unoccupied. A scraggly band of caroling children blocked our progress.

" *'Raus mit* you," Rudi Stammler shouted at them. He reached into his pocket and hurled a handful of coins into the air, over and behind the children so that they scattered in a mad scramble for the money, crawling on hands and knees on the snowy pavement.

"This is it." Rudi preceded me down a steep flight of five stone steps to a narrow door which hadn't seen paint in a long time. There was no sign of a restaurant or café. Not a sound emanated from the building. Fear plunged icy fingers into my heart as I watched Rudi insert a key into the lock. My knees grew weak, and I had a mad impulse to turn around and run back into the Broadway traffic. Frau Anna's warnings about what happened to girls who went about unescorted in the city came back to me. Was this a white slave headquarters? Had I been saved from rape by the sailors only to fall into a fate worse than death itself?

The door opened into a fairyland. Walking into Rudi Stammler's café was like being magically transported back to Bavaria. A candlelit mellowness pervaded a long, low-ceilinged cavern of a room dominated at one end by an enormous Christmas tree, a burning stubby candle on the tip of every branch. Fragrant branches tied with red ribbons hung from the wooden beams. On the walls, surmounting the gleaming dark wooden wainscoting, an artist with a free hand had painted panoramic scenes of mountains with silvery running streams, and city scenes with medieval buildings, Gothic tall-steepled churches, and gabled houses with steeply slanting roofs. As we entered, a cuckoo clock sounded eight cheery notes.

"Oh, how lovely!"

Rudi turned, pleased at my involuntary exclamaation of delight. "Thought you'd like it," he said. "I do my best to bring a little bit of Germany to homesick emigrés."

"You've succeeded very well," I replied. "I could think myself back in a Munich Ratskellar. The atmosphere is very *gemütlich*."

"Come, let me show you." Rudi took my arm and guided me through a narrow aisle between two long wooden tables which ran the length of the room. A number of people were sitting on benches pushed up to the tables, eating quietly and talking. Some wore the loose blouse and flowing scarf of the Forty-eighter. Many sported also the long wavy hair which distinguished them immediately from the American men with whom clipped beards and short hair were in fashion. As we passed, Rudi nodded and greeted them in turn. He did not introduce me, and none asked who I was, although some looked up at me curiously. "Crowd's pretty thin right now," he said. "After the theatre performance we serve a midnight supper."

Max, who had disappeared for a moment, returned wearing a white apron over his finery. The big man nodded to me, beaming, put both hands on the wooden bar and vaulted over it to the other side.

"Max is my right-hand man," Rudi explained. "He doubles as barkeeper and bouncer. Sometimes my patrons become a little rowdy."

As we came back down the aisle, Rudi led me behind the curved bar set in the corner right inside the door. Two waiters in white aprons, each sporting thick handlebar mustaches and shoulder-length hair, were busily filling steins with foaming beer from two giant wooden barrels. Rudi picked one up and handed it to me. "Drink up. You need it after that tussle on the wharf."

The dark brown brew was rich and satisfying. I gulped it down greedily, suddenly remembering that I'd had no supper. I looked longingly at the plates of coffee-colored pumpernickel, pretzels, and sauerkraut which were spread on the wide counter of the bar.

"This lager comes special from Milwaukee, brought all the way by steamboat," Rudi bragged. "My patrons won't drink the pale watery stuff New Yorkers call beer."

The lager reached my blood quickly. My fears subsided, and a warm, relaxed, at-home feeling took hold of me. Loosening the strings of my cloak and leaning on the bar, I smiled up at the little German. "Now about that job—" I began.

"Tomorrow we can talk about it. Right now you should go—" At that moment the door opened wide to bring in a swirl of snow and a group of three people. Rudi beamed from ear to ear and rushed over to greet the newcomers. "Adah!"

"Rudi, you old rascal, where you been keeping yourself?"

What at first appeared to be three men turned out to be one woman dressed as a man, with white ruffled shirt and tight black breeches tucked into shiny leather boots, and two handsomely dressed and handsomely featured young men, who followed on her heels like a couple of well-trained dogs. One of the men was very tall and extremely thin, with great sad eyes, the other not so tall, but with a finely chiselled face.

Rudi left me to escort Adah and her companions to the end of one of the long tables. The woman continued to talk in a rich vibrant contralto. She was striking, although far from conventionally beautiful. Dark hair, a rich brown-black, was swept under a broad-brimmed hat, and pert bangs marched across a white forehead.

"Couldn't open a new play without a bowl of your incomparable chicken soup," Adah was saying.

Rudi signalled to one of the waiters, who disappeared through a door behind the bar. "Elisabeth's had it bubbling all day, just waiting for you, my *Schatzie*," Rudi retorted. "You are already in costume for your role in *Mazeppa*, I see."

Adah looked down at her black trousers and loose white shirt which was opened halfway down to her waist to reveal a good bit of fair white skin. "Yes, it's delightfully comfortable. I'm thinking of giving up corsets and skirts altogether, and scandalizing the whole city. After all, George Sand does it in Paris."

The two handsome men said nothing, merely sat drinking lager from tankards quickly supplied by the waiters. Their eyes betrayed their adoration of Adah.

Adah glanced over at me. "Who's that hiding behind you, Rudi, another of your waifs?"

Rudi jumped up, dragged me over to the table. "This is Sieglinde, who will be staying with us for a while. Sieglinde, meet Adah Menken, New York's favorite actress, who manages to be seductive even in trousers."

The actress lifted finely arched brows. "Well, congratulations on this one, my dear Rudi. She is a considerably better specimen than most of your émigrés." I stared at the woman icily, resentful at being put on display like a prize dog. But in the next moment she smiled at me, revealing two rows of tiny pearl-like teeth, and I melted. I felt the woman's magnetism. No one could be her enemy for long.

"With that magnificent Lorelei hair and that Valkyrie figure, you should have no trouble finding work," she remarked, reaching out a slender hand to take mine. "Or a husband either, for that matter."

I opened my mouth to tell this woman that I already had a husband, but she didn't wait for a reply. Turning to her two companions, she said brightly, "What do you think, Edwin, and you, Edgar?" Before waiting for either of them to answer she addressed me again. "Sieglinde, my child, you have the honor of being presented to Edwin Booth, the most adored actor in all America. You will immediately fall in love with him. Every woman does. And some men too, I understand."

The two men did not join in her laughter. A pair of impressive eyes, blue and piercing as the depths of the

218

ocean, gazed at me. I felt that Edwin Booth was looking into my very soul. "Charmed, Fräulein," he said, rising from the bench and taking my hand lightly in his while still holding the stein in the other. "I look forward to further acquaintance. Please do not be in such a hurry, as are most of Rudi's émigrés, to take the steamboat to Milwaukee or Pittsburgh and become a farmer's wife."

"And this is my other Ed—Edgar Poe." Adah waved to the sad-eyed younger man. "He is unfortunately not an actor, but a poet—and therefore starving. If it weren't for Rudi he would have been in the grave long before this."

Edgar Poe did not rise, gave no flicker of acknowledgement as he watched me steadily, unflinchingly, from deep brown eyes. Dark hair curled softly about his ears. A long thin nose and drooping mustache gave him a lugubrious appearance, much like the image one has of any starving poet. His skeletal fingers cradled the silver tankard of beer as if he would draw strength from the very metal.

The waiter returned, carrying a huge blue and white tureen. With a flourish he placed it directly in front of Adah Menken and lifted the lid. A tantalizing cloud of vapor rose into the air. Adah closed her eyes and sniffed long and deep. "Ambrosia, food for the gods," she said softly.

Three bowls were then set on the table, and Adah herself ladled out the contents of the tureen, Indeed it did appear to be the richest, thickest chicken soup I'd ever seen. Plump yellow noodles and large chunks of chicken floated about in a golden liquid. The three ate noisily, dipping large soup spoons into their bowls. Conversation ceased.

This was a totally different America from the Astor House, where ostentatious vulgarity reigned supreme. These were the artists, the intellectuals, the soul of the country. By sheer dumb luck, I had stumbled into the kind of atmosphere in which I had grown up. Waves of relief flooded my being as I stood behind Rudi watching the tableau in front of me—the handsome, witty people, the kind-hearted roly-poly German, the dying poet.

Suddenly, Poe broke into a spasm of coughing. Deep, wracking, ugly noises came from his slender body. Rudi reached over to pat the poet on the back. "Edgar is drinking himself to death," he remarked, his voice strangely casual. "But it's a free country. A man is allowed to die as well as live. And love, I might add." He gave me a quick, reassuring smile.

His coughing over, Poe returned to his drinking, but kept his eyes fixed upon me. Once again I felt the self-conscious uncomfortable feeling and turned slightly, lifted my eyes to the mural over the bar where one normally expected a mirror. Somehow it looked familiar—the lush greens and golds merging together like that. While the talk flowed on around me, I studied the painting. Gradually the figure of a man emerged from the background. It was a very large person, seated in a dark place with a rounded roof. Like a cave. Giant elbows rested on a stone table, giant hands with a golden fuzz on the backs of them held up the giant head. A pair of black ravens circled round the bowed coppery hair.

My heart started to hammer in my breast. A faraway buzzing started in my brain. It was Lothar sitting up there in that huge painting. Frederick Barbarossa in his cave on Kyffhauser Mountain. "Lift your head," I screamed silently, "lift your head, Lothar, reveal those green eyes. Let me see the smoldering golden lights—"

Adah's voice sounded behind me, seeming to come from a long distance. "Oh, you have noticed our brooding Messiah, Sieglinde. Magnificent, isn't it? Edgar got the inspiration for his poem about the raven from the Redbeard's birds."

A laugh from Edwin Booth. "Yes, he used to sit here for hours on end, staring at those infernal birds. Apparently they signify death, and when they disappear the redheaded giant will come back to life."

Edgar Poe said nothing. Rudi spoke up. "People come from all over the city to look at my Barbarossa. If you like paintings, you must look closely at the others. The Lorelei at the other end, for instance—"

"No, tomorrow perhaps—I feel faint—please may I lie down?" An insistent pain in my forehead had suddenly become sharp, with a cutting edge. I put my hand to my forehead to feel a large swelling.

"Ach, what a *dummkopf* am I." Rudi was all contrition, hitting himself on the forehead with a pudgy hand. "Come, upstairs with you and between the sheets. Excuse us, Adah. See you later, after the show. Right now I've got to get this Lorelei to bed—she's had quite a night, and she's not made of stone like that other one."

"Elisabeth!" The thunderous voice bawled out the name as we left the café for a narrow hallway and started up a steep flight of dark stairs. My mind was in such a whirl I could not speak. I would leave during the night, just slip out the door during the midnight supper. I could not live in a house with the living presence of Lothar.

"Elisabeth, Elisabeth," Rudi called out twice more before we reached the top of the stairs, and immediately an ample-bosomed middle-aged woman with wisps of grey hair tucked into a muslin bonnet appeared. A checked gingham apron covered a flowered housedress. Despite her bulk, she moved lightly, like a dancer, at a half-run.

The soft folds of flesh of her upper arms pressed against me as she nearly squeezed the breath out of me. "Go on," she ordered Rudi, "back to the café. I'll take care of this little one." In less time than it takes to tell about it, she had pulled me into a room, one of many in the long upstairs corridor. I was stripped naked, and a heavy clean-smelling flannel nightgown dropped over my head. I slipped obediently between sheets smelling of sweet herbs.

"How about some schnapps for a nightcap?" Elisabeth bent her sweating face over mine. "Or maybe a cup of cocoa?"

"No, thank you," I replied weakly. "I had some lager downstairs."

She laughed, her plump face dimpling all over. "Ach, you don't need nothing else then. Now to sleep with you, and tomorrow we will talk."

She'd already reached the door when I called out. "That picture of Frederick Barbarossa over the bar. Who was the model for it?"

She threw me a quizzical look. "Model? Who needs one? Every émigré has an image of the great emperor in his mind. Although they talk in the café—the Forty-eighters—of a young man who many thought to be the resurrected Redbeard. Seems he took part in the Munich uprising last year, but he has apparently disappeared since then."

I fell back on the pillow, moaning, the pain in my head nearly blinding me. Elisabeth rushed over and explored the bump with her hand. "That's a bad one. I'll fetch a bit of ice for it."

She danced out of the room, closing the door quietly behind her. I lay perfectly still, willing away the pain. The noise from the streets below, beyond the heavily curtained window, had reached a crescendo. Bells rang, trumpets blared, children screamed, sleigh bells jingled. Below, a

221

faint dull murmur of voices drifted through the wooden boards of the floor. Outside in the hall two people talked quietly. I tried to listen. Maybe they were talking about me. I tried to think about Lothar and the painting. I tried not to think of Lothar and the painting.

As soon as the hall was quiet, I would slip out of bed, put my clothes back on, and walk boldly down the stairs. Annabel would be worried about me back at the Astor House. She might send one of the children down to the wharf tomorrow. I should get back there and tell her about Rosie. The O'Tooles had loved her too. They would be so happy to know that she had found her real mother.

Rosie. Never to see her again. But I could visit. A short steamboat ride, Lauretta had said. I imagined the child right now, fast asleep in a clean bed, just like this one, no more dirty mattress.

My brain would not be quiet. A procession of images flashed on and off like a kaleidoscope. Plans. I must make plans. While I was busy making plans, sleep crept up on my tired body and engulfed me in its loving arms.

Chapter 19

Waking came with a jolting suddenness from a nightmarish dream of Lothar and myself swimming in a violet sea. His gleaming head bobbed beside me, his strong sure strokes moved in rhythm with my own, the lean muscles of his arms glistened wetly. We approached a lifeboat filled with people. He reached it before me, got in, stood up and beckoned.

"Come, Sieglinde, come," he shouted into the wind and the waves. I strained every muscle, stroked as hard as I could, but the faster I swam the farther away the boat seemed to be. My arms became like lead. I could hardly lift them out of the water. The pain became unbearable—

I sat bolt upright in the big bed, massaging the muscles in my upper arms. The pain was very real, as if someone had been pulling at my arms for a long time. Then it all came back to me. Last night on the wharf, those rough sailors had pulled at my arms in two directions at once. A swift arrow of pain darted across my eyes. I reached up to feel the bump on my forehead. It was tender to the touch.

"*Verdammt!*" It must be morning, and I had slept through the night. Now it would be harder to sneak away. There would have to be a little scene with Rudi Stammler. How would I explain why I couldn't accept his offer of a job? Only a madwoman would be afraid of a painting.

Throwing off the heavy quilt, I ran barefooted to the window, my toes curling on the icy floor. Maybe it was still dark outside. I pulled aside the thick draperies and peered through the glass at the street two stories below. The room looked out over an alley which led up to Broadway at the corner. The snow had stopped falling, except for a few stray flakes. The rooftops sparkled in the soft gold of a rising sun. I pushed up the sash to lean out. The air was bracing—cold, clear, fresh. Church bells sounded for early Mass. The day had begun. Well, I'd simply wait until to-night. There was no need at all even to go into the café and look at the Barbarossa picture.

Christmas Day. Already the street was busy. Some children were riding a sled in the alley, where the snow had packed into a shiny track. Their shouts of delight and whoops of joy brought a smile to my chilly lips. Closing the window against the cold, I turned back into the room. A steaming cup of strong coffee would fix up my headache. Maybe I could find the kitchen without rousing anyone. Cautiously, I opened the door leading into the corridor. All quiet. The household was obviously still asleep.

Rushing back into the room, I quickly pulled the flannel gown up over my head and put on the crimson velvet dress. It was dirty and torn in places from the scuffle at the wharf, but it would do. At least it would get me back to the Astor House. I still had the furry cloak too. It would hide most of me. But first, the coffee. The pain in my head had become an anvil. Little black spots swarmed around in my brain.

Before leaving the bedroom, I looked around wistfully. Large bright red roses marched in rows up and down the wallpaper, and there was lots of heavy dark furniture, polished to a dull gleam. A bed large enough fot three people at least, four if they weren't too big. A chamber pot stood sedately in a corner and boasted a painted rosy cover.

I sniffed appreciatively. Everything had that clean, well-scrubbed smell I remembered so well from my Bavarian childhood. Overcome with nostalgia, I closed my eyes, thinking briefly of the dirty, pig-infested alley behind the Astor House, and the vermin-ridden mattress waiting for me at the O'Tooles.

In the dark corridor I slipped quietly past rows of closed doors. Unmistakable snoring sounds came from behind several. On the stairs, I walked along the edges so as not to make any noise. Approaching the door that led into the café I heard voices from inside. I started to run, but it was too late. The door opened just wide enough for a curly blond head to poke itself out.

"Hallo, who's there?" A pleasant, cultured voice with a German accent spoke softly into the semi-dark.

Our eyes met. It was Leopold Siegel, the charming

young Forty-eighter from the *Ocean Monarch* with whom I had whiled away so many carefree hours in the salon.

"Sieglinde! I mean, Baronin Von Edel, is it not?"

He leaned on a broom handle, grinning from ear to ear, his merry blue eyes elated and sparkling in the gloom of the corridor.

"Leopold Siegel," I said, wonder in my voice.

"But how *wunderbar*! But how did you—but of course." He snapped his fingers, nodded his head vigorously. "You are the young lady Rudi brought in last night who so enchanted Adah Menken and her poet."

I nodded. "Were any of your friends saved?" I asked, ignoring his remark about the actress.

The thin, handsome face clouded. "Many of our group perished. You know how it was at the end—it was every man for himself. I managed to swim to a lifeboat."

"So did I," I smiled bleakly. "The ship's doctor tore my dead husband from my arms and literally threw me overboard."

"Apparently the doctor was the hero of the fiery tragedy," Leopold said, reverence in his voice. "He also pushed me off the ship moments before it blew up and sank. Emil, too."

Leopold stuck his head back into the café. "Emil, come here quick, look what Rudi brought home last night."

The short, dark-haired Emil appeared and peered at me glumly through the thick glasses. It was pretty obvious that he was not as happy to see me alive and well as was his friend. "It is good that you were saved," he whispered, "but accept my condolences on the death of your husband the baron."

My heart pounding, I turned again to Leopold and asked as casually as I could, "And the brave doctor, what happened to him?"

Emil answered quickly. "He went down with the ship. A few of us had stayed in the midst of the flames, trying to coax the remaining women and children to jump into the water. He threw many of them into the arms of the men who were swimming close to the ship. But—" the little man's voice broke at the memory—"the last memory I have of that fateful morning was of the tall black-clad figure standing against the orange flames. He could not save himself."

Leopold broke in. "But people keep turning up every

day. Strange thing. Those who could swim got into life-boats and were eventually picked up by vessels that dropped them off at ports up and down the east coast of America. Even South America. It takes them months to work their way to New York."

His words hardly penetrated the thunder in my brain. Lothar dead! Surely he could not have escaped the inferno if Emil had seen him moments before the ship exploded. Surely. It was the end of my false hope that somehow he had escaped and would turn up in New York.

Apparently my face did not betray my churning emotions, for Leopold was whirling around in little dance steps in the corridor with his broom for a partner. He took my arm possessively in his. "But where are you headed at this ungodly hour? Everyone is still in the arms of Morpheus—except myself and Emil who have to clean up the café. Just imagine—cleaning out spittoons on Christmas morning."

Somehow I forced out the words through the thickness in my throat. "I—I was looking for the kitchen—to get some coffee. It seems I got this bump on my forehead—" My hand flew up to my head in a gesture of pain.

"Come, I'll escort you to the kitchen—the real center of this establishment."

He threw the broom after the retreating Emil. "Carry on, my friend, with the spittoons." Then taking my arm as if he were escorting me into a grand ballroom, we made our way into the depths of the building. "The Christmas party went on until five," he prattled on, as we walked. "People just refused to go home. Max ended up throwing some of them right out onto the sidewalk."

His cheery presence had banished the pain for a few minutes at least, but the pain in my heart grew steadily, as the realization of what Emil had told me about Lothar began to sink in.

"You look much the same, ravishing as ever," I said, noting that Leopold wore the billowy blouse and loose neck scarf of the rebel uniform. A voluminous white apron covered most of his front, and the mass of blond curls was smashed under a bright peasant-type kerchief.

"May I return the compliment?" he replied gallantly. "Although you seem a bit thinner." He paused, then proceeded delicately, "How have you been living? And where? And what were you doing on the East River docks?"

"Whoa, there," I laughed. "I'm much too hungry, and in

too much pain to talk about it now. I'm here, safe and sound, and that's all that matters after all, isn't it?"

He looked at me thoughtfully, as he opened a door leading down a steep pair of steps into the cellar. "Yes, yes, of course. We'll speak no more about it now."

As at the Astor House, and in a great many other New York restaurants, the kitchen of the café took up the entire underground level. It looked to be at least a block long. There were no windows, since the café itself was the cellar, the only light coming from numerous lanterns hanging from the rafters. But the whole effect was cozy, rather than gloomy. And the burning candles gave off a welcome warmth, dispelling the ever-present dampness.

Elisabeth's ample form, swathed like Leopold's in a white apron which tied in the back, was bent over a big black cookstove. She whipped around as we entered. "Child, what are you doing out of bed? And who told you to get dressed in that filthy gown? Rudi left orders that you were to sleep all day." She bustled over, looking cross.

"Please don't scold me, Elisabeth," I pleaded. "I'm hungry. And simply dying for a cup of coffee."

"Sieglinde is noted for her hearty appetite," Leopold volunteered. "She's not one of your pick-at-your-food American girls."

The housekeeper cocked her white-bonneted head. "You two are old acquaintances, then?"

"Yes. We met on the ship to America," I replied, "the one that burned and sank."

The woman nodded, as if ship burnings were everyday conversation to her. Returning to the stove, she grabbed a towel and took hold of a large enameled coffee pot. Leopold pulled out a chair and I sat down at a long wooden table. Suddenly the sharp pain in my head flared up again, and I bent low over to the table, cradling my forehead in my two trembling hands.

Three cups of coffee, two fried eggs, three strips of bacon, and a chunk of Elisabeth's fragrant hot bread dissipated the headache. "I was more hungry than anything," I laughed. "Yesterday I ate nothing at all, as I recall."

She eyed me appraisingly. "Leopold was right about your appetite. You'll need it around here if you're going to work for Rudi Stammler. While no slave driver, he expects all his employees to work just as hard as he does," she grimaced, "which is all the time."

227

Leopold had gone back to his work, leaving me to Elisabeth's "capable charms" as he put it. While eating, I noticed the tall stacks of unwashed plates and towers of cups and saucers sitting on a long table along the wall.

"Can I help you, Elisabeth, in some way? Rudi did promise me a job."

"No, not down here in the kitchen. Rudi has people assigned to wash the cutlery and dishes and help with the preparation of food for the evening's business. Wouldn't want to mix up his arrangements. Why don't you just go back up to your room until he gets up?"

It was clear that I was just getting in her way, so after thanking her for the breakfast I made my way back up the stairs at the first floor hallway. At the door to the café I paused and leaned against it, listening. Emil and Leopold were still in there, the noise of furniture moving and general clatter blending with their soft voices. A few feet away the narrow front door of the building led to the outside. It would be a simple matter to keep on walking up the five stone steps onto the sidewalk, turn right and walk the ten blocks or so back to the Astor House. No need to see Rudi at all.

So my head told me, but my feet were like two pieces of stone. They would not move. Inside the door was the curved bar and over the bar was the golden-haired giant. The "brooding Messiah," Adah had called it. My head lifted and a fierce rebellion seized me. I pushed open the door and went into the café. No picture was going to rule my life. Lothar was dead. Lothar was at the bottom of the Atlantic Ocean. Emil had seen him blown up with the *Ocean Monarch*. I did not want to go back to the Astor House, to clean up slopjars and play games with lecherous guests. I wanted to stay here with Rudi and Leopold and Elisabeth.

A half-hour later, I was dressed in a Bavarian peasant outfit with dirndl skirt and brightly embroidered, snowy white blouse. The neckline was low and curved sweetly around my shoulders and across my bosom.

"This is what our waiter girls wear," Leopold said, admiringly. "But I must say you fill it out better than anyone I've ever seen."

A scarf, like Leopold's, covered my braids, and a checked gingham apron protected the blouse and skirts as I helped Emil and Leopold empty spittoons and scrub the wooden table tops and benches. The work was stimulating, the blood rushing to my head and face as I scrubbed. The pain all but disappeared in my arms and head.

The pert little cuckoo clock that hung on one wall chirped nine, ten, then eleven. As we worked, Leopold pelted me with questions. Did the baron perish? How long was I at sea in the lifeboat? Where had I been since then? How had I lived? Did I have any money from the baron's estate?

It was easy to satisfy his curiosity without lying too much. "No, I don't have any money from the baron's estate," I said. "Don't you realize that the new king, Maximilian, would not allow any Bavarian money to be sent abroad? Besides, the baron was able to take out of the country only some family jewels and gold plate. It was in our sea trunks and of course went down with the *Ocean Monarch*."

We sat at the freshly scrubbed table, sipping coffee Emil had fetched from the kitchen. Emil said nothing, merely looked at me suspiciously. I had the distinct feeling he didn't believe a word I was saying.

"But you stood beside the concubine, Lola Montez, the night we stormed that fairy palace of hers, and you were seen not only by me, but by others with her in her carriage." Emil glared at me viciously. "Just what *is* your relationship to that woman?"

"My father was related distantly to the Wittelsbachs," I replied. "My mother died at my birth. When my father died, King Ludwig offered me a place at the court as a lady-in-waiting to his mistress."

Emil banged his coffee mug on the table. "Since when do whores have ladies-in-waiting?"

I flushed, but held my temper. It was important that he not suspect that I was really Ludwig's daughter. "Von Edel asked the king to give me to him in marriage. It was one of Ludwig's last official acts."

Leopold's eyes met mine. Our glances locked for a long moment. "He knows," I thought. "Will he betray my secret?"

"Leave her alone, Emil," Leopold spoke sharply to his friend. "German women know little of politics. Sieglinde was given in marriage to the Baron Von Edel. It was a good match, by Old World standards. Now he is dead, and she is in America to begin a new life."

Leopold's face brightened. "Now you are poor like us, Sieglinde. No more Lola, no more Ludwig, no more baron."

"The truth is, the baron and I were not married very long. I loved him, but he was so much older than I." I reached over to clasp Leopold's hands in mine and gazed deeply into his eyes.

Leopold talked, and I listened, completely fascinated by his stories of the people who frequented the café. "We are the gathering place of artists and intellectuals of all nationalities," he boasted. "They come here for the good German beer, good German food, and stimulating conversation."

Emil rolled his eyes behind the thick glasses. "Ach, the arguments," he said, groaning, "The Forty-eighters may have left their homelands on the other side of the ocean, but they have brought all their political differences with them to America."

"Yes," agreed Leopold, "sometimes tempers get so hot it all ends up in a duel in Washington Park."

"A duel!" I exclaimed. "Isn't duelling against the law, even in America?"

Emil hooted. I smiled at the little man. Apparently he had decided at last to forget the past and to be friends with me. "Since when," he asked, "did the police ever try to stop a duel? They have more than enough to keep them busy; this city is crawling with robbers, murderers, pickpockets, whores—"

"Just like any other in the world," Leopold said excitedly, "but I love New York. A man could make his fortune here."

Abruptly the two men rose from the table and carried the coffee cups to the bar. "Now we must rest," Leopold said, "before the evening's activity begins. You too, Sieglinde. You've been working hard all morning with us. Rudi would be a fool if he didn't put you right to work tonight as a waiter girl."

Alone in the dim room, I sat motionless, gazing at the Barbarossa on the wall. The short curtains on the cellar windows were pulled tightly shut. Only a few candles burned in sconces on the wall. The outlines of the giant bearded figure were barely discernible. Like Lothar, it was part of the past, which was rapidly fading away in the exciting new life of America.

Finally, I too decided to get some rest. But first I walked

230

slowly down the long aisle between the tables, all the way to the unlighted Christmas tree. Rubbing my fevered cheeks against the dark fragrant branches, I stared fixedly at the painting of the Lorelei half hidden by the tree. A good bit of her long golden hair was visible and a part of her arm which held the golden comb. The lower half of the siren's body was encased in scales, so that she resembled a mermaid more than a girl. That moment on the Rhine steamer came back to me, when I had vowed, as I gazed at the real Lorelei rock, that never again would I let love for a man destroy me.

Now that Rosie had found her mother, never again would I need to make the long trip to the East River dock. If Lothar were on this earth anywhere, he would have to find me. I would search for him no longer.

It was all in the hands of fate, both me and my love.

Chapter 20

That night, at the early supper hour, I became a waiter girl for Rudi Stammler. For two hours I worked feverishly, serving a variety of German and American foods prepared in the underground kitchen by Elisabeth and her small army of émigré helpers. By seven o'clock I was able to carry four great steins of beer in my two hands. I wore the peasant skirt and white blouse Leopold had given me that morning, but instead of covering my head with the kerchief, I fixed my long hair in two thick braids which hung down over my shoulders to my knees.

The whole room buzzed with lively discussion, and bits of conversation whirled around me but I was so intent on serving that I could do little more than catch a name here and there. Emil had accused the Forty-eighters of bringing their politics with them, but instead of names like Ludwig, Lola, and Metternich, I heard Daniel Webster, Henry Clay, Zack Taylor. The words "slave" and "free" floated about like birds in the air.

"Who is Zack Taylor?" I asked Leopold, as we stood at the bar waiting for a large order.

His handsome face broke up in shock. "Only the president of these whole United States," he replied, amazed at my ignorance. "He was the hero of the war with Mexico and now everyone looks to him to solve the slavery problem."

"Slavery," I repeated the word slowly. "You mean the Negroes who are bought and sold in the South? What have we in New York to do with them?"

"I perceive, my dear innocent, that there is much you need to learn about your new homeland. The question of owning slaves is tearing the country apart—" He stopped suddenly as the door opened and a new group of patrons entered.

It was Adah Menken, dressed in the same trousers and blouse of last night. Sad-eyed Poe was with her again, but not Edwin Booth. Rudi ran up to them from the middle of the room, bowed gallantly and kissed the actress's outstretched hand. He proceeded to escort them to the far end of the room by the Christmas tree.

"Go over to them, quick," Leopold urged, "she likes you. I'll take care of your previous customers."

As I bent over Adah to inquire about their order, the dark-haired woman looked up, pleased. Then she stretched her neck to kiss me on the cheek. "You look luscious," she declared, "good enough to eat yourself."

I straightened up, conscious that Poe was gazing at my bosom, which rose seductively out of the peasant blouse. "And what sad émigré story have you to tell us?" he asked in his melodious voice. He was already a little drunk and reached out to pull one of my braids playfully.

"You'll get no sad story from me," I replied gaily, tossing my head impishly. "As the daughter of a poor Bavarian farmer, I had no future. Here in America I can become rich."

"Even famous," Poe responded. I listened, entranced at the mere sound of his voice. It was like listening to music, each word a note, carefully chosen and modulated. "Your eyes," he went on expansively, "a man could drown himself in them. Your rounded bosom swells like the earth itself. A man could die happily with his head nestled between the twin hills. That hair, 'tis spun gold, I swear, like Rapunzel, in that story by the brothers Grimm."

Adah put down the stein of beer she'd been gulping, which Rudi had fetched her the moment she sat down. A line of foam etched her finely molded lips. "Please forgive Edgar, my dear," she said to me. "He is inclined to be poetic when he is drunk. Which is all the time. But consider yourself privileged to be spoken of in such lyrical words by one of the greatest poets in America."

Poe continued to stare at me with bloodshot eyes. "You were fashioned by the gods for love, my dear, not for dishing up viands in a dingy cafe."

Adah snorted. "What does she know of love! She is but a child." The luminous black eyes narrowed speculatively as

234

they flew up and down my body. She fingered one of my long braids. "She can't be a day over sixteen."

"Ah—that's the rub. Only children, the very young and innocent, know truly how to love. Only they can surrender themselves body and soul. I had such a love once—" The poet's voice trailed off mournfully.

"Bring me some bean soup, *liebling*, quick, before he turns my stomach." Adah turned toward me abruptly. "What is your name again?"

"I am called Sieglinde."

Poe reared up from the table, his skeletal fingers pressed against the rough wood. "Sieglinde! A noble name! Shades of the Valkyrie. You Germans are so sentimental. Always spinning fanciful myths of great warriors and noble maidens who throw themselves on the fire for love. Like that red-bearded giant on the wall there—" he pointed a long bony finger at the Barbarossa painting—"who's expected to rise from the tomb; like Christ himself on Judgment Day, and save the world."

But suddenly, he fell back down on the table with a thud, his thin brown head face down on the scrubbed wood. "Poor darling," Adah breathed, touching the brown curls softly with her slender fingers, "let him sleep right here. Rudi won't mind. Tonight, when I come back after the performance for my supper, I'll see that he gets home."

After fetching Adah's soup, I left them to see to the other patrons who were now pouring through the narrow door. It had started to snow again and there was much noise of stamping feet in the narrow hall along with vigorous brushing of white flakes from tall hats and cloaks. The café resounded to cheery shouts as people came and went. There was some singing by a small group of Forty-eighters. It was all very exciting to me, and I went about my new duties with a flushed face and happy heart.

About ten o'clock the supper crowd thinned out and Leopold signalled for me to come sit down with him at the table near the bar. He pushed a large bowl of soup in front of me. "Time to stoke your own furnace," he said, making a long face, "the worse is yet to come." The midnight crowd is even thicker than the six o'clock diners. And they stay longer."

The thick bean soup had chunks of chewy bacon floating in it. I dug in greedily. I had been working steadily since five o'clock. Rudi Stammler came up to us and sat down beside me. He was grinning broadly, his little blue eyes dancing in the candlelight. "There is much talk tonight about my new waiter girl," he said, leaning to kiss me lightly on the cheek. "Everyone is dying of curiosity about who you are and where you came from."

I turned my head to look down on the little German, who was at least a head shorter than I. Tonight he was all decked out in a Tyrolean costume, enhancing his elflike appearance. But despite his diminutive stature, there was a certain animal magnetism about him. The forest green breeches fit snugly across narrow hips, so tightly that the bulge of his manhood showed prominently. A brilliantly embroidered vest covered a ruffled shirt, the fabric of which was so thin one could plainly discern the thick mat of sandy hair that covered his chest and extended up to curl out of the open neckline.

I cast my eyes down modestly to my bowl. "I am nobody, really, Mr. Stammler, nobody at all. Just another émigré. In fact, my parents are both—dead." My heart thumped a little at the lie about Ludwig, but perhaps he *was* dead by this time. Nobody knew for sure where the king was, since he had fled Munich for France over a year ago.

"She is the Lorelei of the rock, put into exquisite flesh for our delectation," Leopold shouted dramatically, enunciating his words like an actor on a stage. He pointed to the painting half-hidden by the Christmas tree. "Look, am I not right? Her hair is more golden than the painting."

I opened my mouth to scold Leopold for being so extravagant, but at that moment the strains of music filled the room, and all heads turned toward the bar. A young man, dark and short, with black eyes flashing and dressed in the blouse and scarf of the Forty-eighter, emerged from the green curtain. The flowing white sleeves billowed gracefully as he squeezed a gleaming black and white accordion. His nimble fingers ran up and down the keyboard in a lilting dance melody.

I knew the tune well. It was a peasant dance I'd heard often as a child. Ortrud had often taken me on feast days to the village to watch the men and women dancing in the square. The picture of their whirling brightly colored skirts and the gay ribbons streaming from their hair was one of the brightest memories of my homeland.

Without missing a note, the accordion player now leaped

nimbly on top of the bar and sat down facing the customers, swinging his legs. My eyes widened in amazement as I recognized him. It was Emil! Gloomy, taciturn Emil had taken off his thick glasses and combed his dark hair until it shone like fine leather. He was lost in his music, his head thrown back, his eyes closed.

It was impossible to sit still, as he finished the lively tune with a grand flourish and launched into another folk melody, this one slower and more haunting. I began to hum along with the accordion. My body swayed back and forth on the bench, my feet tapped in rhythm on the bare wood floor.

With the second verse, I started to sing the words: *A maiden in her father's house, she waited for fulfillment, and the call of the earth, one spring morning it came.* The song went on for many verses, telling the sad but familiar story of a maiden loved and betrayed by a faithless lover. Without taking his eyes off me, Leopold leaned over to speak to Rudi. "You need to expand, Rudi, put in a dance floor. Buy up the rest of the block."

Rudi's eyes grew dark, as an angry frown creased his pleasant face. "No, no, a thousand times no," he said in a loud whisper. "Rudi Stammler's establishment will not become just another concert saloon, with naked girls and drunks tearing up the place. Emil's music is enough."

But Leopold would not give up, and as the argument grew in volume I sang louder, conscious now that people were looking at me. Suddenly, the whole room grew silent, Rudi and Leopold stopped arguing, and Emil, without missing a note, jumped down from the bar and walked down to the end of the room where we were sitting, to stand behind me.

Edgar Poe had also risen from his place, wide awake now, and stood on the other side of the table in the narrow aisle. His brooding dark eyes gazed at me transfixed, blazing with suppressed excitement. A few of the patrons left their dinners and gathered round us.

My voice was not strong, and would have been lost in a great concert hall, but in the low-ceilinged cellar room, it was pure, clear, and vibrant. After my momentary panic at suddenly finding myself the center of attention, I lost myself in the music and forgot everything but the story of the tragic maiden. I had lived such a story. My heart was truly in my song. Emil manipulated the accordion skillfully, tempering

237

the volume to suit the modulations of my voice. When at last the song was finished, there was a dramatic silence, then the whole café burst into applause. It grew in volume with cries of "Bravo" and "More, more."

Rudi's face was split wide open in a happy grin. Tears streamed from his little blue eyes. He turned to Leopold and clapped that young man on the shoulder. "*There's* our entertainment, Mr. Leopold Siegel. Emil will play, and Sieglinde will sing. They are perfect together. They got class but—" he thumped his chest dramatically— "they get at the heart strings."

Rudi tore off his peaked Tyrolean hat, threw it into the air, leaned over to crush me to his embroidered chest. My arms flew around his neck in response. The song and the excitement had left me shaken and happy in a way I hadn't been since Lothar and I had been together on Kyffhauser Mountain. As I hugged Rudi, I felt that at last I had come home.

By the middle of January, even the generously gathered, wide-swirling peasant skirts I wore for the nightly entertainment were unable to conceal my swelling figure. I dreaded telling Rudi, fearing he would be furious at my deception and the prospect of losing my services.

The café's business had doubled since Emil and I had started our act at Christmas. In addition to his musical talents, Emil turned out to be something of an artist and painted an alluring picture of me as Lorelei, which Rudi fastened to the iron fence in front of the restaurant. He even pasted rhinestones in the comb to produce a more theatrical effect.

But to my surprise Rudi was elated at the news of my pregnancy. "*Liebschen,* how *wunderbar!*" he exclaimed, pulling me close against his broad chest. "It is only natural that one so beautiful should be so fruitful." Many times, especially when he had drunk more beer than he should, or after an especially moving performance by Emil and me, Rudi would kiss me excitedly on the mouth, shouting, "Marry me, my Lorelei, marry me. Quick!"

But it was all in jest. At least everyone took it that way. Rudi was a kisser, a pincher of bottoms, a slapper of thighs. But that's as far as he went with any girl.

"Once there was a girl, a long time ago, in Germany," Elisabeth told me, "but you must never speak of it to Rudi.

It still hurts, I guess. Whatever happened, Rudi seems to be cured of romance forever. He's all business, just lives for the café."

Perhaps that's why I found him attractive, despite the fact that he had to stretch up on his toes to kiss me. The persistent attentions of Leopold Siegel and other amorous patrons left me cold, but when the little sandy-haired Rudi squeezed me so hard I could hardly breathe, I felt a warmth in my blood and a tingling in my loins.

Now Rudi released me and stood back to survey my figure. "If anything, Sieglinde darling, your added plumpness makes you look more seductive than ever. We will simply devise new costumes as you go along. You'll be able to sing up to the last minute."

So I discarded the variety of folk costumes for more loosely fitted Grecian-type tunics and floor-length robes that fell in soft folds from the shoulder. One night, I came into the café wearing a wheat-colored chiffon sprigged with tiny harvest fruits and vegetables. Round red apples, luscious pears, even green curly-headed cabbages were embroidered right into the fabric. A thick twist of silken rope tied under and across my breasts to outline their opulent fullness.

Leopold's handsome face lit up like a candle. He ran a nervous hand through his curls. "But how marvelous, how perfectly spectacular." His voice rose to a crescendo of excitement. "You are the embodiment of Ceres, the goddess of the harvest. All you need to complete the picture is a sheaf of wheat or a cornucopia of fruits." He threw a wicked, sidelong glance at Rudi. "A passel of dancing girls wouldn't hurt either."

Rudi, who had not hugged me in his usual fashion when I came into the restaurant for the evening, stood by quietly, an unusual brooding look in his blue eyes. Then he slammed his beer down on the wooden table with a bang. "By Jupiter," he cracked, "for once you've hit on something, Leopold. We can do without the dancing daughters, thank you, but the sheaf of wheat I can manage."

So the seductive siren Lorelei of the rock was replaced by the mother goddess Ceres. I slipped into the new role easily, having done it often at Frau Anna's. Every night I sat on the bar, or walked majestically up and down the narrow aisle, resting an enormous bundle of ripe wheat on one arm. The frothy golden tassels mingled with the golden strands of my hair which I still wore down, loosely hanging to my hips. The few times I braided it into the neat coronet brought howls of protest from the patrons.

My only other ornament consisted of a wreath of green leaves of field flowers on my head. Although the wheat was artificial, since it was still the middle of winter, the flowers were fresh hothouse specimens, ordered at great expense each night.

Edgar Poe, the sick poet, was ecstatic. The closer I came to giving birth, the more he idolized me. Every night he sat at the table right in front of the bar, usually falling asleep where he was until Adah or one of his other artist friends came to take him home. The dark-haired actress and the actor Edwin Booth became part of what was known city-wide as the Sieglinde Cult.

"Little old New York has never seen anything quite like you, my dear," Booth remarked, his thin handsome face breaking into a rare smile. "We have more than our share of women who display their bodies for money, many more who sell themselves and their virtue for baubles. But you perform a miracle. You are seductive and refined simultaneously."

Adah agreed. "A pregnant widow who can pack in the audiences that you do——" she sighed. "I'm eaten up with envy." She gave me a long, thoughtful look. "While I really don't want you to take my advice, since the life of the theatre can be hell at times, you really should seriously consider going on the stage."

Thoughts of Ymir and our little skits at Frau Anna's soirées flashed through my mind. I found the idea intriguing. I glowed at the praise from these two, especially from Edwin Booth, who was adored by the most desirable women in America.

But I tried to push all other thoughts from my mind except those concerning the coming baby. Remembering the stormy time of my first pregnancy, and the evenings with Karl's consoling arms about me, I ruthlessly suppressed any violent emotions. I avoided looking at the Barbarossa painting any more than I had to. If by chance my eyes rested on the enormous portrait, I tore them away. I didn't need that extra excitement the bent head of the brooding Messiah always aroused in me.

As soon as the ice broke on the Hudson, I took the river

steamer to visit Rosie and Lauretta Chambers. John Ryan's home was truly magnificent, a fine specimen of the stately homes that lined the upper reaches of the river. A wide veranda surrounded the entire house and enormous willow trees bordered a broad sweep of grass leading right down to the river's edge.

Lauretta urged me to move in with her and Rosie. "Give up that hectic New York nightlife. The city is no place to raise a child. Here you would have peace and tranquility as well as financial security."

"It's very tempting, I don't deny you that," I replied. "But one day you'll want to remarry, and what would happen to me then?"

Her pale face broke into a knowing smile. "How long do you think you can remain single, after the child is born? My brother and I move in a very select circle of wealthy people. You'll be snatched up in a few months, I warrant."

"No, I like what I'm doing," I said firmly. How could I tell this kind woman that the adulation of Rudi's patrons was wine to my flagging spirit, that the thundering applause each night nourished my empty heart?

"Besides, Rudi has been so good to me. I couldn't leave now."

"Well, at least," she said, her words betraying her anxiety, "come out here to have the child. My brother will fetch the best doctors. Healthy as you appear, my dear girl, complications *can* arise."

But I remained firm, and we parted friends. "I think I understand, Sieglinde," Lauretta said as I boarded the steamer for the return trip to New York. "But always remember this—you saved Rosie's life, and if ever you're in trouble of any kind, or become weary of the exciting life you're leading now—"

"I know, I know." I kissed her and Rosie goodbye, and with tears in my own, went back to Rudi's to await the birth of my child.

That man, a strong believer in prenatal influences, insisted that I walk every day in Washington Park. "You need the fresh air and the exercise," he said sternly, "and besides you must see beautiful things. What you look at now will influence the child's mind and body. I don't want him to look like that scarecrow Poe who sits moon-eyed at your feet every night."

The more old-fashioned Elisabeth clucked disapprovingly. "Women in the family way, especially just weeks before their time, should stay at home, and not go parading around in public."

Happily, I obeyed Rudi's command, and ignored Elisabeth's cluckings. There was plenty of natural beauty in the square block of green on the borders of Greenwich village. Ancient wide-branching oaks and chestnuts, towering graceful beeches and poplars bestowed a kindly shade on walkers and picnickers, also providing nesting places for thousands of birds whose songs filled the spring air. Benches sat invitingly beside a small lake where children, supervised strictly by nannies or anxious mothers, sailed their little toy boats.

Ironically, there was ugliness too. Once the site of public executions, the remnants of a wooden scaffold still perched gruesomely on a small rise right in the middle of the park. Children often played on the splintery crossbeams. While I scoffed at Rudi's superstitious beliefs about prenatal influences, I avoided the hill of death, as the place was called. Besides, there was always a mob of people there, listening to the abolitionist preacher Henry Ward Beecher, who left his church in Brooklyn to bring his antislavery message to the man in the street.

Being occupied with approaching motherhood and keeping Rudi's customers happy, I could not bring myself to get excited about the slavery question. The café buzzed with nothing else every night, the arguments pro and con stopping only long enough for Emil and me to perform.

Leopold explained what all the new fuss was about. "Congress has just passed a law which allows a Southern slave owner to come north into a free state and capture his runaway slaves. That means a black man can never be free in any part of America."

"But how horrible," I exclaimed, remembering only too well my own helpless feelings of being enslaved. Lola had owned me, the king had "given" me to her. And the old Baronin von Hohenstaufen had tried to keep me prisoner in her gloomy Schloss.

"What can we do about it?" I asked Leopold.

"Not much, I'm afraid. Some brave men sneak the fugitive slaves into Canada, where our law cannot reach them. But other greedy people hunt them down for the reward money."

One mild afternoon in the middle of April, barely two

weeks before my baby was due, I tucked my hand into Leopold's arm and started off with him on our daily walk. Thoughts of hangings and runaway slaves were far from my mind. The blond handsome Forty-eighter was my usual companion; occasionally, when he was not available, Max or Emil. A decent woman could not, of course, walk alone in the park, or anywhere on the New York streets. I'd learned that hard lesson last Christmas Eve on the East River wharf.

Elisabeth had packed us a picnic basket, which swung from Leopold's free arm. I wore a pretty cotton frock, a long velvet cloak lined with taffeta disguising my condition. Leopold was his usual jaunty self in his flowing blouse, red silk scarf tied loosely around his neck and broad-brimmed hat set rakishly on his blond curls.

"We make a lovely couple, or should I say 'threesome,' " Leopold said lightly, squeezing my hand possessively. "Just say the word, Sieglinde, and we'll tie the knot as soon as it's decently possible."

From the beginning, he'd made it quite clear that he was courting me. And I continued to make it quite clear that I was not interested in anything more than a permanent friendship.

"In October the conventional year of mourning will be over," Leopold said now, "and then you'll have no excuse. The child will be old enough to travel with us on a honeymoon trip."

Quick annoyance swept over me at his breezy presumption, but was just as quickly banished by my real affection for him. Since I had found it futile to argue with Leopold in the past about his ardor for me, I merely laughed now, and said banteringly, "And do you have our itinerary already mapped out? Where shall we spend our first weeks of married bliss? You, me, and the baby, I mean."

He frowned slightly, steering me toward a grassy knoll underneath our favorite giant oak tree which was just beginning to leaf out. I sat down, carefully arranging my wide skirt around me, and leaned gratefully back against the broad trunk.

A violent kick in my abdomen brought a grimace to my own face. "Little Rudi is being obstreperous today," I remarked. "It feels good to sit down." I had decided the week after Rudi rescued me from the docks to name the child after him. Boy or girl, it would be called Rudi, and the kindly little German would be the godfather.

Characteristically he had ignored my reference to the coming child. He continued to be upset over my naming the child Rudi, feeling strongly that the Old World way of naming a child after its father was the proper thing to do. He assumed, as did everyone else, that the child was Von Edel's. But I detested the name Franz, and to call the baby Lothar was out of the question.

Now he settled the picnic basket down carefully between the knotty roots of the tree and, heedless of the curious glances of some children playing nearby, knelt down at my feet. A smoldering but intense longing erased the bantering look from his eyes. He reached out to clasp me around the knees, squashing the thin gauzy fabric of my skirt between his white sleeved arms.

I tensed, knowing I was in for one of his impassioned speeches.

"Darling, sweet sweet Sieglinde," he whispered hoarsely, "I love you more than life itself. You are my very soul. I think of nothing else day and night. You need a lover, you are young, passionate—you are as hungry for me as I am for you."

Shocked and repulsed as always when he got this way, I drew back, and spoke more sharply than I intended. "Please don't spoil our friendship, Leopold. I cannot love you the way a woman should love the man she marries."

Turning away quickly to hide the shame and humiliation I felt for him, very gently I pried loose the clutching hands from my skirt and tore off the checkered cloth from the basket and began spreading out the bountiful meal of roast chicken, fruit, and biscuits.

But as always, he continued to press his suit. His words were clear, pointed, sounding more like a lawyer before a judge than a lover pleading with his mistress. "You are but a child, having known but one man only in your life—and that one worn out and old. Very old."

"Oh, you'd be surprised," I said smartly. "Von Edel was in tiptop condition."

He was back at me again, leaning over the spread-out food. "If you are going to tell me that you ever reached ecstasy with that old aristocrat, I'll have to call you a liar."

Stung now, and furious at being talked to like a child, I lashed out at him. "Now you've gone too far, my friend.

244

For your information, Leopold Siegel, I *have* known the love of a young man, one far handsomer and far more virile than you can ever hope to be."

Even as I said the harsh words, I regretted them, but I wouldn't take them back. His constant wooing was exhausting me.

He pulled himself back once more, leaned against the tree beside me. "Did he have red hair, this extraordinary young man?"

My blood chilled. How could he know? Maybe it was just a wild guess. I stared at him with wide-eyed innocence. "Red hair! Whatever gave you that odd idea?"

His handsome features were contorted in anguish as he replied, "I've seen the way you look at the Barbarossa painting over the bar. The pure naked longing in your eyes is a dead giveaway. Oh, God, Sieglinde, if only once, only once, you could look at me that way."

The long slender hands grabbed mine again, squeezing them so hard I yelped with the pain. "Yes," I flung the word at him, completely exasperated. "But he died. And part of me died with him. The part of me that can truly love a man passionately." I pressed my face against the rough bark of the tree, closing my eyes against the suffering I knew would be blazing out.

There was a long silence, broken only by the shouts of the playing children, the clear, sharp cries of the birds in the lacy branches of the oaks. Finally, I opened my eyes, to see Leopold nibbling on a piece of chicken. His face was that of a schoolboy who has just been scolded for raiding the cookie jar.

Laughter bubbled up in my throat, escaped in delighted peals from my mouth. I let it roll out into the sunny afternoon. Tears streamed from my eyes. My belly hurt so bad I clutched at it with both hands. The whole thing, my being pregnant with a dead man's child, my pretense at being a nobleman's wife, and Leopold's ardent suit—all of it was suddenly unbearably funny.

We finished our meal and continued walking our usual route past the elegant townhouses which faced the park on four sides. Built in the popular Greek Revival architecture, they sported sleek marble pillars and impressive marble-faced front entrances.

"One day I will live in such a house," Leopold couldn't

resist saying, although he didn't add his usual "with you, Sieglinde."

"As if you could afford it," I teased, "on what you make as a waiter for Rudi Stammler."

"Oh-oh," he sang out in a jocular tone. "You don't know all there is to know about me, young woman. The owners of a *very large* beer parlor and concert saloon have made me a very tempting offer. They feel I would be a perfect manager."

"Then why do you remain at Rudi's?" I asked.

"For one thing, I've held onto the idea that I could persuade Rudi to expand, and I would much prefer to stay uptown, where the clientele is a bit more refined. For another—if I left Rudi's, I would never see you, Sieglinde. I'd be involved night and day with my new job."

"Don't let me get in the way of your career, Leopold," I said earnestly. "It is foolish to sacrifice one's whole life for love. Believe me, I speak from experience."

But that night, getting dressed in my Ceres gown for the early supper show, I stood for a moment at the window gazing out into the squalor of the alley. A late afternoon sun fought with the ever-present haze of sooty grime which hung constantly over the city. My nose wrinkled delicately against the smell of burning refuse and manure. Two ragged children pulled a rickety wagon loaded with horse manure they'd picked up off the street. The very poor dried the stuff and burned it for fuel.

My thoughts turned back on the afternoon. Life with Leopold in a house facing Washington Park or perhaps even on a hill overlooking the Hudson would be serene and even beautiful. I had only to say "yes" and presto, I would turn into a gracious hostess, a devoted mother, a loving wife. In bed, in the heat of passion, I could forget for a few moments that there had been another, wilder, sweeter passion. After all, I had to admit that my body had responded like a flame to Ymir, and even to McGreevey. What difference was there between one man and another? Leopold would be faithful, witty, charming, and most important, wealthy.

Angry with myself, weary from thinking and the eternal waiting for the child to be born, I flung myself on the bed and buried my face in the soft quilt. Wasn't it enough? Did I need the sun and the moon too? I remembered bitterly the vow I'd made at the Lorelei rock, standing so defiantly at the rail of the *Rising Star*—never to allow love for any man to destroy me. Now I was letting a memory ruin my chance at a good life.

"Sieglinde, are you all right?" The door opened a crack and Elisabeth poked a concerned face into the room. "Maybe you shouldn't sing tonight. You've been looking pale the last couple days."

I slid nimbly off the bed. "Oh, I'm all right, just meditating," I laughed.

"Ach, the way you jump around," she exclaimed, throwing up her arms in mock horror. "Now remember, at the first twinge—"

"Yes, Elisabeth, you've told me a thousand times. Get into bed, call Rudi, fetch the doctor, *and* the midwife. Don't worry, at the first pain I'll let out a holler that'll reach all the way to the Bowery."

Picking up the sheaf of wheat from the tall chiffonier, I cuddled the rough stalks against my bosom like an infant. I walked clumsily down the long corridor, down the steps, placing both feet squarely on each tread.

I knew myself to be a liar. Desire shivered through my every limb, even now when I was big with child. The naked form that loomed in my fevered imagination was not elegant and slender, with a profusion of blond curls. The tormenting image always assumed the shape of the brooding Messiah, the shaggy redheaded giant of the painting over the bar in Rudi's cafe.

Chapter 21

Emil and I had skipped our usual morning rehearsal so that I could make "one last shopping expedition." Rudi refused to let me go out alone and Leopold was nowhere to be found. I suspected he was avoiding me after our walk and argument in the park yesterday.

The crowds on the street seemed thicker than usual. In fact the crush was so dense Max stopped the carriage in the middle of the street. "You'll have to get to the sidewalk best you can," he called to us as we poked our heads out the door of the carriage.

Emil leaped out, and although he was anything but tall, he was as broad in the shoulders as Max. Enfolding me in his arms against his chest, he pushed me to the sidewalk.

Seeing us safe, Max took off, promising to return for us in an hour. He shouted at us from his high driver's seat. "Make sure you're standing on the sidewalk right here in exactly one hour." He flicked his whip at the big clock which was set into the marble of the building. "I won't be able to wait for you."

As we reached the store entrance, it became obvious what was causing the problem. Henry Ward Beecher was holding forth right in front of Stewart's, his massive grey head towering over the crowd. Shouts of "Dirty abolitionist." "Nigger lover," filled the air.

Emil rushed me inside through the angry-faced mob. "Looks like a riot's about to start any minute. The whole city's in a turmoil. Don't want to get caught in anything like that—especially in your delicate condition."

A.T. Stewart's Department Store was a fairyland to me. Indeed, the magnificent white marble structure looked more like a king's palace than a place of business. All the elite of the city shopped there. It was pure pleasure just to stroll between the shining glass cases, admiring the expensive jewelry, the bright ribbons and trinkets, the bolts of exotic fabrics from all over the world—silks, crêpes, paisleys, cashmeres.

We headed for the ribbon counter at the opposite end of the store. Throngs of fashionably dressed women filled the aisles and leaned against the display counters. Attractive salesgirls, dressed in spotless white blouses and dark skirts, hovered solicitously over this rich clientele.

"So many charming women in this city and I still crawl every night into a lonely bed," mourned Emil.

"No need for you to remain a bachelor another day," I replied, "or Leopold either, for that matter. Plenty of fish in the sea."

"Takes more than wishing—or fishing," Emil quipped, then laughed at his own wit. I glanced at him sideways as we walked. He was far from handsome, not even good looking, with his mousey brown straight hair, and the thick glasses that hid his sensitive eyes. The broad-brimmed Forty-eighter hat that looked so dashing on Leopold only succeeded in making Emil look dumpy. Yet, unaccountably, there was an animal vigor about him, which I found completely lacking in Leopold, Rudi had it too. A quick picture of Emil, naked, in bed beside me, flashed through my mind. I imagined him with lots of body hair. His arms and thighs would be thick and muscular.

At the ribbon counter I forgot romance and devoted myself to fingering the satins, the grosgrains, the cunning ruffled lengths the pretty brunette salesclerk pulled off the shelves behind her. Elizabeth had knitted a bonnet for the baby, and it needed only a ribbon to thread through the crown. I was determined that the child would wear the bonnet immediately after birth. Emil stood quietly beside me.

"Can't imagine that having a ribbon for a bonnet constitutes an emergency," he said, "enough to drag me and Max downtown in the middle of the day."

"Pregnant women have strange desires," I retorted vehemently. "Anyway, this is the last time I can be out. And I didn't want to use an old used-up piece of ribbon for such a lovely bonnet."

Finally settling on a pale satin, I turned around to face the patient Emil. "Let's walk around. We've got plenty of time before Max returns with the landau."

At that moment, a slender young woman, who'd been standing beside me also examining the ribbons, spoke to the clerk in a sharp, querulous tone of voice. "Oh, dear, it's so difficult, you'd think with all these colors I could find one I liked."

The voice was sweet and high, almost a chirp. But unmistakably a Berliner accent. A nagging memory started up in my brain as she went on talking to the clerk. Somewhere, sometime, I'd heard that voice. I whipped around to look, tantalized. Probably one of Rudi's steady customers, and she'd certainly be offended if I didn't greet her.

"Bettina!" My heart almost leaped out of my chest for joy and amazement. It was Bettina, smelling like a hothouse full of roses and all decked out like a gaudy fashion-plate in a pearl-grey moire cape, richly lined with a glossy fur. A bright green moire gown peeped out underneath the cape, and what looked like genuine gold thread wound its way in an elaborate embroidery completely around the wide hem of the skirt. This glittering doll was a far cry from the simple girl in the grey smock I remembered from Frau Anna's, but the coppery curls spilling out from the feathered bonnet reassured me that it really was my dear friend. This time she was not riding naked on the back of a wild stallion, and I could make myself known to her. But there was no need of that.

"Sieglinde! Sieglinde, *liebschen*, what are you doing in New York?"

"Just what you're doing, silly—buying ribbon!"

Then words failed us, and we squeezed each other, tears running down our cheeks, laughing and crying all together. Passing customers and salesgirls looked on, amused. In a city of immigrants, old friends meeting by chance after a long separation was an everyday occurrence.

"Oh, it's so *wunderbar*, so very good to see you," she cried, throwing her head back in her old irresistible off-hand way. The elaborate bonnet slipped down, and the mass of coppery curls gleamed like fiery embers in the light of the massive overhead chandeliers.

A loud noise from behind us told me that Emil was feeling neglected. He cleared his throat twice and waited for introductions. With my arm still curved on Bettina's moire shoulder, I turned her around so that we both faced Emil. The young man's brown eyes behind the thick glasses glistened with anticipation.

"Emil Poesche, may I present my dearest friend in all the world, Bettina——" I stopped, embarrassed, suddenly realizing I had never known her last name. Frau Anna's girls had no surnames. I quickly recovered, however, and improvised, trusting Bettina not to give me away.

"Bettina Schneider."

The pert green eyes swept Emil from head to foot. "You are, I perceive, one of the famous Forty-eighters, the student rebels who fought so bravely, but lost so completely. Strange to see Sieglinde with you."

Fearing that she was about to disclose the whole sordid episode at Heidelberg with the Burschen and my career at Frau Anna's, I quickly interrupted her.

"Such finery, Bettina, such a beautiful gown. You've done well in America, I can tell."

Her freckled face turned beet red, but she said only, "You too, Sieglinde. It seems that we have both found our pots of gold."

Emil, who had not taken his eyes off Bettina's face, now glanced up anxiously at a large clock over the counter. "Max will be waiting for us in a few minutes, Sieglinde. With the traffic as thick as it is today, it will take us some time to get back to the café." He looked inquiringly at Bettina.

"Perhaps your friend would join us for *Mittagsessen*, or as they say in America, dinner?"

"But of course." I was overjoyed at the idea. "Bettina and I will have so much to talk about—so much time to make up for."

She smiled prettily and replaced the fallen bonnet demurely on her curls. I had forgotten how devastating her dimples could be. They had the predictable effect on Emil.

"And just where is the café?" she asked.

"Rudi Stammler's, at Bleeker and Broadway. Emil and I both work there."

There was a momentary silence, then a look of shocked recognition swept her face, and she blurted out, "Sieglinde, you are the famous Lorelei, the girl who sings with the sheaf of wheat. Why, you're the talk of New York."

I blushed and said modestly, "Emil is the real musician. It's his magic with the accordion that makes our act so successful."

"Men like Edgar Poe and Edwin Booth do not come every night to gaze at me," responded the homely young

252

man, who now took his turn at blushing. He had taken off his large hat upon entering the store and his sable brown hair gleamed smooth and thick. Bettina's wide-spaced green eyes stared boldly at him. Emil opened his mouth to speak, but apparently being uncertain how to deal with this forward young woman, closed it again. A foolish smile split his face.

"Max will be waiting," I said sharply, tearing them both out of their trance. Tucking one arm under Emil's and the other under Bettina's, I walked resolutely between them toward the front entrance.

Emil wisely volunteered to sit up on the high seat with Max, leaving the inside of the carriage to me and Bettina, with the excuse that two ladies who haven't seen each other in more than a year would find a masculine presence a distinct nuisance.

But his face was bright as he said it. Bettina laughed, flirting outrageously with both him and the burly Max. My heart was light. I felt like singing right there in the middle of Broadway as Max and Emil helped me onto the high step to the inside of the landau.

Once inside the closed carriage, however, all the animation left my redheaded friend, and she gazed somberly out the little square of window, avoiding my eyes.

"You remember, Sieglinde, how I once told you that I considered my body my talent, and that I was not ashamed to use it as other people use their brains of musical abilities."

"Bettina darling, don't tell me anything—there's no need." I laid my gloved hand on hers, which was trembling in her lap.

"Oh, but I must." The beautiful green eyes swam with tears, which flowed unchecked down her freckled cheeks. "It's like an answer to prayer, Sieglinde, bumping into you in Stewart's. I'm at the end of my rope. I can't stand the life I lead—"

Her head dropped and I reached out instinctively to pull it against the mound of my belly. I laughed uproariously. "I don't have any lap for you to cry into, Bettina. As you can see, I am very much pregnant."

As I had expected, her sobs quickly dissolved into laughter, and she told me in a few words the story of her life since leaving Germany with such high hopes. "Working as a hotel chambie is such hard work," she pouted, "and the

253

wages so little—well, at Frau Anna's you know, we lived like queens. So-o-o-o," she drew out the word with a sigh, "I became an entertainer, and a prostitute."

She buried her lovely tear-stained face in my belly, ashamed to meet my eyes. Her muffled voice mumbled the rest of the story, which I already knew. "Sieglinde, I ride naked every night on a horse at the Astor House. In front of a roomful of men."

I stroked the coppery curls and said gently, reassuringly, "You did a lot worse than that at Frau Anna's, if I recall."

"But it was so glamorous there, so intimate, so professional!"

I nodded, although she couldn't see me. The lump in my throat kept me from saying any more just then. I myself was remembering Ymir, and Herr Grauberg from Hamelin, the little man who had regained his virility when I got myself all wet as Lorelei.

Pulling a scented hankerchief from her gold net reticule, Bettina lifted her head and blew her nose vigorously. "They bring me presents, they feed me, buy me clothes, but they don't ask me to marry them!"

It was the simplest thing in the world to persuade Bettina to give up her job at the Astor House and come to work for Rudi. The whole matter was settled by the time we reached the café. Emil was more pleased than anybody.

Chapter 22

The tantalizing aroma of fresh hot coffee combined with an awful racket from outside the building to tear me out of a deep slumber. A hot dry wind blew in through the open window of the bedroom. "What's going on out there, an earthquake?" I muttered groggily.

"Wake up, it's the Fourth of July," Bettina shouted at me from across the bedroom where she bent over little Rudi's cradle. "Your first in America. I got here last year just in time for the fun."

"The Fourth?" I echoed. "Oh, yes, Independence Day. Fireworks, cannon, parades—Rudi told me all about it. Does this go on all day?"

"And far into the night," she replied, laughing at my consternation. She picked up the child, wrapping him securely in the light blanket, and brought him over to the bed for me to nurse. "And a wonderful day for a christening too. Little Rudi will get his name the same day his country got hers."

"High time too," I said. "He's over two months old. But Rudi thought it a clever idea to do it on the Fourth. That way we can have one big extravagant party."

Bettina stood looking down at us as the little mouth hunted and found the nipple. The child began to suck greedily. "He makes as much noise as the firecrackers outside," she laughed. "You are so lucky, Sieglinde, so very lucky, to have such a beautiful baby."

"And healthy as a young colt, too," I murmured gratefully.

"He's always hungry," she said wonderingly. "How do new mothers manage to do anything else?"

"They have wonderfully kind, helpful friends like you," I

replied reaching out to clasp the hand that lay on the bed cover. Since that April night she'd come home with me from Stewart's, Bettina had slept with me in the big bed, moving after Rudi's birth to a cot brought by Elisabeth. She was alone with me the night my pains came upon me, and had with her own hands brought Lothar's child into the world, long before the midwife arrived. It had been an easy birth.

We had become like sisters, I felt closer to her than I ever had to any person since my nurse Ortrud. Two months of wholesome food, regular meals, and peace of mind had transformed the former prostitute. Her lovely green eyes had lost that hungry, haunted look, and she fairly bounced around the café like a heifer in a grassy spring meadow.

She was proving to be Rudi's most popular waiter girl. "I'm making almost as much money as I did at the Astor House," she exulted. "Rudi's customers are big tippers."

More than a little part of her happiness stemmed from her relationship with Emil. Several times I'd awakened during the night to find her cot empty. Once she crept back into the room to find me awake, cuddling little Rudi back to sleep. She blushed sweetly, like a sixteen-year-old going through her first crush. "I guess you know where I've been," she said, her eyes sparkling. On her face was the soft radiant look of a woman who has just been loved.

"Bettina dear," I said, "I couldn't be happier. Why don't you and Emil get married? That way you wouldn't have to wear out the carpet going back and forth."

"You know, it's strange," she said dreamily, "he isn't at all what I had always imagined my ideal lover to be. He's anything but tall, dark, and handsome."

"Don't question, Bettina," I replied softly, thinking of my own difficulties. "Love strikes unexpectedly, when you least expect it. Just accept it, and be grateful."

"Oh, I'd get married tomorrow," she said quickly, "but Emil—he's so oldfashioned about it. Says he has to have a nest egg before he settles down. At least enough to rent a whole house for us."

She'd leaped out of the cot and taken the baby from me to put him back in the cradle. I looked up enviously at the tousled curls, the flushed cheeks, the soft lips. She had just been thoroughly kissed. I was wretched with envy.

"What about yourself?" she said, returning to the bed.

"Rudi looks at you like a starving Turk. You need to get married lots more than I do."

"He hasn't asked me."

"Pish, tosh," she said, imitating a favorite expression of Edwin Booth's. "As if he needed to. Ask him. Just move over in bed some night, when he comes in to play with the baby."

She was right, of course. Since the baby's birth, Rudi's manner toward me had changed drastically. No more the fatherly hug and kiss when we met. He never touched me at all, which in itself spoke volumes. The pale blue eyes under the sandy brows glittered with a new intensity, which I recognized as wanting. But he remained, at all times, the perfect gentleman.

Now Bettina was bustling about, getting dressed for the christening ceremony. "The priest said ten o'clock, and it's already nine." She walked briskly to the window and pulled it shut.

"Don't need all that noise. Besides there's precious little breeze coming in anyway, just that horrid gunpowder smell."

"Rudi has to be in the parade by noon," I remarked, putting the baby down at the foot of the bed, and swinging my legs out. "He wanted me to sit all dressed up on the firehouse hose carriage, but I put my foot down. It's called the *Lorelei*, after me—and the real one of course."

"He's sure proud of that thing," she agreed. "But no point in making a spectacle of yourself. Let him get somebody else, if he wants to win the prize. Maybe he can put a dress on the horses." We both laughed.

Like practically every New York merchant, Rudi was a volunteer fireman. Many nights the café would empty out for an hour or two, while all able-bodied men ran to put out a new conflagration somewhere in the city—usually the Bowery or one of the tinder boxes in Greenwich Village. Each company of firemen had its own hose carrier and water carriage, which they painted with colorful scenes—mostly buxom women—and decorated elaborately with flowers and streamers for every parade.

Bettina had finished dressing herself in a pretty light cotton frock sprigged with summer flowers. "Not as elegant as I would like for a chirstening," she said, as she brushed her red curls in front of the mirror, "but it's too hot to put on silk or even moire."

"You look ravishing," I declared firmly, admiring her fresh beauty. "I bet Emil can put his hands around your waist."

She dimpled at me, smiling her thanks at the praise. Then she came back to the bed to pick up the baby. "Now to get the guest of honor dressed for the big occasion."

She put little Rudi down in the cradle, where he commenced to wail, pulled open a drawer in the chiffonier and drew out a long lacy christening gown. Elisabeth had unearthed it in one of her numerous trunks in the attic.

"Here, let me help." I walked over to the cradle and picked up the squalling infant. The little mouth, which had been wide open with rage, immediately closed. I kissed away two fat tears which had slid down the downy cheeks. Kristina had been about his age, just a little past two months, when Karl had carried her on his back to Mannheim. Two months of precious life she'd had. But she'd been a quiet child, who seldom cried. I swallowed the hot lump in my throat.

"That infernal banging outside has my baby all upset," I said irritably. "You'd think there'd be some other way to celebrate our country's birthday." I pressed the soft face against my neck, savoring the feel of the young flesh on mine. Having a baby, holding a baby, nursing a baby, feeling the pull of the mouth on my nipple—these things were the most sensual experiences in my life.

"He's likely to really raise the roof when the priest sprinkles all that holy water on his head," I said now.

Bettina made a clucking sound with her tongue. "Not with all that thick red hair he's got. He'll never feel the water." She took the baby from my arms. "It's a godmother's job to dress the baby. You just go back to bed to get some more rest. The party tonight's going to be a real humdinger. It's your first public appearance, remember."

I nodded and slid gratefully back between the sheets, pulling up the thin summer blanket. For tonight Rudi had thrown open the café; all drinks and food would be "on the house."

"Rudolph Franz Andreas Von Edel," Bettina repeated the names slowly, deliberately, her green eyes sharp and thoughtful. She pulled the long white garment swiftly over the baby's head and buttoned the tiny buttons which ran all the way down the front.

Then she said abruptly, in a deceptively soft voice, "Seems to me you've left out a very important name."

"What's that? Isn't three enough for one little boy?"

"Lothar."

"Lothar?" I said smoothly. "Why should I call my baby Lothar?"

I looked at her warily, as she plunked herself and the baby down on the bed. She lifted the little legs and drew on a pair of knitted stockings, then some soft white leather shoes which Emil had fashioned especially for the occasion.

"Because he's the baby's father, that's why." Holding the child with one hand, she ran a tiny comb through the little thatch of soft coppery curls.

"He could be your child," I said, hedging for time. "Your hair is exactly the same color."

"But he isn't," she answered testily. "He's yours—and this Lothar's whose name was on your lips moments before the child emerged from the womb. And in case nobody's ever told you, my dear, you talk in your sleep."

"Lothar is dead," I said stonily. "This child was conceived during my marriage to the baron. Therefore, according to law, he belongs to the Von Edel family, and will bear that name."

"There is talk in the café," Bettina continued, "about a Lothar von Hohenstaufen, a giant of a man with a shaggy red beard to his waist. Some think him to be the legendary Frederick Barbarossa—you know about *him*, of course."

"Yes, yes of course. The painting over the bar. But so what? Are you implying that this—this Lothar von Hohenstaufen was my lover?"

Finished with dressing the child, Bettina stood up. She and little Rudi made a handsome pair in their chirstening day finery. I jumped out of bed and faced them in my rumpled nightgown. Pulling the child out of her arms, I held him high in front of her startled gaze.

"Look. Look at this child, Bettina. He's handsome, strong, healthy, and from all indications, highly intelligent. Do you want him to be known as a bastard? Even in America, the land of the free, to be illegitimate is to be nothing. Worse than nothing."

My voice rose to a shout. A fierce rage burned within me, a fire born of agony and despair that the father of my child was not here to see this day.

"Darling, darling, don't carry on like this. You'll spoil

your milk." Bettina's face had gone white, as she realized she had struck at the truth buried deep in my heart. Her voice dropped to a whisper. "It's just that certain people— Emil, Leopold, Rudi—have guessed that this Lothar, the leader of the rebel Burschen back in Bavaria, was at one time your lover. But we love you. We are your friends, your family, Sieglinde. We'll keep your secret."

By seven, the café was packed to the rafters. The whole German-American colony had come out for the christening, it seemed. According to custom, a wreath of hemlock hung on the door, a charcoal sketch of mother and child adorning the center. Gifts for little Rudi were piled high on a table set up in the hallway.

Well-wishers came from all over New York to toast my newborn child, and I received them like a queen, holding court in a large wooden chair decorated with red, white, and blue streamers and covered with a deep blue velvet cloth. My dress was a wheat-colored silk in the newly popular sleeveless Grecian style. Soft folds of creamy fabric fell from gold clasps at my shoulders; a golden rope encircled my waist and tied across and under my bosom. The neckline was high, edged with gold embroidery. A thick golden bracelet encircled my left arm, in the shape of a viper with rubies for eyes. It was Rudi's gift for the new mother.

"I feel more like Cleopatra than Sieglinde," I said, as Rudi slipped the bracelet on my arm.

He shot me a brooding, enigmatic glance. His sweating fingers lingered on the soft flesh of my arm. He made an impressive picture himself in a Bavarian mountain costume. His powerful thighs were encased in short *lederhosen*, leather breeches. Black woolen socks reached halfway to the knees. Embroidered suspenders crossed a creamy white shirt and thick tufts of sandy hair pushed boldly out of the open neckline.

"You are neither Cleopatra nor Sieglinde," he muttered under his breath. "You are woman incarnate." A shock of memory ran through me at the words. Ymir had called me that—woman incarnate—during our lovemaking at Frau Anna's. A tumultuous wave of desire swept through my loins at the remembrance of Ymir's hard body against mine. As I returned Rudi's gaze and thanked him sweetly for the gift, the desire shot up past my loins into my breasts, my shoulders, my arms.

Shaking, I clutched the wooden arms of the chair. Rudi had suddenly become a man I wanted.

He moved away then, and I saw no more of him that night, busy as he was with the crush of customers. From time to time, his jolly shouts of laughter could be heard above the noise. He was in heaven tonight, for many reasons. Not only was his star attraction back—I had promised to sing a few patriotic songs tonight—but his other pride and joy, the *Lorelei* hose carrier, had taken the prize for the most beautiful carriage in the Broadway parade.

No hot food was served that night, but the five waiter girls, supervised by Bettina, darted about the long candlelit room, keeping steins and mugs filled with beer, their short red skirts flying. Rudi had finally given in to Leopold's pleas to "modernize" and had permitted the girls to wear the high shiny leather boots which were the vogue at all the concert saloons.

But the blond Forty-eighter was not here to savor his triumph. A few days after he proposed to me for the last time in Washington Park, he departed for his new position at a downtown saloon and *biergarten*.

By eight o'clock, the bartenders had emptied three oaken kegs of Rudi's dark Milwaukee lager and two giant fans had been set to blowing at the far end of the room, right under the Lorelei painting.

Edgar Poe came alone, his friends Adah and Edwin Booth being out of town on speaking engagements. "Pennsylvania," he wailed, comically spitting out the word. "A sooty, godforsaken, bug-infested river town called Pittsburgh!"

"Pittsburgh," I exclaimed. "Why, I know someone there, a very dear friend from Bavaria. Last year I was saving up to visit her."

The poet knelt at my feet and kissed my extended hand. His lips were hot and dry, his mocking brown eyes luminous with fever. He suppressed a cough and moved back a few paces.

"You are not well, my friend," I cried, compassion filling my heart. "Bettina," I called out as she ran past, "fetch Mr. Poe a drink, quickly."

"Brandy, if you please," Poe murmured drowsily. "Beer just fills the stomach, does nothing for my blood."

He sat down at my feet and rested his dark head against

my golden slippers. "I have missed you sorely, my Venus," he said, "That is why I am dying. Now that you have emerged from your cave of motherhood, I will soon be well again."

His cheek on my knee was hot. I reached down to touch the burning forehead as one would a sick child. "Would you like to see the infant?" I asked impulsively.

The eyes that lifted themselves to mine were ablaze with a fierce new light. "To see the fruit of your womb would be a feast for these jaded eyes."

"Not now," I said, smiling as always at his poetic extravagance. "Rudi wants me to sit here and receive my guests. Later, about ten, when it is time to feed little Rudi again."

By ten, the place was in an uproar, and nobody missed me when I slipped from my throne and, followed by the now thoroughly drunken Poe, went upstairs to tend to the child. The gloomy poet had never taken to wearing the new bright styles of the men of fashion—the embroidered vests, ruffly silken shirts, tight satin breeches. Now he made a somber black figure as he stood gazing down at the little Rudi. The infant, just awakening, made little snuffling noises. Two tiny fists shredded the air over the cradle.

"Red hair," Poe said. "Where did that come from? You are so blond. Looks almost Irish, he does."

"The baron was red in his youth," I responded easily.

"Another brooding Messiah is what he looks like," Poe declared. "Got the build for it too. Big for his age, if I'm any judge of babies."

"Not for my child," I lashed out fiercely, grabbing little Rudi up from the cradle, pressing him against my breast. "He's going to be just another American citizen. Like his mother and his godfather."

"Sorry," Poe said soothingly. "I just assumed that every mother wants her child to grow up to be someone important." Then, changing the subject, he said sadly, "I have no gift for the child."

"You could write a poem. That would be a gift for the ages.

"Yes, yes," he whispered, inspired. "A poem for the Day of Naming. I'll do it before I sleep."

There was a long silence. Neither of us moved. He was obviously waiting for me to bare my breast. But I continued to press the infant's face against my neck, ignoring his hungry whimpering, keeping him away from the brooding glance of the dying man. I wanted Poe out of the room, away from the presence of my child. I regretted having asked him upstairs.

"I—I will not be returning to the party," I said at last. "Please tender my regrets to anyone who asks. I must be alone with my baby."

Poe left finally, with a deep, gracious bow. I listened to his lurching footsteps in the corridor and then down the steps. A momentary sense of shame enveloped me. I should have accompanied him; the poor man was so drunk he might easily fall and break his neck.

But his persistent adoration was beginning to annoy me, as had Leopold's. I didn't want to be worshipped like a marble goddess on a pedestal. I wanted to be loved for what I was—a real, live, breathing woman.

The Grecian dress did not open in the front, so I pulled it over my head, after laying the still wailing child down on the bed. His little face was beet red now from crying for his milk. The tiny fists flailed at the air over his head and pushed themselves finally into his wide-open mouth.

"Do you know how adorable you are?" I whispered to my baby. "Right now I want no other love but yours."

The window had been closed all day against the noise and smell of the celebration. The room was a furnace. I blew out the single candle on the bedside table and, running to the window, threw open the sash. A strong breeze was blowing off the river. Impulsively I whipped off the thin linen shift and stood naked in the open square of window. The biting air played about my sweaty breasts, like the brisk, demanding hand of a lover.

"New York, I love you," I shouted into the din of the street below. The citizens were still hard at it celebrating their Independence Day with rockets and cannons and drums. Then I turned back to my waiting child.

Chapter 23

Slowly, I came awake, I felt as though I were crawling on hands and knees through a twisting dark tunnel. As Lothar and I had crawled out each morning from our Venus Cave, after a night of lovemaking. A rough, warm hand, slippery moist, was caressing my neck in a steady, kneading movement. Round and round, the thumbs digging urgently under my fall of hair.

"Lothar." I spoke the name drowsily, unwilling to open my eyes, revelling in the delicious pleasure of the hard touch.

"No, dammit. It's not your precious Redbeard come back from his watery grave. It's me, a real honest-to-god man." The voice was husky, throaty, deeply accented.

"Rudi!"

My eyes flew open to gaze directly into his, which glistened wetly an inch from my own.

"Rudi," I gasped, "what are you doing here this time of night?"

Without answering, he straightened up and threw aside the light cover I had pulled over the child and myself before we both fell asleep.

"The first thing I am doing," he chuckled, "is removing this infant and putting him back where he belongs."

"Be careful," I whispered, "you'll waken him."

With the utmost care and gentleness, as if it were something he did every night of his life, Rudi lifted the baby and carried him back to the cradle.

Then he was back at the bed staring down at my nakedness. His intent was very clear, but I waited for him to make the first move.

"The time has come, Sieglinde, for you to become a

woman once more. A child at your breast is one thing, a man, quite another."

"You're drunk, Rudi." I laughed a little. "You won't be able to perform. You know what they say."

I watched hungrily as he removed the lederhosen, the boots, the high stockings, the white shirt. He wore no undergarments. Finally he stood before me in the half light from the window, completely naked.

"Well," he said, "drunk or sober, we'll take a stab at it, won't we? Tonight's the night we exorcise the ghost."

"The ghost?" I asked innocently.

"*Ja,ja*, the ghost of Lothar von Hohenstaufen, Lothar the magnificent, Lothar who gave little Rudi the red hair. Any fool knows that handsome child never came from the loins of old Baron Von Edel."

He leaped upon the bed, his heavy body right on top of mine.

"Rudi," I groaned in mock protest, "get off, you're too heavy."

Hands pressed into the mattress, he hoisted himself up so that his thick thighs spread out on either side of me. His eyes were fixed intently on the dark triangle between my hips.

I bit back a smile. By this time I was thoroughly aroused, but wanted him to make the first move. What kind of lover would he be, this fortyish emigrant who prided himself on being no woman's slave? As I watched, his manhood, which had been soft and flabby moments before, sprang into life, became rigid, uptilted, the soft fleshy tip glistening with his desire. The sandy bush of hair reached down all the way to his hips, narrowing from the chest into a triangle to surround his manhood like an aureole.

"Yes," I bleated in a strangled voice, "Please, Rudi, please."

He fell upon me once again with a force that knocked the breath out of me. The hardness was inside, rested a moment, as if gathering force, then the broad muscular hips swivelled powerfully to move the hardness in and out and around. The furry mat of hair pressed against my swollen breasts. I rose to meet the pain, as my back arched against his moist, pulsating body. Waves of pain and pleasure worked their way up and down my spine.

My head dug fiercely into the pillow. I strained with all

the pent-up desire of eleven months without a man. My fingers kneaded his rock-like buttocks as our passion and intensity mounted.

For a long time afterward, we lay side by side, like two statues. Rudi slept, snoring softly. I dozed myself, only to awaken to his hands moving restlessly up and down my still moist body. A fierce tongue licked my nipples, sending shivers of ecstasy to my loins and thighs.

"Drunk eh?" he laughed wickedly. "This drunk is ready for another round."

Rudi's thick work-hardened fingers explored my body as if it were a new continent, touching nerves that had been dead for a long time. A marvelous feeling of contentment pervaded my entire being. I had a man again. I was a woman again. The ghost had been laid to rest.

"We will be married the first day of Oktoberfest," Rudi announced the next morning.

No one at the café was in the least surprised when Rudi moved into my bedroom. Bettina was relegated to Rudi's old room. She didn't mind at all. "It's closer to Emil's room anyway," she dimpled.

Elisabeth was enchanted. "It's about time," she exclaimed, "but be sure to tie the knot soon. Rudi is as healthy as a horse, but you don't want him dying on you or changing his mind. At least not until you're legally entitled to his money."

Many simply assumed that I was marrying Rudi for his money. The café was doing better than ever, and Rudi, like any other far-seeing man in New York, was buying up property, especially on the outer reaches of Broadway and Fifth Avenue.

Barely a week after he'd moved into my bed, and we'd announced our engagement, he purchased an extensive piece of land thirty miles up the Hudson. "Right where the Croton River empties into the Hudson," he said proudly. "Someday it'll be worth a fortune. In ten, twenty years, I'll be ready for the life of a country squire. We'll leave this dirty, crowded city for the wide open spaces."

For our present needs, he bought one of the Washington Park townhouses, looking just like the others in Millionaire's Row. A wrought-iron fence surrounded a patch of green grass; marble steps led up to the Grecian portal. Slender pillars reached from the sidewalk to the second story. Best of all, the long deep garden in back was shielded from street sights and noises by a six-foot hedge of glossy green privet. Little Rudi could enjoy the fresh air in the utmost privacy.

The present occupants could not vacate, however, until early September. We would have three weeks to redecorate to our own taste, to buy furniture, to find suitable servants. "By the first day of October, I'll carry you over the threshold," Rudi told me proudly.

But I was troubled. Somehow buying the house seemed to make a reality of something that still seemed more like a dream. I could hardly deny the strong physical attraction between me and Rudi. My body glowed all day from our bouts of passion at night. I throbbed with vitality. But my mind would not rest.

When I mentioned my doubts to Bettina, she scolded me. "Jitters, that's all that's the matter with you. Don't be a goose. Rudi's the catch of the century."

"But I married Lothar, in the sight of God, on Kyffhauser Mountain," I protested. "It seemed so sacred at the time, and—"

"And what?" she prodded.

"Lothar could still be alive. There is nobody to prove he's really dead."

The look she gave me was one of complete exasperation. "What you went through with Lothar was just a silly ceremony performed by two younsters in love. What did the man ever do for you but get you pregnant and disappear?"

She was right, of course. But I felt a need to talk, to get away, to think about this important change in my life. If I refused to go through with the wedding, it would mean the end of my career as a singer. At any other saloon in town but Rudi's I would be expected to sing and dance half-naked or worse. Perhaps other "duties" would be involved also.

If only there were a priest, or someone older, wiser in the ways of the world. Someone impartial, that I could talk to. If only I had a mother! Of course! Sister Paulita was just a few days' journey away in Pittsburgh. Surely it would not be a difficult journey. Poe said that Adah Menken and Edwin Booth traveled back and forth all the time.

On fire with my idea, I ran into the café early one morning in the middle of August. Rudi was up on a ladder supervising the installation of gas wicks. The whole building was being piped for the new kind of illumination, and the café would be closed down at least until September. Long narrow lengths of iron pipe were strewn all over the floor. Rudi peered down at me from his high perch in the darkness of the rafters. "What is it, Schatzie? You shouldn't be in here with all this stuff lying around. Wouldn't want you to trip and break your pretty neck."

I clutched the ladder with both hands. "I want to go to Pittsburgh to visit Sister Paulita. She runs an orphan asylum there."

"Pittsburgh," he roared. "What the hell for? And just who is Sister Paulita?"

"She was once like a mother to me. A girl likes to talk to her mother before she gets married."

He looked down at me, aghast. "You're making jokes," he said in mock dismay. But he climbed down and took me in his arms and kissed me long and hard on the lips. The workmen grinned. It was plain to anyone with eyes that the hard-headed Rudi Stammler had lost his noodle over this golden-haired Valkyrie.

"If that's what you want—all right" he sighed, "though I don't pretend to understand why you want to leave me right now. But I guess it'll be all the better when you get back."

So it was arranged that Max, the bouncer, would accompany me as far as Pittsburgh, on his way to Missouri. Rudi would fetch me home in a month or so. A week later, after a long, uncomfortable trip by train and canal boat, little Rudi and I sat in the dark parlor of St. Joseph's Home for Orphans in Pittsburgh. Max stood at the window, too restless to sit, anxious to be on his way. The hired carriage waited for him at the curb on the street below. Rudi was fretful from the extreme heat and the absence of his familiar cradle. I held him on my lap, crooning softly. I looked out the window at the Allegheny River glistening far below at the bottom of the steep hill on which the Home was built.

Soot from the steel mills covered the city like a black shroud. My clothes and the child's were heavy with it. I longed for a bath and a cool drink. What a dreadful place to live in, I thought. Poor Sister Paulita. She must miss Germany dreadfully; the air in the Bavarian Alps was so cool, clean, and fragrant. But I had to smile as I noticed the neat rows of vegetables right in the front yard of the

Orphan Asylum. Fluffy heads of cabbage, lacy carrot fronds, rich green beet leaves spouted bravely up into the sooty air.

"Sieglinde, *liebschen*!" Suddenly there she was, the black-sleeved arms crushing me and the baby against the white wimple, the dear familiar smells of starch and soap plunging into my nostrils, bringing back tears of fond memory. As I clung to this dear old woman, it became clear to me why I had to see her before I married Rudi. She had been part of my childhood, she had loved me as if she were the mother I never had. She would tell me what I should do. She would tell me if I should put away my dreams.

We both cried a little, then she released me. "But this is a miracle," she said, her voice husky with emotion, "that you are really here. And a child—oh—" She took the baby from my arms and turned to Max, who stood waiting to say goodbye. "And this is the husband, the father of the very fat little boy?"

Max blushed painfully and I said hurriedly, "No, Sister, Max is just a friend who did me the kindness of escorting me to Pittsburgh. He will board a steamer for St. Louis tonight."

Her old eyes twinkled behind her spectacles. "Oh, everyone goes to St. Louis, it seems. I understand there is a new little Germany being built out there in the west, along the banks of the Mississippi. But here, too, we have so many emigrants yet, so many orphans."

By the time Max had climbed back into the carriage with a last wave of his hand, the baby was crying lustily for his dinner. I looked at Sister Paulita appealingly. "The child must be fed, Sister, and I must wash this grime off both of us before I say another word or listen to your story. At any rate we have a whole month at least."

She lifted a work-reddened finger to rub her forehead underneath the white coif. It was a gesture I remembered well, and my throat tightened now as I saw it. "Yes, so much has happened," she sighed, "so very much, since the night of Corpus Christi, that terrible night when you disappeared."

We wound our way through long narrow corridors, through broad dormitories, filled with row upon row of white bedsteads. Sister talked softly about the hard times they'd had when they first started the orphanage. "It's a constant battle to keep the little stomachs full, and the dirt and soot off their little bodies. The coal makes people rich, but—" she heaved a deep sigh—"sometimes I long desperately for the lovely wood fires of Bavaria."

Sister Susanna had given up her room for me, a narrow cell with a single window thick with grime, a simple bed, a small chest of drawers, and a commode. With the high iron crib they'd moved in for little Rudi, there was barely room to walk.

But the size of the bathroom more than made up for the cramped sleeping quarters. Ten iron tubs were set right against the walls. Water was brought in through pipes which came from the well outside in the yard. At one end of each tub were brass handles to turn the water on and off.

"Of course, we'll have to fetch hot water from the cellar or the kitchen," Sister Paulita said apologetically. "Maybe some wonderful day, hot water can be piped in too."

"Why, even the wealthiest homes in New York City cannot boast of such luxury." I gasped in surprise and admiration. "Most of us there still plunk ourselves into round washtubs, and carry water up two or three flights of steps."

She explained that a wealthy doctor in the town had left the bathroom to the orphanage in his will. "He knew that if he had given us the money instead, we would have spent it on something else.

"It must be a godsend," I said, "with all these little ones to wash." And it was for me, that night.

Quickly peeling off the baby's crusty clothes, I immersed him in warm soapy water, then fed him before handing him over to a solemn little orphan girl to carry back to the bedroom and put to sleep. She would stay with him until I came to bed myself.

Leaning back luxuriously in the warm soapy bath, I remembered other baths—the ones Lola had taken in her erotic green and pink tiled room, the rubdown Heinz had given me that first day at Frau Anna's, and the baths at Schloss Kyffhauser. Karl would drag the tub in front of the fire, and with his gentle hands on my naked flesh rub my unhappiness away.

Supper was a simple meal of soup, cheese, and thick homemade bread. We sat around a large wooden table in the nuns' dining room, which opened right off the big kitchen. The children ate in large rooms on the other side of the yard.

"The older girls and the novices take charge of the orphans at meals and supervise their playtime in the yard or inside when it rains," Sister Paulita explained. "After we eat, I'll take you around the building. Two years ago we had nothing but an old barn. Now we have a fine three-story brick structure. We've accomplished so much with the help of the Lord."

"Not to mention King Ludwig's bag of gold coins," chimed in Sister Elfreda, who was much thinner than when I'd last seen her at Lola's party.

"Oh yes, of course, that was a start," Sister Paulita admitted, "but what a frightening night." She rolled her eyes in horror. "Cannons were going off, guns, swords, bricks—anything the people could throw. We were lucky to escape with our lives, let alone with the money—but it all worked out for the best."

The young Sister Susanna asked the question the others were avoiding. "How did you escape, Sieglinde? It was rumored that you were captured by the rebels."

I kept my eyes on my plate. How could I shock these dear women with the actual story of my abduction and rape, and the affair with Lothar? Not to mention the Burschen at Heidelberg and Frau Anna's. So I said simply and smoothly, "Oh, Baron Von Edel hid us—the king, the Countess von Landsberg, and me—and later got us all to safety."

"Countess von Landsberg." The young nun repeated the name, her thin face squinting in an effort to recall.

"She was also known as Lola Montez," I said tersely, then pushed back my chair. "Sisters, you'll have to excuse me—I'm really quite exhausted from the journey, and my child will be needing me."

Immediately Sister Paulita rose too. "How thoughtless of us to question you about that terrible night. We'll speak no more of it. You are here, safe in America. That's all that matters now."

We walked together through the babies' dormitory to get to my bedroom. Iron-grey cribs were lined up in two long rows down the center of the large room.

"Where do they all come from?" I asked, my heart constricting at the sight of so many little ones without home or parents.

"As I said before, right from the doorstep. And the priest sometimes sends us children whose parents have been

272

taken, and there are no relatives who are willing to care for them. Many come from emigrant ships which have been sunk, or which have suffered a great loss of life crossing the great water. The sailors throw the children into the life-boats, while the parents perish."

My heart was full, thinking of my own lost Kristina, as I walked slowly between the rows of cribs. Most were asleep, their tousled heads sticking out of the light summer blankets, but some were wakeful, fretting with little strangled whimpers. "They are all so tiny," I murmured. "Do they ever get out of these cribs? Does anyone ever hold them?"

"Of course," she replied, "but we cannot replace a real mother and a real father. The older orphan girls help out, at least until they themselves leave to find employment in the town."

A young girl in a grey orphan smock bent over a crying child. She made crooning noises, patting it softly on the back. Another sat in one of two wooden rocking chairs set over by the windows.

We were going through the door into the corridor, when a piercing scream made us turn around. One of the children was standing up in the crib, rocking back and forth violently on her feet. Shriek after angry shriek poured out of her little mouth.

Sister Paulita heaved an exasperated sigh. "Oh, dear Lord in heaven, it's Kristina again. We'll just have to move her upstairs, although we usually keep them in the crib room until they are two."

The orphan girl who had been sitting in the rocking chair got up, put down the sleeping child in her arms, and moved quickly toward the shrieking baby whose screams now filled the room. "Still, still, Kristina," she scolded in a sharp commanding voice. "You've had your supper, and now it's time for sleep. You'll wake up all the others, you naughty girl."

I had to see this child, this Kristina, this noisy one. Sister Paulita followed me as I walked back into the room.

In moments I was face to face with the squalling Kristina. The long white gown was rumpled from her thrashing about the crib. Tears of rage poured out of her tightly closed eyes. Two rows of glistening baby teeth shone white against her red lips. A veritable thatch of bright red hair was cut short just below her ears in a straight line all around her head. I leaned closer, hardly daring to breathe.

She tossed her little head from side to side and the silky hair brushed my cheek.

My throat was so thick I could not bring myself to speak. Red hair, not yet two, an orphan, she was called Kristina—somehow the whole thing was like a crazy dream, a fantasy created by my lonely heart. She could be Irish. *But I had to find out.* I had never actually seen the graves of Karl and Kristina. I had simply believed what Frau Anna had told me. "Sister," I whispered painfully, "Sister Paulita, where did you get Kristina?"

Without asking for permission, and before the amazed eyes of the orphan girl, who had continued to scold the child, I reached down into the crib and lifted the little body right out over the top of the iron bars. Two fat little arms immediately encircled my neck. The crying drifted off into hiccups. The wet face was pressed tightly into my neck. Half afraid to look at her eyes—half afraid to find out that they were not green with flecks of gold—I rocked her gently back and forth.

Sister Paulita blurted out, obviously shocked at my behavior, "Why, from a ship. Last September—or was it October—I can't remember exactly—"

"Are her parents dead?" I interrupted rudely. "Could I adopt her?"

"Why—why, we'd have to ask Karl about that. He says her parents are still alive in Germany somewhere."

"Karl!" I stared wild-eyed at the woman. "Did you say Karl?"

"Yes, Karl brought her to us. Sieglinde, dear, are you ill? Come, sit down over here."

The nun led me to a rocking chair and pushed me and the child gently down into it. There was a little table by the chair on which an oil lamp was burning. Now that my heart was certain. I was no longer afraid. I turned the child's face so that the light from the lamp fell upon it. The eyes were tiny cups of tears. Even in the dim glow of the lamp, the golden flecks shone brightly in the sea-green depths.

All at once a marvelous peace and contentment enveloped me. That this child was my Kristina was beyond all doubt. By some crazy coincidence—Sister Paulita would call it a miracle—she had been taken out of Germany by Karl and brought here for me to find her.

"Sister, who is this Karl? And where is he?"

It took only a few minutes for the nun to tell how the big black-haired man showed up at their front door one morning, asking for food and shelter for himself and the child, promising to work his way.

"Karl was sent to us from heaven," she concluded. "He does all the heavy work, much of the shopping, helps with the boys. I don't know how we'd manage without him."

Kristina had fallen asleep, exhausted from her tantrum, the cropped red head snuggled against my white blouse.

The orphan girl broke in, "Karl went into town, Sister, to the tannery. The tanner promised us a lot of scrap leather to put new soles on the boys' shoes. Don't you remember?"

"Of course, well, he'll be along soon. He seldom lingers in Pittsburgh after dark."

"That's why Kristina was making such a fuss," the girl said. "Karl always comes every night to sing to her and kiss her goodnight. When he doesn't, she carries on something fierce."

There was a little silence as I continued to rock Kristina back and forth on the wooden floor. I was in a world of my own. I stared up at Sister Paulita with glittering eyes.

"Please leave me, Sister. I want to wait right here for Karl to come back. I—I'll explain everything later."

The nun shook her head, puzzled, but there was a ghost of a smile on her face. "At my age, nothing surprises me. You always were a strange one, Sieglinde, full of mystery. I never could tell what you were thinking about."

Gradually darkness filled the squares of windows. The storm which had been threatening all day finally broke, but Kristina slept on through the thunder and the lightening.

"Sieglinde, Sieglinde, *Gott in Himmel*! Is it really you? Or is this a dream?

I smelled him before I saw him, the same leather-tobacco-sweaty odor of him. Karl's black curls bent over me, his pale blue eyes wide in amazement from behind thick round spectacles. The ugly red strawberry mark glowed in the lamplight.

"Karl," I said stupidly. "You have glasses now?"

He chuckled softly. "Yes, isn't it wonderful? All those years I was nearly blind and didn't know it. But you, darling, how did *you* get there? I thought you were dead."

"And I thought you were," I wept.

Tears of happiness gushed from my eyes. Karl lifted me

and Kristina out of the rocking chair and clutched us to his massive chest. We stood swaying back and forth, both of us sobbing helplessly.

Kristina began to whimper. "We're suffocating her," I said.

"Put her back in her bed," Karl whispered gently, "and we'll go somewhere and talk. She'll sleep until morning. No one can take her from you now."

"Or ever," I said fiercely, raining soft kisses on the soft flesh of the little face and arms.

Karl's room was in the cellar. "Best room in the whole orphanage," he boasted, "cool in summer, warm in winter." He proudly showed me the rest of the underground area—a dark square room half-filled with shiny black lumps of coal, a fruit cellar with preserved summer bounty packed in jars lined up snugly on shelves. A row of iron sinks bordered one stone wall. "Takes a lot of scrubbing and washing to keep two hundred orphans clean," he said. He pointed with pride to a hulking square brick furnace. Metal pipes led from the furnace up through the ceiling to the rooms above.

"Not many homes have central heating like this," I remarked. "Even the finest homes in New York depend upon grates in every room."

"Built this one myself," Karl bragged, his big face beaming. "I modelled it after one in the mayor's home." Then he led me to a corner behind the furnace which seemed to be filled with pieces of lumber. "My next project is a workshop where I can do the shoe repairing, build simple furniture, fix broken toys. The good Sisters do their best, but they are only women, after all."

"Karl," I exclaimed, dismayed at what he was saying, "you're coming home with me. To New York. I won't hear of anything else. You can't live out your life in this dirty city, working in an orphan asylum."

He took my hand firmly in his, led me back to his room and sat me down on the bed beside him. He grasped me gently by the shoulders and looked deep into my eyes, his voice soft but urgent. "Do you think it's humanly possible for me to live in the same house or even in the same town with you? Knowing that you belong to another, that you bear another's children? That another man's arm's are bringing you pleasure?"

I was silent. In my selfishness I had thought only of myself, of how much I wanted Karl with me, to help me with the children, to comfort me in times of loneliness and need.

He went on, "Here I have found my fulfillment. A purpose to my twisted life. I, who can never father a child, am a kind of father to hundreds of little ones."

We talked away the night, his big hands holding mine as if they would never let go. I drew strength from them to last me the rest of my life.

The tale of how he and Kristina escaped from the Polizei in Mannheim was quickly told. It was the story of so many caught in the fires of revolution.

"When I couldn't find you on the wharf, I went to the Polizei. They laughed at me, saying they had enough to do without looking for every runaway wife. I raised such a commotion about it, however, that they threw me in jail. To cool off, they said."

"And Kristina?" I asked. "How did you feed her? Did she go to jail with you?"

"They tried to put her in an orphanage, but I wouldn't let them take her from me. The Mannheim jail was packed with men, women, children, anyone who was involved in the street fighting. I looked for a woman with an infant and gave her my share of the miserable food in exchange for sharing her milk with Kristina.

"Luckily, after a few days they emptied the jail, said they couldn't afford to feed us all. The woman and I—she had no husband—found a room in the city, and lived together until I could earn enough money to pay her passage to America. Her child died. It was a sickly little thing. But your redheaded Kristina," he grinned, shook his head, "thrived on it all. I signed on as a seaman on the ship, and that way we got here three months after you and I fled the Schloss."

"It all seems so incredible. I thought never to see you again, or the baby. Now here you both are, hale and healthy."

"A miracle," he agreed, his voice bright with wonder. "But one learns that life itself is a miracle."

"This woman, what was her name? Where is she? I must repay her, I have money."

"Mary. That's all the name she would tell me. Minutes

277

after we landed in New York, she disappeared. By that time the child was weaned, a bit early at seven months, but as I said, Kristina is strong and healthy."

"Did you love her, Karl? I whispered.

"Who?"

"Mary. The woman you lived with."

The pale blue eyes darkened with pain behind the spectacles. "Love her? How could I? There is only one love in my life, or ever shall be." He punched his big chest dramatically, like an actor on a stage. "You see here a man with no heart. You tore it right out of my body long ago on Kyffhauser Mountain."

He was so comical in his seriousness, I broke into laughter. "Karl, Karl," I cried, "there is too much love in you to give it all to one person." I hugged him and kissed him soundly on the cheek. "Someday, Karl, you will find a woman who, like you, is deprived of the physical side of love. Many people marry that way—for companionship, to set up a home together."

He shook his head so hard the black curls danced. "No, no, you cannot know, you cannot understand, you who is loved by everyone. But enough of me. What about you? How did you come to America?"

I told him, in halting but calm words, about the Burschen making me their "goddess," of my rescue to Frau Anna's, of Von Edel finally bringing me to America. Or almost bringing me, since the poor man died on the voyage. I skipped most of the painful details of my experiences, embellishing just enough to make it all sound convincing. I told him nothing of Nathaniel McGreevey and his desertion of me, or of the hard time afterward with Rosie.

It was all best forgotten now anyway, I assured myself. Nothing could be gained by sharing my bad memories with this devoted man. Thinking about the indignities I had endured would only make him grieve all the more that he had been unable to protect me, as he had promised.

We sat close together on the narrow bed, my head on his shoulder, his strong arms holding me tight. I dared not look at his face as I talked. "The baron married me," I lied, "because he had always wanted me for his wife. On Corpus Christi Night when the Burschen attacked Lola's palace, he even asked my father, the king, for my hand in marriage."

"And the child, your new little one asleep upstairs, he is then the new Baron Von Edel!"

"Legally, yes," I nodded. "But in America, Karl, there are no barons, or kings, or princes."

"Legally. What does that mean?"

"That he is not the baron's child, but Lothar's." I spoke in a rush. "Lothar and I were together on the ship. The baron was deathly ill from the seasickness, and confined to his bed." Karl's eyes were gazing at me shrewdly. I stumbled on, "Well, so both of my children belong to Lothar, both have his red hair, his giant build——"

"And Lothar? He died, too, in the fire, as did the baron, your husband?"

I shook my head miserably. "I-I'm not sure. Oh, Karl." Then I was sobbing out my doubts, my uncertainty, my agony over not knowing for sure if Lothar were still alive somewhere, drifting around the world, perhaps, out of his mind, not knowing who or where he was.

Karl listened quietly, holding me tightly until my trembling ceased.

"Karl, what should I do? I came here to ask Sister Paulita for advice. I still love Lothar, in spite of everything that's happened. I——I promised to marry Rudi Stammler. He will be a wonderful husband and father to my children. We'll never want for anything. He'll build a fine house, we'll even be wealthy. The children will have all the advantages of a fine upbringing, tutors, servants, highly placed friends. Can I deny them that?"

"But you do not love Rudi as you do Lothar." It was a flat statement, brooking no argument.

The big man paced back and forth nervously, like a prowling lion in the jungle. His voice was loud and angry.

"You don't know the first thing about love, my beautiful child. You have been a wife, you have known many men, you have borne three children, delivered them in pain and travail. Yet——" Karl stopped, leaned down to where I sat on the bed, shook a long calloused finger in my face. "Yet you are ready to marry one man while your heart belongs to another."

"But how long must I wait?" I cried out in torment. "It's been a year. Leopold Siegel saw Lothar in the flames just before the boat exploded. Surely he is dead."

"How long? How long?" Karl's face wrinkled up in

279

thought, the ugly red birthmark glistened with sweat. "The legal period of waiting, I understand, is seven years. For a spouse. But for a lover—there is no set time. Only the time of the heart."

He knelt down by the bed, clasping my knees between his arms in a vise-like grip. "How long does your heart say, Sieglinde?"

His eyes locked into mine. I stared into them, hypnotized. "Forever," I wailed, the word trailing off mournfully.

"Well, then," he was up and pacing again, "let's hear no more talk of marrying the rich and influential Rudi Stammler. Kristina returned from the dead, I returned from the dead, Lothar will return from the dead."

My heart had stopped beating as I listened to his words. He sounded like a prophet foretelling the future. I had to believe him. I wanted to believe him.

Rudi would have to wait.

Chapter 24

But Rudi would not wait.

We faced each other angrily in the darkened, deserted café the night of our return from Pittsburgh. After putting the children to bed upstairs, I had discarded my dusty traveling clothes for a cool silken wraparound robe which I was accustomed to wear when nursing little Rudi.

"Are you mad, woman?" Rudi exploded. Sparks fairly flew from his sandy mustache and his usually mild blue eyes were stony. "You dare to ask me to wait—to live under the same roof with you after—" he paused dramatically, drew a deep breath—"after we have known each other in the flesh?"

The strong work-scarred hands grabbed the silk of my robe as he pulled me close and rained kiss after bruising kiss on my lips. His tongue darted to the utmost recesses of my mouth, insisting on contact. My flesh leaped in response, for we had not been together for over a month.

He released me so suddenly I fell to the floor. "What do you take me for," he thundered down at me, "a damn plaster saint? You are mine, I took you, you belong to me—*me*, do you hear? Not some damn dead Redbeard."

The smell of cigar butts, the day's accumulation of dirt and dust, tobacco juice, and spilled beer drifted around me as I lay there, looking up at Rudi in his rage. He stood over me, one leg on either side of my body.

"All right, my little king's bastard, you listen to me now. All your life you've been handed love on a silver platter. Men's tongues literally hang out for you. You're beautiful, desirable, completely maddening."

Falling to his knees, still straddling me, he started pulling off his tight breeches. His intent was clear. I stiffened. He had only to touch me, I knew only too well, and my

281

loins would become warm, moist, receiving. I dug my elbows into the hard wooden floor, brought myself to a sitting position. "Rudi, don't do this thing," I pleaded. "You're hurt and angry right now, but give yourself time to think about it. It will all seem different in the morning—"

With the palm of his right hand he pushed me back to the floor, with the other hand he tore open the loose robe. My nipples stiffened in the cold air. The smell of his lust filled the close air of the café. His mouth was touching mine. He hissed against my lips, "You are a whore. Putty in the hands of any man who desires you."

They say the truth hurts. At that moment I felt my soul being ripped from my body. With a swift movement he thrust into me, then reared up again resting his hands on the floor. He slapped me four times on the face. Warm salty blood poured into my mouth. He had cut my lip. Genuinely frightened now of what he would do to me, I pummeled at his back with my fists. But my puny hands might have been snowflakes trying to break down a locked iron door. He was a mindless, savage animal.

Unutterably weary from the long train journey from Pittsburgh with two small children, I finally stopped fighting him, and lay receiving him like a docile mare. My fingers uncurled out of the fists they had wound themselves into. My cold erect nipples softened at the touch of his lips.

Incredibly, as Rudi moved in and out of me with practiced strokes, as his thick tongue pushed in way into my mouth, piercing waves of sweet sensation ripped up and down my spine. My back arched from the floor as if it were not part of my body. "Deeper, deeper, Rudi," I moaned, "Faster, faster." I yearned for the ecstasy to come. In minutes, he exploded inside me. His hoarse cries of triumph filled the empty café.

I had been raped. I had not wanted this man with my heart or my mind. But my body had shattered into a million shivering pieces at the touch of his loins. I despised myself. I was a slave to passion. I closed my eyes in the agony of self-knowledge.

Rudi lay heavily on top of me, the breath rasping in spurts in and out of his lungs. He said nothing. He knew, too. Leopold had been right, all along. I needed a man. All the time.

Rudi stood up at last, adjusted his breeches, then bent down politely, like a courtier in a king's ballroom, to help me to my feet. He did not move to touch me, although I longed to hurl myself against his broad chest and to sob out my torment and self-loathing.

"Forgive me, *Schatzie*," he murmured, suddenly his old kind self again, "for doing this thing to you. But such foolish talk—not marry me, of course you will marry me. What else can you do?"

As we walked up the stairs together to bed, my heart broke with every step. I hated Rudi for showing me what I really was, yet I loved him for the man he was. I loved him for raping me. It was all very confusing.

Curled up in the big bed together, he continued to lecture me quietly so as not to wake the children. He explained patiently that if I tried to leave him, he'd see to it that I could not work anywhere in New York. The children and I would starve, or be forced to depend on the charity of others.

There were other threats, pronounced in the same smooth sweet tone of voice. "Certain people in the pay of the Prussian kaiser," he said, "would be most interested to know that not just *one,* but *two* royal children are alive and well in Rudi Stammler's café. Children who might grow up to threaten the Prussian power in Germany.

That the warning was real and menacing, I was convinced. That Rudi loved me, and the children as well, in his way, I also knew. But he loved his honor more. My jilting him would be an insult he could not tolerate—an insult to his manhood, his name, his reputation.

The first day of October, 1849, dawned clear and brilliant, a perfect Indian summer day.

A perfect day for a wedding, a perfect day for the opening of the annual harvest festival, so dear to the hearts of Germans everywhere. Like *Fashung* in the spring, Oktoberfest was a time to throw over the traces, to get drunk, to sleep with your neighbor's wife whom you've been ogling all year long.

By eleven o'clock in the morning, I was Mrs. Rudi Stammler. The ceremony itself was brief and private, a mumbling clerk in a dusty City Hall office doing the official honors. Rudi wore a black suit and I a simple blue moire street dress with matching hat. Bettina and Emil were our only witnesses.

By noon I was back in my upstairs bedroom, changing

for the real business of the day—the wedding reception and the Oktoberfest festivities which Rudi had arranged to kick off the month-long celebration. The renovation of the café had been completed in September. The new gas wicks and mantles looked very impressive, and were considerably safer than the candles, which had always been such a fire threat.

Kristina and little Rudi had been packed off to the Washington Park House, in the care of a young émigré girl Rudi had engaged, called Anneliese. But I was uneasy about leaving them with her, although she had assured me that she knew everything there was to know about children, having been the oldest of ten back in the old country.

Bettina sensed my nervousness as she helped me into the elaborate Oktoberfest costume I would wear the rest of the day and far into the night. As my only bridesmaid, it was her duty to dress me on my wedding day. Tomorrow she would assume her new responsibilities as co-manager of the café, along with Emil. The two of them would have complete charge of the entertainment, the waiters, the cleaning-up. As before, Elisabeth would supervise all the cooking and meal preparation.

"But Rudi, what will I do?" I protested, feeling left out. My singing duties were not very arduous.

He smiled, a lustful gleam lighting up his little eyes. "You are to look gorgeous and seductive every night for my patrons. And afterwards, just be warm and ready for me. I expect a new little Stammler every year."

Bettina pushed me into the big armchair where I had always nursed little Rudi and started pulling out the hairpins from the triple coronet of braids I had worn for the ceremony. My long heavy tresses fell to the floor. I'd have to wear my hair loose and flowing, in keeping with the peasant costume of heavy black silk. The sleeves were long and full, with ruffles falling down over the hand, the neck high and snug, with even more ruffles brushing my chin. It was hot and confining.

"Can't get the kinks out of all this hair," Bettina groaned, plunging the ivory-handled brush into the tumbling mass that sprang like a live thing from the loosened braids. "But Rudi says it must be smooth and shining like a lake of gold."

"Rudi says, Rudi says," I shouted, mocking her. "Please, Bettina, stop, at least for one day, telling me what Rudi says." I flipped a thick strand of hair with my hand. "I like the kinks; girls in Germany have kinks all the time. Makes them look virginal."

The pert freckled face puckered up into a frown and a look of anxiety filled the green eyes of my friend.

"What's the matter with you, Sieglinde? You don't act very much like a brand-new bride. Aren't you feeling well? I think you weaned little Rudi a little too fast."

"Oh, I'm fine, it's not that," I replied. "It's just that—well, I thought being married to Rudi would give me more time with the children. I feel guilty leaving them with that girl all day."

Hiking the chair over to the nine-foot mirror which was one of Rudi's many wedding presents to me, I gazed thoughtfully at the two of us. In spite of the frown, Bettina was radiant. Since her marriage to Emil more than a month before, she had filled out, putting on at least ten pounds. Her bosom was fuller, her hips more rounded, and her green eyes had lost the haunted look. She now looked like a woman, a very seductive one at that. By contrast, the heavy peasant costume, modelled after the kind worn in Rudi's native village, made me look like a dumpy, frowzled Hausfrau, just off the boat from Germany.

At last my hair was done to Bettina's satisfaction, lying in thick glistening swatches like molten gold down my back. Across my shoulders she fastened a wreath of moist glowing red and white asters, set into a circle of glossy green leaves. Long narrow ribbons of red, white, and blue streamed from the wreath.

"There." A radiant smiled crossed Bettina's face. "You look very bridal—and quite authentic, which is what Rudi ordered."

"Not very sexy," I replied, "but anyway, being bridal is a bit silly, don't you think? After all, I've had three children, three husbands—" I stopped, unable to go on, great sobs welling up within me.

Suddenly Bettina's arms enfolded me, clutching me fiercely but tenderly to her white-shirted bosom. Neither of us spoke. She knew of course that I was thinking of another man, another husband, another time. But Lothar was dead, our love with him, and I would be Mrs. Rudi Stammler forever.

After a long time, my sobs dwindled to whimpers, and I pulled out of her arms and gazed at my reflection once more in the mirror. "Jitters," I murmured softly, "just plain jitters. I'm such a goose. Rudi is everything any girl could want."

"Everybody cries at weddings," was all Bettina could say. "Come on," she urged then, pushing me out the door. "Time to meet your public."

It was true, I thought, as we climbed into the landau for the ride to the park, Rudi would be everything to me—the father I never really had, the uncles, the cousins, the brothers—and of course he was still a passionate lover. Since the night he raped me on the floor of the café, he had been his old kind, considerate self.

And the children adored him. No matter how busy he was with affairs of the restaurant, he took time to play little games with Kristina, to fondle little Rudi. He never returned from a shopping trip downtown without fetching both of them some expensive trinket or toy.

"You'll spoil them to death," I protested each time, but he merely smiled indulgently.

"Don't worry, when there's need for it, I can be a stern father too."

How well I knew that, I thought ruefully. No, Rudi was not perfect, but—if only Karl had not put the nagging thought of Lothar returning into my heart. Well, even if he did come back from his watery grave, even if he had been rescued and showed up to claim me, he had no legal right to me, or the children either. He had deserted us. I could resist him. I had to.

Chapter 25

Rudi had taken over all of Washington Park for the big day. A gaily decorated bandstand towered over a wooden dance floor erected right on top of the grass. A rifle shooting contest was the main feature of the afternoon, the winner of the most direct hits on the targets to be given a month's free drinks and food at the café. In addition, games and contests had been planned for the children.

Edgar Poe was there, I noticed, as Bettina and I took our places near the bandstand. Like a black phantom he wandered around, his long pale face thin and drawn. Of late he seldom ventured out of his Greenwich Village room, so I was surprised to see him.

He walked solemnly up to me and bowed from the waist in his usual courtly manner. "Hail, Ceres, Queen of the Harvest," he proclaimed in a low baritone voice which seemed too strong for the rest of him. "For your wedding, Sieglinde, I would crawl from the very grave itself."

My heart ached for him, and I felt the same dark shadow as on the night of the christening, when he had stood in my bedroom gazing somberly at my baby.

By midafternoon all of the men, some of the women, and even a few of the children were thoroughly drunk, having emptied six kegs of rich dark beer. Poe had long since fallen asleep under a golden-leaved oak. The brisk clear air of the morning had given way to a muggy afternoon. Puffy grey clouds flirted with the sun. A storm was brewing. I sweated profusely under the heavy costume. I longed to pile my hair on top of my head and plunge my head into a bucket of ice water.

Leopold had won the shooting contest. He was handsomer than ever in a magnificent costume of blue broadcloth. The coat was of the new fashionable claw-hammer type, with long tails almost to the ankles in the back. The breeches were of a lighter satin and fitted his slim thighs like a second skin. He towered over the crowd like a Teutonic god.

"Well, Leopold," I greeted him, as he came to the bandstand to receive the certificate granting him free food and drink for a month. "Perhaps we'll be seeing something more of you now. You'll have to come to the café to take advantage of your prize."

His blue eyes clouded over momentarily before resuming their old mocking look. "I'm afraid, Frau Stammler, that my duties as manager of the Bluebird Concert Saloon preclude traveling uptown very often, but I'll see that the prize is not wasted. Each day I'll send some poor émigré to partake of Elisabeth's cooking."

A marionette show had been scheduled for the early evening on the bandstand, a type of entertainment that marked any festive occasion in Germany. But already many people were leaving the park with anxious looks at the cloud-thick sky. Pretty soon, the crowd was so thin that I suggested to Rudi that we move the rest of the party to the café.

No one objected, least of all Rudi, who was more than a little drunk himself. It was almost midnight, however, before the puppeteers got their gear set up in the space behind the bar at the restaurant.

Rudi and I sat on identical throne-type chairs facing the Barbarossa painting. The long tables which usually filled up the floor space had been carried into the cellar for the evening, and benches and folding chairs were set up close together for the audience. Some of the people who had gone home had apparently returned, because in moments it seemed that every seat was filled, and I looked out on a sea of upturned faces.

The reds and golds of the bearded "brooding Messiah" towered eerily over the improvised stage. I was dizzy with exhaustion as well as with the burden of the heavy dress. My sleep the night before had been fitful. "Rudi," I said abruptly, "don't you think it's time we got rid of that gloomy painting of the Redbeard? After all, it's ancient history now, we're in America, and all that should be forgotten. How about something more modern, more cheerful? A village on the Rhine maybe, or a Black Mountain scene."

He turned and kissed me wetly, soundly, on the cheek. "Anything you say, *Schatzie*, at least for tonight. But I'm afraid my patrons would put up a howl you could hear from here to Kyffhauser Mountain and back."

The magic of the play-acting banished the exhaustion and the loneliness from my mind, and with the rest of the audience I stomped my feet, clapped my hands, even put my fingers in my mouth to whistle when the curtain finally rang down. It was a long time before anyone noticed the commotion at the front door of the café. I turned to the door to see a striking woman, all in black, moving slowly, snakelike, through the crowd toward me and Rudi. The people sitting in the chairs moved aside to make a path for her.

Now she was a few feet away, and even through the smoky haze her violet eyes glittered stunningly in the gaslight like rare jewels, sapphires from an imperial crown. Or like the eyes of some otherworld beast of prey, such as one sees in illustrations in books of fairy tales.

She was dressed as a dancer, with a very full, short black skirt composed of countless tiers of ruffles. Slim, gracefully curved legs were encased in flesh-colored silk stockings. Black satin slippers covered her tiny feet. A pile of glossy black hair erupted into ringlets that fell around the bare flesh of her shoulders and neck. Her slim white arms extended toward me.

"Sieglinde, my darling child, this is indeed a miracle. It is really you?" Her fingers grasped both my hands, brought them up to touch her cool cheeks. Her beautiful face was heavily made up, the eyes heavily outlined with blue-black kohl.

"Lola! Lola Montez!" I scarcely breathed the name, but it rang out like a bugle call in the silent room.

Rudi sucked in his breath sharply at my side. His arm crept around my waist. My brain whirled with fear and dread of what he would do. How many times had I heard him exclaim that if Lola Montez ever came to America, he would hunt her down like the viper she was, and run her through with the sharpest sword he could find! My eyes flew up to the pair of crossed swords which hung on the wall under the Barbarossa painting.

Lola was speaking again, the clear bright voice echoing sharply, each word clear and distinct. I felt once again the old sick-to-the-stomach feeling of being nothing but a worm in her sight. "You are such a naughty girl, Sieglinde, for emptying out my theatre tonight. When the curtain went up, and I saw all those empty seats, they told me that everyone in New York was at Rudi Stammler's helping him celebrate his marriage to his golden-haired Ceres."

"I-I'm sorry, Lola. I didn't mean to—" I stopped my apology. Why should I feel sorry for *her*? My voice grew firm and strong. "The king—Ludwig—is he in America with you?"

Before answering, she leaned forward and kissed me deliberately, slowly, on both cheeks, then on the mouth. Attar of roses rose up to fill my nostrils, bringing back memories of afternoon baths in the erotic gold bathroom, magnificent parties in the salon of the fairy palace on the Barerstrasse.

Then she stepped back, threw back her lovely head and laughed her throaty scornful laugh. "Ludwig? That old fool? God only knows where he is. Most likely in his grave by now. The last I saw of him was that Corpus Christi night two years ago when he ran like a scared rabbit out of my palace, away from the Burschen."

An audible ripple of shocked amazement ran like a live thing through the men and women seated all round us. Although they were Good Americans, their hearts were faithful to Ludwig. He had been their king, and this glorified whore was insulting his memory. The rumble built up till it sounded like a swarm of angry bees, but Lola, ignoring the threatening noise, raised her voice to shout over it. "Adah Menken has been raving about some girl, a genuine Valkyrie, she said, who is enchanting all of New York, but—" Again she threw back her head and laughed boisterously, "I never thought it would be *you*, Sieglinde. The little girl who used to draw my bath water and clean out my tub! But it just proves that anything can happen in America. Just imagine, a king's bastard rising to such heights."

Rudi stepped forward now, releasing his hand from around my waist. He pushed his red angry face right into Lola's.

"Madam, I must ask you, for your own protection, to leave my café immediately, If you remain, if you utter one more insulting word to my wife, I can't be responsible for what happens to you."

A number of men had moved forward stealthily, not speaking, their faces set and tense. Like a pair of bodyguards, Emil and Leopold stepped up at either side of Rudi. Leopold bowed stiffly to Rudi. "Your pardon, Herr Stammler, but this woman has insulted not only your wife, but our beloved King Ludwig. The honor of Bavaria must be avenged."

Turning to Lola, he approached her, grabbed both her white arms and lifted her with a mighty heave right on top of the wooden bar, setting her down like a doll. His voice rang out like a battle cry. "I demand satisfaction. Name your weapons, woman."

A moment of stunned silence was followed immediately by a tremendous uproar as the men began to shout and call out obscenities and suggestions on what to do with her, even offers to fight in Leopold's stead. "Death to the concubine! Give her the whip, just like she'd done herself to many a Burschen! Kill, kill, kill, kill, kill . . ."

Time had rolled back two years to that dreadful night of death and rape in Munich. Lola screamed, attempting to climb down from the bar, but a solid wall of bodies blocked her way. She was trapped. Gradually over the din, I made out the words she was shouting. "Ymir, Ymir, help me."

A tall dark man emerged from the murky shadows by the door and pushed his way through the crowd. Bounding up gracefully onto the bar, he pulled Lola's writhing figure from Leopold's arms, and, holding her in front of him like a hostage, pointed a gleaming pistol directly at Leopold.

Ymir! After the shock of seeing Lola pop out of the past like a black witch out of the forest, Ymir's presence seemed perfectly natural. Karl was right. Eventually everyone would turn up in America.

Ymir's long, lithe, sensuous form never looked better in tight satin breeches of a muted fawn color. The strong, finely chiselled nose, the penetrating grey eyes, the broad sweeping forehead, the rich black hair falling thickly to his shoulders—it was all just as I remembered.

He looked like an avenging angel. He never even glanced in my direction. The familiar deep baritone rang out over the noise and shouting, the hand holding the pistol never wavered. "Any man who has a quarrel with the Countess of Landsberg must deal with me. In the absence of King Ludwig, I am her protector."

Hoots and hollers and titters followed this announcement. "Well, just look at the fancy man threatening us." A voice from the back of the room shouted out, "Maybe your pimp will fight for you, whore. I challenge him to a duel. Anybody for knitting needles?" More guffaws and rude laughter.

Again the chanting and the stomping of feet. "Pimp! Pimp! Pimp! Fight! Fight! Fight!"

Rudi came back to life at this point. He shoved in front of Ymir and Lola. He raised his hands for order. "American men don't fight with women. I demand that you let these people go quietly."

But the crowd was a mob now, beyond all reasoning. They were thirsting for blood. It had been a long time since the last duel; the police had been ordered to crack down on the practice. Now the men could smell it in the air. Leopold whispered in Rudi's ear, then jumped back onto the bar, stood tall and blond over the mob, as he shouted, "I accept the challenge from the black-haired chevalier. Since he is already brandishing a pistol, pistols it will be."

"No, no!" I shouted up at Leopold, then turned to clutch Rudi. "It's not a fair fight, Leopold is a crack shot. The poor man will be killed. It's murder."

Rudi pulled me roughly out of the room, through the little door in the bar and into the curtained-off space behind. The shouts of the men rang in my ears. My heart pounded in fear for Ymir's life, Ymir, the sweet, gentle, passionate man whom I had once loved, and who had loved me when I needed it most.

"Sit down here and be quiet," Rudi hissed, then, "No, go upstairs to bed, and let men handle men's business. This is out of your hands."

I stood stock still, staring at him, unwilling to comprehend that all this madness was actually happening. He gave me a mighty shove. "Do I have to carry you? Now upstairs with you. You must obey me now. I am your husband."

Blinded with tears of rage and frustration, I ran up the stairs and into the bedroom, slamming the door behind me in an attempt to drown out the noise from below. I dashed to the window and threw it open. People were pouring out of the café onto the sidewalk, heading toward Washington Park. Most of the men were drunk, their passions at fever pitch from the piled-up hatred and resentment of years against Lola and her treachery. But it would not be Lola who was punished. She would escape untouched! It was Ymir who would be murdered!

Throwing a cloak around my shoulders, I crept back down the stairs. I must save Ymir, somehow.

At the park, the crowd was already at the mound of execution, men and women pouring out of the neighboring houses, attracted by the shouts and calls. Mothers with children, blankets thrown hastily around babies clutched to their breasts, doddering old men and women, many in their night garments, took up every inch of grassy slope. Even if the police arrived, it would take a regiment to disperse this crowd. If indeed the police would even try! Talk was they liked a killing as much as the next person.

"Please—let me through—please, I am Mrs. Rudi Stammler, please may I pass—" I elbowed my way through the crowd, but even as I got to the center of the excitement, the fateful mound itself, I knew I had come too late.

Two shots rang out almost simultaneously. Silence descended on the crowd, and I emerged at last to the little cleared-off space to see Leopold's tall figure outlined in the moonlight. Lola was nowhere in sight. I ran quickly to the fallen figure at the other end of the clearing, and sitting right down on the grass, put Ymir's dear dark head into my lap. Tiny bubbles of blood edged the corners of his wide lips.

"Get a doctor, please, someone, quickly," I shouted into the mob. "He is still alive."

The long brown fingers straightened out from their fists of pain and wound themselves tightly into mine. "Sieglinde, dearest—" The handsome face grimaced in agony.

"Please, Ymir, don't try to talk, save your strength. You'll need every ounce. Oh, God—"

Then a man was bending over us, his ear pressed against the snowy white of Ymir's ruffled shirt, where an ugly crimson stain had begun to show. The doctor shook his head, lifted Ymir's eyelids one at a time, peered into them by the light of the torches which several men held over us. "The bullet has penetrated the lungs," he said quietly. "There is nothing to be done."

"A priest, a priest," someone shouted. "Someone fetch the priest. The poor man must not die without the sacraments."

Ymir lifted up his head weakly, like a sick puppy, then flopped down again in my lap. "No, no priest, just you, Sieglinde," he whispered, "only you. I want to go into eternity with the memory of your lovely face imprinted on my heart."

"Ymir," I sobbed, "please, please—why did you do it? How could you tie yourself up to that awful woman?"

A ghost of a smile played about his lips and eyes. "She

paid me well. I had no money. I gave my life savings to the Baron Von Edel to take you to America. Two thousand florins, which I had put aside to start my own business."

Shock and horror rippled through me. The pain of it was unbearable.

"It was your money then, and not the baron's?"

"Yes." The word was mumbled as he buried his face deeper into my lap.

My arms tightened around his shoulders. I cuddled him close, as one does a dying child or a beloved doll. "But why, Ymir, why, why? Why didn't you tell me? Why didn't you escape with me to America? I loved *you*, not the baron."

"Because, you little goose, I loved you more than anything in the world, including myself. I wanted you to be somebody important, not the wife of an ex-pimp and prostitute trainer."

I was silent then. There was nothing more to say. Gradually I became conscious that Rudi was standing over us. In the presence of death he too was silent. Later there would be questions. Rudi's eyes, too, were bright with pain.

But for now Ymir alone filled my heart. Rudi's questions would have to wait. A priest had arrived, kneeling beside us in the grass. He mumbled the Latin prayers over the dying Ymir, who ignored him, choosing instead to gaze steadfastly into my face. The bloody lips were moving, as if with a great effort. I bent my head low to catch his dying words.

"To die with honor," he whispered hoarsely, "after a life of dishonor. What more could any man wish? And in the arms of his beloved."

Then he was gone. A long trembling shook the beautiful body of my friend and lover. With one last burst of energy, he released his fingers from mine and reached up with a feeble hand to tug at a strand of my hair.

Chapter 26

How long I sat there, numbed and frozen, my head bent over the lifeless body, I could not tell. Time had stopped. As if in a dream I stroked the black hair, the still warm cheeks.

Then Rudi was prying me loose. "Sieglinde, please, dear, you are making a spectacle of yourself. There is nothing more you can do for your friend."

The crowd parted respectfully for us as we made our way out of the park toward our elegant new house where Anneliese and my children were sleeping. Out of the corner of my eye I saw a blue-coated policeman heading toward Leopold. They would arrest him, he would spend the night in jail, but it was only for show. In the morning he would be released. If there was any trouble, well, Leopold was rich now and could buy his way out of anything. Even murder.

As we walked my mind churned with a procession of imagines from the past: Ymir and I in the edelweiss room, Ymir instructing me in the arts of lovemaking, Ymir, who was named after the first living being of the North, the land of my mother.

We reached the wide marble steps of our new home. Rudi let go his tight grip on my hand. "Now go inside, *Schatzie*, and take a headache powder to calm you down. Don't leave the house any more tonight. I must make the arrangements for burying the body of this poor man, since his friend Lola Montez has apparently deserted him."

His voice was ragged, edged with pain, thick with un-asked questions. He turned and walked a few steps away from me, then whipped around to ask, "Just what was this man to you, Sieglinde?"

"Nothing," I said tonelessly, "Nothing you have to

worry about, Rudi. He helped me when I needed help desperately. But now he is dead, and is best forgotten."

With that I turned to go up the gleaming steps through the wide oaken doors, into my new home.

I went into the front parlor and sat down facing the cold fireplace. It was foolish to think that the thing would end with burying Ymir.

Rudi wouldn't be home till dawn at the earliest. Suddenly an unbearable restlessness seized me. Tormented by my thoughts, I stood up, raced to the front door, and hurled myself back down the marble steps. Automatically I turned toward the café. The streets were deserted. Now that the fun was over, everyone was home, tucked snugly in bed, husbands besides wives, children in their iron cribs. Only Ymir and I were wandering souls, he on the back of a wagon, me walking ghostlike through the gaslit New York streets.

I was a bastard and a whore, no better than Lola Montez. People would talk, wondering why I had picked up the bloody dying head. Many had been close enough to hear what Ymir and I had said in those last moments. Rudi's honor would be ruined. His wife would be known as a whore, or at least as the sweetheart of a pimp.

In minutes I was at the corner of Bleecker and Broadway, under the shiny new gas lamp that illuminated the intersection. The stormy weather of the late afternoon and evening had vanished. The sky was clear, a million stars glistening brightly overhead. I looked up.

"Dear Mother in Heaven, what am I to do? Everything I touch turns to dust. Ymir is dead because of me, Lothar despises me for what I am, now Rudi too, when he finds out about my life at Frau Anna's—"

I pressed my burning forehead against the cool iron of the lamppost. The streets were quiet, traffic for once practically stopped. Even the long omnibuses ceased rumbling back and forth between midnight and five. A few straggling drunks wandered across the street, but paid me no heed. Just another streetwalker, they were thinking, looking for another customer. Then something caught my eye from across Broadway. A tall burly figure was walking swiftly toward me from the direction of downtown. Fear stabbed at my vitals, as I remembered the sailors on the wharf last Christmas.

The walking man emerged from the dark street into the

circle of gaslight. Even before the light struck the coppery beard, I knew it was Lothar. The beard was a mere skeleton of its former lushness, jutting out a bare few inches from his chin. He stood before me on the curb, a dead man who was suddenly very much alive. But it was too late. I was now and forever Mrs. Rudi Stammler.

"Sieglinde, is it you? Here, alone on the street?"

I looked up at him dumbly, the words forming in my brain, refusing to come out of my mouth. He reached up a hairy hand to grab my shoulder, shook it slightly. "Am I too late for the wedding then?"

Dreamlike, I moved into his arms, which opened automatically to receive me. At first we did not kiss, but clung together like two drowning people in the middle of an ocean. I lifted my hand to stroke his cheek, outlined the long scar with my finger, and finally pressed my lips against his cheek.

Suddenly he came to life and moved his face so that his lips brushed mine. The rough feel of the coarse red hair against my chin and lips was like a torch set to my body. Our bodies strained against each other, his hard manhood pushing, pushing, pushing, until the iron of the lamppost bit cruely into my back. Then our lips met, our tongues clashed, darting in and out of each other's mouths as we tried desperately, feverishly, futilely to join our bodies, to become truly one person. His kiss was long, hard, bruising, but somehow strangely tender and sad at the same time.

Every nerve in my body sprang into new life. The horrible events of the night, Lola's reappearance, Ymir's death, seemed now part of a nightmare. It hadn't really happened. "Lothar, Lothar," I murmured against his lips, "my true, my only husband. You have returned from the dead."

He drew back with that swift panther-like movement of his. The green eyes gazed miserably into mine. "You are another man's wife now, Sieglinde. My ship had not been docked more than a few minutes when the news reached me. Everyone in New York was talking about the wedding of the year."

"No, no, *liebling*, it is no true marriage. Rudi forced me into it. I wanted to wait for you, but he wouldn't let me."

With my two hands I clutched at the heavy pea coat and tried to draw him to me once more. But he resisted, plucking my tense fingers, one by one, from the rough wool of the coat. "No, no. Our love was never meant to be. It is forbidden by the gods. We had our moment of glory on Kyffhauser Mountain. I—" His voice cracked as the agony of our situation struck him fully. "I simply wanted to see you once more before heading west."

"West?"

"Yes, St. Louis. There is much work there, I am told. Work that needs to be done."

"But you can't go. It's inhuman." My voice rose to a shriek. Several people passing by looked at us curiously. Realizing how irrational I was becoming, I changed my tactics, remembering it was emotion, not reason, that worked best with Lothar. I thought of the time on the *Ocean Monarch*.

"At least you must see your children, Lothar, both of them. Surely even *you*, dedicated as you are to your work, must be at least curious to see your own flesh and blood." I paused, then added softly, enticingly, "They are beautiful children, both of them, Lothar, with your red hair, your giant frame."

"Two?" There was amazement in his voice. "But the *Grossmama* told me that the boy had died."

"He did, but I gave birth to another boy nine months after our few days together on the ship. He is yours, Lothar, all you have to do is to see him to know that. Your red hair, your giant frame, your eyes."

Conflicting emotions worked over his face; in the gaslight the long scar quivered as he struggled for control of himself. "Yes," he said finally, "of course. A man gives up very much, Sieglinde, sometimes all that he loves—" He stopped, swallowed hard against the pain, then continued. "Lead me to them. I will look upon them before I go."

My heart filled with happiness. Once he saw our two beautiful little ones, all thoughts of leaving me again would vanish from his heart. We would go off together in the night, the four of us. By the time Rudi came home at dawn, we would be lost in the vastness of the city.

Taking his hand firmly in mine, I led the way back toward the park and the house. The watchman was just passing, announcing softly that it was two o'clock and all was well.

Yes, indeed, all was well, my heart echoed joyously. All was well. I stole a glance at Lothar's face as we started up the marble steps to the magnificent wooden doors of the house Rudi had bought for his wife and children.

The gas mantles in the foyer were turned low. The dark wood balustrade of the curving stairway gleamed dully in the soft light. Without a word, without even taking off my cloak, I led Lothar upstairs.

The door to Anneliese's bedroom was wide open, to enable her to hear the children more easily if they should cry out. We stood in the room and looked down at her. Her soft brown hair was spread against the pillow. She did not wake, and we crept stealthily out again.

We went swiftly to the spacious nursery where Kristina and little Rudi slept side by side in identical cribs. I could hear Lothar's heavy breathing as we entered the room. We stood together, hands still firmly joined, looking down on the children. My heart was filled to bursting. They were so beautiful, these products of our love. Now that he has seen them, my heart sang, he would have to be made of stone to leave them. And me.

Suddenly Lothar whipped around and ran out of the nursery as if pursued by demons. He bounded down the stairs, heedless of the noise his heavy boots made in the quiet house. By the time I had reached the foyer and stood beside him, his hand was on the crystal doorknob. Hurling myself against him, I pinned his body against the hard wood of the front door. Our eyes clashed. His were filled with surprise and unutterable hurt, while mine were hot with anger and determination. "Lothar," I whispered, "are you mad? How can you leave me now? We belong together, you, me, and the children. I'll wrap them up warmly, and we can be on the morning steamboat, on our way to the Mississippi."

Despite the obvious suffering on his face, his voice was cool as he replied, "Let's not tussle like a couple of sailors, Sieglinde. You'll wake the girl and the children."

But I babbled on, incoherently, pleading with him. He must not go back into the night to disappear forever from my life. "You might at least explain, Lothar, where you've been, why I've heard nothing from you all this time. Surely you can't deny me that."

His hands left my shoulders, dropped limply to his side. "You don't really need me, *liebschen*. You have a husband, and if you don't love him, there are others."

"But it's *you* I love, Lothar, only you. Remember what we said on Kyffhauser Mountain—you are mine, and I am yours, nothing on earth or heaven above can change that."

The familiar words had the predictable effect. The bearded face gradually took on a stonelike impassive expression. He was slipping away from me again. Desperately I cried out from the depths of my being, "Don't you want me, Lothar?"

His answer was a moan of agony. "Don't want you? Don't I want to breathe? To eat? To sleep? You are a part of every breath I take, you are in every drop of blood which flows through my veins . . ."

Then we were down on the marble floor of the foyer, our bodies writing together in mutual wanting and lust. My shaking fingers unbuttoned the heavy sailor's jacket, his hot searching hands were up under my heavy black skirt, probing, stroking, demanding. His hot moist lips covered mine and I spread my legs to receive him. "Lothar, Lothar," I moaned against his lips, "you cannot split one body in two."

But again, with that swift panthery movement, he was on his feet, blazing down at me. "I cannot take you here, like a dog in the street. Someone will come—but I must taste your body once more before I go away forever."

"Come." Again I took his hand and practically ran with him through the foyer, into the kitchen and out into the garden. There was an arbor at the far end of the garden, a latticed enclosure, shielded from the street by the high privet hedge. There we could be alone to enjoy our passion.

The chill night air struck my hot face and I looked up joyously at the October moon. We ran quickly down the brick path. In moments we were on the wooden floor of the arbor. Lothar took off his heavy coat and spread it under me, then lifted my skirt over my head. In a moment he had thrust inside me, and we reached our mutual fulfillment quickly, spontaneously, at the mere touch of each other's bodies. In his usual way at our first joining, he did not touch my lips or my face but leaned on the floor, spreading his hands on the floor, his head to the skies, as if invoking some mysterious god of love.

For long exquisite timeless minutes we lay joined flesh to flesh, bone to bone, the life force draining from his body into mine. I felt as if I too had come back from the dead.

Then he rolled swiftly off my body, fell heavily beside me, and closed his eyes. He slept. Contentedly, I propped myself up on one elbow to gaze rapturously down at my lover. My heart tightened at the sight of tiny lines of suffering around his eyes and mouth.

He was only twenty, but seemed much older. What had he endured? In what distant barbarous places had he been? A tiny groan emanated from his half-open mouth, and I reached out to encircle his body tenderly, protectively. This big man was little more than a boy, although he was two years older than I. Because of his size, and his keen intelligence he had always been a leader of men. But it was a leadership, I was convinced, which had become a burden to him. The mission to restore the Hohenstaufens to Bavaria, both in battle and by siring an heir, had consumed his young life.

"Never, never, never," I whispered fiercely into the thick hair which spread out on the wooden floor, "never will I let you go. Not now." Then dropping back on the floor beside him, I fell asleep.

When I woke, he was gone. I stared dazed, unbelieving, at the empty place beside me. The coat underneath me was gone. The bare wood of the arbor floor was cold and damp. I searched the little place frantically for a note. Nothing.

Bettina was waiting for me in the kitchen wrapped in a warm morning robe. She said nothing, merely lifted an eyebrow and poured me a cup of fresh hot coffee. With trembling fingers I lifted the cup to my lips, took a few scalding gulps then blurted, "Is Rudi—?"

She nodded. "Upstairs. Fast asleep. I told him you were in church, praying for Ymir's soul. He swallowed it, too tired to question it, I'm sure." She gave me a long piercing look. "I've been worried sick about you. For a while there I was sure you'd run away, but when I saw the children were still in bed I knew you'd be back. Where have you been?"

"With Lothar."

"Lothar?" Her eyes widened in amazement. "He's here, he's still alive?"

"He's very much alive," I nodded miserably, the hot tears spilling out of my aching eyes, into the steaming coffee. "But he's gone again. Oh, Bettina," I began to wail like a spanked child, "Bettina, he's left me again. This time for good."

"Oh, you poor thing, what a night this has been for you." She dashed to my side of the table, clasped me to her and let me sob out my grief.

When at last I calmed down, she said, "All the same, you'll have a powerful lot of explaining to do about Ymir. The whole town's buzzing about the way you ran to him and let him die in your lap, his blood spilling all over you."

Blood! I'd forgotten about Ymir's blood. Numbly I looked down at the black silk skirt. Ugly brown splotches of dried blood were spread out all over it. Lothar and I had made love with Ymir's blood between us.

Bettina started pelting questions at me. "Where has Lothar been all this time? It's been over a year. Where did he go? What do you mean, he's left you again for good? You're another man's wife now, Sieglinde. You can't forget that, no matter what."

I lifted my head from gazing at the bloody skirt and looked boldly into Bettina's bewildered green eyes. "No more questions, Bettina. Rudi knows all that he is going to know. I have served him well in the past and I will be a dutiful wife, even a faithful one. Beyond that, I owe him no explanations about Ymir, or Lothar, or—or anything."

As I turned to leave the kitchen, I shot back at her defiantly, "As for the rest of them, all of New York, I don't give a damn what they think."

The midafternoon sun was streaming brightly through the tall window of our new bedroom as I woke to find Rudi glaring down at me. I had fallen asleep the moment I'd crawled naked into the big four-poster beside him, taking time only to throw off the uncomfortable peasant costume I'd worn almost twenty-four hours. In his face was a mixture of love, hurt, wondering. "Start talking," he ordered.

"About what?" I parried, sleepily.

"Explain why in God's name you made a spectacle of yourself, and a fool of me, by throwing yourself on the ground beside that pimp and picking up his bloody head?"

My lips tightened into a thin line. I would tell him nothing. Not if he killed me for it. I would not pollute Ymir's memory by telling Rudi about Frau Anna's and what Ymir and I had meant to each other. He would never understand.

"Speak, woman!" my husband roared, his left hand grabbing my chin in a hard cruel grip. "I demand an explanation, the whole story."

"Ymir and I were friends in Mannheim. He helped me

escape from the Burschen. Then he made it possible for me to come to America."

An evil smile creased Rudi's broad face. His sandy mustache twitched in amusement. "And what did you give him in return, my little whore?"

The shrill voices of my children sounded from the garden behind the house. It seemed like a warning signal. I must not drive Rudi to a murderous rage. I'd heard of husbands killing their wives for much less than I had done. "We were friends," I said calmly, "nothing more. What I did in Washington Park was an impulsive act of Christian charity." I paused to let that thought sink in, then went on dramatically, "How would you like to die alone in a strange country, with no one to comfort you at the end?"

For a long agonized moment, Rudi stared into my eyes; then, deciding there was no answer there, he moved his body over mine, spread his hands on either side of me, and took me fiercely, silently.

I lay supine, exhausted, thinking of Ymir, of Lothar, of life, of my children, of my bleak loveless future. I would live, somehow, and somehow I would find Lothar again. No matter how many times he rejected me, our time would come.

PART IV

St. Louis

Chapter 27

July 4, 1855. I sat in my blue and gold bedroom on the second floor of the house on Washington Park and dressed for the big party to be held that night at the café.

Another year, another Fourth, another celebration of a nation's independence. Seven-year-old Kristina sat on the four-poster bed, her long legs tucked under her Indian fashion, and watched me, her Lothar-green eyes glinting with excitement. "Oh, Mother, you are so beautiful," she exclaimed.

"You are too, darling," I said, leaning over to kiss her freckled forehead. She pursed her mouth, knowing full well that she was too large for a girl, her hair a shade too red. But I knew that someday she would capture men's hearts.

Five-year-old Rudi ran in circles around the room, in and out of the heavy carved furniture, whooping and hollering like an Indian. They both had been studying about the American native tribes with their tutor, Sebastian, and could think of little else day and night.

I was a wealthy matron, Rudi having become a millionaire in the past few years, his shrewd land purchases paying off handsomely. And as I measured my reflection in the massive gilt-framed mirror, I had to admit that the years had not marred my beauty. My cheeks were still round and firm and needed no rouge to brighten them. My figure, if a little fuller than previously, still curved artfully in the right places.

Rudi was a good husband and father, denying me and the children nothing. I still sang at the café each night, the old haunting songs of the German homeland. Men still desired me; many stared brazenly at me when I walked the streets of New York or sat in the park with my children. Some even made advances to me, sensing that the rumors of my relationship to Ymir had a solid foundation. But I remained chaste, a devoted wife and mother.

With Rudi, it was different. Realizing finally, after months of trying, that I would never love him passionately as I had Lothar and it was only my body he claimed every night in the big bed, Rudi turned to other women. Anneliese had been the first. He had quickly gotten the little émigré nursemaid with child and packed her off to a cottage in the country where he visited her occasionally. The bastard would share equally in his fortune, along with my two children, whom he had legally adopted.

What could I say? I had given him no child, my womb having closed up after the first years of fruitfulness. As the years passed, Rudi's husbandly demands became less and less frequent. The fires of my own passion had died. My loins were cold. I felt nothing for no man, an occasional fitful dream all that was left of my longing for Lothar. My coldness did not seem to bother Rudi; on the contrary, he seemed pleased at my new self. "At least I don't have to worry about your being unfaithful," he remarked.

Now I could look straight at the Barbarossa painting without flinching.

My reverie was interrupted as the bedroom door opened to reveal the heavy figure of Martina, the buxom Black Forest girl who had replaced Anneliese as nursemaid for the children.

"Come now, Kristina and Rudolph, time for your supper and bath. Then bed."

Immediately the two of them set up a howl of protest. "But it's the Fourth of July, Martina, and Mama promised we could watch the fireworks tonight."

Martina's fat face creased in a frown. "Did you indeed say such a thing, Frau Stammler?" she asked, incredulously.

"I'm afraid I did, Martina." I smiled at her shamefacedly. The young woman reminded me so much of Bettina and we had become more like friends than mistress and maid. The gold in California had lured Emil and Bettina away from New York, along with half of the émigrés who used to come to the café. A slim, wily little man named Joseph had taken over managing the café.

"The fireworks display is scheduled for nine o'clock, as soon as it's dark enough," I explained to the upset Martina. Although she'd been in America five whole years, the woman still couldn't fully identify with the wild celebrating on the Fourth. To her it was a lot of dangerous shooting and foolishness. She said as much as she hustled the children out of the bedroom and headed downstairs to the kitchen where she would stuff them with good solid German food she'd cooked herself. She insisted on doing all the cooking for the children. They responded by growing like weeds, both of them threatening to become taller and broader than their father himself.

I kissed the children, and settled back on a velvet chaise lounge to rest for a bit, again invoking memories of the past—a habit I'd developed through the years since Lothar had disappeared from my life forever. With Bettina and Emil gone, their occasional letters being the only evidence they were still alive, my life seemed empty and barren. Karl wrote faithfully every month from Pittsburgh, but refused to come to New York, even for a brief visit. Edgar Poe had died a few weeks after that dreadful night that had brought Ymir and Lothar and Lola Montez back into my life. Lola had barely escaped from New York with her life. Her exploits were well known. She'd sailed around the Horn to California, with still another lover, and after a brief if spectacular career dancing for the woman-starved miners in the mining camps, she had dropped from sight.

And Lothar? From time to time people spoke in hushed whispers about a mysterious German with a long bushy red beard who lived in a palatial mansion atop a hill overlooking the Mississippi River. In St. Louis, they said. He was reputed to be a dealer in runaway slaves. Since the passage of the Fugitive Slave Law in 1850, capturing runaway slaves for the bounty and returning them to their so-called owners had made many a man rich.

But it couldn't be Lothar, I told myself. No matter how desperately he wanted to restore the Hohenstaufen fortunes, he wouldn't engage in slave trafficking. I closed my eyes against the terrible thought. Also against the rumors that he had taken a slave wife, a beautiful octoroon, who had borne him several children.

We had loved each other, Lothar and I, but had never really known each other as persons. Maybe it was possible that, driven by his dedication to his homeland and his destiny, he would do such monstrous things.

Rising from the chaise, I shook my head to banish gloomy thoughts of the past and moved to the head of the curving stairway to descend to the party already in progress below. The scene which met my eyes as I descended to my guests seemed to me a fairyland of wealth and beauty. Men and women milled about, brilliantly dressed in the latest fashions, the women in wide-swirling bell skirts, many with hoops, the men in bright blues and greens, with heavily embroidered vests. The émigrés had long ago given up the Forty-eighter costume of white silk blouse, flowing tie and broad-brimmed hat.

Leopold advanced from the crowd to greet me, his blond curls glistening in the reflected light of the giant crystal chandelier. His slender fingers pressed mine and his blue eyes glittered with desire. He still loved me, after all this time. In spite of his wealth he had never married, had never even taken a mistress. There was even talk that he was not quite a whole man. But people loved to talk, no matter what the subject. The café buzzed every night with arguments on politics, on slave states and free, on the latest scandal from New York or Washington. Bavaria and Lola Montez and Ludwig and a resurrected Frederick Barbarossa were long forgotten.

Or so it seemed. A few remembered. Rudi steadfastly refused to remove the "Brooding Messiah." The golds and greens of the beloved mythical Redbeard still hovered over the wooden bar.

"Sieglinde, you are exquisite," Leopold murmured, bowing deeply from the waist to kiss my hand. My gown was of imported Belgian lace, cut to reveal my swelling bosom, the ribboned neckline barely clearing my nipples, the heavy skirt falling in graceful creamy folds to the floor. I had decided when they first appeared that hoop skirts were not for me. I was fully aware that my simple costume made every other woman in the room look overdressed.

"And may I return the compliment, Leopold." I smiled up at him. Leopold was one of the few men to whom I had to raise my eyes. "But you disappoint me again. Where is your companion? Surely you could find some beautiful young maiden to accompany you tonight."

He shook his head, laughing, but his eyes were veiled. "Shall we say I am waiting for the fortress to fall?"

Changing the subject quickly, I remarked, "What is the gossip tonight? The crowd seems excited about something, or is it just the usual Fourth of July boisterousness? And where is Rudi?"

310

I looked anxiously through to the parlor and the sitting room beyond. Rudi was nowhere in sight. My eyes filled with annoyance. He had promised to help me entertain the guests. Surely he could leave the café for a few hours at least.

"Still at the café, apparently. You know it's pretty busy on the Fourth, and then there was the clean-up after the parade—" We both turned as the front door burst open.

It was Joseph, wild-eyed, shouting like a madman. He spoke in German as he was prone to do when excited. "Frau Stammler! Herr Siegel!" He pushed through the crush of people to where Leopold and I stood under the candelier. "There's trouble, in the streets, a riot—" He stopped for breath, unable to go on.

Leopold grabbed Joseph by the arm. "Speak, man, just where is the riot? Is Herr Stammler in any trouble?"

Calmer now, Joseph told the story briefly, speaking now in English. The guests crowded around listening intently.

"It started across the street at the theatre, right after the afternoon performance of *Uncle Tom's Cabin*. Some anti-abolitionist swine started throwing stones, rotten vegetables, eggs, anything they could get their hands on at the people coming out of the theatre. A fight started and the police were called."

Leopold was becoming impatient. "But how does that concern Herr Stammler and the café?"

"Herr Stammler came out onto the street and invited the theatre people, along with the cast of the play, to seek protection in his café."

I gasped, sudden fear for Rudi's safety stabbing at my heart. His abolitionist feelings were well known; in fact there'd been rumors that he had made the café into a way station for the Underground Railway. Several times I had noticed black men and women being fed in the kitchen, but had not bothered my mind about it, thinking it was only Elisabeth's big heart that was responsible.

In fact, on more than one occasion, Harriet Beecher Stowe herself, the author of the famous book, had been Rudi's honored guest at the café. She was a small pretty woman with brown hair curling softly about a pleasant face. Amazing that a little person like that could stir up such a hornet's nest!

"You must come," Joseph was pleading with Leopold.

"The police are there, but cannot handle the mob. I'm afraid of what might happen."

Soon we were all running down the sidewalk after Joseph, past the Greek porticoed houses bordering the park, cozy supper fires gleaming through the lace-curtained windows, past bunches of little boys sitting on the curbs with their tiny firecrackers. "Pop-pop-pop," they shouted, accompanying the noise of the exploding rockets.

The acrid smell of gunpowder hung heavily in the New York twilight. The distant sound of a fire bell shattered through the noise of exploding rockets. As we drew near the café, the shrill clanging grew louder, more insistent, and by the time we reached the corner of Bleecker and Broadway, the fire carriages were there, huge bay horses plunging through the dense crowd at the intersection.

Thick billows of black smoke poured out of every window of the café. Leopold's hands reached out to grab my shoulders. "Stop here, Sieglinde, don't get any closer. The firemen will do what they can. I'm sure Rudi is safe, and the others."

Then he was gone, himself plunging toward the conflagration, muttering, "Damn slavers did this."

By now at least six fire wagons were there, and water poured from a number of hoses onto the building. But the smoke continued to pour out, and soon tongues of red and orange flame leaped out of the upstairs windows. I looked at the window where my bedroom had been. There I had given birth to little Rudi, there I had first known my husband's body.

Rudi! Frantically I pushed my way through the crowd to a group of firemen struggling with a large hose. "My husband, Rudi Stammler, have you seen him?" I yelled.

One of the firemen looked at me, his blackened face surprised at my presence. "You must get back, Frau Stammler, or you will be injured by the horses or the water. I'm sure your husband managed to escape the flames. Now, please—" With a rough hand he pushed me back, and then Leopold was leading me away, back through the crowd onto the street.

We stood there watching as the combined forces of six fire stations managed to bring the blaze under control. The café itself was a shell, but at least the neighboring houses were untouched.

But there was still no sign of Rudi.

"Maybe he's gone to the house to reassure you," Leopold murmured consolingly. I nodded dumbly, watching as some of the firemen entered the building to look for bodies. I had often wondered what would happen if a fire ever broke out in that long, low, narrow cellar, and the kitchen—so far underground.

"Elisabeth," I screamed. "Elisabeth, Elisabeth, Elisabeth!" I became hysterical, unable to stop shouting her name. Leopold struck me on the face once, hard.

"Stop it, Sieglinde. We can do nothing now but wait."

Hours later, as I sat in my parlor, they came to me with the news. Rudi was dead, his charred body having been recovered in the ruins. Elisabeth too. Or at least they thought so, for no trace of her had been found. Rudi had died in his beloved café. I could imagine him trying to save as many of his patrons as possible, waiting until the last minute to make his own escape.

"The smoke got to him before the flames," Leopold said gently, his voice heavy with unshed tears, his hand stroking mine. "It's always that way. His clothes were hardly singed. I'm sure he felt no pain."

"No pain," I echoed dumbly, "no pain, what a blessing."

I stared up at Leopold dumb with grief. "Where is he? Where is Rudi's body?" His hands tightened on mine as he replied, "They've taken him to a home behind the café." His voice broke. "We had to get him out of there."

Jumping out of the chair where I'd sat like a statue for hours, I made for the door, shouting as I went, "I'm going to the café to bring my husband back here where he belongs."

"Don't be a fool, Sieglinde," Leopold shouted at me as I ran down the marble steps to the sidewalk. "The mob is still there—at least some of it—the police can't be everywhere at once."

"What would they want with me?" I panted, half-running in my eagerness to reach the burned-out café.

"You were Rudi's wife, they figure you were in on it—the whole business of the Underground Railroad has got the slavers in an uproar. They're out to get everyone they can. It's not safe to walk the streets."

But I was too blinded with rage to listen to reason. Bad enough that there would be no funeral as befits a man of his standing. The police had forbidden any public gatherings. But to lie in a stranger's house!

Leopold was shouting at me, grabbing my hand in an effort to slow me down. "What do you want down there anyway?"

"I don't know, I don't know." How could I explain to him that I had to see it, that I had to see what the filthy rabble had done, when I didn't know myself. But yes, there was a reason—

"Besides," I said, "Elisabeth is still in there, you said they hadn't recovered her body. The least I can do is to pray over her ashes."

The street and sidewalk in front of the café were still wet and slippery from the fire hoses. Papers, pamphlets, bits of blackened wood and loose brick from the building were strewn about. A small crowd of spectators stood on the corner of Bleecker & Broadway chattering excitedly. As Leopold and I approached, they became silent and eyed us angrily, menacingly. Swallowing hard against fear and nausea, I marched down the steps into the narrow doorway that now gaped wide open.

"Let's not spend any more time here than we have to," Leopold muttered with a fearful glance back at the crowd. "They smell like trouble to me. His face was white, his lips set in a thin line.

The water on the floor soaked the hem of my gown so I picked up the heavy lace with my hands and raced toward the bar. The putrid smell of burned food and human flesh hung heavy in the chill air. The Brooding Messiah was gone. Where once the giant coppery head had leaned on the massive hairy hands, where once the black ravens had circled overhead in the mountain cave, where once the muted greens and golds of the Barbarossa painting had reminded Rudi's patrons of their German heritage, there was nothing but a black, charred, blistered wall.

What years of pleading on my part had failed to do, the hungry devouring flames had done in seconds. Heartsick, I gazed sombrely up at the wall behind the bar, desolation like a stone weighing heavily on my heart. It was as though a door had closed in my life—in the life of all German-Americans in New York, all those who had come to Rudi's place to drink, eat, be merry, and dream of the past. It was a door that had been closed and locked forever. No more could I gaze on the Redbeard and yearn for my lost love.

Leopold stood beside me, his arm clutched tightly around my waist. I shivered in the early morning dampness, my feet in their dancing slippers cold and clammy from the water on the floor. Leopold was talking again, pushing me with his arm gently toward the door. "If you're thinking of rebuilding, I would advise against it. Sell out and take the money——"

But his words rolled right through my numb brain. I was thinking of that snowy Christmas Eve six years ago—a whole lifetime it seemed—when Rudi had brought me here, bruised and desperately lonely. With trembling hand I touched the charred table where Adah Menken had sat with Edwin Booth and dear dead Edgar Poe.

"What are you called, dear?" she'd asked.

"Sieglinde," I'd replied, and served her a bowl of Elisabeth's steaming chicken soup. I whipped around to stare at the walls where once mountain villages and tall church steepled churches had been painted in fresh, glowing colors. The Lorelei was gone.

A giant fist of pain squeezed my heart. Waves of dizziness washed over me and I was crying, like a child lost in the forest, loud, wracking, tearing sobs. "Got to get you out of here," Leopold's voice grated in my ear. Picking me up swiftly in his strong arms, he made his way through the debris to the hallway. By the time we had climbed back up the steps to the sidewalk, I had regained my senses, and worked my way out of his arms to my feet. The crowd had grown from a handful on the corner to a throng that filled the entire intersection.

A tall, ugly man with a patch over one eye blocked our passage. He held up a large placard which read, "Cash for Negroes."

"Let us pass," Leopold yelled at him. But the man simply spread his legs and waved the sign back and forth tauntingly.

He stuck his face right into mine. Several other people crowded round him as he jeered, "Well, look at the whore in all her fine clothes! Lace and all! How many niggers you got hidden in that fancy house of yours?"

"Yeah," a woman's shrill voice cut through the noise of the crowd. "Let's go see. Nigger-lover's wife deserves just what her man got!"

Something thick and hot struck me on the cheek. I reached up dazedly and picked it off. It was tar. Even as I watched it drip onto the Brussels lace of my gown, a ripe tomato splattered on my bosom. Then Leopold leaped past me, to stand in front of me, his body shielding me from the crowd. He brandished a gleaming black pistol in his right hand. "I'll shoot the next person who lays a hand on Frau Stammler," he shouted at them, meanwhile pushing me back down the steps into the burned-out café.

"You're not the only one with a gun," the shrill woman's voice came again. "Let's tar and feather them! Both her and her fancy man."

The sharp crack of a gun going off split the air, bringing a sudden silence. Flaming tongues of fear raced through my body. I whipped around and grabbed Leopold's arm, deflecting his aim just as his gun went off. Then we were in the café, running through the water-soaked debris toward the stairs which led to the downstairs kitchen, desperately hoping the darkness would provide some protection from the guns of the mob. Just as we reached the door to the stairs, I stumbled over a piece of wood and fell into blackness, conscious only of a tremendous, shattering pain at the back of my head.

A low, soft, feminine voice was the next sound I heard. "I think she's coming back to us, Doctor." Silky fingers stroked my forehead, as I struggled upward through layers of pain and darkness. My whole head was on fire. A giant hand was pressing down on my eyes, pressing so hard I could not open them.

"Wh—wha—what?" I finally managed to say through parched lips.

"Sieglinde, darling, don't talk, don't move." The voice was so soft and sweet. Whose voice? Puzzled, I started to cry in frustration.

"You are all right, the doctor is here. You are safe now."

I knew that voice—cultured, with the precise intonations of the native New Yorker. I forced my eyes open to look into the smiling but anxious face of Lauretta Chambers. She was wringing out a cloth into a blue flowered basin on the bed. Then she placed it gently on my forehead, brushing my lips tenderly with her wet fingers.

Seeing me fully awake, her smile broadened. "You had a nasty crack on the head, dear. We thought for a while we'd lost you."

"Can't kill a Valkyrie," I murmured half to myself.

Lauretta leaned down to put her ear to my lips. "What did you say, Sieglinde?"

"Oh, nothing, it was nothing at all."

"Well, that murderous anti-abolitionist mob was dispersed by the police finally, but not until they managed to do even more damage to the café. Some ruffian threw a rock at you, nearly split your head wide open."

I turned to face a short, grey-haired little man, who was obviously the doctor. He was washing his hands in another basin held by a maid. My hand crept out of the covers and reached up to encounter thick bandages completely swathing my head. My hair had been unbraided and lay in confusion all around me on the satin coverlet.

Returning my stare, the doctor handed the towel to the maid, walked over and sat on the edge of the bed. "You'll be laid up for a while, Frau Stammler, but apparently there's been no concussion." He grinned, patted my hand and got up to leave. "You're talking quite rationally now, at least."

Rationally. That's what Leopold had said, that I wasn't rational. Leopold! Where was he? And my children? That angry mob had yelled something about going to my "fancy house"—I drew myself up to a sitting position and spoke against the drumbeats of pain that pounded in my head. "Leopold," I shrieked, "where is Leopold? He's dead, and my children, too and you're hiding it all from me."

Throwing back the blankets, I swung my legs out of the bed. Both Lauretta and the doctor rushed to push me back under the covers. "Leopold is fine, Sieglinde, and so are the children. He was lucky enough to get hold of a closed carriage in the alley behind the café, and told the driver to race like the wind. The carriage stopped only long enough to hail another one to fetch the children and Martina. The crowd was on foot, remember, and couldn't keep up with you."

I pulled on her arm, so that her head was bent close to mine, forcing her eyes to look deep into mine. "Lauretta, swear to me you're telling me the truth."

She looked at me intently, her pretty face working with emotion. "By the life of my child you saved from the depths of the ocean, Sieglinde, I swear."

Relief swept through me like a giant river and the flood gates opened up inside me. I cried helplessly, great tearing sobs, as I had done in the café when looking at the blackened walls. "Let her cry," I heard the doctor say. "It'll clear her brain."

Dimly, through the pain and tears, I heard Lauretta and the doctor go out into the hall where they remained talking softly. Gradually my sobs subsided, and I lay back on the pillow, closed my eyes, and thought about my future. I would be wealthy. Even after providing handsomely for Anneliese and his child, Rudi was rich—no, he was a millionaire. Dear, sweet, kind Rudi who had loved me so much he had kept his abolitionist activities hidden from me, not wanting to involve me, and thereby endanger me.

I had betrayed him and my marriage vows by withholding my heart from him. My heart was Lothar's—Lothar who dealt in human flesh. A shudder of revulsion shook me as I remembered the signs on every lamppost—*Cash for Negroes.*

Horrible! That Lothar lived, while Rudi was dead.

If only I could have returned Rudi's love! But how could I give something that was not mine to give? That had not been mine since the moment on Kyffhauser Mountain when Lothar had lifted the rough monk's garment and taken me on the fallen leaves?

Chapter 28

Rosie Chambers placed a bowl of steaming soup on the marble top of the commode by the bed and tiptoed over to the window to draw the draperies against the night. The draperies were a rich crimson velvet, and she made a pretty picture leaning against them in her white and blue sprigged muslin.

She was twelve now, I thought, a young woman. Soon she too will be loving and being loved. My heart ached for her at the same time it rejoiced for her. She had her mother's patrician good looks. She would not lack for admirers.

"Rosie," I called out. "How wonderful, how perfectly wonderful to see you!"

Like a young deer, she leaped from the window to kneel at the bedside. Her brown eyes glowed with happiness. I'd seen her off and on through the years on my infrequent trips upriver to the Chambers mansion on the Hudson, but after she'd been sent away to boarding school, she was often missing from the house.

"Tante Linde," she whispered, kissing me on the lips and brushing her firm young face against mine. Her cheek was cool, like a mountain spring.

Then she straightened up to reach for the bowl. "Mama says I am to feed you *all* of this soup. And no back talk from you, either," she dimpled at me.

Arranging the pillows so that my head was lifted slightly, she proceeded to feed me spoonful by spoonful. "Mmm," I murmured, "pea soup. My favorite." The thick green mixture warmed me all the way down. I felt my strength returning.

I waited until the bowl was empty before asking the question I'd been holding back. With the soup in my stomach, I felt prepared for bad news if it were coming. In spite

319

of Lauretta's swearing, a nagging premonition about Leopold and the children's safety still lurked in my mind. "The children, Rosie, Kristina and little Rudi, where are they? Are they with Leopold?"

"No," she replied quickly, "they are sound asleep. It's already nine o'clock. You've been sleeping all afternoon. The doctor gave you a sedative."

"And Leopold?"

She shrugged her slim shoulders. "I don't know exactly. He left the house right after he delivered you and the children."

Once again, with the hot soup warming my innards, I drifted off into blessed sleep, waking to sunlight streaming in the tall window. My eyes were clearer than they had been and I could see the silver ribbon of the Hudson gleaming at the foot of the hilly expanse of lawn that led down to the water's edge.

The shrill treble of childish voices drifted up from the lawn into my window. I could distinguish Kristina's prim little girl accents, and Rudi's louder boyish shouts, mixed in with Martina's stern guttural German-English.

"Still!" she was saying. "Be quiet! you'll wake up your mama with your noise." I smiled, knowing them safe and secure here, miles upriver, away from the city mobs. Then my heart lurched, as I realized that they were now fatherless. Orphans!

Rudi was gone. Although he'd been only their foster father, he'd loved them deeply and they had loved him. Their real father, on the other hand, had deserted them. I shut my mind against him. That door was closed and locked, burned down, along with the Barbarossa painting. But my heart ached for my children. I knew what it was to grow up without a father. Ludwig had been generous to me and looked out for my welfare, but a bastard is still a bastard. I turned my head from the window as the door opened and Leopold's tall form moved swiftly to the bed. Leopold! He loved me still, I knew, and deeply. He would be a wonderful father.

As if reading my thoughts, Leopold knelt down and drew both my hands tenderly but firmly into his. They were warm and comforting; his smile showed two rows of dazzling white teeth. He looked so young, so healthy, so virile.

"Oh Leopold," I exclaimed, attempting to lift my head to

kiss him, "how can I ever repay you for risking your own life to save me and the children too?"

He pushed me back on the pillow, leaned down, and kissed me firmly on the lips. His lips were soft and warm like his hands, and a glorious comfort filled my heart. My thoughts raced ahead. After the usual year of mourning, Leopold and I would marry.

Abruptly, I wrenched my mind away from that. Guilt was tearing at my entrails, guilt that I could think of another man before Rudi was even in the grave.

"Leopold," I said abruptly, "what about Rudi's funeral? Have any plans been made?"

The handsome face clouded. "Sieglinde, as you already know, the police have forbidden all public gatherings, and there can be no funeral. A group of Rudi's old friends have already buried him quietly in St. Benedict's Cemetery in Brooklyn."

I nodded, mutely, unable to speak for the pain in my throat at the thought of Rudi Stammler going to his final rest in such an undignified manner.

The hands holding mine tightened, and Leopold said nervously, "Sieglinde, you must leave this place, as soon as the doctor says it's safe for you to travel. You and the children are in danger even here."

"But where will we go?" I stared at him wild-eyed, the terror I had banished from my heart now returning in full force.

Releasing my hands suddenly, he stood up and walked to the window, looked out at the river, his back to me. He seemed afraid to meet my eyes.

"Sieglinde," he said in a strong firm baritone as if he were making a speech, "try not to be shocked at what I am about to say. As Mrs. Rudi Stammler, you will never be safe from the anti-abolitionists. As Mrs. Leopold Siegel you will be free from harm. I have taken a house much like this one, a few miles further upriver. Five bedrooms, a spacious veranda completely surrounding the house, perfect for the children. And you'll be close to Lauretta."

His words dropped into the quiet room like a hail of bullets. As he finished and the full import of what he was saying hit me, ripples of shock coursed through me. He had said exactly what I had been thinking, but I recoiled at hearing the thoughts spoken right out. Thinking was one thing, saying another. And doing it, actually becoming

Mrs. Leopold Siegel, was something I thrust out of my mind like a bad dream.

"You can't be serious," I sputtered, dry-lipped, "a woman cannot—a respectable woman cannot marry while her husband's body is still warm."

"These are not ordinary times," he exploded, turning from the window to hurl himself across the bed and press my face between his slender hands. His usually well-groomed blond curls were unkempt, falling over his brow into blue eyes that were clouded with a mixture of pain and desire.

"*Gott in Himmel*, woman, what's dead is dead. We are alive, you and I, and I'm determined to keep us that way."

Then he was kissing me, his warm tongue darting in and out of my mouth, his sensuous lips wide and soft and moist. I lay like a stone until he was finished. He straightened up finally.

"Forgive me, *liebschen*, for old times' sake. But you must do as I say."

Do as I say! The words had a familiar ring. Lothar was fond of saying things like that. And yet when Leopold said them, resentment and something akin to hatred flared up within me.

"My head is pounding, Leopold. I can't argue with you now." I bit back the fierce sharp words that rolled around on my tongue. This man had saved my life and my children. He was my friend, and I could not hurt him.

Lauretta came in just then, and Leopold excused himself. Noting my agitation, she said, concerned, "What has he been saying to you, darling? Has he asked you to marry him?"

I nodded, too miserable and ashamed to speak.

My friend stalked around the room angrily, fussing with the pitcher of water and the basin, wiping my face with the wet cloth. She rubbed so hard, I finally laughed out loud.

"There can't be that much dirt on me, Lauretta, that you have to rub my skin off."

"Oh! Men!" she gritted between clenched teeth. "They think every woman needs a man to protect her. They like to think we can't live without them."

"Leopold tends to be dramatic," I reminded her. "Don't be angry with him. Don't forget he was one of the famous Forty-eighters, always looking for a battle to fight or a war to win."

She fetched a brush and began stroking my tangled hair vigorously. Twin spots of red filled her cheeks. Her eyes sparkled from her excitement, eyes which were a deep, rich, warm velvet brown, just like mine and Rosie's.

"Why have you never remarried, Lauretta? I'm sure you've been asked."

For long moments she stroked busily, arranging my golden hair elaborately over the satin cover. Finally she said, in a musing tone, "One love in a lifetime was enough for me. I am a one-man woman." She threw me a sidelong glance. "I guess you find that hard to understand, Sieglinde, you who have had so many lovers."

"No," I said in a small, weak voice. "I understand perfectly."

Her eyes met mine in a long meaningful look. At that moment our souls were bared to each other. I had often thought that Lauretta knew more than she was willing to say about my activities on The *Ocean Monarch*.

"You are an immensely wealthy widow, Sieglinde," she went on. "Don't tie yourself down to another man so quickly. Anyway it's not decent to marry so soon. You should be in mourning for at least a year."

Lauretta Chambers still wore mostly black, reserving bright colors for holidays like Christmas and Easter. Even now, at home, her black costume was relieved only by touches of white lace at the neckline of her simple frock. She moved gracefully, like the lady she was, to replace the hair brush on the tall chiffonier. I watched her thoughtfully. Could I become like her, sober, dedicated to my children, chaste for the rest of my life? Never knowing another man?

"Leopold seems to think it's dangerous for me to stay here, so close to New York. He wants me to marry him and move to a big house further upriver."

She turned from the chiffonier, her eyes blazing. She walked swiftly back to the bed and gazed at me long and hard, her brown eyes luminous in her pale face. "Go away," she said.

"Away?" I echoed, stupidly. "Where?"

"Yes, just go away from here, far, far away."

"Where?" I repeated. "Where could I go, with two children and a maid?"

She sat down on the bed, a sudden smile making her radiant. "To Pittsburgh, to Sister Paulita." She was so excited with her inspiration that she practically shouted the words. "To Karl—your oldest and dearest friend, as you keep telling me."

Then it was my turn to shout, despite the pain in my head. "Come here," I ordered, then hugged Lauretta Chambers with all my might.

Leopold was furious, his pale complexion turning livid as I told him of my decision to travel by boat to Pittsburgh to visit Sister Paulita and Karl.

"You're being irrational," he yelled, using once again his favorite adjective. It was a week after I'd been hit by the rock, and I was sitting on the wide lawn watching the children at play.

"The slavers haven't forgotten how many fugitive black people Rudi helped to escape to Canada. They're bent on revenge, and—" he shook his blond head vehemently— "they'll follow you all the way to Pittsburgh if they have to. And beyond."

"Leopold, I can't live the rest of my life in fear," I fumed at him. He could be irritating, I thought. Then, contrite, I pulled him down on the grass beside me. "Give me time," I pleaded. "Just a little time, six months or so, then I'll come back and we'll be married, and live happily ever after in your palatial white house on the Hudson."

"You're making fun of me," he said dejectedly, his eyes boring sadly into mine. "You need a man, Sieglinde, you can't go running about the country, a lone woman with two children."

"I have Martina to help with the children," I said tartly. "We're not in the old country, Leopold. This is America. I can do as I please, go where I please. I am my own woman."

"Are you, Sieglinde?" His voice was harsh, tense.

"Am I what?"

"Your own woman! While you're on the river, why stop at Pittsburgh? Why not go on down the Ohio and then the Mississippi to St. Louis?" Leaping from the grass, his lean form towered over me, his face black with rage and torment. He had lost me, and he knew it.

"Yes, that's where you're really headed for. St. Louis, and that criminal Redbeard who lives like a sultan on top of a hill." Leopold bent down to grab my arm so tightly I cried out with the pain.

324

"I hear," he added, "that he keeps a regular harem of blacks and browns and even some almost-whites. And manufactures his own human beings to sell."

With that he was gone, striding furiously down the hill to the road where his private carriage waited to take him back to town and the Bluebird Concert Saloon.

As I busied myself preparing my things and the children's for the journey to Pittsburgh, I thrust Leopold's vindictive words to the back of my mind. Irrational, was I? Maybe. But for the first time in years, in fact, for the first time since I had left my native Bavarian mountains for the court at Munich, I felt completely, blissfully free.

To see Karl again after all these years! No matter how many times I'd begged him, several times even sending him the money for passage, he had refused to come to New York to visit me and the children. He'd spent the money on the orphans.

The children knew, of course, that Rudi Stammler was not their real father, that they were adopted. They would have found out sooner or later, so we had told them the truth, adding, at Rudi's suggestion, the story that their own father had been a sea captain and had died on a long voyage. They never questioned, accepting as children do what their parents tell them. Leopold was mad if he thought I would even consider taking them to St. Louis to meet a man whom I would have to introduce as their "real" father and who was a criminal—a cruel, inhuman man—at that!

The *Freedom* was a handsome white steamer I'd seen many times plying gracefully up and down the Hudson. Many times I'd envied the passengers crowding her decks, milling about in their holiday clothes. They would lean over the rails and wave at the children along the banks.

Now it was our turn to wave to Rosie and Lauretta standing at the river's edge with white handkerchiefs fluttering. Soon Lauretta's was at her nose, since she'd been weeping on and off all morning. Leopold had not come to see us off. My heart was heavy that our parting had to be this way; I knew only too well what it meant to be rejected.

"*Mein Gott*, we're moving!" Martina shrieked. The nurse stood beside me, her plump round face fearful as the gangplank was drawn and the funnel blasted three times to signal that we were on our way. Since her Atlantic crossing, which had been stormy, she'd sworn never to "set foot on the water again." But her love for me and the children overcame her fears.

My heart was light and happy at the thought of seeing Karl and Sister Paulita in a week or so. My joy must have shown in my face, for several passengers looked at me admiringly, smiling and nodding at the antics of Kristina and Rudi as they pranced around the wooden deck with Martina in hot pursuit. I knew we made an attractive-looking family, the two redheaded children bursting with health, the roly-poly Martina, and the tall, golden-haired widow, whose frock, although completely black, outlined a curvacious figure.

Since the Erie Canal had been built, making it easier to travel to the Great Lakes and to the West beyond, the Hudson River steamers had been doing land-office business. We had booked a private cabin, but many people—families with children and aged parents—slept right on deck, their meagre belongings piled around them.

In the long salon, where food was spread out at all hours on the long tables, the smell of cigar smoke and whiskey brought back sharp memories of the *Ocean Monarch* and the Forty-eighters, and of Nathaniel McGreevy too, who had saved me and then left me.

Martina sniffed at the sharp masculine odors. "I t'ink I eat in the cabin," she said, and departed soon after with a loaded tray. I laughed, thinking of Von Edel and how he tried to make me eat in the cabin.

Little Rudi had turned into a little question box. "Mama, let's stay on the boat forever! I hate New York—I hate my school—when will we see some wild Indians?"

Kristina clung to me, shying away from the other children on board. She seemed to miss her adoptive father more than the boy. She and Rudi had been very close. The two of us spent most of our time sitting on deck chairs gazing out at the lush green hillsides and the graceful mansions, all with wide verandas and sloping green lawns. Small boats rocked gently at the water's edge.

"When we come back from our visit, we will live in such a house," I promised her. "And you may go boating every day the weather is fine."

She was silent, as if she too could detect the lie in what I said.

Chapter 29

In no time at all, it seemed, we were at St. Joseph's Home for Orphans, being driven up the long cobblestoned hill to the brick building, blackened now by years of soot and grime, and into the waiting arms of Sister Paulita.

After the initial flurry of greetings the children were dispatched to eat supper with the orphans, while I sat at the round kitchen table with the nuns and Karl. Martina had preferred to remain with the children, feeling, she said, "strange around nuns."

"I'm sure you're accustomed to more elaborate fare in New York," Sister Susanna apologized as she dipped the tin ladle into the big tureen of soup, filling my wooden bowl to the brim. "We don't have much meat, maybe once or twice a week at most."

The delicious aroma of cabbage and onions filled my nostrils. "Mmm," I exclaimed, "it's heavenly. I haven't tasted soup like this since leaving Bavaria."

I turned to smile at Sister Elfreda, knowing her to be the cook. She was thinner and older, but her blue eyes still sparkled in the old merry way.

"Where is Sister Emmanuel?" I inquired, suddenly missing the old nun who had nursed me through my childhood sicknesses.

"Gone to her eternal reward," Sister Paulita answered softly. "We lost her two years ago in the terrible spotted fever epidemic. So many little ones died also."

"Yes," murmured Sister Susanna," so many die, so much sickness, but—" she shrugged her black shoulders in resignation—"it is God's will."

Karl spoke up for the first time since we had sat down, his voice indignant, even angry. "Sickness of the body is one thing, and may be God's will, Sister, but the sickness in men's souls, the terrible evil which makes them buy and sell their fellow human beings like so much cattle, that is the work of the devil!"

"Karl is very active in the Underground Railroad," Sister Paulita explained. "Pittsburgh, being on the Ohio, is an important way station in the chain of hiding places."

My eyes widened as I stared at my beloved Karl. The slavers killed Rudi, and my heart contracted with fear for my friend. "Karl," I breathed, "it is so dangerous, the work you are doing."

His pale blue eyes darkened. "A man must live for something," was all he said. The thick black curls were touched with grey, and in spite of the ugly red birthmark, he seemed to have grown more handsome with the years. There was a natural dignity about him. A wild thought pierced my brain, like a lightning bolt from heaven. I could marry *him*—what matter if we could not be as other married couples? We'd have each other, and the children.

Sister Elfreda was talking again,

"How long will you stay with us, you and Martina and the children?"

"As long as you will have me—I mean," I stopped, flustered and uncertain, "My plans are indefinite."

Sister Paulita interrupted, reaching over the table to cover my hand firmly with her own work-scarred hand. "Siegelinde has experienced a great loss. The rich suffer from death as much as the poor, Sister. At such times a person must have time to think of the next step."

"We will pray for you," the young novice who was serving the meal bent down to murmur in my ear. I looked up at her sweet face, sudden tears blurring my vision. She was so young, so innocent, so pure. What did she know of human passions and the destruction they could work?

After the meal, Karl disappeared to attend to some chores, and I made sure Kristina and Rudi were safely bedded down. They were overjoyed at having so many new playmates.

"You know, Mama," Kristina said, as I bent over her bed to hear her nighttime prayers, "I have the strangest feeling I've been here before."

My eyes filled with the remembrance. "You were," I replied. "I'll tell you all about it someday."

Finally, I reached the second-floor room where I was to sleep, and throwing off my dusty traveling clothes, I slipped on a clean flannel night garment. There was no heat in the bedrooms and although it was early August, the night was chill. Wearily, I stood at the tall window looking out into the black fog that completely obscured the Allegheny River at the foot of the hill. My mind flew back to the sunny banks of the Hudson. Could I live here, in such a dirty city? I shivered, but whether from the cold or apprehension at my uncertain future I couldn't tell.

A soft knock on the door brought me out of my reverie. Moments later Karl's muscular arms were wrapped tightly around my shivering form. I rubbed my cold cheeks against the leather jerkin which he still wore. The smell too was the same—tobacco and sweat and horses.

Finally he released me, walked over to the door to slide the bolt, then led me to the bed. I lay down on the narrow mattress and he stretched out beside me. "Just like old times," I murmured, choking back the tears of happiness which sprang unbidden to my eyes. My lips touched the birthmark, my hands stroked the mass of curls, my body clung to his hard firmness.

I felt his own body tense, then relax; his giant arms pressed me ever closer. We talked, that way, for hours, while the fog rolled up the hill from the river into the little room, covering us with a moist, remembering coldness.

"Even the fog is like the top of Kyffhauser Mountain," he chuckled. "But one gets used to it. In fact I'd miss it if I ever had to leave."

"My children are fatherless now, Karl," I said sadly. "Let me stay here with you. Forever."

His hands gripped my shoulders to shake me gently in reproof. "Kristina and Rudi are not fatherless," he said angrily. "Their father is alive and well. You know it as well as I."

My response was quick and bitter. "He has disowned them many times. They will never see him or even hear of him, not if I can help it."

Rolling off the bed with a quick movement, Karl strode to the window, turning his back to me. "This is a sin," he said into the night. "It is not your God-given right to deny them the knowledge of their father."

"He has denied *them*. Besides, Rudi is their legal father. He adopted them, and left them wealthy and secure for life.

"Lothar is wealthy now, from what I've heard," Karl replied, turning back now to sit on the bed beside me. "You must at least take them to St. Louis to see him."

It maddened and frightened me to hear Karl say what was in my own heart, what I had been afraid even to admit to myself. "They do not need Lothar von Hohenstaufen and his filthy money," I choked in my anger, but whether my anger was against him or myself I couldn't tell. "Their father is a monster, he sells human flesh for profit."

The pale blue eyes drew closer and closer.

"They are flesh of his flesh, your children. Bone of his bones. Blood of his blood."

"As I am." I moaned, burying my head in the hard pillow, not wanting this man to see my own pain.

His voice was soft now, but insistent. "Do you still yearn for Lothar?"

"Yes," came my muffled reply. "But I can deny my body. I have conquered the flesh. I have felt no desire for six years. I am like Sister Paulita and the others." I whipped around to face him defiantly.

"Ho! We'll see about that!

Before I could stop him, he had lifted the flannel gown over my head and plunged his big hairy hands into the soft flesh of my bosom. Then the hands traveled downward to my abdomen, making little circles there and on my hips. He lifted me from the mattress to cup my buttocks as in a cradle.

Furious at his attack, I struggled desperately, but I was no match for his lionlike strength. Short little grunts came out of his mouth, and then he was sucking on my nipples, first one then the other, hungrily, voraciously. Each pull of his warm moist lips on my nipples was matched by the familiar tightening in my loins. I dared not cry out for fear of arousing the nuns. What would they think of their beloved Karl, and the mourning widow?

Moans of pain and ecstasy soon were coming out of my own mouth. I arched toward him, waiting for the familiar stroking of the pulsing place between my thighs. He waited, as my moans increased in intensity. With one giant hand he pushed me back on the pillow, while the other worked feverishly but expertly at the dark, warm place.

As if with a will of their own, my legs parted wantonly, spreading wide on the bed, my thoughts not on Karl and the hand that was stroking me to fulfillment, but upon great bushy red beard which had covered my breasts while a hard silken manhood had plunged into my body. "Yearning, yearning, yearning," I panted, senseless of what I said. And then as I neared fulfillment, the name, the forbidden name came to my lips. "Lothar, Lothar, Lothar."

Karl fell asleep immediately, his rough cheek pressed wetly against my bare bosom. Gratefully, I pressed my lips to the crisp dark curls.

"Thank you, Karl," I whispered, "thank you, once more, for proving that I am a woman, whatever else I might be."

Since there was no mirror in this convent room, I turned my head toward the tall window and the darkness beyond.

"I am Sieglinde," I repeated, "daughter of King Ludwig of Bavaria, love mate of a prince, mother of two living beings born of that love. No—three," I corrected myself, uttering a silent prayer for the tiny body which was now part of the dust of Kyffhauser Mountain.

Dawn finally lit up the square of window and the sharp wet smell of the river and the smoke of the steel mills penetrated the little room. Karl slipped out of bed, leaning over first to kiss me gently on the forehead. I pretended to be asleep. I knew now what I had to do.

The night clerk at the Planter House Hotel knew immediately who I was looking for.

"Mr. Staufen? Of course. Everyone in St. Louis knows him." He paused, cleared his throat importantly. "Or should I say," he added, "everyone knows *about* him. Few of us have ever actually *seen* him."

"Oh?" I lifted my eyebrows in what I thought was a look of casual surprise. "Is he then so—unfriendly?"

"Unfriendly?" The man wrinkled his forehead, as if searching for the proper word. "I would say, rather, mysterious." He smiled, nodded his head vigorously. "A fabulously wealthy recluse who sports long red hair, long red beard, who no one has ever set eyes on, at least in the light of day—yes, madam, I would call that man mysterious."

While the clerk busied himself fetching a carriage to take me and the children to the mysterious Mr. Staufen's residence, I related to the children one more time the story behind our visit to St. Louis. Now that he had said the name Staufen (obviously a shortening of Hohenstaufen), I knew with a dread certainty that it really was Lothar up there on a hill overlooking the river. It was really he who was the infamous, fabulously wealthy slave trader.

331

Martina had decided at Pittsburgh that she did not want any more water travel, especially into the wilds of the southern United States. She'd taken a train back to New York. So the three of us sat at a little table sipping hot chocolate.

"Mr. Staufen is an old friend of Lauretta Chambers," I lied to the children, "and I promised to pay him my respects upon our arrival in St. Louis."

Rudi's green eyes danced with excitement. "When are we going to see some wild Indians, Mama? You promised when we got past the Ohio River that we would see them."

I smiled at him indulgently. He, much more than Kristina, had been excited about our trip down the Mississippi. "We'll ask Mr. Staufen when we see him, darling."

The carriage was painted bright red, and the well-matched grays were high-spirited. They fairly galloped through the nearly deserted early morning streets. The children had been up at the crack of dawn, and I hadn't closed my eyes the entire night.

The journey downriver had been exhausting, with Martina gone, and the sight of so many fugitive slaves being returned to their masters had depressed me. Some were manacled to various parts of the ship, and at every stop along the way more were herded on board, with grim-faced white men whipping their naked backs as one would a horse who wouldn't move fast enough. At one point a beautiful young black woman with a child at her breast jumped into the muddy waters of the river, drowning both herself and her baby. Death, to her, was preferable to slavery.

"Why are those people chained up like that?" the children had wanted to know. I'd brushed aside their questions, distracting them with stories of how I used to swim in the deep lakes of the Bavarian mountains.

The carriage soon left the river road for the narrow twisting streets of the old town. Soon we were climbing up the hill, past neat brick houses with starkly whitewashed front steps and potted plants at every window. The pungent smell of malt signalled the presence of a brewery nearby. Where there were Germans, there would be beer. My heartstrings caught as I remembered Rudi's kegs of Milwaukee dark Bock.

It seemed like hours since we'd left the hotel. The horses plodded now against the steep grade of the road. The fog had lifted and a hot sun beat down on us. We had no parasols.

Kristina fidgeted. "Will we soon be there, Mama?"

"I don't know, dear, I have no idea how much further it is. But I promised—and a promise is a promise." I touched her hand consolingly. That much of my story was true. I *had* promised. But it was Karl I had promised, not Lauretta. Karl had extracted my solemn promise, my hand on a Bible he had in his cellar room, that I would at least *see* Lothar.

At last! A dignified dark wooden sign bore the legend STAUFEN MANOR. We were here. The carriage turned into a driveway fashioned of red bricks set in a geometric design, curving between gigantic trees whose lacy foliage hung low, brushing our faces as we passed. A sudden impulse seized me. This whole idea was sheer madness! "Stop here," I shouted at the driver over the noise of the carriage wheels.

The man swivelled to stare at me, open-mouthed, his eyes blazing white in his black face. "Lawd, Ma'am, 'scuse me, but th' house is way up dere som'eres."

"It doesn't matter," I said heatedly. "I want you to turn this carriage around and take us back to the city."

The children were also staring at me as if I had taken leave of my senses. Rudi's face was so mournful, it was almost comical.

But it was too late. A very tall, young man, his half-naked black body glistening with sweat, broke through the thick bushes at the side of the driveway. He was followed immediately by a boy, also black, who looked to be about Rudi's age. The smell of moist earth filled my nostrils. In the man's hand was a spade encrusted with dirt. They had apparently been digging. Over their heads I could see flower beds set in an expanse of lawn and a gleaming marble fountain. In the center of the fountain a statue of a woman leaned gracefully toward the sun, holding in her arms a vase from which streams of water flowed into the basin of the fountain. It was exquisite! I could not tear my eyes away from the sight.

"Mama, Mama!" Kristina tugged at my sleeve.

Suddenly, I realized that the two slaves were waiting for me to speak first. "Is this the residence of Herr—I mean, Mr. Staufen?"

"Yes, ma'am." The older slave bowed stiffly from the waist. His voice was soft and musical.

I looked searchingly at the boy beside him, who was staring wide-eyed at Rudi. Was this one of Lothar's brats by his octoroon?

"Does the massah 'spect you?" the slave asked politely.

"Yes—I mean, no—well, in a way," I finished lamely. The driver of the carriage was regarding me suspiciously. "Mr. Staufen is a dear friend of a dear friend of mine in New York, and I promised to pay our respects during our stay in St. Louis."

A large bird with bright red plumage flew past us. The whole place was filled with the sound of birdsong. It seemed like a fairyland, a place from some other world, set down in the middle of Missouri.

I turned to the driver and ordered him to wait for us. "We will walk from here," I said. "It's such a lovely day. And the grounds are so beautiful."

As we started to climb out of the carriage, a man on horseback burst through the shrubbery at the spot where the two slaves had emerged earlier. At the sight of us, he pulled back so savagely on the reins that the animal, a handsome chestnut mare, rose straight up in the air, pawing frantically. "Whoa there, Nancy," shouted the man.

In the next instant a pair of giant dogs appeared and leaned forward expectantly at us, teeth bared, waiting for the command from their master to charge.

"Kirnis! Lumpi!"

It was the same strong, deep, commanding voice. My senses reeled and I seemed to be back on Kyffhauser Mountain, on that September dawn when Lothar and I had walked hand in hand to his baronial Schloss. And I felt the same rigid terror upon seeing the dogs with their saliva-dripping jowls and hearing their threatening growling noises. Kristina whirled to bury her face in my black skirt and Rudi's hand reached, trembling like a leaf, for mine.

With that sinuous, panthery movement that wrenched my heart right out of me, Lothar slid down out of the saddle. He handed the reins to the slave. "Achilles, Nancy's had a busy morning," he said quietly, in a much softer tone than he had used with the dogs. "Take her to the stables and rub her down good!" Then he turned to fix his eyes on me and the children. "I'll escort Frau Stammler and her children to the house."

We stood, our glances locked, for several long moments,

334

transfixed at the mere sight of each other. He looked the same, although subtly different. Older, but somehow more distinguished. The mane of copper hair no longer fell thickly, carelessly to the broad shoulders, but was cut off bluntly, neatly, just under the ears. The shaggy beard that had once tumbled in a brilliant cataract to his waist now surrounded his leathered face elegantly, no longer than five or six inches, but it was still very full, each single wiry red hair seemed to vibrate. A very thick mustache covered the space between the high bony Hohenstaufen nose and the wide sensuous lips. But it was the eyes that mesmerized me into the past. As I gazed, conscious only of his presence, losing all sense of time and space, I once again was sucked into their sea-green depths.

He opened his mouth to speak, but closed it again, and tearing his eyes from mine strode ahead of us up the driveway. We followed, the children clutching tightly to my hands. In a moment, we turned a corner to view the house for the first time.

I gasped in astonishment and sheer pleasure. I had expected the traditional white-pillared, stately plantation house like those I'd seen on both sides of the river on our journey from Pittsburgh. What I saw was an enormous pile of black rock rising out of the earth, as if it had sprung naturally from a seed planted by a master builder. The large square stones sparkled in the sun. Long, narrow casement windows covered the facade of the building. Towers loomed into the sky at either end of the building. It was the Schloss Hohenstaufen transported, it seemed, stone by stone, from the Black Forest to Missouri. Instinctively, I looked around for the moat and the bridge.

"Why—why," I finally managed to say, in a weak stammer, "you have duplicated it—exactly!"

Lothar still did not speak, but walked ahead of us with the same rapid long-legged stride through the massive wooden doors into a dim, cool, entryway. He yanked on a bell pull by the front door, then finally turned to us. With a quick violent movement he threw himself on his knees to the gleaming parquet floor.

Kristina and Rudi had let go my hands, once they were assured the dogs would not devour them. Now they stood open-mouthed at the kneeling giant, whose hair was the same color as theirs. Lothar smiled broadly, for the first

335

time, and with both powerful arms, reached out to encircle both of the children. He swept them to his broad chest, buried his lips first in one coppery head, then the other. "Welcome, children, welcome home."

Chapter 30

A very large, very fat black woman now appeared through a doorway at the far end of the entry. She approached us, two rows of stark white teeth splitting her face in a wide smile. A spanking white kerchief completely swathed her hair.

Lothar lifted his head from the children and spoke to the slave. "Lucinda, our guests will want to refresh themselves before luncheon is served. They have just come from a long journey—" his eyes forced themselves up to mine once more—"yes, a long journey indeed."

"I don't have to wash. I washed this morning at the hotel." Rudi's young voice sounded loud and bold in the semi-darkness.

Lothar threw back his head and laughed uproariously. "Of course you don't need to wash. That's for women. What boy ever does?" He swooped the boy up onto his massive shoulders and strode out the front door. "My son and I are off to the stables. We'll return at the sound of the luncheon bell."

As Kristina and I followed Lucinda up the broad stairway to the second floor, I asked, "Are there many in the household? Slaves, I mean?"

She was silent until we reached a large bathroom complete with tubs, a commode with several porcelain basins, and a black and white tiled floor. "No," she replied pleasantly, "They's jes' four of us. Me, Achilles, Maybelle, and o'course the boy Frederick."

"Frederick? What an odd name for a slave."

"Yes'm," she said smoothly, "tha's what ev'ryone sez. But Massah Lothar, he say he had a li'l son onc't by that name. So, when Janet left her babe here, tha's what Massah Lothar calls 'im."

I plunged my face into the cold water the slave poured into the basin, not trusting myself to say another word. Frederick was the name of our first son, Lothar's and mine, who lay dead in Kyffhauser Mountain.

Lucinda left us, promising to return to show us to our rooms. There would be time then, I decided, to tell her we were not staying the night, that indeed we had brought no change of clothing with us.

Kristina spoke for the first time. "Mama, is Mr. Staufen Rudi's father?"

My heart stopped, as I realized the time had come for the truth. Lothar had called Rudi his son. Obviously, he had every intention of claiming them again—at least for a while.

"Yes," I said dully, willing away any emotion from my voice. "Mr. Staufen is Rudi's father." I turned to pull Kristina to my breast. At seven, her head reached past my waist. "He is also *your* father, Kristina."

I don't know what I expected, but certainly not the calm, pleased acceptance that I got. "I thought so," my little daughter said. "I thought so all the time."

The luncheon bell, a loud cowbell, was sounding over the estate as we walked with Lucinda back down the stairway. A very old slave was bent over the balustrade, polishing the intricately curved posts. Her hair was a frizzled grey, and she moved slowly, almost painfully, at her task.

"This 'ere's Maybelle," Lucinda explained. She ailin' and cain't do much. Jes' some cleanin' and cookin'.

"Why doesn't Mr. Staufen sell her then?" I asked. "Since she's not profitable any more?"

The slave's startled eyes flew to mine, then she quickly covered her face with an impassive mask. Without answering, she led us into the dining room.

Lothar and Rudi were already seated at the long table, every inch of which seemed to be covered with delectable foods. There was crisp fried bacon, slices of cold ham, potatoes fried in the German manner with sliced onions and pepper, and several kinds of fragrant hot breads.

Kristina seated herself directly across from her father. "Were you in a fight, fa—" she stopped, suddenly embarrassed, "Mr. Staufen?"

"A fight?" He smiled at her inquiringly.

"Yes, you have such a long scar on your face."

Lothar reached up a finger to touch the scar, musingly.

"Oh, that." The smile disappeared, and he finished in a sober tone, "Someday I'll tell you all about it, Kristina."

Deciding it was about time to straighten out the confusion in his mind, I looked directly at Lothar and said in a loud, firm voice, "We cannot stay the night, Lothar, we have brought no luggage, and our carriage is still waiting——"

The shaggy brows lifted in mock surprise. "I have dismissed your driver, and dispatched Achilles to the Planter House for your things." He turned to look at the children again. "You and your mother will be my guests—my honored guests—indefinitely."

After luncheon, the children ran out with the boy Frederick, who was ordered by Lothar to show them the animals and the farm. Then he excused himself, bowing stiffly in my direction, saying he had some things to attend to and that he would not return until very late in the day.

Lucinda fixed a light supper for me and the children, Lothar still being absent. His large retinue of slaves must be occupied in the fields, I decided, and there was obviously a "slave quarters" somewhere, such as I'd seen along the river. I remembered them vividly—rows of ramshackle wooden shacks with dirty children and animals wandering around.

The children had come into the house exhausted from their afternoon with the boy Frederick. Lucinda took them in hand, leading all three of the little ones up to the third floor where they were to sleep. I puzzled about the slave boy not coming back down the stairs, but figured I'd find out eventually what was going on with him. If he indeed was Lothar's natural son, as I suspected, I preferred to put off knowing for sure, as long as possible.

Alone in the big house now, still anxious about Lothar's long absence, I walked out the front door onto the grounds. There was an iron bench at the foot of the fountain I'd seen earlier in the day. I sat down, my mind and heart in a whirl. What could I do? How could I tell my children that their father was a slave dealer? And that we must leave this beautiful place soon? Quickly. Tomorrow. I knew only too well the power of Lothar's charm. He would enchant them as he had enchanted me.

Night descended with the suddenness of the southern climate. But I still remained, listening to the tinkle of the water into the basin of the fountain. A few night birds called their haunting songs to each other, but otherwise the silence was overwhelming. I dozed, resting my head on the cool, iron back of the bench.

Gradually, I became aware of sounds in the night. They seemed to be voices, a low, dull murmur, coming from the foot of the driveway. I lifted my head to look, but the thick shrubbery hid everything from view. After a few minutes, the voices faded, and the crunching sound of carriage wheels turning on the bricks echoed sharply in the night. Probably Lothar returning from his errands, I decided sleepily, then leaned my head back again, unwilling to move to go into the house.

Achilles' voice was the next sound I heard. "You bes' come in the house, ma'am," he said softly, reaching out to touch me gently on the shoulder. "You lik'ly to catch your death out 'ere."

. Waking up with a shock, I felt the chill run through my bones. I had walked out without my cloak. "Achilles," I asked, as we walked rapidly back toward the house. "Why don't you run away?"

We were at the front door now, and he turned to stare at me, the whites of his eyes gleaming bright in his black face. He drew himself up to his full height and looked down at me. "I loves Massah Lothar. He lik' a father to me. I don' have to run."

Upstairs in the huge bed chamber Lucinda had taken me to after luncheon, I opened my trunk and pulled out a long, warm, flannel gown. The night air streaming in through the open window was cold and damp with the smell of the river. Lucinda had pulled the covers to the foot of the bed, and placed a candle in a glass shade on the bedside commode. The whole effect was cozy and inviting.

Stripping myself of the sweaty traveling clothes, I splashed cool water from the commode basin on my burning breasts and face and slipped the gown over my head. The sleeves were long and full, tying at the wrists, and the neckline high. Ruffles around the neck reached to my chin. I decided against the muslin night cap which went with the gown and slowly, wearily, pulled the pins out of my coronet of braids and let my hair fall loosely around my shoulders.

Strolling over to a long mirror set right into the wall, I gazed thoughtfully at my reflection. "You are Sieglinde," I started the old familiar speech, then abruptly dropped my head into my hands and wept. "You are Sieglinde," I sobbed to myself, "a fool."

The octoroon. Where was he hiding her? In the slave's quarters? What did he take me for? Did he think that I would resume my life as his wife, knowing what he had become? His continuing absence irritated me. Suddenly, the sound of carriage wheels drifted up from the hill once more, and the low mutter of voices. I ran to the window, peered out into the darkness, but could see nothing. The fog from the river covered the view from the bottom of the hill.

I threw myself on the bed, weeping in rage and frustration. A deep sleep enveloped me, along with all my fears.

The spring föhn is blowing deliciously cool on my face as I run down the forest path with the little basket of spring flowers which Ortrud has fixed for me. I will place them at the feet of the stone Virgin in the grotto by the lake. My feet are bare. I am dressed only in a thin shift reaching to my knees.

But I have no fear, for I am fourteen, and have never known a man.

Suddenly, a giant shadow blocks out the sun. A man stands right in the path, his powerful legs spread wide apart. He knocks the flowers from my trembling hand, then reaches out his gigantic hairy arms to pull me roughly to his body.

He is completely naked.

My own scream woke me from the dream. Sweat poured down my face onto the silken pillow.

Lothar stood at the foot of the brass bed, gazing at me somberly, his giant form outlined by the flickering light of the single candle. He was naked, the short beard seemed to run right into the hair on his chest and neck, the hair on his chest reaching down to join the hair around his hips, then down along the long muscles of thigh and leg. The only part of his body which was not covered with red hair was his face, and the thin curving scar. The hair glowed like the brass of the bed in the yellow light of the candle. His manhood was hard, strong, outthrust.

I lay still as a stone, hardly breathing. My lips opened

341

but the words I said were not the words I wanted to say. "What was all that noise outside just now—the voices, the carriage?"

"A shipment of slaves," he said, in a matter-of-fact voice.

Revulsion seized me, and I buried my face in the pillow, unable to look at him any longer.

"I guess," he said, without moving to touch me, "it's time for an explanation, my Valkyrie. Yes, I deal in human flesh, as they say up and down the river. But not in the way you think."

"What other way is there?" came my muffled response from the pillow.

"This mansion is a key waystation on the Underground Railroad. Just as Rudi Stammler's café was before the rabble burned it down."

My head came up. I looked at him fiercely, "You expect me to believe that?"

"Yes," he replied, his voice shaking now with emotion. "Yes, I do! All this magnificence, this mansion, the vast estate, the black men and women who pretend to be slaves—it's all a false front to deceive everyone into thinking that I am a bounty hunter."

"How do you get them out of St. Louis?" I said sarcastically. "Do you simply march them through the streets to the docks and load them?"

"No, you beautiful little fool. All our rescues are made at night, the slaves are taken to the steamers—most of which I own, by the way—and secreted on board. Sometimes we have to chain them to keep up the pretense. Sometimes we hide them below decks."

I was sitting bolt upright now, not wanting to believe this incredible story, but—knowing Lothar and his outlandish ways in the past—feeling instinctively that it was all true. Every word.

"Where did you get all the money, then, for all this?" I asked scornfully, swinging my arms wide to sweep the beautiful bed chamber.

"My *Grossmama*. Surely you remember her! After you stole away with her grandchild and her beloved Karl, she simply pined away and died. From starvation, Klaus wrote, but—" his faced worked at the memory, "but what does it matter now, all of that? It's part of the past."

"And the past is dead," I said dully. All the dreams of Bavaria, of restoring the Hohenstaufens, are dead and buried. Like all my beloved dead—my son, Ymir, Rudi. All dead.

Lothar left the foot of the bed, walked over to the window and gazed out into the dark. "King Maximilian sent me the money from the sale of the Kyffhauser Mountain and suggested I put it to good use here in America. After my year on the slaver ship that picked me up from the wreck of the *Ocean Monarch*, I knew what my new mission was to be."

I reached out my arms toward the naked form at the window. "We were so young, Lothar, and so—young," I finished.

There was a long waiting silence. What was Lothar thinking? What about the octoroon? Was that too a made-up story, to fool the anti-abolitionists? There were still so many questions in my mind. But they could wait until tomorrow. Or the next day. Or the day after that.

The tall, powerful, naked figure at the window looked terribly lonely, and I thought I detected a trembling in the rippling muscles. "Let the dead be dead," I said softly.

He turned then and fell upon me, pressing his sweet mouth to mine. We kissed for a long, shivering eternity. Then, lifting his lips from mine, he murmured, "Yes, yes. The future belongs to the living."